CAPTIVE OF LOVE

Trying to control herself, Jessica attempted to hold back the sob that shook the length of her body. But as her gaze rose to the man holding her so tenderly and she saw only gentleness in his features, for a moment she was truly lost. So much had happened to her so quickly, and she was so tired and frightened. Now here was her abductor, a horrible Indian, looking down at her with such tenderness that she wanted to weep aloud for the feelings that were assailing her.

Star Hawk bent his head and gathered her soft, pliant lips with his own. The stream swirled gently and warmly around them and the moon softly cast a golden hue over the forest. They clung together, their lips bound, their bodies melded, as all time and eternity stood still only for them. . . .

Destiny's Splendor

Kathleen Drymon

ZEBRA BOOKS

KENSINGTON PUBLISHING CORP.

To Sharon Ezell Collier
I raise my cup to you, dear cuz (perhaps filled with a Miami Whami),
For you have ever been a true friend, since our childhood.
Love you, Kathleen

Prologue

THE BLACKFOOT HILLS

A fine, thin sliver of moonlight touched gently down with lighted splendor, lending a softly golden hue to the soft earth and setting a sparkling diamond glitter on the lush green grasses. Gentle winds touched the branches of tall, majestic pines. The star-studded velvet night revealed the presence of a tall, straight, bronzed Indian chieftain as he sat alone and unattended, his back braced against one of the towering trees. His ebony eyes gazed off into the distance as he peered down the gentle sloping valley to where his village lay in quiet repose.

He held himself erect as his lips formed a silent prayer to the Great Spirit. He thought of the preparations that his people had taken for the winter months ahead: the meats that had been cured and tended and the lush hides that would be their warmth and clothing. Everything about him seemed to sing in the night air of peace and contentment. With a large sigh, he thought of himself. As his father before him, he had been chief to his people for many winters now, and they had known great prosperity under his guidance. He had led his warriors against their enemies and had won great victories. His coups numbered many. The songs and stories sung around the campfires by the shaman of his tribe told of his boldness and honor. And now, with the first signs of the approaching winter that would shelter them in the arms of the fleecelike snow, he thought of his reasons for being alone here this evening.

His midnight eyes looked at the birthing hut that had been built well away from the rest of the large village of tall tepees, close to the river's edge. His wife, Singing Moon, the woman of his heart, was at this very moment laboring greatly to deliver his first child. He, Golden Eagle, had awaited this time when he would sit alone with only the company of the Great Spirit and the fathers of days long past to ponder upon the wondrous gift that he would shortly be receiving. He had sought many things through prayer and fasting from that day, months ago, when Singing Moon had greeted him with the news that he would be a father. Many seasons ago he had taken his wife from her father's lodge and onto his own sleeping mat as his bride, and for many winters they had both thought that they would never be allowed the great pleasure of being blessed with a son. But now, with the event so close at hand, he had many worries. He had sought out a sign in the past few months, going often to the great shaman of their tribe to question him about the route he should seek. He would need to know much to be a true and good father to his child. If his child were to be a son, he would have to be doubly diligent in his teachings. For his seed would one day lead his people, and he had learned over the past years that wisdom and understanding were absolute necessities in a great chief of the mighty Blackfoot nation.

Again the agate eyes shut and the lips moved with barely audible words, which were carried high upon the wings of the gentle night breeze. His own father, and his father before him, had passed upon the star path many years before and were now in the paradise hunting ground with the Great Spirit, and Golden Eagle knew that they were at this very moment interceding on the behalf of his people. With this thought foremost in his mind, he added his prayers aloud to those of his ancestors. His love was great for the people of his blood, and Golden Eagle knew with the sureness of his efficient mind that there were many threats that would come against them, against their very existence. He had dreamed several times of a day when the white-skinned and pale-eyed men would come to their lands in droves—not as it was now, when only a few were seen now and then trapping or hunting on the mountains. The future was unclear to Golden Eagle, and he desired some sign from his fathers that they would remain watching over his people.

With the finish of his prayer, his dark eyes slowly opened. His breath clutched in his broad chest as his gaze settled on a pale hawk of an abnormally large size sitting on a sturdy branch in the tree before him. Its talons were long and curled around the pine bark, its yellow gaze possessive of the forest around it, and hard. The large animal looked on the man sitting below him, and at the same moment, Golden Eagle felt the slight prickling of his flesh as he heard the shattering, piercing scream of his wife. The large wings of the hawk rose up to the very skies, and then the bird flew straight up. Golden Eagle's eye fol-

9

lowed it until it seemed to disappear in the moonlit clouds. As his ebony gaze held on the heavens, he beheld a rare sight. The silver fire of a twin pair of shooting stars raced across the velvet cover of night. And as they seemed to join together, for an instant, Golden Eagle saw the mighty hawk swoop high and clutch out his long talons at the stars. Then, with a shower of glimmering brilliance, the hawk and stars seemed to join and then explode with a silver light throughout the heavens.

His large chest pounding from the racing of his heart, Golden Eagle knew that his quest for a vision had been fulfilled. Slowly and unsteadily he rose to his feet, as though drunk. He staggered from the sheer power of the vision. For a moment he gulped at the cool night air, trying to clear his head. Then he made way toward the birthing hut. The signs that the Great Spirit had sent to him could only mean that he had a son, a child who would be a strong and invincible as the fierce hawk. Surely the very heavens themselves would be on his son's side throughout his life, for what else could the twin stars mean? Had they not been a sign sent to ensure that the child would walk a straight path as a great leader of his people?

An elderly, wrinkled woman met Golden Eagle at the flap of the birthing hut. "Your son, my chief." She held outstretched in her hands a tiny infant. "Your wife, Singing Moon, is well and sleeping."

Golden Eagle stood outside the birthing hut, his chest swelling with pride as he looked at the tiny, perfect features of the child he had so long desired. With a tentative hand he reached out and touched the soft, delicate skin of the pink cheek. "Star Hawk." He spoke the name aloud and with some wonder at his own choice of name for his son. Golden Eagle's dark eyes rose to the older woman, called Cloud Dreamer.

"Star Hawk will be a proud name, my chief. One day this tiny boy will be a worthy leader of his people." The old woman spoke softly.

Golden Eagle knew that this woman, Cloud Dreamer, besides being a healing woman of their tribe, had also been given the gift from the fathers to see into the future. As the warrior chieftain looked deeply into her wrinkled features, he saw that she was seeing much in the small bundle in her arms. "I shall speak to the shaman about my vision of my son's birth, and he will relate it to the village. There will be much feasting and rejoicing, for I, Golden Eagle, declare to all that one day Star Hawk will reign over the Blackfoot nation, and his name will be one that none shall forget!"

SWEET OAKS PLANTATION —
OUTSIDE OF NEW ORLEANS —
THREE YEARS LATER

As the night breeze softly swept over the coast, gently circling the tall, three-storied house and whistling a lonely sigh over the curved front porch, a tired gentleman lowered his large frame into a wicker rocking chair. After only a few short moments, he again rose to his feet and paced about the long veranda, stiffly and slowly. As he moved back and forth, his heart raced fiercely in his chest and his ears strained for sounds coming from within the large house. He mumbled again and again, prayers to God, who he knew would hear him and would help his wife with her laboring pains.

He stepped off the veranda and slowly walked across the trimmed and tended grounds toward the small forest glade not far from the house. He had always found the cool copse of trees a sanctuary of sorts for his weary soul. It was a place where he could be alone with his thoughts and his plans for his plantation, Sweet Oaks, and the large family that he and his wife, Hope, wished one day to have.

His frail, delicate Hope had spent the day in labor, and now, with the descent of the evening darkness, his light, gray-blue eyes again looked upward through the trees.

The midwife had declared again and again to him throughout the long day that this was usual for the first child. "Sometimes," she had sworn, "it can be two days before a babe will make his way." But still, Dennis Coltin felt his tension mount with each passing moment, and knowing nothing else to do, he began to pray once again.

"Ye be a-wanting me to send a lantern out there to ya, Master Dennis?" The call came from the large house and reached Dennis's ears when he stood in the dense glade. "I be a-sending old Bartram out there to ya, master. Or, best ya be coming on back to the house and sitting fur a spell in the parlor now, with this night air a-coming from the coast. Ye needn't be a-catching yer death with the missus in there a-trying her best to get shed of that youngun." The middle-aged black woman, called Marcy, who had come with Hope as part of her dowry, stood upon the front porch and called out across the stretch of lawn. She had watched her master's movements from the front parlor window. He always wanted to go to the forest glade, she knew, when he

12

was troubled, but she thought it best that he not be all alone at this time. The missus might be needing him at any moment, and if he were in the forest, she and Bartram might not be able to find him fast enough.

Dennis Coltin knew that the large black woman only wished to offer comfort. Stepping back from the forest, he called to her, "Nay, Marcy, I am fine. I shall be back at the house in a moment." Marcy went back into the large brick house, hurrying to her mistress's chambers to see if the end was near.

The evening wore on in slow, halting moments. Dennis Coltin, back again on the veranda, was about to give up his pacing and seek out his own assurances that his Hope was well. His steps took him to the front railing of the porch and his light eyes looked out on the rolling lawns of his property. Then, without will, they rose to the heavens above. At that same instant, a loud, piercing scream came from the brick house. Feeling the coldness of rippling goose flesh covering his entire body, he shut his eyes for the barest instant, a terror-filled pain in his chest. But as his reasoning returned and he knew that he had to reach his wife's side, a spectacle in the skies held him immobile.

The blue-black blanket of the night covered the heavens, bespeckled with the brilliance of a thousand stars. At the highest point, Dennis's blue-gray gaze beheld the splendor of twin falling stars racing across the firmament and piercing together with a brilliant display of sparks and glimmering eruptions. For a moment, Dennis Coltin's breath clutched in his chest. The meaning of this rare sight was lost upon his mind. But as he heard the cries of a babe within the house, his breath left his lungs in a single gasp.

13

Surely this was a sign given to him of some vast importance concerning his child, he thought. And even if it wasn't the strangeness of the moment would be forever imprinted in his memory. With one last glance up into the skies, he quickly went through the large house and into his bed chambers.

The pale-haired woman in the large bed in the middle of the large room lay shaken and weak. The elderly midwife held a small form bundled up in the crook of her arm. As the chamber door opened and closed, the pale-haired woman looked at the man striding across the gleaming wood floor. "It is a girl, Dennis." She smiled weakly and then lay back against the pillows. "I know that you had thought that the first would be a boy. I am sorry."

Dennis Coltin made his way to his young wife's bedside and tenderly kissed her soft brow. "A girl child with the looks of her beautiful mother will please me very much, my love." As her eyes shut with the tiredness of her long ordeal, he stepped to the woman holding his tiny infant. Looking at the small, wrinkled pink features of the babe, he grinned with pleasure. "Jessica Star Coltin," he murmured aloud as his large hand tenderly reached out and caressed the small tuft of pale red-gold locks on her tiny, perfect head. The name seemed perfect for this tiny being, and as the twin stars again came to his thoughts, he wondered what her future would hold.

Chapter One

The small forest glade was a cool haven from the bustle of activity. The damp, sweet-smelling earth and canopy of trees offered a welcome respite from the heat of the late summer day. And as the young woman bent and gathered a variety of plants, she sighed aloud with pleasure.

"Miss Jake, Miss Jake," The call came to the young woman's ears and her silky blond-red head turned, her creamy, beautiful features showing a touch of exasperation at having been disturbed. "Miss Jake." Again the call came. "Ye be out there in them woods again? Miss Jessica Star, you best get yerself out here this minute. Yer Cousin Edmond sent word that he be arriving at Sweet Oaks most any time now."

Straightening, the girl made a sour face as she thought of her cousin. His dark, menacing features left her with no desire to make her presence known. But knowing that it would do her little good to hide from him, she gathered up her basket in the crook of her arm. She would not wish for Edmond to find her in this sheltered glade with no one about to protect her. She well remembered the times in the past when

15

his manner had caused cold chills to dance over her body, and she knew that his intentions were not those of trusted kin. Nay, given half the chance, her father's relation would set upon her without mercy.

"I am here, Marcy. I will only be a moment." She straightened her gown of sprigged muslin and started down the path. With a sigh of wistfulness, she let her silver-blue gaze circle about the area once again. These woods were the only place she had found any pleasure in the year since her parents' death. The outer world had nothing to offer her. She always had to caution herself to be strong and keep her wits about her.

"There ye be, child. I done thought fur sure that ye be lost this time for good," the large black woman scolded as Jessica stepped from the forest glade. Marcy took hold of the basket in the younger woman's arms, and then her large brown eyes saw the grass-stained gown that earlier this morning had been fresh and pretty.

No answer was forthcoming in response to the elder woman's concern as the young girl docilely followed along toward the large brick house. Jessica was wondering why her cousin was seeking her out at Sweet Oaks. Was he once again bringing one of his gentlemen friends out for her consideration as a possible husband? A slight shudder coursed over her delicate form at this thought.

As a settling quiet encircled the forest with the young girl's departure, a moccasined foot stepped out from behind a towering oak tree. The ebony eyes of a bronzed-skinned warrior looked at the small area where only seconds before the beautiful, copperhaired woman had knelt gathering plants and herbs. His chest swelled and fell with deep breaths as

16

he heard the gentle singsong of her voice coming to his ears from the distance. The large black woman who had sought the young woman had called her by the name of Jake at first, and then Jessica Star, and with the sound of her name in mind, his heart began a fierce, beating tempo.

He had lingered for a small time here in this glade to rest his horse, and had thought to admire her rare beauty while he stood hidden. But now he felt a strange loneliness filling him. And for a moment he wished he had made himself known to her, to see her reaction as he stepped in front of her, perhaps catching his own reflection in the brilliance of her strange-colored eyes. Shaking his dark head, he knew that such an action would have been unwise. She would surely have screamed her fear and brought others to the glade, and he would have taken to his heels or stood and fought off his foe to a bloody finish. Either way, the beauty that she had created in his thoughts would have been shattered for all time.

Turning away from the spot that had so shortly before been occupied by the lovely creature, the lone Indian brave started toward his large black stallion. He had much to do. He had been sent to this area by his father, and he could not afford to linger or let anyone know of his presence. He had information to gather for Golden Eagle and nothing could be allowed to get in his way. The whites were coming in vaster numbers toward his people's land, though there had been little threat thus far to his village high in the mountains. His father, Golden Eagle, was a wise man who wished to know the thoughts of other tribes as well as whatever he could find out about the white men, to whose numbers there seemed to be no end.

As he jumped on the back of his horse, he again recalled the gentle curves and winsome look of the woman he had been silently watching. Even her name remained with him: Jessica Star. It seemed to vibrate in his thoughts as he pulled his mount around and started from the depths of the forest. Silver eyes and flowing, burnt-gold tresses seared his memory.

Jessica entered her chambers and found an inviting bath set out before the hearth and a fresh gown laid out on her bed. She called, "Marcy, did the message say what Edmond wished this time? I am weary of his constant parade of men since my father's death. I pray that this is not another one of his constant harassments for me to wed a man of his choosing."

Marcy sighed aloud, not knowing what she could do to ease her young charge's plight. She and all of the house servants here at Sweet Oaks held the same uneasy feelings where Cousin Edmond DeVaugn was concerned. It was truly a shame the display of men that her cousin had foisted upon Jessica in the past months. There had been old men; fat men; tall, thin men; men with surly dispositions wishing for a wife to do their bidding; and men looking like bookish monks. But all the men had something in common. They were older than Jessica, and when they stepped inside the doors of Sweet Oaks, their eyes were alight with thoughts of what they would gain. Shaking her dark, kinked head, Marcy replied, "The boy yur cousin sent only be saying that Edmond would be arriving to speak with you in private this afternoon."

18

Slipping out of her gown and into the warm, scented bath, Jessica leaned back against the rim of the wooden tub. "I grow tired of his ceaseless talk of how I should do my duty as a woman and become a wife and mother. And of those that he would tie me with." A frown appeared across her brow and the softly parted lips pushed into a downward pout. "Why is he so intent upon seeing me wed to someone of his choosing?" she mused aloud, not expecting any reply.

"They be a sorry lot, that be fur sure, honeychild. I only wish the old master were still alive to see the deeds of his cousin that he so trusted with yur care. To be a-thinking that master Dennis thought that he could entrust yur care into his evil keeping."

Again Jessica was pricked with sad thoughts of her mother and father's death. It was still like an open wound, each time she remembered their kind and loving faces. The pair had died together, a little over a year ago, in a carriage accident. Since that afternoon, Jessica's whole world had seemed to change rather swiftly. Her father's kin, Edmond De-Vaugn, was named in Dennis Coltin's will as his only living relation here in the colonies. As such, he had been left the full responsibility of seeing to Jessica's needs, and those of Sweet Oaks, until she was of an age to handle everything herself, or until she married, when then all would fall to her husband.

Her bath finished, Jessica stood back from her dressing table mirror and watched as the black woman brushed out her hip-length red-gold curls.

"I think I be a-hearing a carriage pulling up out front now, Miss Jake." The elderly black woman used the pet name that she had given Jessica as a young child. "Ye best be a-hurrying. Mr. Edmond

19

would not be a-thinking twice of coming up them stairs to fetch ye if ye be a-keeping him a-waiting long." The boldness of Jessica's cousin was clear to Marcy when she thought of his actions in the past months.

Jessica nodded her head in complete agreement and started quickly from the chamber. Marcy was only a few steps behind, intending not for a moment leaving her young mistress alone without herself or one of the other servants in the parlor while Edmond DeVaugn was there.

"Show Edmond into the front parlor, Marcy, and see if Penny has something cool to drink. The heat of the morning is still lingering, and I am sure that the ride from town will leave my cousin with a large thirst."

"Yes ma'am, yes ma'am. You just be a-settling yerself, and I be a-bringing Mr. Edmond in here in a moment." The black woman turned around and left the parlor.

Jessica walked about the small parlor, her steps leading her to the double window that faced the coast. She gazed at the large rocks that rose threateningly along the cliffs of the property bordering Sweet Oaks. Her thoughts were in disarray, as she wondered what her fate would be in the cruel grasp of her Cousin Edmond. Was he here today to bring her news of another would-be suitor who would be calling upon her? Would he again demand that she consider a stranger for her husband? With a soft, brooding sigh, she laid her forehead against the cool glass.

Edmond DeVaugn quietly entered the front parlor, Marcy leaving his side to hurriedly fetch the refreshments. The dark, piercing eyes of the slim man sought the figure of the young woman standing alone across the room. She seemed slight, almost childish in her appearance as she stood with her back to him, but he knew better. She had soft charms and a figure that was womanly. Her ice-blue gown molded perfectly to her willowy, shapely form. For a moment, Edmond once again cursed his luck. Several years ago, not knowing he would become her guardian, he had married a woman whom he had thought weak and incapable of tending her own finances. He had been misled. For, in fact, his quiet little Hester had quickly risen against him and had fled to her family, drawing their protection around her and refusing to release him from their vows or give him even the smallest amount of her family's fortune. If not for this, he himself would have wed this girl and put an end to his scheming to gain control over this vast plantation and her father's wealth. As it was now, he would have to choose a man to wed the chit, one who could be easily manipulated to allow him to remain in full control of all of the finances of the Coltin estate.

A small noise drew Jessica from the window. She saw her Cousin Edmond standing quietly against the door, studying her with that calculating look that inflamed Jessica for a reason that she could not fathom. "Edmond," she greeted him, pulling herself together and bracing her spine for this interview. "I was sent word that you wished to speak with me, though I see little that we could have to discuss. Is there some business matter you wish to relate to me?" Her fine golden brow rose inquiringly. Jessica knew that her cousin was not about to discuss any business matters with her. Since her parents' death she had been kept totally in the dark about the transactions of her father's interests in New Orleans.

"Indeed, Jessica, there are matters that I wish to discuss with you, but I assure you I am fully capable of handling all of the family business." His dark glare settled on her as he took a seat on the small satin sofa, stretching out his long, thin legs. His gaze held upon her as she crossed the small parlor with an elegant stride. Straightening her skirts, she sat down on the edge of a chair facing the sofa.

Jessica folded her hands primly within the folds of her gown as she awaited the words that she knew would be forthcoming.

"It would appear that once again, my dear cousin, you have rejected another suitor. Ansil Towns told me only this morning of your cool manner toward him and even mentioned something to the effect of having been sent from Sweet Oaks in a rather un-friendly manner?" The dark gaze pierced her with quelling intensity.

Stiffening her backbone, Jessica looked with pink-ened features at the man across from her. How had her father ever trusted this blackguard with his wealth and family? "Indeed, cousin." She tried to appear haughty in the face of his intimidation. "Your Mr. Towns was rude and insulting. His hands pawed over me as though he had a right to make such bold overtures."

"You must learn, sweet Jessica, to try and react differently to the attentions of your gentlemen suit-ors. Do you think that once wedded you will be left to your own icy reserve? A husband surely will have the rights to, as you say, paw you at his wish." There seemed to be evil amusement in the dark eyes as he watched the blushing face across from him.

"Perhaps when I am married, but not before!"

Jessica seethed inwardly at his crude manners. "Beside which, Edmond, you have but beset me with older, bumbling oafs who seem to desire nothing more than a young woman to fondle. Why is it that you wish so desperately for me to wed, Cousin? And why one of these fools that you have brought before me? Am I not a woman with a will of my own? Do you think me so hard to look upon that I shall not be able to find a man for myself when I so desire one?" Her gaze rested on him. She would not abide his insults and she would make her thoughts known to him as she had in the past. He did not cow her.

Relaxing more fully upon the sofa, Edmond DeVaugn looked at the beauty of his cousin. Aye, he had no doubt that she could easily find one to become her mate. With her looks, any man would willingly bend a knee before her. But this was not the way his plans were laid out. He had kept her here at Sweet Oaks with only servants for company, not allowing her any visitors other than the ones that he wished her to have. "I have been given the task of seeing to your future, dear cousin, and I take this responsibility close to heart. Your father left you in my care, and I shall be the one who decides what is best. In the plans I have charted out for you, I feel that you should wed shortly. I do not wish you to live forever here at Sweet Oaks all to yourself. You should have a normal, happy life."

"There is plenty of time for me to wed, Edmond. I see no reason for your rushing me and besetting me with such unwanted suitors."

Rising to his feet, Edmond glared down at his cousin with an intimidating look. "You will do as you are told, Jessica. Upon the arrival of the next gentleman that I send, you will present yourself in a ladylike manner. I shall not have any more talk brought to my ears of your rudeness and ill-bred actions."

Jessica did not respond to his demands. Her silver-colored eyes were blazing with fury. She kept them lowered, looking at her folded hands, not allowing her cousin a glimpse of her anger. This was always the outcome of his visits. His threats came boldly to her ears, and when he left, she forgot them. The next gentleman coming to her home received the same treatment as the one before him.

Dennis Coltin's will had stated that his daughter, upon her twenty-first birthday, would become totally responsible for herself and her estate. She would care for Sweet Oaks and the numerous ships and warehouses in New Orleans. Going over all of this in his mind, Edmond knew that he had only two more years before he would lose control. He was becoming quite rich with his handling of Jessica's affairs already, and he had no intentions of being cast aside. Time was wasting away, and he could ill afford for the young chit to linger much longer over the choice of a husband.

"If you do not mend your ways and accept with some gratitude the help that I am offering you, Jessica, I shall be forced to take it upon myself to set the matter to rights."

This statement brought her blue-silver eyes up to his face. "Aye, I see that you are interested now in what I have to say. I shall not much longer be patient with your willfulness. Your rejection of so many gentlemen is a shame for you and myself to bear. I will pick the best of the lot and arrange the matter of your marriage myself if this keeps on."

Jessica gasped aloud. "You would not dare! I

would refuse, and you certainly cannot force me into an affair that I wish no part of."

"Do not count on this, my dear." Edmond circled about the room, then stood before her once again, his small, glistening black eyes resting boldly upon her décolleté. "If I am pushed, I shall bring you before a priest tied and bound. The gift of gold is ever a persuader to the good men of the clergy here in New Orleans."

"Nay! I shall not be forced in this matter. I will marry when I find the man whom I want to share my life with."

"Heed my warnings, dear cousin, and heed them well, for I will tolerate no more of your spoiled actions." He started toward the portal just as Marcy was bringing in a tray. "A gentleman by the name of Gaylord Fuller will arrive here tomorrow noon. See that he is well entertained." The warning was clear as Edmond DeVaugn stormed through the front foyer and slammed the front portal with a resounding bang.

"Nay." Jessica whispered, the sting of tears dampening her silver eyes and slowly making a path down her creamy cheeks.

Marcy glared at the retreating figure of Edmond DeVaugn. "There, there, child." She went to Jessica and tried to comfort her the best that she was able, but even she knew that there was little she could offer in the face of the bold threats Jessica's cousin had made. It was as though this horrible man had the right to do as he wished and they were all powerless to do anything about it.

The rest of the afternoon dragged past with the ever present threat hanging about Sweet Oaks of what the morrow would hold. Jessica retired early to her chambers and to her dark thoughts. Life seemed to hold little happiness for the young girl. With thoughts of her black-hearted kin darting through her mind, she finally slept as the slow hours ticked by on the mantle clock.

Gaylord Fuller was one of the worst of the lot of would-be suitors that Jessica's cousin had thus far presented to her. His balding pate and bespectacled, red-veined eyes seemed to add to his age. His manner was most forward and annoying, as the manners by many of those who had come to Sweet Oaks before him expecting to find an aging matron but instead finding a beautiful young woman with flaming curls and silver eyes.

Marcy was not many steps away from the parlor as she pretended to dust a small statue in the foyer. Her ear was turned toward the parlor door in case her mistress were to call. Jessica glared at the man sitting next to her on the small sofa. "Take your hands off me, Mr. Fuller." She gasped aloud as she pushed away the large, greedy hands that were trying to wrap about her shoulder.

"Now, now, deary. Your cousin Edmond led me to believe that I would find you most willing. You be needing a husband, and I be the man for you, missy." The elder man's eyes gleamed with thoughts of a wedding night with this young beauty. He would regain his youth with the feel of her tender flesh next to him.

"You surely go too far!" Jessica tried to rise to her feet but was held in place by a hand that was much stronger than this man's appearance would lead one to believe.

26

"Edmond did mention that you might be a touch reluctant, but he also said you had little choice in the matter. I warn you now, my dear, be warm and receptive, and all will go much easier for you as my bride."

With all her might Jessica pushed against his chest as the yellowed teeth and foul-breathed mouth started to descend upon her own. With a loud breath, she won her freedom as she offset her attacker, causing him almost to fall from the sofa.

Jumping to her feet, Jessica glared down at the man now sitting alone on the sofa and trying to straighten his disarrayed clothing. "Take yourself out of my house this minute, Mr. Fuller!" she shouted, her finger boldly pointing to the doorway. With her words, Marcy appeared in the portal.

Gaylord Fuller, assured by his memory of Edmond DeVaugn's promise that his cousin was in need of a husband and that if he desired her she would shortly belong to him, sat back against the sofa with a lecherous grin, Aye, he would enjoy taming this firebrand. His wife of twenty-five years had died a year ago. He had found her a boring shell of womanhood, always willing to do his bidding in what ever avenue he directed. It would be a pleasure to show Jessica Coltin who was master.

"Mr. Fuller, ye had best be taking yerself from Sweet Oaks as the missus be telling ye." Marcy stepped between Jessica and the older man. He looked as though he had not heard her. But the elder black woman felt confident as she glared at the intruder. She had sent word to the stables for Bartram to come on the run to help the missus, and she knew he would be barging through the front doorway any moment.

His face flustered and reddened at being so intruded upon by a servant, Gaylord Fuller rose to his full height, pushed his spectacles back on his stubby nose, and pushed out his chest as though he had every right to be in this parlor and treating Jessica Coltin in any manner that he wished. "Here now, you old black wench. Get yourself back to the kitchen where you belong. This is none of your affair. Your mistress and I have some business to settle." As soon as he wed this chit he would teach this old black woman her place in his household.

The door was suddenly knocked open and a small group of black men stormed into the front parlor. "Miss Jake!" A shout covered the downstairs portion of the large house as a large, burly black man pushed his way forward, three younger black men following his hurried steps.

"We be in here, Bartram. Come quickly now and help this gentleman find his way out to his carriage." It was Marcy who gave the orders for Gaylord Fuller's removal. She stood back and watched with a fiery glint in her brown eyes as the room filled with Sweet Oaks' protectors.

Gaylord Fuller sputtered with outrage as he was surrounded by the large blacks. His rhumey eyes settled on Jessica. Seeing her small smile of thanks toward her people, he seethed, "You will be regretting this day, miss. Yes indeed, when your cousin hears of your treatment of me, he will set you aright."

Jessica did not care that this foul old man would report to her cousin. Right now, all she could think of was that she was at last safe from his greedy hands and horrible mouth.

"And don't you be thinking that you have seen the

last of Gaylord Fuller, either. Edmond will arrange everything, and you will be mine soon. You and your people will regret this day, I assure you, madam." He shook off the black hands on his arm. He glared once more at the young girl, then left the coolness of the house, followed closely by the procession of black men.

Feeling tears of relief slowly making a path down her cheeks, Jessica sat down on the sofa. She wondered what would be the outcome of *this* afternoon. Had Edmond been serious in his threats to force her to wed the man of his choice? Or had he only been trying to force her hand? She knew she could put nothing past him. He was an evil and vile man, and one not easily duped or ignored. She knew for a certainty that she could expect a call from Edmond DeVaugn in the very near future.

Just as the afternoon sun was beginning to descend, Jessica shook herself out of her lethargy. She decided that a walk would do her good. She had determined that she would face her cousin as best she could, knowing that upon the morrow he would arrive at Sweet Oaks in a fury. He could not force such horrible men upon her and think that she would easily allow their advances. She was not some harlot or loose woman to allow their vile hands upon her person, and Edmond would surely have to agree.

Reaching the shade of the forest not far from the large brick house, she slowly began to walk down the same path where the day before she had picked herbs and plants for her medicine basket. Her thoughts were clouded with the horror of the afternoon and her face showed her worry. This quiet forest was the only place where she could find a reprieve from a world that threatened to overcome her.

With a large sigh she sat down on the cool ground, mindless of the destruction to her gown, and leaned against a large pine tree, shutting her eyes with the quiet of her surroundings. What was she to do, she wondered, her mind continually returning to the subject of her cousin and the few recourses that were open to her.

Perhaps she could flee, she thought, as she had so often in the past year. But where would she go? How could she survive alone and without even Marcy to see to her needs? She had always had Sweet Oaks and her people to give her comfort. How could she just turn her back on them?

But if not escape, what was she to do? Marry some horrid old man of her cousin's choosing and live out the rest of her life bound and tied to a man she would surely loathe? Silent tears coursed down her cheeks.

"Jessica Star, why do you weep so?" A gentle voice filled the quiet forest as a tall Indian warrior bent over her. With a tender hand, he wiped the tears that roamed freely down her creamy cheeks.

Gasping aloud, Jessica's eyes flew open. Not believing the sight before her, she tried to bolt from her lowly position on the ground.

"Do not fear me." The tanned fingers stayed her with a firm but gentle hold on her shoulder.

"What do you want of me? And how do you know my name?" Jessica's tears halted as she was assaulted with this new problem.

"I watched you from the forest path yesterday as you picked your herbs. I heard the black woman call your name." He did not tell her that he had been plagued by her vision since yesterday and had been drawn back to this forest spot, hoping that she would appear.

"Then you have been spying on me," she stated incredulously, not understanding what this man could want of her. "But why on earth would you wish to watch me from afar? Why did you not make your presence known yesterday?" Jessica had been raised hearing stories of the terrible Indian tribes in this country, and though she remembered all of the frightening tales, she did not fear this man before her. There was something in his gaze that burned with concerned and tender intensity.

"Why do you weep here alone in the forest?" His black eyes sought out her every feature, wondering at the pain that would cause her to seek such seclusion to shed her tears.

Shaking her gold-red head, Jessica wiped at her tears with the back of her fist. "I did not think anyone was about," she whispered. Over the past year she had tried not to let the servants at Sweet Oaks glimpse the sorrow that seemed upon occasion to overwhelm her. For that reason, she had at different times sought out this quiet forest glade. Here, alone, she could be herself and allow her true feelings to show.

Again the long dark finger traced the path of her cheek. "I wonder at the sorrow of a young girl's heart. What pain could be so great?"

Hearing the soft concern in his tone, Jessica, for the first time since her parent's death, wished to share her feelings with someone else. She had forced herself to be strong throughout the adjustment after the accident and throughout all of the harassment by her cousin. Not once had she had a strong shoulder to lean on, and now something in the handsome, bronzed features before her showed understanding and caring. "I-I do not know where to begin." She spoke so softly that the Indian had to bend closer to make out her words. His dark gaze held her own, not forcing her to continue but willing her to share a portion of herself with him.

Seeing his intense look, Jessica tried to pull herself together. "I truly should not be telling you any of this. It is my own affair, and it's best that I work out my own problems."

"Why should you not let me listen and perhaps help you in your time of need?" the Indian questioned.

"But why would you wish to help me?" She could not fathom his kindness. She had always imagined that an Indian brave would be strong, powerful, and full of wrath, if she ever met one. This man was indeed strong, for his very look spoke of power and strength, but he seemed to have a tender nature. "My cousin Edmond has plans to force me to wed a man I do not want." There, she had said what was bothering her. Though she knew this man could not help her anymore than any other could, at least she had unburdened herself.

"But why would your cousin wish you to take a mate that you do not desire? Has he offered much for you?" The Indian had been raised with people who indeed married off their daughter in a like manner. But oftentimes the maiden was allowed to choose her husband. Surely, if she did not wish the match, her family would consider her feelings.

"There has been nothing offered. It is *my* property and wealth that my cousin wishes to hold on to, and the only way for him to do this is to wed me to a man he can control." Jessica felt the tears well up again in her silver-blue eyes.

The Indian felt his own heart wrench at her show of tears. "I do not understand why your cousin would wish to join you with this man. Has he not wealth of his own?" Before he could speak further, there was a call for Jessia from the edge of the forest.

"I must go now." Jessica rose to her feet, assisted by the Indian brave. As she turned to follow the path, she looked back in his direction. "What is your name?" she called softly to him.

"I am called Star Hawk." His strong, masculine voice touched her and filled her with a warm inner feeling of peace.

"Star Hawk." She marveled as she turned about and fled the forest. She ran into Marcy as the large black woman set out upon the path in the hopes of finding the girl.

"I was beginning to get worried about you, child. The night air will be falling and you be catching a chill iffen you don't have a shawl." So saying, the woman wrapped a pale yellow shawl around the younger woman's shoulders.

Jessica's silver gaze turned once more toward the forest, feeling the caress of those dark, ebony eyes following her up to the house.

That evening as Jessica lay on her soft down bed, she let her mind dwell on the strange meeting with the Indian in the forest. For the first time she had met a man she could share her feelings with. Though he was not one of her own people, she gave this fact little thought. He had been kind and understanding in her time of need, as no other had been. Even her kin seemed set against her. But the Indian had given

33

her a small moment of reprieve from the dark world that threatened her.

Closing her silver-blue eyes, she tried to find some much needed sleep, but all she could envision were the bronzed features of the Indian called Star Hawk. Even his name had a special meaning to her, as her own name was partly the same. Snuggling deep within the coverlet, she thought of the story her father had told her about the night of her birth. How he had glimpsed the two soaring stars that had blended together as one. He had always told her that her destiny would be special. Even the stars had claimed it at the exact moment of her delivery into the world.

But now, with a long sigh, she knew that her future held little but unhappiness and misery for her. If Edmond had his way, she would be bound forever to an aging brute, and whatever she could have become would be taken completely out of her hands.

As the dark clouds scuttled across the velvet sky and bared the moon from shedding its light, Jessica slept. Within the valley of her dreams she was freed from her tormenting thoughts and worries.

A lone dog barked in the distance as a tall figure slowly made his way to the large brick house. His dark gaze traveled up to the second floor of the massive structure. Cautiously he began to climb hand over hand, up the trellis that trailed with clinging ivy. His vision and hearing were alert for any kind of intruder.

The bronzed hands touched the windowsill of the opened window, and with little effort he pulled his large, muscular body up and over the edge. His light steps, now free of his moccasins, padded across the floor. As he reached the bed centered in the middle of the chamber, he stopped still within his tracks. His eyes gazed upon the girl beneath the soft silken coverlet.

She was truly beautiful. This Jessica Star had cast a mighty spell upon the brave warrior, and he was powerless to do aught but be drawn to her. He drank in her vision as though one starved of all nourishment, allowing his dark eyes to roam over the silky texture of her long copper-bright tresses, and as his eyes gazed on her sleeping features, he had to keep a firm hold on himself. Her face was perfectly heart-shaped and her skin was soft and creamy. He remembered that afternoon when he had gently wiped the tears from her cheek, how satiny had been the feel of her flesh. Her nose was small and straight, with the slightest uptilt. Her lips, softly pouting in her sleep, were as pink and delicate as a gentle blooming flower. Her chin he studied for a moment, seeing the strong tilt that told of her inner strength and purpose. She seemed all things to this Indian brave. She was a woman of beauty and inner passion that he had never seen the likes of before. And though he had warned himself since the day before to flee this place and to go back to his father's village, he found that his steps had been led back to the forest where he had first seen Jessica Star.

With a quickened breath he let his heated gaze settle lower on her body. The satin coverlet outlined her figure and left little to his imaginings. She was not a large woman; perhaps some would even call her small, but she was built with a womanly figure that caught the male eye and held it with a strong pull of longing.

Without will, his hand slowly reached out and touched the silken strands that lay so gently on the pillows. His fingers felt their softness, and gently pulling the tresses to his cheek, he inhaled their delicate scent.

Star Hawk understood little of his motives as he reached out to the woman on the bed. He had thought the afternoon through about what she had told him of her cousin's plan to wed her to another, and a fierce inner need to keep her to himself had overcome him. How could he allow another to glimpse her as she was at this moment in her sleep, so beautiful and innocent? Could he leave this place knowing that another would one day claim her as wife and have the right to do as he wished with her young, beautiful body? With this thought, Star Hawk placed his hand across her mouth and slowly gathered her up tightly in his arms.

Slowly pulled from the outer regions of her sleep, Jessica tried to fight her way to reality and free herself from the grip upon her. But as she pushed the coverlet from herself, for she thought that this was the reason for her imprisonment, her silver-blue eyes slowly opened. Feeling the hands upon her and her mouth held tightly shut, she realized with slow, mounting fear that something horrible was amiss, and she began to fight.

"Shhh," Star Hawk whispered in her ear. "Do not fear, little one. I shall not harm you."

Realizing quickly who her attacker was, Jessica tried once again to gain her freedom, pushing and kicking out with all of the strength that her body possessed, as the fear mounted within her. This was a savage Indian in her bedchamber, her mind screamed with sheer terror.

Her attempts were of little concern, as Star Hawk started back toward the window with Jessica in his arms. But as he looked at the trellis, he shook his dark head, knowing that this route would be too dangerous. He would have to steal through the house if he had any hopes of taking this woman with him.

Upon silent feet he started from the chamber, his dark eyes shifting in every direction as he went down the hall. Holding the soft form tightly against his chest, he hurried down the stairs, his ears straining to hear any signs that others were about at this late hour of the night.

With frantic glances Jessica looked around the hallway and down the stairs, praying that Marcy or one of the other servants would be up for some reason and see her struggling in the arms of this horrible man. But as they reached the front foyer and he eased open the door, she felt her tears fall with the realization that no one was to come to her rescue.

His gait quicker now, Star Hawk ran across the lawn and toward the forest to gain his horse. Jessica was still held in his arms as though she weighed no more than a small sack of flour.

With eyes filled with fear, Jessica looked back toward the dark outline of her house. Her heartbeat quickened with each step that took her further away from all that she had ever known and loved.

In only a few minutes, the Indian with his burden climbed on the back of a large black stallion. "Come, my friend, it is time we return to our homeland." He called softly to his animal. Then, with a kick to his flanks, the mighty beast was set into motion.

The forest passed out of sight and the horse quickly made his way across fields and pastures. Star Hawk finally eased his hand from Jessica's mouth, though his arms still held her about the waist as she sat before him upon his mount.

"Let me go!" Jessica screemed aloud, as soon as the hand was gone from her lips and she could take a deep, fresh breath of air into her lungs.

She received no reply to her demands, only felt the tightening of the arms about her. "You must take me back to my home at once!" She turned her face to look into his dark features, seeing only the ebony eyes looking further ahead in the direction they were bound. At that moment, Jessica remembered those eyes as they had looked this afternoon. She had thought this man kind and tender. How could she have been so fooled? Why had she not fled when she had first seen him and then sent Bartram and the other servants to make sure that he was gone from her property? If she had, surely she would not be in this situation now.

Twisting her body about, Jessica, feeling her anger and frustration building within her body at the sure knowledge that each step his horse took was taking her farther from Sweet Oaks, began to pummel his hard chest with her small fists. Her shouts for freedom circled about on the night breeze but, like her futile abuse upon his naked chest, they were unheeded.

As she kept up her barrage, Star Hawk, finally having had enough, pulled the stallion to a halt. His piercing eyes stilled her movement and her calls for help. He spoke for the first time, softly but sternly. "If you are not still, I shall tie you. And if you are not quiet, I shall gag you." The words were spoken easily, as though he would be little concerned if he were forced to take such actions.

"But why are you doing this to me? You cannot

38

just take me like this. Marcy and the other servants at the plantation will not know what has happened to me. You must return me before it is discovered that I am missing. I promise you, I will say nothing, only bring me back to Sweet Oaks." She pleaded with him, hoping that she could penetrate his hard heart.

For a moment Star Hawk felt sympathy settle over him for this woman. But knowing that there was no recall to his actions now, he reached out and gently brushed the stray strands of hair from her face. For the first time he looked upon her now uncovered form. She was wearing but a short, thin satin nightgown, which clung quite fetchingly to her luscious curves. "You are mine now, Jessica Star. I, Star Hawk, shall care for you from this day forth."

This Indian must have thought that she had wanted him to take her away from all the troubles that were assailing her, she thought. She should never have talked to him, she thought, knowing now that it was too late. "Nay, you must listen to me, Star Hawk. What I told you this afternoon did not mean that I desired to leave my home. I want to be returned to Sweet Oaks. I do not want to go with you." The true horror of the moment was settling upon her with frantic urgency. She was being abducted by an Indian warrior!

"You will learn in time to accept your fate." He smiled kindly at her. "Many other tribes take white women as prisoners and slaves; though our village does not practice this, I know that those women learn to adjust to their new lives."

"As a slave!" Jessica gasped aloud. "You cannot take me as your slave." She tried to throw her body from the horse and out of his arms, but all that movement caused was his arms to tighten more securely about her bosom.

Kicking the flanks of the black stallion, the Indian set the horse into motion once again. "Keep still," he stated to Jessica in a strong and commanding tone.

With large tears trailing a path down her face, Jessica could do nothing but what he bid her, unless she wished to be tied and gagged as he had threatened.

The large stallion soon carried the couple out of the area. Jessica found herself exhausted from her lack of sleep and her fear, and with her head nodding, she found a sturdy pillow on the chest of her abductor.

Star Hawk sighed softly as he guided his horse, his senses filling with the clean, sweet scent of the woman in his arms. She smelled of wild flowers of a fresh spring day, he thought, inhaling deeply of her woman's essence.

Star Hawk had thought little of what he would do with this woman once he had captured her. All he had known was that he could not leave her to the fates that were evilly closing in on her. Deep inside he knew this woman called Jessica Star was to become a part of himself. Their fates were linked somehow. He could not return to his village without her.

For a moment he thought of what his people and his father, the chief, would say on the matter of the white woman. His tribe had never taken the white-skinned people among themselves. His father would be angry and would try to talk him into releasing the girl or selling her to another tribe. With these thoughts, Star Hawk's arms tightened about the woman. She belonged to him now, and he would not let anyone take her from his side. He had proved himself time and again as a worthy warrior to his people, and there was no one that could best him in a fight or on a hunt. So he had no fear. He knew that he would give his very life to see that this woman stayed beside him.

It was not until the sun was just beginning to lower in the sky that Star Hawk made camp along a small stream. Setting Jessica on her feet, he allowed her a few moments to herself as he made a small fire and tended to his horse.

Having had only small stops throughout the day to take a bite of food or have a moment of privacy, Jessica now went to the water's edge and splashed some of the cool liquid over her face. She knew that after the day's riding she had to appear haggard. Her hair was tangled and she still was wearing her nightgown.

For a moment she looked at the nightgown and grimaced at the dirt stains that were scattered on the satin material. Oh, how had she come to such a sorry state? she questioned herself. She who had thought that being forced to wed an old, unwanted man was the worst thing that could have happened to her was now being forced to endure the more horrible of hardships.

"Come to the fire and eat, Jessica." The Indian stepped to her side, his dark eyes taking in her tired appearance. "You will feel much better with your belly full."

"I am not hungry," she mumbled softly. Indeed, the very idea of food made her feel ill.

Reaching out, Star Hawk took hold of her forearm and lead her to the fire. "Sit and eat." His voice was a command that already Jessica had learned to obey. He handed her the fare and she reached up slowly and took his offerings.

Star Hawk sat across from her and watched her every movement. His dark eyes lingered on the way in which her small fingers daintily picked at the dried venison and sweetbread. Everything about this woman interested him.

As they finished their meal, Jessica did indeed have to admit that she felt somewhat better. At least now her belly was not empty, she thought as she eyed the Indian across from her.

The bright moon filtered through the trees and lit the small camp area. Star Hawk rose to his full height, his hand reaching out toward Jessica as he stated, "Let us go to the stream and bathe. You will feel better, and sleep will come easier once you are cleansed."

Jessica held back, her silver eyes enlarging with her fear of this man. "Nay, I do not wish to bathe. I am fine as I am." She tried to ignore the hand reaching out toward her.

With a quick movement, Star Hawk gathered her up into his arms. "You must learn that I do not wish you any harm. I only wish for your well being. You will feel better after you have bathed and brushed the tangles from your beautiful hair."

Trying to push away from him, she shouted her fury, but her protests were ignored as Star Hawk strode with her to the stream's edge. He shed his leggings and moccasins, and boldly walked out into the center of the stream. Gaining the deep part of the water, he let Jessica drop into the warm depths.

Gasping aloud as she went under the water's surface, Jessica shouted her outrage. "You horrible beast!" she stormed, feeling the thin material of her satin gown sticking to her body. "You have ruined

42

my gown. What am I going to do now?" Tears came easily to her bright silver-blue eyes. The loss of her gown seemed to her the last bit of punishment that she could bear.

Star Hawk tenderly ran his fingers through her long copper-colored hair, helping to cleanse and untangle the mass. When he saw her tears, he brought her up tightly against his chest. With her trembling he knew of her great fears. "I shall care for you, Jessica Star. Do not worry about your clothing."

Trying to control herself, Jessica attempted to hold back the sob that shook the length of her body. But as her gaze rose to the man holding her so tenderly and she saw only gentleness in his features, for a moment she was truly lost. So much had happened to her so quickly, and she was so tired and frightened. Now here was her abductor, a horrible Indian, looking down at her with such tenderness that she wanted to weep aloud for the feelings that were assailing her.

Suddenly Star Hawk bent his head and touched her soft, pliant lips with his own. The stream swirled gently and warmly about them, and the moon shone softly, casting with a golden hue over the forest. They clung together, their lips bound, their bodies molded as all time and eternity stood still for only them.

It was Star Hawk who broke away from the searing hold that joined them together. He had known from the first moment he had set eyes on this woman that he would be ensnared by her beauty and innocence. But not until this very moment did he realize how lost he truly was to her. Never had he kissed a woman who made him feel the way this one did. She caused a fire deep in his veins, a burning flood of

43

feeling unleashed from a deep, stirring well, and overriding all his inner senses.

Jessica also stood shaken. She had felt little tenderness and love in this past year, except that given to her by the people at Sweet Oaks. With Star Hawk's hands on her and his mouth sealed across her own, she felt completely a woman, cherished and protected from the cruelities of this world.

"Finish bathing before the night air causes you to chill." Star Hawk's words broke the quiet of the night. His voice sounded harsher than he had intended, but he felt his body quaking with the need to hold her again. He was a mighty warrior of the Blackfoot nation, and these feelings were new to him. In his past he had taken women to his sleeping mat with little thought. Those that were willing played the game well and appreciated his talents in the art of lovemaking. Those who were maidens and who held back for an offer for their hand he had shunned, somehow not desiring marriage. Until this moment Star Hawk had had little need for anyone who would cling to him and demand of him. But with Jessica he had done nothing but offer her his protection and care. In his confusion now he allowed his manner to be curt and hard. He did not know how to handle such strange feelings.

Jessica looked into his foreboding features and hung her head, sinking her body into the water until she was up to her neck. She tried the best she could to wipe the dirt and grime of the day from her limbs. Her hair was another matter, and try as she might she could not seem to get the tangles out.

Star Hawk stood at her side and waited patiently. When he saw her trying to run her fingers through her hair, he reached out himself and did the job

44

easily.

The bath completed, Jessica started back to the small campfire. Star Hawk stopped her and lifted her easily into his arms, pulling her cool body closely to his chest.

He looked down into her face and saw her sheer beauty shining in the moonlight. He moaned softly, and his lips devoured hers. His tongue, with slow movement, slipped between her small, white teeth and sought out the hidden crevices of her warm, sweet mouth.

Jessica was lost in his fiery hold, her senses swirling and inflamed as she was kissed as she had never been kissed before. The heat of his mouth surrounded her as his tongue sent thrilling ripples of delight coursing down her spine.

Feeling her response to his kiss, Star Hawk eased her down on the soft grass near the stream. He pulled her damp body tightly to his chest, letting her feel the proof of his manhood as he boldly pressed against her. His hands traveled down the loose top of her gown and lightly touched the swelling mounds of tender flesh that seemed to strain at his fondling.

With an indrawn breath, Jessica felt her senses expand. The feelings that this man was evoking sent her on a steamy path of no return and her inner self told her that he was all that mattered. She pressed against his hand, her own tongue now circling and dancing around his. As his hand lowered to the throbbing center of her being, she felt she would surely swoon, so wonderful were the feelings that were consuming her.

Seeking and exploring, Star Hawk caressed his way to the warmth of her womanhood, his fingers gently probing as he seared her face, neck, and breasts with his heated tongue and kisses. But as he inserted a finger within the warm nest of her precious jewel, the tight membrane of her maidenhead halted his passions. His ebony eyes gazed deep into her passion-filled features.

Without a word, the large Indian brave bent and gathered the small woman into his arms. At the small blazing fire he set her on her feet and went to his saddlebags. He returned with a shirt made of leather hide. Gently he reached out and pulled the gown over her head, his heated glance traveling her body's length as she stood naked before him. Again he felt overpowering lust seething through him. Quickly, so as not to allow such feelings completely to overcome him, he drew the shirt over her body, lovingly tying the thin leather thongs at the neckline.

"Thank you," Jessica mumbled, her eyes still gazing at his face in wonder. He had a power that completely turned her upside down and inside out. His touch was tender and inflaming at the same time. She wondered what had stilled his flaming ardor of only moments before. Even now in the glowing light from the small fire she could read the heated lust in his dark eyes. What kind of man was this, she wondered. Here she was alone and powerless, and still he held back.

Stretching out his sleeping mat near the edge of the fire, Star Hawk pulled Jessica down upon the softness of the pallet. Holding her between his mighty thighs, he pulled a comb from his bag and gently began to untangle her length of gold-red hair.

The ordeal of the day and now the warmth of the fire pulled a tired haze around Jessica's senses. Star Hawk stroked her tresses until they gleamed brightly in the shimmering glow of the fire. She covered her mouth with her hand as she yawned.

Star Hawk smiled at her with a tender tilt to his sensual lips. "Lie down, Jessica Star." He gently pulled her down and wrapped his body around her to share her warmth and to ensure that she was well protected.

In moments Star Hawk heard the easy breathing of the woman beside him. Rising on his elbow, he looked down into her tender, worn-out features. She seemed so innocent and vulnerable. He desired nothing more than to pull her closely to his chest and to protect her from any harm that might come her way.

Many strange emotions had assailed him since first seeing this woman, and he now tried to sort them out. There was some strange power about her that left him feeling unsure of the actions he should take. Like down by the stream. Why had he not taken her then? But when he had touched her maidenhead, strange thoughts had stilled his actions and cooled his ardor. He could not force himself on this woman, even if she were willing. There was something about this Jessica Star that seemed a part of him. He could no more defile or dishonor her body than he would his own. So thinking, he wrapped his body around hers, sharing his warmth with her and allowing himself the pleasure of drowning in her fragrant tresses.

Chapter Two

Just at the break of dawn, Jessica's silver-blue eyes slowly opened and her slim body stretched out fully on the soft sleeping mat. Then, with the sun streaming through the treetops and the sound of the early morning calling of birds and crickets, the full realization of her whereabouts brought her fully upright.

She was not at Sweet Oaks in her own chambers, surrounded by all her familiar possessions — no, she was here in this wooded forest with a fierce Indian abductor. Looking about the small campsite and noting that she was alone, her thoughts went swiftly to a means of escape. Then she glimpsed the Indian's large black horse grazing on the grass that bordered the stream. Perhaps she could reach the horse before Star Hawk returned and she could somehow climb upon his back and find her way out of here.

But as Jessica started toward the horse on slow, cautious feet, her gaze came upon the busy figure of Star Hawk near the water as he cleaned and gutted a rabbit, obviously for their breakfast.

As though feeling the silver-blue eyes upon him, Star Hawk turned about, and with a smile of greeting, he started back toward the camp and the fire. "Good morning Jessica. I found us some meat that should be much more to your liking than the strips of venison we have shared thus far."

Disappointment rose in her chest, but as the ebony gaze held her own she felt a flush cover her features when she remembered what had occurred at the stream last evening. How could she have succumbed so wantonly to his charms? She must have been much worse off than she had realized, her senses feeble and more easily led in her exhausted condition.

Star Hawk saw the pink flush that touched her cheeks and his smile deepened as he boldy strode toward her. She was lovely even upon first awakening, he thought. "You may freshen up, if you like, while I put the rabbit over the fire." His gaze took in his leather shirt that went to her knees and left her shapely legs and feet bare to his hungry view.

Seeing his lowered gaze, Jessica hurriedly went past him toward the water and once there splashed water over her face and arms. She wondered about this strange man. She had to admit that he had thus far been gentle with her. Though she had only the expectation of being made a slave once they reached his village, she had so far been treated well. But her memory of the night before reminded her of a new fear as she thought of how easily she had lost herself to his touch. Once again she could feel the searing touch of his lips upon her own, his heated tongue gently probing and seeking. She had never in the past been kissed by any man other than her father. And those had only been the tender endearments of a loving parent — never had she been so overwhelmed. She was fully confused by her own actions and responses to this strange man who had stolen into her home and taken her from the life that she had always known. She had thought in the past that only a woman of ill repute would give herself so easily to a man without the bond of wedding vows. But if Star Hawk had not himself put a halt to the rising passion, she knew that she would not this morning be the same chaste girl she had been yesterday. She would gladly have given herself to him in their moment of heated embrace, and she admitted to herself that she had desired to know the secret pleasures that awaited her. She had not wanted him to cut off the feelings that he was evoking.

Some small noise drew Jessica's attention from her own thoughts as Star Hawk approached the water's edge. "The rabbit is cooked. Come to the fire and share the meal with me. We must get on our way shortly."

Jessica stared up at this tall, muscular, handsome man with some inner qualms. This man was more of a threat to her than were her Cousin Edmond's horrible plans for her future. At least, with the sorry group of gentlemen that Edmond had brought before her, she had been able to keep her senses intact. Her feelings had remained her own, though they were unpleasant and filled with anger. With Star Hawk's dark eyes upon her, she jumped to her feet and hurriedly rushed past him, hoping that he did not somehow read her thoughts and feelings in the look that she had bestowed upon him.

Star Hawk followed her hurrying form with his gaze, and he stood and watched her retreating back, not fully understanding what was troubling her. He had thought that after what they had shared last evening they would have formed a special closeness.

For within him there was a warm glow when he looked upon her. She was what he needed to fulfill his being. Had she not also realized this? he wondered as he slowly made his way back to the fire and looked at her as she sat upon his sleeping mat.

"You must listen to me, Star Hawk." Jessica's voice was barely above a whisper, her eyes downcast and looking upon her hands folded within her lap. "You have truly made a terrible mistake by bringing me here with you. You must return me at once to Sweet Oaks. I am sure that everyone is looking for me, but if you return me I can make up a story that they will believe. I will never tell them that you took me during the night from my bed. Perhaps I can say that I went for a walk and lost my way." Finally, her eyes rose, as she had to see his reaction to her pleas.

Bending over the glowing coals, Star Hawk took the rabbit from the spit, and cutting it in half with the large knife strapped to his side, he offered her a portion. After sitting back on his haunches, he took a bite of the savory meat and then looked at her. "Jessica Star, I am not able to return you to your people."

"But why not?" she questioned quickly, putting her own food aside, for she had no appetite.

"Listen to me, my little flower, and listen well, for I shall not change my mind, nor shall our course be diverted. From the moment that I set eyes upon you, I was drawn to you. I tried to leave the spot where I first viewed you, but I had to return." As she would have interrupted him, his hands went up to stop her. "From the first I knew that you were the woman who would stand at my side. Even your name, Jessica Star, tells of our linking upon the paths of our fates."

51

Her name leaving his lips held a bold caress, but Jessica tried to put it from her thoughts. She had to persuade him to release her. She could not go with him to his village, she had her own life back at Sweet Oaks. They were of different worlds. "You are wrong, Star Hawk. You have your own people and life, and I do not belong there."

"And do you belong in a world where your kin leads you down a path that you do not desire? Do you not know that this is not to be your destiny?"

Jessica opened her mouth as though she would have replied, but was held quiet by his gaze.

"You are mine!" His voice held the same firm commanding tone that she had heard before.

Shaking her head back and forth, she tried to deny his words, though some inner voice told her of the truth of his statement. "Nay, I belong to no one."

With a simple movement Star Hawk was next to her, his arms wrapped about her and his lips slowly descending with a greedy seal. "Mine," he whispered aloud next to her mouth as he released her.

For that moment with his lips upon her own she lost her reasoning, but as he released her she pulled her senses about her, knowing that this indeed could be her last chance for freedom. She had to convince him to release her. "I shall be no one's slave!" She leaped to her feet and glared down at him.

But as quickly his hands were upon her upper arms, holding her body still against his own. "You are mine, now and forever." Letting her go, he bent and gathered his sleeping mat, and with a loud, piercing whistle he caused his large stallion to leave the lushness of the high green grass and come beside him, awaiting Star Hawk's attentions.

Crystal tears slowly slipped from Jessica's eyes as

she stood back and watched as Star Hawk packed his supplies upon his mount's back. And the full realization hit Jessica that she was not going to be set free. Her life was in this man's hands, and he was far more stubborn than any other person she had ever met in her past. The only way that she would gain her release was by escaping. But she knew by the way that he constantly watched over her that this was going to be nearly impossible.

Star Hawk turned about and appraised Jessica's full form. He came to her side with a pair of leather breeches. Reaching out a tender hand, he first tried to comfort her. "Your tears are wasted, Jessica. There is no cause for them. I will allow no harm to come to you, there is no reason for fear." His voice was tender and consoling as he saw the sobs that were shaking her. He pulled her up tightly against his broad chest, trying to relay some of his inner strength to her.

His strong, hard body lent Jessica the comfort that she needed and giving in for a full moment to her total pain, not only about her abduction but for what she had suffered over the past year, she gave vent to her feelings.

Star Hawk knew that some inner agony was tearing Jessica's soul, and with tender ministrations he gently let his fingers run through her long copper tresses, his lips softly murmuring soothing words against her forehead. As her weeping let up he looked into her tear-streaked face, his lips silently kissing each eyelid and tasting for himself the salty moisture of her pain.

Swept away in his loving embrace and the tenderness of his touch as his mouth lowered upon her own, Jessica found her arms wrapping about his muscularly corded neck, her body molding tightly against his.

"Oh my Silver Star," he breathed aloud, holding her as though he would never let her go. "I can never release you, for to do so would be to destroy my own inner self." With this he lifted her up into his arms and carried her toward his horse.

With no words spoken he helped her to pull the leather breeches over her naked legs and tied a rawhide strap about her tiny waist to help keep them in place. Star Hawk again lifted her in his arms, this time placing her upon his horse in front of him and mounting. He kicked the stallion into motion.

Jessica could say nothing, barely able even to think with the closeness of this man. She had thought that her reactions to him had been from her exhaustion and low feelings, but now she had to wonder. For at this moment she should be fully in charge of herself, but with the slightest touch of his hand she seemed to melt against him. He indeed was proving to be a threat to her peaceful existence.

The rest of the day was consumed with fast traveling, only a stop in the late afternoon for a respite and then back again upon the stallion's back heading in the direction of the Blackfoot village. It was late that evening when Star Hawk pulled Jessica down upon his sleeping mat and again molded his long hard form about her. At last she softly questioned him about the things that had been bothering her since first she had met him.

"How is it that you speak English so well?"

With a large sigh, Star Hawk let his ebony eyes settle upon his beautiful captive. "My father, Golden Eagle, is the chief of our people, and he is well known for his wisdom and strength among the Indian nations. When I was but twelve winters old, he sent me to a trading post that was run by a white man. His name was Ollie Bengiman, and my father trusted him as an honorable man, which I also found him to be. My father paid him well with many furs and much gold for his care of me. For four winters he taught me much. I learnt his tongue and the way in which the white eyes count their numbers. During the summer days I stayed with my village when the tribe moved higher into the mountains, but my winters were with Ollie Bengiman, and we became friends during this time."

"But why on earth would your father wish you to learn the white man's ways and language?" Jessica was curious. She had heard stories of Indians, and all that she had ever heard was that they wished to remain to themselves, not desiring the influence of the whites.

"My father had many visions of the whites invading our lands, and since one day I shall also be chief of my people in my father's stead, he thought it wise that I know much about their ways."

"Your father sounds very impressive."

"Yes, he is a mighty chief of our people, but he is aging quickly, and I shall soon have to take his place. I only pray to the Great Spirit that I shall be half as wise as Golden Eagle."

Jessica held her own counsel about this man she was lying next to, his strength and tenderness enveloping her. "Are there many white slaves in your village?" Some small spark of hope appeared in the silver eyes. Perhaps if there were others like herself she could somehow form a plan of escape with one of them.

Slowly shaking his dark head, Star Hawk responded, calling her by the name that he had first called her that morning. "There are no others, Silver Star." And seeing her features fall, he added gently as he lightly caressed her chin, "My father has always believed that the presence of whites would weaken and contaminate our tribe."

"But surely he will object to your bringing me to your village then?" Now Jessica was beginning to feel the assault of another deep terror, far greater than that of being held a mere captive by this man lying next to her. She now knew also that she would be unwelcome and more than likely hated by the Indian chief himself.

"I will care for you. Do not worry needlessly about anything." He kissed her forehead as he gently pulled her tighter against his long, hard frame. This was all that he could offer her at the moment. For he himself was unsure of the welcome they would receive. All that he knew was that this woman would remain at his side.

"You must release me!" Jessica tried to push away from Star Hawk but found his arms like steel bands wrapped about her body. "Do you not see that you can not take me with you to your village?"

"I see only that you are mine. Now let us sleep. I grow weary of this talk, and we shall rise early in the morning." He again snuggled her up close to his body, ignoring her futile pushes against his chest as he allowed his senses to fill with the clean, sweet scent of her hair and body.

There were another three days of hard riding during the day light hours and then sharing close contact during the nights, but finally late one afternoon Star hawk pulled the large black stallion to a full

56

stop at the top of a small knoll, his dark gaze going down into a valley wherein his village appeared. The large pointed teepes dotting the area along the river and the peacefulness of the scene filled his chest with a homeward longing.

"We shall take the time to freshen ourselves before we go down into my village." He wished for his father to see them both in the best possible way. The dust of their days of travel did little to enhance their appearance.

Jessica knew better than to object to his wishes; she had already learned, if nothing else in the past days, that what this man wanted he got.

The large, imposing village of the Blackfoot tribe had been laid out during the winter months next to the river, and it was to this river that Star Hawk now led his mount. Keeping away from the village to allow himself and Jessica some privacy, he helped her from the horse's back, his hands going to the leather shirt that covered her beautiful body.

With a surprised glare, Jessica whirled about as he made to pull the shirt over her head. And stepping back a few steps, she stammered, "Please could I have only a few moment's privacy?"

Her voice was low and Star Hawk almost had to strain to hear her words, but with a small smile he shook his dark head. "There is little need for you to hide from me. I know your body, now after these days of having you next to me, as though you were a part of myself. And besides, I do not wish to leave you alone, in case one of the braves from my tribe should come upon us. I would not wish to have to kill one of my own people over you, my dove. But certainly any man who lays eyes upon your beauty will be lost and will dare anything to gain you." With

57

this he pulled the shirt over her head, watching the way the blush spread over her delicate cheeks and down her slim neck and over the tips of her firm, full breasts.

Jessica was left without any choice in the matter. She saw the dark gaze upon her upper body, and as his hands reached out and untied the rawhide strapping and her breeches dropped to her ankles, she turned about and rushed into the river's cool, crystal depths.

Star Hawk chuckled aloud at her quickly retreating back, her shapely buttocks bringing the rush in his loins to a full boil. He clasped an iron grip upon his desires and waded out into the water as she disappeared from his view. With a large sigh, he cleansed his body and washed out his long straight hair. His dark gaze was now thoughtful as he watched Jessica also rid her body of the days' dust and cleanse her own hair.

When he finished his bath Star Hawk stood along the riverbank and waited for Jessica to step out of the concealing water.

Knowing that she would have to stride toward him naked she held back.

"Do not linger; you will get a chill, for the sun is lowering and the coolness of the night air will make you ill. Come and let me dry you and then you can dress."

Shaking her head in rebellion, Jessica blushed at his words. Had this man no sense of decency? Did he not understand that she wished to tend to her own needs? But by the strong set of his handsome features, she knew that he would not relent, and with the increasing coolness of the air, she began to feel goose flesh over her body.

"Do not make me come back into the water to get you. I am already dried and there would be little sense to my getting wet again. You surely know that I will stand here and wait until you allow me to help you dry and to dress."

Jessica's silver eyes looked upon the tall, muscular near-naked form of the Indian standing upon the riverbank. And slowly, the golden-red curls nodded. Indeed, she knew that she was powerless to do aught but what he desired. What matter *if* she stepped from the freezing water and into his waiting arms or allowed him to come the few feet that separated them and carry her to the river embankment? With slow, halting steps she started toward him, her head held down, her face flaming from her complete embarrassment.

"There, my Silver Star, this is not so bad now, is it?" He tenderly drew her from the water and with ease began to dry her body with a soft piece of fur.

Jessica could not speak as his hands went over her entire body, leaving not a fraction of it unattended. And as he gently dried the junction between her legs and her rounded buttocks, he felt the quivering of her slim body as Jessica experienced the stirrings of her response to this man's gentle caresses.

"Oh, if only I could this moment satisfy these longings within our bodies," Star Hawk mumbled as though to himself.

Jessica tried to pull back as she realized what he meant, but with a firmer hand Star Hawk quickly finished with the tormenting job he had set for himself. And helping her to pull on his shirt and breeches, he took up his comb and stroked her waist-length curls until they crackled and shone like gold. He then fashioned her hair into two long braids and

59

tied strips of leather to hold them secure.

Placing a light kiss upon her brow, Star Hawk set her from him and let his dark eyes go over her critically, viewing what his father and his people would see at their first meeting of this woman. And as his coal-black eyes took in her beauty, he felt his chest expand with his pride. She was lovelier by far than any other woman he had ever seen, and those of his village would surely think the same. "Let us go." He spoke softly, taking her arm and steering her toward his horse.

"Are you sure that you will not release me, Star Hawk, before it is too late?" The silver eyes that looked up into his face were pleading for him to reconsider. "If it is a slave you wish, you have but to send to my Cousin Edmond, and he will send you enough gold that you can afford to buy all of the slaves you wish. I am a very wealthy woman; there are ships in New Orleans that belonged to my father and are now mine. Edmond would give you whatever you wish if you will release me." Tears sparkled in the depths of the eyes that were begging him this one last time to release her before he took her to his village.

"I do not wish a slave, and your money does not interest me," came the reply as Star Hawk lifted her onto the back of his horse.

"Then what is it that you do want of me?" The words broke from her lips in the form of a sob. What could he wish of her, she wondered as he climbed atop his mount and his body molded about her own. He did not seem to desire her as a woman, as she had at first expected. For after that first night near the stream when she had thought that he would make love to her, he had seemed to not be affected by their close contact. Even while she was naked and standing helpless before him, he seemed only to treat her as though she were a child or a favored sister. What was it that he had planned for her? Was she to be the slave of another? Had he bought her to this village to wait upon another's demands? Perhaps his father? The chief who did not wish for whites to be in his village and to contaminate his people with their presence? Was this some cruel trick of Star Hawk's that he was set upon playing with his father? She was confused at this moment, she did not know what to think.

"Surely what I offer is not as bad as what your cousin would foist upon you, my little Silver Star?" His words were spoken softly as he turned her face toward him and gently wiped away the tears falling over her cheeks. "Would marriage to an old dried up man or one that is fat and blusterous be more to your liking than being here with me in my village?"

For a moment Jessica thoughtfully went over what he was saying. What was he offering her? That she should stay with him here in this Indian village? But in what capacity? Would she be his slave? His mistress? With this thought a part of her being filled with dread, but at the same instant a small fire seemed to ignite within the center of her being as she again remembered the feel of his lips upon her mouth, his long tan fingers roaming over her body and bringing her being to life with emotions that she had never known existed. "Will I then stay with you, Star Hawk?" The fear of the unknown forced her to question him. But at this moment the full realization hit her that she would, of course, choose to stay with this handsome, young, and gentle man, rather than return to Sweet Oaks and the fate that Edmond held

61

in store for her.

For a full moment Star Hawk did not answer her question. His eyes seemed to sear her with their intensity as he devoured her every feature. What was it that he had to offer her, he wondered in that moment. He had taken her from her home and had brought her here to his village. A village in which one day he would rule. But what of this day? His father, the mighty Golden Eagle, was the leader. What would he say to his son's desire to keep a white woman for his own? Could he speak of a future to her when he knew not what would greet them? He knew, at this moment, only that he would allow no one to take her from him. Even Golden Eagle would be denied if he demanded such a request of his son. He would be forced to take her from his village, and then he would have even less to offer her.

"I stay in the tepee of my father, Golden Eagle." He finally broke the quiet that had built between them.

This seemed to say it all to Jessica. With a soft sigh she knew that her hopes of staying with this handsome abductor who had stolen her from her home and had also, she feared, stolen something even more dear from within her breast, would not come about.

"There is a woman in my village — Cloud Dreamer, who has no husband nor sons to bring her meat for her fire. She is a healing woman, and that is mostly how she earns her food. She will be glad to have you in her lodge."

Another stranger, Jessica thought to herself, and, seeing some of her thoughts easily in her eyes as he kicked his horse's flanks, Star Hawk added, "She is a kind woman, Silver Star. She works hard and will welcome you as her daughter." He tried to offer her some small comfort as he viewed the misery that was consuming her.

There was little more that Jessica could say, since she knew she could not sway him from his purpose, though she did not, in fact, know what his purpose was. Had he brought her to his village as this old woman's daughter? It made little sense to her why he would kidnap her and bring her these many miles for someone else. But if, in fact, some of what he claimed was true, perhaps this woman called Cloud Dreamer would indeed be kind and accept her. For she surely needed a safe haven for the ordeal that she expected to endure.

Star Hawk's heart went out to the small woman pressed so closely to his chest. He wished to offer her more, but at the moment he did not wish to raise her hopes and then have them dashed. He would confront his father with his desire for Jessica and then see where his intentions would lead. Deep down he doubted that Golden Eagle would refuse him once he saw how adamant his only son was on the matter of the white girl. For Star Hawk, being Golden Eagle's only son, had grown up under his father's guiding and loving hand. There had never been anything that his father had refused him when he had seen his true desires.

The darkness encircled the large encampment of tepees as Star Hawk slowly led his stallion toward the towering structures and open fires in the village. As they entered the enclosed circle the familiar smells and sights assailed him. Shouts reached him as his people saw his black stallion approaching, and with much excitement and curiosity several young boys ran along the horse calling up to Star Hawk about the woman behind him, her fire braids and light-glistening silver eyes stoking their wonder.

Their calls were shouted out in a language that Jessica had never heard, and this left her even more frightened than she had been earlier, and Star Hawk, feeling the trembling of her body against him, gently bent down near her ear and whispered, "Do not fear little one. I shall be by your side at all times."

With only these words for her to hold on to, Star Hawk led his horse to the center of the village and before a large tepee he pulled the animal to a halt. He dismounted and then pulled Jessica down to stand at his side as a large crowd began to form about them. He started toward the large, imposing structure.

But before his hand rested upon the flap that was secured as a door, a tall, stern-looking Indian stepped from within. As his eyes rested upon Star Hawk, the craggy visage softened and his hand reached out and clasped his son's.

He spoke to him in their language. "It has been too long, my son, that you have been gone from us." He smiled as he nodded his graying head. "Your mother will be pleased that you are again home and well."

Star Hawk responded in kind, standing before his father and chief and loving the elder man as only a son could. "Yes, father it has been long. There is much that I have learned in my travels, and I hope that we can talk later this eve. And I am also most eager to greet my mother, Singing Moon. Is she also well?"

Nodding his head slowly in answer, Golden Eagle

for the first time let his agate eyes go to the woman at his son's side. And though he was surprised as he looked upon the beautiful white woman standing so silently, he did not in any way show his thoughts. He had learned long ago to be patient, for in time he always learned what he needed to know.

Star Hawk saw that his father's intelligent and lively eyes rested on Jessica, and quickly he introduced them. "Father, I would have you meet Silver Star." And then, in English, he spoke to Jessica, "Silver Star, this is my father, Golden Eagle."

Jessica had been silently listening to the exchange between Star Hawk and the elder man, realizing instantly that this man had to be his father and the chief of this village. His bearing and demeanor were proud and strong, and anyone, at first meeting him, would know him to be something special. Nodding her head, she softly murmured, "I am pleased to meet you, Golden Eagle." But as he did not respond, she looked to Star Hawk.

With a few words, Star Hawk, speaking in the Indian language, told his father what Jessica had said, but as the black eyes still did not acknowledge her greeting, Jessica nervously clasped her hands together in front of her.

Seeing her fear and feeling sorry for her, Star Hawk spoke to his father once again. "I shall take Silver Star to Cloud Dreamer's tepee. Then I shall return to you, Father, and we shall talk. There is much that I must explain to you, my chief." Oftentimes in the past Star Hawk had called his sire his chief when he wished to show the elder man that he respected his wisdom and counsel, and though he knew his own mind on the subject of this woman, he wished his father to know that he would listen to his

65

words with an open mind.

Golden Eagle slowly nodded his head. Dismissing the pair and turning his back to them, he again entered his lodge.

"What did he say?" Jessica whispered as Star Hawk led her through the crowd of curious faces grouped about and started toward the opposite end of the village.

"Nothing," was his only reply.

"What do you mean nothing?" Jessica's nerves were tightly strung and the meeting with Golden Eagle had all but undone her.

"We but greeted each other, and I asked about my mother's health. We shall talk after I have seen that you are settled in Cloud Dreamer's lodge."

"But surely he said something about your bringing me to his village?"

"He will only speak on the matter after he hears my story. Do not worry so, Silver Star. I have told you already that I will see to you. And you must begin to learn my language; I grow weary of your pestering me on every hand about what is said."

"Pestering you?" Jessica pulled back and glared at him, feeling the hurt of his words like a physical blow. "I did not ask to be brought here, you unfeeling brute. If you had left me at Sweet Oaks I could not be pestering you now. And I have only asked you once, anyway," she stormed at him, at last finding an outlet for her fear and pent-up frustration.

Star Hawk chuckled at her fine display of temper. "Augh, but you have cast a spell upon me, and I was powerless but to bring you with me." He watched as she quieted and her face turned to flame at his gentle, caressing words. "Come, Silver Star, if we linger much longer Cloud Dreamer will be upon her mat and we shall have to awaken her."

Jessica kept her thoughts to herself. This man was so contradictory. At one moment he brought her anger to the surface, and then, with a few words, he could set her whole body atremble. Was it he, in fact, who had set a spell about her? she wondered fleetingly as he led her along with him to the end of the village.

As they approached the tepee set closest to the river, a young boy hurried toward Star Hawk and said something to him. At Jessica's look he smiled to reassure her. Then he held aside the flap at the front on the tepee and motioned her to enter. He followed her in. There was no one inside and he indicated to her that she should sit down on the fur mat on the floor.

"How do you know that Cloud Dreamer will wish me to stay here with her? Perhaps she likes living alone and will not want an intruder?" Jessica questioned, her voice sounding childlike to Star Hawk's ears.

With an easy movement he sat down next to her, drawing her body next to his own as though to comfort her with some of his own strength. "She will welcome you and learn to love you. Why must I tell you this? Do you not know that anyone would want you near them?"

With a small sigh Jessica allowed his arms around her as she laid her head against his sturdy chest, hearing the steady beating of his heart and feeling totally secure in his strong arms.

It was only moments later that a short, drawn woman bent with age entered the tepee. Seeing the sleeping white woman in the arms of Star Hawk, she went over to them. "Place her upon my sleeping couch and let her rest," she instructed Star Hawk, her wise eyes watching the tender concern of her chief's son as he carried the woman and gently placed her upon the fur-covered couch.

Stepping back to the fire, Star Hawk watched as the woman quickly began to brew a simmering stew, the flavorful aroma filling the small tepee and setting Star Hawk's stomach growling.

"Why do you bring this white woman to my lodge, Star Hawk?" Cloud Dreamer finally stood up from her cooking with a bowl in her hand for her guest.

"She is not just another white woman, Cloud Dreamer." Star Hawk's dark gaze held hers for a full moment as he reached out and took the food that she offered him. "She is the complete circle of my life span. Her name is Jessica Star Coltin, I call her Silver Star, for her eyes are the color of the blue-silver of smoke."

Cloud Dreamer was the same woman who had helped with the delivery of Star Hawk so many years ago, and at this moment she remembered that night as though it where only yesterday. Again she thought of her feelings at the time when she had presented the babe to his father, and she could hear his words about the twin stars racing through the heavens. She had known at that moment that the child in her arms would have a different future than the others of their tribe. And now she knew, as he did, that this woman surely was meant to play a part in his life. But she also saw more: days of pain and hurt for her young chieftain where this woman was concerned. She also felt in these moments an emptiness around his leaving his village to fulfill his destiny. But as her mind cleared she again saw the gentle care that he had given to the golden-haired beauty. The future could not be swerved from its course. The happiness that would be there would overcome all the grief and pain.

"Your Silver Star can stay here in my tepee, Star Hawk. It will be good to have the company of one so young."

"And you will teach her our ways and tongue?" he questioned as he set the bowl aside, now empty.

Nodding her gray head, the elder woman looked upon him with piercing black eyes. "Have you spoken to Golden Eagle about your plans for the woman?" she questioned, already knowing what the young man had in his thoughts. "He has always shunned the presence of the whites, will he take her as his daughter?"

Star Hawk did not answer quickly, but gave careful thought to his words as he spoke. "Silver Star is not only beautiful but wise and strong. She will learn quickly and be worthy of Golden Eagle's people."

"But what of your people, Star Hawk? What of the day when you will be the chief of this tribe? Will your braves follow you to war against the whites when your woman at our side is of their color and race?"

"My people will be her people." His voice was strong and commanding, leaving no room for doubt or argument on the subject.

And with a long sign of resignation, for Cloud Dreamer saw that there would be no changing his heart, she gathered up the used bowls and placed the stew to the side of the fire. "I must get some sleep now, for Spotted Fawn's youngest son is sick and I shall have to return to her lodge with the morning light."

Rising to his feet, knowing that all had been said

and that Cloud Dreamer would do as he requested, Star Hawk went to his horse and pulled his sleeping mat from its back. He went back inside and spread out the pallet and the furs on the other side of the tepee. Going to Jessica, he gently gathered her into his arms, enjoying the softness of her against him as he carried her to his own mat. And without waking her, he tenderly settled her within the folds of the soft furs, his dark eyes lingering caressingly over her innocent features as she slept, totally exhausted.

Cloud Dreamer observed it all, and with a deep sigh she settled herself upon her own couch, her eyes following Star Hawk as he slowly rose from the girl's side and went through the flap of her tepee. She had dreamed many dreams of this young warrior, and she knew that one day he would be a fierce and honorable leader among her people. In these dreams she had at times glimpsed a golden hand upon his arm. She had not known until this very moment that the hand belonged to this woman, Jessica Star.

The meeting between Golden Eagle and Star Hawk went much as the younger man had expected. After Star Hawk had greeted his mother, his father had talked at length with him about the things he had seen on his trip, and then Golden Eagle had lightly asked what his son was going to do with the white woman called Silver Star.

Star Hawk sighed aloud as he rubbed down his horse, going over again his father's reactions to his calm words, when he had told the elder man that he intended to make Silver Star his wife.

Golden Eagle had been furious with this news. His face had darkened and he had quickly tried to sway his son's decisions, first attempting to reason and then shouting that a tribe such as theirs needed strong leaders; his line would be made weak by the blood of the whites. This woman would rob Star Hawk of his strength and his children's strength.

But Star Hawk had remained steadfast in his decision. He had already gone over in his mind all that his father would say to him, and he had an answer ready for each statement. He told Golden Eagle that Star Hawk would become one with them; her people would be his people, and their line could only be stronger, for she was wise and strong as well as beautiful.

But Chief Golden Eagle was not convinced. He was not willing to allow his only son to take a white woman to be his wife, the mother of his children. "Why must you marry the girl? Take her as your slave for a time until you tire of her, and then you can sell her to another tribe." His voice had softened as he had offered this means of turning things about.

Shaking his dark head, Star Hawk had adamantly refused. "She is worthy to be my wife. She has known no other man, and I shall not degrade her in the manner that you speak of." Feeling his anger beginning to mount, Star Hawk had risen to his feet, knowing at that moment that his worst fears were to become reality. He would have to take Jessica and leave his village.

His thoughts must have been apparent to Golden Eagle, for as he saw his son, full grown and a strong warrior, rise to his feet, he saw his dreams for the future being dashed all about him. This son was to rule his people one day. He had taught him well, and Star Hawk had proven himself as strong and invincible as any brave from time long past. Was he going to, in a moment of anger because of a white woman, destroy all that had been between them? Would he jeopardize his people because of his own anger and desires?

"Nay, my son, do not leave in anger." He reached out and drew Star Hawk back to the fire. "You are a man now, and you know deep within your heart the best path to follow. There is no reason for a father and son to fight when you have been gone from your village for so long. If the woman is with Cloud Dreamer, she will be well tended. She will have the protection of my village. See to your horse now and then return to our lodge and sleep. Your mother has long worried over you and will rest in peace knowing that you are across the fire from us."

Star Hawk had nodded his dark head, going through the tepee flap without another word spoken. He had been glad that he had not had to say the words that would have sent him from his village and his people, for though he loved them dearly, he knew deep down that nothing would keep him from claiming Silver Star for his own.

Chapter Three

Jessica awoke at the first light of the new dawn. She was pulled from her slumber by the slight noises about her, and as she opened her silver-blue eyes, she glimpsed an old woman standing near the entrance of the tepee. The woman's features began to break into a smile and, nodding her head, she spoke some words that Jessica did not understand. Quickly, the old woman bent and was gone from the lodge.

Sitting up on the sleeping mat, Jessica looked about her, realizing that the small woman must have been Cloud Dreamer. Jessica looked down at the pallet that she had slept on and saw that it was the same sleeping mat she had shared these past few days with Star Hawk. Thinking of the strong Indian brave who had brought her to this village caused her features to soften. She brought one of the furs up to her cheek and felt the softness of the tiny hairs. She inhaled deeply of the strong, male scent that seemed to linger on his belongings. She again imagined his dark eyes settling on her and his soft and gentle voice soothing her fears away.

Jessica had met many men in her young life, thanks to her Cousin Edmond, but none had ever affected her as this strange Indian had. He seemed the most gentle of men, and she could not remember a time when she had felt so protected and secure as she had sitting in front of him upon his horse or when he had wrapped his arms about her when they settled in to sleep for the night. But knowing that these feelings were wrong, she tried to push them from her thoughts. It was not seemly for a young girl to harbor such thoughts about any man, let alone an Indian. Still, she felt the warm afterglow of his presence surrounding her as she sat on his sleeping pallet.

Soon, she rose from the mat, her light eyes settling on the small pot near the fire of glowing coals. Cloud Dreamer must have left her something for her breakfast, she thought as she looked into the pot.

But feeling little hunger, she looked around at the strangeness of her surroundings. She wondered, with a tremulous sigh, what was in store for her. Here she was, Jessica Star Coltin, alone in the confines of an Indian village. Knowing that there were no other whites here whom she could befriend, she did not know what course she should take. Surely this nightmare would have an end.

She stepped to the entrance of the tepee and stepped out into the brisk morning air. Most of the village remained quiet at this time of the morning, and she wondered what could have drawn the old woman from her warm home at such an early hour. Again her thoughts went to Star Hawk. Was he also sleeping peacefully? Did he think that his captive was being well cared for, until he desired to seek her out for whatever pleasure he might have in mind?

Feeling deep anger and despair mounting from the abuse that she had suffered thus far, she took a deep breath of the fresh air. No one seemed to be watching her, so why not just leave this madness behind her? she reasoned. She was near the river here at Cloud Dreamer's tepee, and all she had to do was circle about and head southwest. That direction should sooner or later bring her to some sort of town or settlement.

Having made this decision, she quickly went back into the tepee, her eyes seeking supplies she might be needing. She could not possibly set out without some kind of shoes for her feet. She spied a pair of moccasins and a smile broke her lips. Surely the old woman would not mind her taking the shoes, she thought as she pulled them onto her feet.

Once she had the shoes on, she went back to the pot of food near the fire. Whether she desired food or not at this moment, she knew that it might be some time before she would have another meal.

Taking the bowl that had been set aside for her use, she filled it to the brim. She tentatively tasted the thick gruel, but after the first bite, she greedily consumed the contents. It was a good and rather sweet creamy mush that more than filled her empty belly.

When she finished, she started one last time toward the entrance. But her silver eyes turned back as though with a will of their own and settled on the sleeping mat across the room. Again she could feel the touch of Star Hawk's hands on her soft flesh, his hard, unyielding body pressed tightly against her own as he had shared his warmth with her on their journey to reach his village. With a groan of pain and something akin to regret, she forced such thoughts from her. It would do her no good to think of such things. She was his captive. A girl stolen by an Indian, nothing more. If she did not wish to be made a slave to one of these dreadful people, she knew that she had best be quick to seek her freedom. It would not be long before the whole village would be awake and stirring, and she needed to be as far away as possible before anyone discovered she was missing.

Jessica stepped away from the tepee and started toward the riverbank. She would gain the water's edge and then, under cover of the brush and the trees, she would circle about. When she reached the river, she let out a pent-up sigh of relief, for thus far no one had seen her venture away from the village. But as she hurriedly began her way down the river, she was jolted to a dead stop, her heart beating wildly in her chest as a broad, but rather short Indian stood before her on the path, blocking her way. His face had a grin that sent terror shivering down Jessica's spine.

He said something and pointed to her, his hand boldly reaching out and grabbing hold of the long red gold hair that she had, in her hurry, forgotten to bind around her head. His dark eyes seemed to devour her with pure animal lust as they traveled over her body. She was still wearing Star Hawk's shirt and breeches, so much was hidden from his sight. But this did not seem to detract from her beauty in the least to this savage. He slowly pulled her toward him as he gathered more of her hair within his grip, winding the strands about his wrist.

Jessica's silver eyes were twin saucers of fear. She opened her mouth to scream, but before she could utter a sound, he pulled her tightly against his hard, broad chest, and without a second's hesitation, his lips branded across her mouth. His assault was hurtful and demanding as he ground his teeth against her lips. His large fingers grabbed her chin in a hold from which she was powerless to break free.

Fear overcame all other thoughts as Jessica struggled with her captor, hitting out at him with her small fists, kicking and trying to pull her trembling body from his grip.

It was with a mixture of horror and relief that in the next moment the hold upon her broke and she was all but thrown to her knees. Her silver-blue eyes watched as the terrible Indian was pulled from her side and Star Hawk stood above him, glaring with features as cold as slate down on the shorter man. "You dare to touch my woman!" The voice had a deathlike chill that was not warmed by the bright sunlight filtering through the treetops.

Cunning Wolf watched Star Hawk carefully and with some fear. He had seen the younger man fight many times in the past, and he had witnessed first-hand while on a raiding party the daring and strength of his chief's son. But when he thought of the fire-haired woman he had been pulled away from, his fury rose to tremendous heights. "She is the woman of whoever can claim her." He spat, rising to his feet. With a quick movement, he pulled a long, sharp-looking knife from his breechcloth.

A fierce, animallike cry filled the air as Star Hawk pounced on his adversary. His battle cry sent chills of apprehension down his opponent's spine. Jessica sat trembling with fear as she watched the two circle each other and then come together in heated battle.

The fight was over in moments, but to Jessica, the scrambling and tussle for dominance seemed to last for hours.

It was Star Hawk who at last rose to his feet, his

glare of black rage fixed on the lifeless form at his feet. Cunning Wolf's own knife protruded from his chest, his blood running down his broad body and staining the earth red beneath him.

And as Star Hawk's black eyes settled on Jessica, she at last let out her breath and her tears began to flow, her sobs filling the quiet of the morning air.

Star Hawk felt little remorse for the deed that he had done. Cunning Wolf had ever been one to try to disobey orders and to rebel. The man who dared to touch what belonged to him was not to be reasoned with. But now, as he looked at Silver Star and saw her terror and pain, his chest vibrated with a tenderness that left him mute.

Never had he fought over a woman. Never had he been so consumed with such fierce hatred as when he had come looking for her and found Cunning Wolf holding her in his arms. On silent feet he gained her side and with pity looked at her crumpled form. His hands easily gathered her to his chest as he took her away from the scene of blood and death. She was his and he would dare any to try and take her from him. But now he knew that she needed his tenderness, for her sobs filled him with swift pain.

Her tears were not only for what had just happened, her near destruction at the other Indian's hands and her witness of his death and the power that Star Hawk possessed, but also for all that had happened to her in the past few days. Her sobs were loud and without control as she buried her face in the strong naked chest.

Walking quietly down the path and away from the body of Cunning Wolf, Star Hawk did not speak for some time. He held Jessica comfortingly, his large hand that had so easily caused a man's death moments ago now tenderly stroking the golden-red curls that hung about her tear-dampened face. His direction seemed aimless as he walked along the river's edge and let her cry out her grief and fear.

Finally some control seemed to settle about Jessica as she gulped back her whimperings and sniffed aloud, her face still hidden in Star Hawk's chest. He sat down on the soft grass with his back pressed against a large tree as he held her tenderly in his strong arms.

For a time Jessica did not move, daring only to breathe as her cheek rested on his swiftly beating heart. The sleek, bronzed skin rippled with muscles that comforted her and offered her the shelter that she so desperately needed at this moment.

Star Hawk sensed her recovery as he felt the quivering of her body lessen. Gently he placed a finger beneath her chin and tilted her face up toward his. He saw for himself the pain and fear still reflected in her silver eyes. The eyes that he loved so much—their silver brilliance haunting him day and night, until he could do nothing but think of this woman. "Your fear is wasted, Silver Star." He spoke softly, his ebony eyes pleading with her to trust him.

"If you had not come when you had. . . ." She shuddered to think of what would have happened if Star Hawk had not found her in the arms of the cruel Indian brave in time. "But to kill him." Her features paled as she looked at the handsome face before her. How could this man at one moment be so tender and gentle, and at the next a fierce killer?

"I am sorry that you were put through this. I promised you that I would let no harm come to you, and I did not keep my word." He lightly caressed her smooth cheek. "I went to Cloud Dreamer's tepee to find you and you were not there. I thought that you had gone to the river for water and that is when I came upon Cunning Wolf with his arms about you." His voice was tender, but inside Star Hawk again saw the vision of the other Indian touching this woman that belonged only to him.

"Did you have to kill him, though?" Jessica choked back another sob that threatened to overcome her.

"No one will ever touch you but me." His words were pulled from him and settled about the wooded glade with firm intensity.

"But I was not searching for water, I was trying to run away from your village. I do not wish to stay here." Again tears filled her silver eyes.

As though not surprised by her statement, Star Hawk lightly wiped the tears away as they fell on her cheek. "I would have done the same, but you will learn in time to love my people, for they will also be your people." His eyes seared her as he watched for her reaction to his words. "You are mine." As he said this he reached behind his neck and untied a small strip of leather from which hung a silver amulet. The markings showed a fierce-looking hawk, his talons clutching a brilliant star. "My life is only complete with you at my side, Silver Star." He gently pulled her up and secured the necklace around her neck. "None of my tribe will doubt that you are under my protection now. My strength and promise of protection are given witness by this gift that I give unto you." His fingers gently caressed the soft skin next to the piece of silver that hung between Jessica's full breasts.

She could barely breathe as she looked into Star Hawk's face. He seemed to overpower her with his

80

nearness and gentle touch. As his lips slowly began to descend she tried to fight the sensations that he was arousing within her. It was not right that she should be so affected by a man not of her race — a man whom she had only a short time ago witnessed killing another.

Star Hawk clasped his fingers lightly beneath her chin. "I wish but to erase thoughts of another's touch on you." His lips gently touched her own, banishing the memory of the other man's hurtful abuse of her mouth.

Jessica sighed at the tender assault, her breathing beginning to grow ragged as the kiss lingered on. Her senses filled with the tender touch of his fingers that lightly caressed her jawline and the smooth column of her throat.

Star Hawk finally pulled back and looked into her face. She seemed desolate for a moment, empty and lost. His mouth this time covered hers with a hungry hold, his tongue easing through her soft lips and small white teeth and seeking out the fine nectar and honeyed taste of the woman in his arms. She was the rarest ambrosia to him, the finest of wine swirling throughout his entire body. For a moment he lost all reasoning as his lips rained kisses over her brow, the soft satin texture of her cheeks, the contours of her slightly uptilted nose, and along the smooth hollows of her throat. But swiftly he again returned to her lips, setting aflame his need and passions.

Jessica was lost, drawn into his caresses and devoured by his building passions. She had no thoughts but of this man in her embrace, not that he was Indian or savage, but that he gave her the most rare of pleasures. His lips pulled her along on the tide of his ravaging desires and left her breathless and wanting more. Her body trembled with her own passion, which she knew little about, but from the very center of her belly she felt the sweet tugging of some unknown wanting.

Star Hawk's lips took him from her soft, pliant lips and down the softness of her creamy throat once again. His mouth felt the coolness of the amulet about her neck and then the sweetness of her flesh as the swell of her bosom strained against his leather shirt. With a slight motion he untied the fastenings of the leather straps. His hands gently touched the twin globes of softest flesh as his kisses showered over her.

Jessica felt drained, totally consumed by this man and his tender assault on her body. She sighed her pleasure as his mouth touched the rose peak of her breast, his tongue circling and inflaming until she strained toward him and he gently filled his mouth with her softness and suckled gently. Her body now writhed in his lap, her soft moans of pleasure gently filling the air.

It was again Star Hawk who pulled back. Jessica's silver eyes slowly opened and she sought to pull his mouth back to her. But he smiled gently at her, gathering her tightly against his chest. "I shall not take you here in the woods." He slowly tied the leather straps of her shirt back in place and with a smile He gently touched the silver amulet. "My claim upon you will be sealed soon, my little Silver Star. Then we will have a lifetime to get to know each other." At her blush, he softly kissed her swollen lips.

Now that reality had settled in once again, Jessica wondered at her reaction toward this man. How could she have been ready to allow him to go even further? What possessed her when his strong, but oh, so very gentle lips touched her own? Was it a madness beyond her control, or did she truly desire to lose her feelings of propriety with him? Slowly shaking her head, she wondered about herself.

"We should be getting back to the village. It is already past the noon hour, and Cloud Dreamer will wonder at your long absence. I also must tend to Cunning Wolf's body." he gently eased Jessica to her feet.

For the first time Jessica thought what it might cost Star Hawk to have killed one of his own tribe. "Will there be trouble over your rescuing me?" she softly asked, holding her breath with fear that some terrible retribution would befall him as soon as they returned to his village.

"It was a fair fight, and he died by his own knife. My father and others of our village know of Cunning Wolf's ways, and they will not blame me for his death. I will, though, offer his mother two of my horses as a payment for her loss."

"Is this how it is done in your village?" Jessica was amazed that a man here could so easily take another's life and then make a payment for that life with animals.

"Not usually. For there is truly no reason for me to give Cunning Wolf's family anything. He attacked me and what belongs to me." Here the dark eyes tenderly caressed her as he pulled a stray curl from her cheek. "But I have plenty of horses, and Cunning Wolf's family could use them, and the pain will be lessened."

Looking at this man, Jessica saw a kindness and wisdom that seemed completely out of place for an Indian savage. But before she could say anything further, he pulled her hand with his own and started the slow walk back along the riverbank and toward the village. Her first attempt at freedom had been lost, but strangely enough she did not feel the disappointment that she would have expected.

"It was good, my son, that you gave Cunning Wolf's mother the horses. She has always been a kind woman and a friend to your own mother." Golden Eagle looked across his lodge fire toward his only son.

It had been three days since Star Hawk had killed Cunning Wolf, and this was the first mention of it that his father had made. Star Hawk nodded his head in agreement with his father's words. Knowing that the old man had more on his mind, he sat quietly awaiting his next statement.

"Have you given more thought to your plans for the white girl?" The question was softly asked, as though Golden Eagle was afraid of all these few words could stir up. He had tried for the past few days to encourage his son to go hunting with a small party of braves, thinking perhaps with his absence that the girl would somehow disappear, or that Star Hawk would come to his senses when he was away from her. But his son had refused to go far from the village, claiming that he had been gone far too long on his last trip and did not wish to leave again for a time. Already Golden Eagle could imagine his son's strength sapping from his limbs with the power of the white woman with whom he spent his time during the days, walking about the village and down near the river. The elder man's fear was growing daily that soon it would be too late. Star Hawk had already killed one man because of his Silver Star, and there was no telling how many more would die by his hand before this woman's power was purged from his soul.

"Silver Star is mine, given to me by the Great Spirit, and she shall become my wife." Star Hawk's voice was strong as it carried across the fire to his father.

"And what then of Bright Lilly?" The old man now felt the full gaze of the alert black eyes across from him. "Have you so soon forgotten her?"

"What do you mean, have I forgotten her?" Star Hawk seemed baffled by the question put to him, his thoughts allowing no other woman into his mind, except Jessica.

"Have you then spoken to Bright Lilly and told her that you wish another? Have you perhaps offered her also some of your fine horses to ease her pain and your own conscience?"

For a moment Star Hawk was taken aback by his father's blunt words. As he looked at the weather-beaten features, he sighed aloud. "There were no promises made, Father. Whatever Bright Lilly thought was from her own imaginings."

"Do you disclaim that you bid her to wait for your return?" The old man's eyes searched his son's face for the truth.

"I but thought to keep her from my sleeping mat by putting her off until I returned."

At the angry glare from his father, Star Hawk added, "She was willing to give herself to me, but I turned her away, knowing of your closeness to her father and also thinking to give myself more time to think things through."

"You agree, then, that you did have thoughts of

85

taking her as your mate?" Golden Eagle put aside his son's words about Bright Lilly's trying to give herself to his son without the joining ceremony. If things worked out now as he wished, all of that could be forgotten.

"I had thoughts of finding someone to share my life with, I admit that freely. I am not a boy any longer, and I think often of the future."

"And this future you thought of sharing, was it with Bright Lilly?" The old man's question was harsh. "Can you still not see what a fine mate and mother to your children she would be? She would serve you well, as your own mother has me these long years we have been joined."

"It is not Bright Lilly whom my heart desires. It is Silver Star who will be the one I take to my sleeping mat as my woman. From the first time I set my eyes on her, I knew that she was to be mine." There was a faraway look in Star Hawk's eyes as he again envisioned Jessica picking her basket of herbs in the forest glen near her home.

"There is an easy way, my son." As Golden Eagle paused he saw his son's eyes rest on him. "Listen to my wisdom as you have always in the past. You will be the leader of this tribe one day. Your full strength and wisdom will be needed at all times. You will have to stand without flaw for your young braves to follow you into war. Your orders will not be heeded if you cannot be trusted."

Star Hawk nodded his dark head, having heard these same words often in the past when his father had talked to him about the grave responsibilities of being the chief of a mighty nation.

"Now those of our tribe would willingly go where you would lead because you are the son of Golden

Eagle and you have proven yourself many times to be stronger and braver than any others. But one day, things will not be as we have known them. The white men are coming with the might of the mighty buffalo herds on the empty plains, and one day you will have to lead your people against them. If not, they will destroy our people and our name will be no more. You alone have the power and the wisdom to lead your people to victory, for your name already is chanted around the other tribes' campfires. You are known throughout the Indian nations and will be able to band our allies together and rise up against the poison that tries to infect our people."

"On that day, I shall do all I can for my people, my chief." Star Hawk knew the truth of his father's words. He was able to see for himself the fast-approaching day drawing near.

"That is why I say to you, my son, that you cannot take this white woman as your wife."

As anger settled about Star Hawk's features, Golden Eagle held up his hand.

"Hear me out. You can have the woman of your heart, this Silver Star. But you must be joined with one of your own. Take Bright Lilly as your first wife and Silver Star as your second. You will sire strong, fierce warriors with Bright Lilly, and still you will have this Silver Star at your side."

The features of the young Indian woman vividly came to Star Hawk's mind. He had seen her often in the village during the last few days since his arrival, but he had had little time for her. He remembered the veiled, hungry looks that she cast in his direction, and the long, silky black hair that flowed down her back. She was indeed beautiful, but he had never really considered her as his wife. And now here was his father telling him to take her first and then Silver Star. He had known others of his tribe who had more than one wife, but he had never thought of himself as one to want more than his desires demanded.

Before he could form the words in his mind to speak to his father, Golden Eagle silenced him. "Think upon the matter. It will be your decision. But see that whatever you do will be for the good of your people."

Leaving his father's lodge, Star Hawk slowly made his way toward the river and Cloud Dreamer's tepee. His mind was confused by the large responsibility that lay heavily upon his shoulders. The very life of his tribe depended on him and the decisions he would make for the future. So it was with a heavy heart that he entered the tepee of the healing woman. His eyes sparkled with ebony fire as he saw the woman across the small structure bent on her knees and grinding a mixture in a small bowl.

Jessica was intent on the job given to her by Cloud Dreamer, so she did not hear the silent steps of Star Hawk. In the past three days since her attempt at escape had been botched, she had tried to make some adjustment to her new life here in Star Hawk's village. She enjoyed sharing this tepee with the elder woman called Cloud Dreamer, and she was learning much from her kindness and patience.

Each day the elder woman set aside her afternoons to help Jessica learn more of the language that was so strange to her tongue. Slowly, she was improving. And, as Cloud Dreamer knew no other words except her Indian language, Jessica was shortly able to understand the names of those things in the tepee.

She was also enjoying the woman's knowledge of

healing herbs and potions. Jessica herself had helped with tending to the sick at Sweet Oaks, her own mother having instructed her about certain plants that could ease pain and help bring about healing. But Cloud Dreamer seemed to know everything there was to know about sickness and healing, and she was constantly in demand. Jessica enjoyed the small jobs that the elder woman gave her to do.

"What is it that you brew there, my little witch? A potion to entrap a weary soul? Is not your beauty enough to ensnare, but now you need more to aid you?" Star Hawk's soft lips nipped playfully at her neck.

Jessica jerked away from him, startled, as she had not heard him enter.

Chuckling low in his chest, Star Hawk pulled her to him. "It is I, Silver Star. Did you think that I could sleep this night upon my lone pallet without seeing your beauty one last time this day?" He turned her around and sought the sweetness of her full, ripe lips.

Once again Jessica was amazed at the hold this man had on her senses. She seemed to melt against his large, sturdy frame, his nearly naked body sheltering and warm as she felt the firm muscles of his torso.

"I see that your potions are working," he whispered against the side of her lips. "But set them aside and come with me for a walk. The night is not too cool and the moon is full. I would like your company at my side for a short time."

"But I promised Cloud Dreamer that I would finish this for her." She looked down at the bowl of herbs that she was slowly grinding into a fine powder.

"She will understand your need of enjoyment. Come with me." He took hold of her hand, his ebony eyes leaving her powerless to resist him.

They strolled in silence for a time, the beauty of the river shining silver as the moon caressed it and the shimmering stars glittered their reflection on the water. Shortly, Star Hawk halted, and pulling Jessica down on his lap alongside of the riverbank, he snuggled her against his naked chest. A large sigh of contentment came from his lips.

"There is much that I would share with you, Silver Star." His words touched her like a soft caress, making her aware that he wore only a simple breechcloth for covering. Her own doeskin dress was tightly molded over her buttocks, which now rested upon his groin.

Feeling the flush of confusion, Jessica tried not the think of the passion that she found in his strong arms, but tried instead to concentrate on the mirrored stars in the water's reflection. "My father said that on the eve of my birth, at the exact time that I left my mother's body, twin stars flew across the heavens and collided together." She almost whispered the story, her silver eyes gleaming as sparkling gems in the heavens.

"My father also told me this same story." Star Hawk spoke just as softly.

Turning in his arms, Jessica looked at his handsome features. "But however did your father know this story of my birth?" She was confused to think that Golden Eagle knew this about her life.

Star Hawk lightly caressed her cheek, his eyes locking with her own. "The night that I was born, the very moment that I left my mother's body, twin stars raced across the heavens and collided together.

That is the reason for the name of Star Hawk. My father had been seeking a vision, and that evening while he awaited my birth, a great hawk rose before his eyes to the very heavens and seemed to clutch the twin stars before they showered the velvet heavens with sparkling brilliance." As he spoke, he seemed not in the least surprised that she had told him of the same story of her own birth.

Jessica touched the amulet that was tied about her neck, not having once taken it off since he had placed it there. "Is it so common a thing, then?" she whispered, for she was indeed awed by the similarity of their births.

"No, my Silver Star, it is not common. The Great Spirit linked our destinies together the night of our births, and that is why I know you to be my own. The fathers led me to your home and to you that day in the forest as you gathered your herbs."

"But however do you know this?" She looked deep into the black eyes before her, finding everything he was telling her so overwhelming.

"I have known forever that a part of myself was missing, and not until I looked into your silver eyes did I realize what that part was. You, Silver Star, are my life. Without you, I am lost."

Jessica sighed and relaxed against his strong chest, digesting his words and savoring their meaning in her mind. She had never before felt that she belonged to anyone, not truly, even her mother and father. Oh, they had showered her with love and affection, but was it not the same with her as it had been for Star Hawk? Had she not always felt a deep emptiness inside of her until she had seen this bronzed, tall Indian that afternoon in the forest?

For a time, Star Hawk held her close, each rejoicing with the feel of the other. "You will be my wife, Silver Star," he gently said. He did not ask her nor desire any answer from her, but merely stated the truth of what would come shortly for them.

Jessica felt her heart racing as she looked at him. "How can this be? I am a white woman and you an Indian. Does this not matter to your people? Your father? Is it not enough that we can be near each other?" She thought of the hurt that could be caused by a union between them. Not once did she think of herself as a white woman marrying an Indian, and what the white world would say and think of her if they knew.

Star Hawk read her concern for him in the depths of her silver gaze, and slowly his lips rested on hers, tasting the sweet, life-giving substance of her soul. "It is not enough to be near you each day. I must make you completely mine. I wish you in my own lodge. My heart longs to hear your soft voice singing gently to my children."

Stinging tears touched Jessica's eyes at that moment, and she longed for nothing more than to live with this man, not caring about the obstacles that would be presented to them. Anything would be worth the picture that he so clearly painted for her. She could see herself in his tepee, his tender dark eyes upon her and her arms filled with his baby.

"There will be problems, though, I do not fool myself. My people must become your people or else, one day, I shall have to turn myself from leading them." The seriousness of his statement hit Jessica as she stared up into his face.

Slowly, she nodded her copper head. "What must I do, then?" she softly questioned, her trust given over to his keeping.

With a large sigh, Star Hawk gently caressed the gold-red curls about her face. "You would do as I ask of you?" He had never before held such trust in his hands as he did this moment when he looked into the love-filled eyes before him. "And what if I ask you to become my second wife?" He forced the words out.

Unexpectedly, the words hit Jessica. With a gasp she pulled back from him. "You are already wed to another?" She could not believe this man could so play with her feelings. Did all that had happened between them mean nothing to him? How could he have a wife and lead her on as he had, asking her to become one of his two women? This was worse than anything that Edmond had ever asked of her.

All her thoughts were so easily read on her beautiful features that Star Hawk lost his heart even further to her. "No, I have no other woman. I was but wishing to see if you would honor my wishes, even this one, if I asked it of you."

Relaxing back in his arms, Jessica searched her mind for the answer. "I would be willing to learn all of your ways and to accept your people as my own. I have already come to love Cloud Dreamer. But to share you with another?"

"You would ever be first in my heart."

Still Jessica held back. Why did he desire an answer to this terrible question? Was he going to wed another before her? Had he someone else he cared for? "I will try to do this thing that you ask of me, Star Hawk." As she said this, a great sadness filled her heart. How could she share this man with another, when her heart beat night and day for his name, for his touch? Could she easily sit by while he gave his attentions to a young, beautiful Indian maid?

"I do not wish to hurt you, Silver Star," he said softly next to her ear, while inhaling the sweet scent of her soft, curling tresses.

"Could you so easily share me also, Star Hawk?" She put the question to him, wanting him to understand why she held back.

Her reply came swiftly as she saw the black rage slowly engulf his handsome face, his eyes a black storm as he thought of another man touching this woman. "No other shall lay a hand on you!" he swore as his mouth greedily sought her lips.

When he released his tight hold on her, she whispered, "You have your answer."

Star Hawk knew then that he would have to disappoint his father, and if the need arose, he would willingly give up all his horses to Bright Lilly's family. His Silver Star would be the only woman for him. There would be only one mate for Star Hawk, for this woman in his arms was the reason for the very beating of his heart.

As Star Hawk had expected, Golden Eagle was furious when he told him he refused to take two wives and that as soon as possible he would be joined with Silver Star. The mighty chief of the Blackfoot nation had shouted and raged, but in the end he could do nothing but accept his son's decision.

For the next two weeks, preparations were made for the wedding of Chief Golden Eagle's son to Silver Star. A new tepee was made, hides stretched and sewn together, poles cut and erected. The excitement of the whole village was centered on the happy event. Everyone whispered about the white woman who had captured the heart of the daring and handsome brave.

For the past week Star Hawk and a group of young braves had been up in the mountains to hunt. At the foot of these mountains was where Star Hawk planned to erect a lodge that would shelter him and Jessica for the first days after they were joined. He had laughingly explained to her that it would be much like their honeymoon lodge, for they would be alone in an isolated area that he would pick. During this separation, Jessica's thoughts had been constantly on Star Hawk, remembering each tender word he had spoken to her, each light caress, and the fiery embrace of his lips. It was in this mood of reflection, as Jessica sat upon her mat and lightly rubbed a hide into smoothness, that Singing Moon, Star Hawk's mother, came to Cloud Dreamer's tepee.

It was the day before the wedding was to take place, and as of yet, Jessica had not met Star Hawk's mother. She had only stood before his father on the evening she had arrived in the village. Mostly, Jessica had stayed in Cloud Dreamer's lodge, helping the elderly woman and learning all that Star Hawk wished of her. She had determined in her mind that she would be a good wife to him. She would try not to embarrass him in any way or cause him to regret taking her for his wife. Now as the pleasantly rounded smiling woman came into the tepee, her head nodded first in greeting to her longtime friend Cloud Dreamer. Then her dark eyes turned toward Jessica. Seeing the young woman busy at her work, she silently made her way to stand in front of her, and as Jessica's gaze rose from the hide across her lap to the woman before her, she almost wept aloud at the realization that this was Star Hawk's mother.

She had truly been dreading this meeting that she knew would eventually come. Little had been spoken to her about Singing Moon other than that the elder woman was of a kind and generous heart. Now as Jessica saw the motherly, warm face before her, she hurriedly set the hide aside and rose to her feet.

"Greetings, Singing Moon," she softly welcomed the visitor in the Indian language. At Cloud Dreamer's smile, she knew she had said the right thing.

"You are learning our language well, Silver Star." The elderly woman motioned Jessica back to her work and sat down upon the mat. "My son has spoken much of you, and I can see now why he is so taken with you. You are a very beautiful woman."

"Thank you," Jessica responded, holding the tanning spoon but not returning to her work as she watched the other woman.

"I wish my son's happiness above all things, Silver Star. He tells me that he cannot be happy unless he is joined with you. I hope that you feel these same feelings for him?" Her fine, dark brow drew upward as she awaited the answer from the young girl. She had prayed that Star Hawk would not be hurt by this joining of bloods, and she was determined now to know of the girl's feelings. Was her son forcing this union because he desired the girl so badly, or did she also feel stirrings in her heart for Star Hawk?

Jessica felt her face softly blush as she remembered Star Hawk's parting kiss, his lips and tongue branding her with a fiery intensity that left her trembling. Even after he had ridden away with his friends, she could still feel his lingering warmth. Slowly nodding her burnt-gold head, she spoke. "I have never known anyone like Star Hawk. From the

96

first I was drawn to him. He has filled a void in me. I know little of loving a man, but when Star Hawk is near, I can think of nothing but him. Even when he is not around, I think of him often." She did not fully tell this woman the truth, how, with each drawing of her breath her thoughts were consumed with Star Hawk's face—night and day.

Singing Moon seemed pleased with her answer. Reaching out, she patted the fragile, pale hand in Jessica's lap. "Your path may have many forks, child, but I will pray always that your love for each another will see you through." She began to unwrap a bundle and pulled forth a white doeskin dress, beaded at the top with tiny silver stones shaped like little stars. Jessica felt the swift sting of tears touch her eyes. "Star Hawk told me the story of your birth, which was much like his own. That is the reason for the stars. For I believe as he does that your destinies are linked and your path will be straight when you walk it together. I hope you do not mind my making your wedding dress?" In her dark eyes there were also misted tears.

With a brilliant smile, Jessica reached out and touched the soft dress and then her arms were wrapped around the gentle Indian woman. "Thank you so much," she whispered. "Not only for the dress, but for your acceptance of me as your daughter."

Cloud Dreamer also wiped at tears in her eyes. She had known that as soon as Singing Moon met her son's woman, she would love her well. Did she not herself already feel as though Silver Star was her own daughter? The girl's nature was sweet and good, and always she was willing to help and never did she complain. Cloud Dreamer was teaching the young

97

girl all that she knew about healing. One day she would have to leave this world, and she wished to be assured that another would take her place here and see after her people. This girl had the heart to care for others, no matter their coloring or tongue.

Singing Moon did not stay long. After visiting with Cloud Dreamer for a short time and then promising Jessica that she would return upon the morrow to help her ready herself for her new husband, the elderly Indian woman took her leave.

For the rest of the afternoon Jessica felt happier than she had ever been. It was as though she had gained a whole new life. She kept thinking of the kindly woman, and her silver eyes kept straying to the beautiful white dress.

It was late that evening when Jessica heard the hoofbeats of several horses riding through the village. With baited breath she waited, her eyes watching expectantly for the entrance flap of the tepee to rise and for Star Hawk to enter.

Some time passed, though, before he was able to make his way to his love, for many braves of the village stopped him and jokingly congratulated him about the wedding. When he finally made his way to Cloud Dreamer's lodge, he was met by Jessica as she threw herself into his outstretched arms.

He squeezed her tightly against his chest, delighting in the feel of her softness. "You have missed me, Silver Star?" He grinned as he questioned her, looking deeply into her gentle eyes.

With a sob, she nodded her head, her arms wrapping around his neck and pulling his mouth down upon her own.

This was the first time she had displayed any boldness toward him and Star Hawk felt his insides melt with the feel of her need for him. "I am sorry that I did not come back sooner, but many of the younger braves dared several of us to a hunting game. I could not let their boastful threats and bets go unanswered." He smiled down at her, hoping she was not displeased with him for leaving her for so long.

"You are back now. That is all that matters," she whispered, again finding his lips.

Star Hawk knew instantly that he had to keep control over what was happening. It would be so easy for him to take her now while she was so sweet and loving and Cloud Dreamer was not present in her lodge. But thinking of the beautiful spot where he had erected their joining lodge, and of all the wondrous delights he wished to show this woman in their mating, he held back. He did not want her any less, but demanded more of himself than to take her without being joined in the marriage ceremony. "Tell me what you have done in my absence." He sternly set her from him, his eyes devouring her but his hands lowered to his sides. "All went well?" He now thought of her safety, as he had many times in the past week. Had she strayed from Cloud Dreamer's tepee and found herself in harm's way?

"Everything has been fine." She smiled, and taking his hands, she led him to her sleeping mat. For a moment, Star Hawk seemed to pull back with fear of what would happen if he came near that mat with her so near at hand. "Come, Star Hawk, I wish to show you what your mother brought me." Jessica looked at him strangely, not knowing why he would pull away from her. For a moment she thought perhaps he no longer desired her. Had he changed his mind about marrying her while he was gone from the village?

Some of her fears much have been written on her face, for Star Hawk gathered her lightly in his embrace. "You are so beautiful and tempting, my Silver Star. I only pray that tomorrow comes quickly. Thoughts of you are nearly driving me mad." He lightly fingered the silver amulet that hung from her neck and announced to all that she was his.

Jessica received her answer. Her face flaming, she was now the one to pull away. "Your mother visited Cloud Dreamer's tepee this afternoon, and she brought me my wedding dress." Her attention turned again to the sleeping mat, where the white dress was laid out. As Star Hawk saw the beauty of the dress made by his mother's own hands, his dark eyes shone with his happiness.

"And my mother? She loved you also the moment that she saw you?" His question was more of a statement, and as Jessica smiled into his handsome face, he had his answer.

"Oh, Star Hawk, I love her so. She was so kind to me, and she understands everything. She even said that she will pray for our happiness."

This woman's happiness was all that mattered to this fierce, savage warrior at the moment, and as he held her against him he grinned, "Was there any doubt that she would love you, my little Silver Star?"

Chapter Four

The soft whispering north winds touched lightly among the tall pines, shaking the high needles and calling a smooth song of greeting down into the peaceful valley. The black-velvet night was alive with the brilliance of a thousand stars, and a full orange moon cast its light upon the evening as Jessica prepared herself for her coming wedding.

Cloud Dreamer's tepee was full of Indian women who had come to help the bride of Star Hawk to prepare herself for the joining ceremony. Most of the women Jessica had not met before, having kept their distance from the white woman with the strange fire hair and glittering silver eyes, for they were not sure what position she was to occupy among them. But as word had traveled about the village the night before that Singing Moon herself had visited her soon-to-be-daughter and had even made her wedding dress, most of the fear and nervousness was banished among the women of the tribe.

Young and old came to offer their help, each seeming to have an idea or a talent that the other did not have. It was the younger women, those married and those still maidens, who laughingly led Jessica to the river and bathed her body and washed her long hair, not allowing her to help in any way, but giggling and joking among themselves, for they too had gone through this same bathing ritual before their own joining ceremonies.

Many of the younger maidens hung back, not helping with the bathing but taking part by being at hand, some looking upon Jessica with envy in their eyes for capturing the heart of such a strong, handsome warrior as Star Hawk, and still others watched the golden woman with a touch of awe. Her long gold-red-fire hair curled about her body as she was washed, and her cream, smooth pale skin shimmered in the moonlight, holding them speechless.

One of the maidens, however, looked darkly upon the white woman who had stolen the heart of the man she had loved for as long as she could remember. Bright Lilly stood with the other young women, but there was no smile upon her lovely face, was no sparkling in her large, dark eyes, which held, rather, an icy foreboding.

She had waited these weeks since Star Hawk's return to his village for him to come to his senses and to come to her father's lodge and seek her out. Her father had told her that he had talked with Chief Golden Eagle, who he had spoken with his son, trying to dissuade him from his idea of joining with a white woman, but their talks had led nowhere. Star Hawk had stood adamant in his decision. He would wed the white one.

Bright Lilly was sure that Star Hawk had been swept up in a spell that the white woman had cast upon him. She had heard the talk that Cloud Dreamer was teaching Silver Star the art of healing and that the girl had already known of herbs and plants from her own people. And now, as she stood along the riverbank and watched as the moon shimmered its golden light upon the woman, she knew that she was right. A spell of evil had been cast about her beloved, and no one seemed to know this but her. With one last glance in the woman's direction, Bright Lilly started back toward the village, her mind working hurriedly on a plan that could again win her Star Hawk's favor.

With the finish of the bath the women wrapped Jessica in a large buffalo robe and hurried her back to Cloud Dreamer's lodge. With one accord they reached out to dry her body and hair. This completed, they rubbed her down with a smooth lotion that had a sweet flower scent. Her hair was brushed until it seemed to sparkle and crackle before the fire, and then she was helped into her dress. Her matching moccasins of a white doeskin were placed upon her feet, and then Star Hawk's mother, Singing Moon, herself came to Jessica's side. She took up the comb and stroked the red-gold tresses, her fingers working smoothly and quickly as she braided three long strips of hair on each side of her face. And then from her own hair the elder woman pulled out two pale blue hair combs. She pulled the braids to the crown of Jessica's head and secured them with the combs. The rest of her tresses she brushed out and down the length of her back, letting the full mass hang to her slim waist.

"You are a beautiful bride," she whispered and lightly placed a kiss upon Jessica's cheeks. "Make my son happy, Silver Star." There were tears in the elderly eyes as they looked up into the beautiful features of the young woman before her.

With tears in her own eyes, Jessica hugged the

103

mother of the man she loved. "I will," she promised, before she was pulled from Singing Moon's grasp and led out of the tepee.

It was toward the center of the village that they led the trembling bride-to-be. Jessica's silver eyes searched for a sign of Star Hawk, but as she was brought before Golden Eagle standing proud and erect before a large center fire, and the faces of all the citizens of the village looked upon her beauty with disbelief, for a moment she felt some small fear. Where was Star Hawk? Surely he would not be late for their marriage. She looked about again but could not see him through the crowd circling about her and the chief.

Golden Eagle reached out his hand slowly, almost, Jessica thought, as though he dared not touch her white skin, but finally holding her arm, he brought her to his side. His visage was stern and solemn as he turned and looked past the mass of his people standing about waiting for this most special occasion.

Jessica gasped aloud as she saw Star Hawk and an ancient, bent man coming toward them. Star Hawk also wore the white clothing of doe hide, his shirt much like her own dress, and she knew that Singing Moon would have made her son's clothes, as well. But what drew her attention was the fact that his usually long braided hair was worn loose about his face and shoulders, the long sable blackness boldly shimmering. His handsome, bronzed face was painted on one side with a lone star of silver, and another streak of silver ran down the length of his straight nose. On the other cheek were painted three dark straight lines. As he approached her with his head held high, his muscular torso seemed to strain against the restrictions placed upon him by his clothes. He seemed to tower over everything with his height and strength, and he looked primitive and savage to her.

What was she doing, she thought as he came to her side and the man who had walked along with him placed his old, trembling figure before the young couple. Was she truly to wed this Indian? Had she been lost in a dream for the last weeks and not realized what she was about? How could she, Jessica Star Coltin, join herself to an Indian—and one as fierce as Star Hawk? Had she not seen him kill another man? What on earth was she doing standing here in the center of this Indian village and marrying Chief Golden Eagle's son, the man who would one day himself lead this village? She should be at Sweet Oaks this very moment in the softness of her own down-cushioned bed, the bed she had known since her childhood.

Star Hawk smiled down upon Jessica as the old man began to chant and shake a small clinking instrument, his strong hand gently reaching out and gathering her own. He felt her trembling and saw the paleness of her features, and at that moment her silver eyes looked up into his face, making him catch his breath with the sheer brightness of her beauty.

As Jessica looked at Star Hawk her fears seemed, in that second, to melt away. He was the one who had offered her security and happiness when all about her seemed to be tilting crazily. She had felt only joy while in his presence. Though he was fierce and hard, he had not been so with her. She had known little love since her parents death, until she had met this man that afternoon in the forest glade. He had given her joy and a feeling of belonging. More than her own kin had in the past few years.

The ceremony seemed to pass by in a whirlwind. Then the old shaman was giving his final blessings and prayers to the Great Spirit, and Star Hawk grasped Jessica tightly against his long frame. "You are mine now, little Silver Star. For now and forever; even throughout eternity our love shall be binding."

Jessica felt tears stinging her silver eyes. She was touched to her very heart by his words. But before she could tell him of her own feelings, a young brave of smaller stature than Star Hawk stepped toward the large fire and to the couple, his hand holding the reins of a beautiful sorrel mare.

"My wedding gift to you, Silver Star." Star Hawk took the reins and thanked his friend for bringing the horse to them. "Her name is Red Wing," he added watching the display of feelings crossing her lovely features.

Jessica could not believe her eyes as they settled upon the mare. "But I have nothing to give to you," she whispered as she reached out her hand and ran it down the smooth, velvety nose of the fine animal.

"I need only you. You are the gift I have been given by the Great Spirit. I need nothing else to complete my joy." His ebony eyes looked upon her with such a tender, loving hold that Jessica wanted nothing more than to throw herself into his arms at that moment, but with all of the village still standing about and watching, she could only smile her feelings within her gaze.

"Come and let me help you to mount. We shall leave now for our joining lodge." Star Hawk gently lifted his wife onto the back of the mare, and at his shrill whistle, his own large black stallion came galloping through the crowd. Among the shouts and well wishes of the tribe, Star Hawk led Jessica from the village and toward the mountains that his tribe used during the hot summer months.

Star Hawk desired a secluded spot to spend the first days with his wife, and with the help of some of his friends he had built a cozy lair for the two of them. The only problem that he now had was that it would take them some time to reach the foot of the mountains, and in that space of time, he was on his horse and Jessica was on hers. With the realization that this woman was now his wife, he could hardly bear the matter of the small separation between them. With that thought, he reached over and pulled Jessica from the back of her mare. Settling her before him, he gently nuzzled her neck. "I cannot bear to be apart from you."

Jessica felt the same. So much had happened so quickly she did not know how to sort out all of the thoughts in her mind, and as she rode along, the stark reality of the turn of her new life settled upon her with a cold chill. But as Star Hawk took her up upon his own horse and she felt his arms go about her, all such thoughts fled with the touch of his body next to hers. He held a power over her that was so complete that there was left no room for worries of any kind.

Gently he kissed the side of her neck, letting his lips caress her jawline and then lightly run over the length of her cheek, at last settling upon her soft, full lips. "I have waited forever to do this; to kiss my wife."

The smile that she bestowed upon him filled his chest with an unbounded happiness. "Is it far to where we shall have to travel?" she questioned softly, enjoying his attentions.

"At this moment I wonder what possessed me to

107

build our lodge near the foot of the mountain, when I could have placed it closer and had been done with this ride shortly." His long, tanned fingers lightly touched the softness of her cheek.

Jessica settled more contentedly against his firm chest, feeling the rapid beating of his heart, which at the moment matched her own. This was her wedding night, and she could only imagine what it held in store for her. Star Hawk thus far had proven the most gentle of men, his touches and kisses sending strange feelings throughout her body. The anticipation of the new bride swept over her, keeping her nervous and not a little curious.

Feeling total happiness with his life now that this woman was finally his bride, Star Hawk held her tightly against him, pushing his horse to a faster pace with thoughts of their journey's end. He could be content himself with letting his hands run through her free, flowing hair and her softness in his arms.

Jessica trustingly fell into a peaceful slumber with the warmth of Star Hawk's large body encircling her, her thoughts at peace. Her body relaxed and was lulled into a contented sleep as the large black stallion brought them closer to the foot of the mountains.

The moon was full when Star Hawk slowed his horse and then finally stopped. He gathered up the woman before him and lowered his body to the ground. "We are here my love," he whispered lightly against her sweet-smelling hair, his senses already swimming with her nearness and the fact that she now fully belonged to him.

Jessica smiled softly as her silver eyes opened, her

hands winding themselves about his neck as she enjoyed his arms about her body.

With a chuckle for her sleepy innocence, Star Hawk carried her into the lodge. Putting her down upon the soft sleeping mat that he himself had fashioned days ago, he went to build a fire, for the chill of the structure settled upon them as they entered through the small doorway.

As the fire came to life, Jessica sat with a fur wrapped about her shoulders, her silver eyes going about the room. To her surprise she found that it was not a tepee made of hides, but in fact a building that was much like a small cabin. Made from hewn logs, the windows and door were covered over with stretched deer hides. "I am surprised that we are not in a tepee," she said as she watched Star Hawk building up the amber coals.

His dark gaze smoldered as he looked across the small space of the room to the woman sitting upon his sleeping pallet. She was so incredibly lovely that it nearly took his breath from his body. Her small, soft form snuggled into the furs, and her face, her creamy smooth skin and gently tilted eyes, created such a pull over his senses that he dared to believe that finally she belonged solely to him. "I thought to make you more comfortable with this kind of lodge." His voice was husky as he answered her, belying the fact that he was consumed with her presence.

"But what of you?" Jessica asked, her eyes now realizing that this kind of man thought of her comforts before his own. "Are you not more at ease in the lodge of your people? I would have been as well satisfied to spend these first days together in the shelter of a tepee." She answered softly, feeling the stain of a blush upon her cheeks with this small confession.

"When I lived with my friend Ollie Bengiman I lived in his home and I found much comfort there. In fact, perhaps even more than I had upon my own sleeping mat in my father's lodge. Wherever you are, I will be happy." He rose to his full towering height, looking across the now warming fire that he had placed in a small pit in the center of the single room.

Jessica felt the full nervousness of her limbs as she stared across the cabin at her husband. He had not as yet washed the paint from his face, and his dark hair flowed down his muscled back. In that moment, she again felt the savageness of his being. His power seemed to encompass the small room and leave her totally breathless.

Some of her fear was obvious in her gaze as her silver eyes looked upon Star Hawk's face. With a small sigh he went across to the other side of the cabin where there was a small pouch resting upon the dirt flooring. Stretching, he pulled his decorated shirt over his head, his body turning about once again to face his wife. "I shall tend the horses and wash at the stream. I will not be long." He thought to give her a few moments alone to settle herself.

Watching him leave the cabin, Jessica sat still for a time, her thoughts a jumble. She again wondered what she was doing with this man. Only now she knew that it was far too late for any doubts. She had joined herself to this man as his wife. Though it had been an Indian ceremony, she had understood some of what had been said by the old shaman of the tribe. He had asked blessings from the Great Spirit over their union—which she knew was the same as asking the God that she had been raised to pray to, to bless their marriage. There had been much more

110

that she did not understand, but she did know that all of Star Hawk's village, and he also, considered her his wife.

Stepping from the sleeping mat with a nervous glance back down at the soft pallet, she went to the leather pouch that Star Hawk had laid his shirt over, and taking up the soft white hide shirt, she folded it and put it inside, her hands feeling about for a comb.

As she found what she was looking for, she stepped nearer the fire, her hands rising up and pulling the delicate worked combs from her copper tresses. She could envision Singing Moon as she had placed them in her hair, and the softly spoken words came back to her: "Make my son happy." There had been a plea in the gentle voice, telling of a strong young man who had always been loved but had never found the happiness that he had been seeking.

Combing out the red-gold curls, Jessica was lost to all but her thoughts. Could she make Star Hawk happy? Would their life together as man and wife be the happiness he had been searching for? A small noise drew her attention at that moment toward the entrance of the cabin, and with a start Jessica saw a lovely young Indian girl boldly step into the room.

No words were said for a full moment as the two women stared across the small space at each other. Jessica saw the coldness of true hate in the dark gaze across from her, and involuntarily she stepped back from the small pit fire.

"You have taken what is mine." The words were spat out in the Indian language. Slowly the girl lifted up her hand, which had been hanging down at her side, and a long, wicked-looking knife was revealed held tightly in her fist.

111

Jessica gasped aloud. "What are you talking about? I have taken nothing that belongs to you. I do not even know you." Looking past the girl, her silver eyes went to the door flap.

"Do not think that Star Hawk can help you. He is tending his horse. When he returns he will find only your body to mourn. He will not share any pleasures with you this night!" The dark-skinned girl advanced a step, her coal-black eyes watching the face of her victim as though she had dreamed many times of this same scene that was being enacted.

"But what is it that you think I have done?" Jessica was truly frightened. Perhaps she could defend herself from only the girl, but the blade that she grasped tightly in her hand was another matter altogether. She knew little enough about fighting, let alone defending herself against a knife.

"You should know before you die, white woman!" The girl took another step in Jessica's direction, her anger now contorting her beautiful features and making her appear hard and cold.

Looking about now in true panic, Jessica tried to find herself a weapon to use or something with which to at least shield herself from her attacker.

"You took Star Hawk from me. He was to become my husband!"

"What are you saying?" For a second Jessica forgot the wicked-looking hunting knife that the girl was now waving. And then her thoughts turned to the eve when Star Hawk had spoken about taking her as his second wife. Was this the girl he would have chosen to be the first? "But if he wanted you as his wife," she ventured, thinking to stall the girl somehow until Star Hawk came back to the cabin, "he would have wed you. You surely know that Star

112

Hawk does as he wishes. I could not have kept him from you if he had desired you for his wife."

For a second the ugliness of revenge was swept from the girl's features and Jessica caught a glimpse of the true beauty that she was, as Bright Lilly remembered the time before Star Hawk had brought the white woman to their village. "He did desire me before you came. He had bid me to wait for his return. We would have been joined together this night if you had not come back with him. You have cast some horrible spell upon him that has made him forget Bright Lilly." Again her face contorted with anger and hate for the white woman standing across from her. "But soon after he has mourned your loss, he will again turn to me. He will find me willing to give him warmth and comfort. And he shall find pleasure within my arms."

Feeling her own anger rising with this woman's words, Jessica stood straighter. "You are insane! Do you think that Star Hawk will easily take the killer of his wife to his heart? He will shun you, if he does not kill you himself," she seethed, taking the fur from about her shoulders slowly and holding it in her hand, knowing that this would be her only means of protection from her attacker.

"He will not know that it is I who has put the knife through your white witch's heart." And at that moment the girl ran toward Jessica, the knife held upright. With spellbound eyes, Jessica watched the shining blade coming toward her.

Star Hawk entered the cabin at that exact moment, his black eyes filling with the scene of Bright Lilly attacking his Silver Star, and with the sound of his mighty war cry filling the small space of the room, he threw his body full upon the Indian

113

maiden, his huge fist slamming down upon her arm as it clutched the knife and sending her reeling beneath his heavy weight.

With wide, staring eyes Jessica watched the scene before her, daring to allow her breathing to resume as she saw Star Hawk grasping the knife from the girl's hand, his other hand he wrapped about the slim throat. The vengeance in his eyes was terrible to behold, intent as he was upon bringing the attacker completely down. "No!" Jessica screamed as she saw the girl slumped upon the dirt floor. Then, fully regaining her senses, Jessica ran to Star Hawk's side, her arm grabbed hold of the hand about the girl's neck, and her pleas for Bright Lilly's life slowly penetrated the void of blackness that had taken over the warrior's brain. Slowly the large hand relaxed, and Star Hawk's gaze turning toward Jessica.

"You are unhurt?" he questioned before fully turning the girl loose.

Nodding her copper head, Jessica watched still with a sense of horror as Star Hawk stood, his dark eyes going over her form to ensure that she had indeed been untouched by Bright Lilly. And then his gaze lowered to the woman at his feet.

"She wanted to kill me," Jessica finally whispered aloud, the tears now starting to fall in earnest from her eyes.

"She will be punished for her foolishness." Star Hawk went to Jessica and gently placed his arms about her. "Her father will tend to her when he hears of her treachery."

"No, Star Hawk." Jessica wiped the tears with the back of her hands. "She is in love with you and thought that she would one day become your wife." Pulling from his hands, she bent to help the Indian

114

girl sit up. "I know full well the feelings that she is suffering."

"She was given no reason to think in this manner." Star Hawk's words pulled Jessica's eyes to his face, and seeing there the truth of his words, she felt a great weight being removed.

"She is indeed very foolish then, but not deserving of harsh punishment. You have already given her enough cause to doubt the wisdom of her actions," she said.

Bright Lilly stumbled to her feet, her head lowered as large, crystal tears filled her dark eyes. She had thought in that moment under Star Hawk's hands that she would die, but the white woman had saved her from such a fate.

"You will never again come near my woman." Star Hawk spoke harshly in the Indian tongue to the young girl. "Silver Star is mine, given to me by the Great Spirit, and no hand shall touch her in harm. The next time that you dare such an act, I will not allow you from my grasp, not until your very last breath is gone from your body."

Bright Lilly raised her head and looked upon the fiercely stern visage of the man she had loved for so long. She knew without a doubt that he was lost to her forever. He spoke the truth of his claim upon this white woman. The spell that she had cast about him was so binding that it left him blind to any other. He would kill even his own people for her, she thought as she remembered Cunning Wolf's body being brought to the village. A shudder passed over her. Nodding her dark head, she slowly made her way to the entrance of the cabin. "I will not again seek out your woman," she whispered through her bruised throat.

With her departure the couple settled down with the quiet about them, neither speaking as they looked at each other. Star Hawk again envisioned the blade of the large knife held out toward his love and felt the sharp pain of the loss he might have suffered, and Jessica, seeing only the full horror of the past few moments, with a small sigh found herself wrapped within the circle of Star Hawk's large, protective arms. He had washed, and once again he wore only the leather breechcloth that hid only a small portion of his body. The paint now gone from his face and his hair tied back with a small strip of cloth, he was the same man who had held her close so often in the past weeks. And Jessica laid her cheek against his chest and felt the rapture of his heartbeat.

"You are mine, Silver Star." The words were softly murmured in the tiny cabin, and as the ebony eyes looked down upon her with warmth and love, Jessica could only nod her head in total agreement.

With slow steps Star Hawk led her toward the sleeping mat, the furs invitingly laid back about their feet. His hands, with a gentleness that always amazed Jessica in one so strong, slowly began to unlace the ties of her dress and raise the white doeskin material over her head, leaving her bare before his loving heated gaze.

"The very first time I saw you by the river that night, I thought you the most beautiful of women, and now you seem even more so," he breathed, letting his dark eyes roam over her red-gold curls down her slim white throat, to the fullness of her budding breasts, over her flat belly and shapely long legs. She was truly perfection, he thought as he gently eased her down upon the sleeping mat. His hands reached

116

out and loosened the lacings of her moccasins, his fingers lingering on the soft flesh of her legs, as she at last was fully unclothed.

Jessica felt her face turn to flame with his gaze so bold upon her naked body. The light from the fire made everything discernible in the small cabin. She saw the look of hunger and passion in his gaze, but she also saw more in that moment. There was a look that held her, a look of total belonging, of love and adoration, and with a cry she held her arms out to him, wanting them to share their feelings.

With but a single pull Star Hawk allowed his breechcloth to fall from his body, his tall, broad frame standing for a full moment next to the sleeping couch as he watched his wife's silver gaze roam over his body.

He was magnificent! Jessica's breath clutched and held in her chest as she looked from his handsome, tanned face down the corded muscled neck and the expanse of hard, powerful chest to the growth of short, curly hair that wound down from his navel and encompassed the strength of his throbbing love tool. Pulling her eyes from that part of him, she made herself look further, to the long, muscle-rippling thighs and legs. Then once again her sparkling eyes rose to his, seeing there a flame of storming desire that totally possessed her.

With their gazes still locked tightly upon each other, Star Hawk lowered his body down upon the sleeping mat next to his wife's, his long frame fully stretched out. He felt the softness of her woman's curves next to his harder form.

It was only for a moment that they could bear to

withhold themselves from each other, and with a racing heart Star Hawk lowered his lips to the soft, sweet petals of Jessica's mouth. At first the touch of their lips joined was gentle, as though to reassure and to caress. But shortly their searching turned to liquid fire as his tongue boldly entered the sweet cavern of her mouth, seeking out the soft hidden crevices of her sweetness.

Jessica did not resist. As in the past, whenever Star Hawk had kissed her, she felt herself melting from within, her body turning to a soft, molding clay for his hands alone. Her mouth joined his, her tongue tasting him.

Hearing the soft moaning of her release to him, Star Hawk rained kisses over her soft face, his passions swirling to a towering inferno as his mouth lowered, inflaming her skin where his lips touched it, going across her throat and down to her full, straining breasts.

And with the feel of his mouth and tongue touching the soft mounds, Jessica pulled his dark head closer toward her, her body atremble with this moment's pleasure. His hands seemed to burn across her body as they touched and sought out hidden spots, caressing until she writhed beneath him, seeking that which she knew little of. But the torment of her senses cried out for some form of release.

His long, tanned fingers slowly wound their way down over her belly, causing a shudder to course over her whole body. They then lowered to the nest of her womanhood and she gasped aloud. He had touched her once before in this same spot, sending her emotions to a shattering height, but he had pulled back that night. Now there was no pulling away as his fingers sought out her sheath of warmth, the very fountain of her being.

Moaning aloud, Jessica was totally lost to his sensations that he was causing to erupt within her, his mouth upon her body, his fingers gently probing and tantalizing until she felt the heat of her body's passions flooding her entire being. Her small form rose from the soft mat to gain a closer feel of his long frame.

Not wishing to hurry these first moments of love for his wife, Star Hawk did not heed her moans for fulfillment. He desired her to be on fire for him, totally consumed with her want of his body and the need for their joining. So, with a gentle movement, he pushed her down against the mat, his mouth now searing over the rest of her flesh, his tongue making small circling movements along her smooth ribs and across her tiny belly. Lowering, he lightly kissed and tenderly nipped the inner side of her shapely thighs.

Not believing that anything could compare to the feelings she was now experiencing, Jessica clutched out at the fur coverings, her head thrown back and moans of pure pleasure coming from her throat. But as his mouth covered the joining of her being, where only seconds ago his fingers had been bringing her to passion, she knew that there indeed were more feelings left for her to discover.

His tongue and lips tantalized and devoured, bringing her to the very pinnacle of rapture and sending her over toward the descending edge of unreason.

Knowing at that moment that his own body demanded the release that only the joining with this woman could bring him, Star Hawk rose above her, his body held so that his manhood gently lay against the moistness of her womanhood. His lips lowered and held hers once again with a hold that spoke fully of his feelings, and as he gently pushed into her warm pulsing sheath of love, he felt his heart soar, and at that moment he would have shouted aloud his war cry of victory, for never had he felt so complete. No other woman had ever brought his body so close to this trembling peak of ecstasy.

As his enlarged rod of love entered her tightness, Jessica felt the sharp pain of her maidenhead being torn, but with his keen sensitivity, Star Hawk had stilled his body, his mouth now gently lulling her toward the passionate burning of moments ago. As his tongue plunged in her mouth and circled and sought out, she felt her body beginning to respond. Slowly at first she moved, and feeling little of the stinging pain, she moved again, more fully against him, as though seeking out an elusive delight.

The second that her membrane of virginity was pierced, Star Hawk had stilled his movements. His dark gaze had seen the small searing pain cross her delicate features, but he had allowed her the time needed to adjust to his manhood within her, and his mouth had kept a steady assault upon her own. He soon felt her body's movements, but still he lingered, wishing her to accept him fully, not wanting to cause her any more pain but desiring to express all his love and feelings, and to share them with her.

It was not long that he held back, for Jessica's passion for him was as fierce as his own for her. She clutched at his back, her small nails digging into his flesh with a welcoming sting that brought his body fully against her own as she slowly moved in unison with him.

Looking deep into her passion-filled features, Star Hawk began to move his body against hers, increasing his bold rhythmic stroking. Touching the chords of her inner emotions. Leaving her lost to all but his purpose.

Gathering the slight curve of her buttocks in his large hands, Star Hawk pulled her body more fully to his own, allowing more of him to enter into her depths. With the feel of him completely filling her body, Jessica cried aloud to the darkened cabin, her satin-smooth legs now wrapping about his hips, helping him to gain the full prize. Her body, of its own accord was trembling with the sheer ecstasy that was consuming her, and then, with a surging thrust within, she was sent to the never-ending heights through the turmoil swirling about her.

Her body felt liquid, the very center of her being seeming to burst with a thousand sparkling bursts of jeweled lights. She was sent spiraling—spiraling toward the outer reaches of the heavens and showering down about the stars. Her molded form quaking uncontrollably with this new assault upon her senses, she tasted fully for the first time being a complete woman.

Star Hawk gloried in savoring the delight of knowing that she had fully shared the completion of their joining, and as his dark, fathomless eyes held her wondrous beauty, he also was swept over that thin precipice of fulfillment, his sensations seeming to be pulled from within, swirling in dizzying brilliance. He released an animallike groan of total satisfaction as his seed was pulled from his loins and showered into his wife's womb.

Clasping her tightly against his chest, as though disbelieving the wondrous reality of their bodies' joining, Star Hawk placed adoring kisses upon her face, her forehead, her eyelids, her cheeks, and then, with the gentlest of touches, he caught her lips to his own.

"Is it always thus?" Jessica softly questioned as he kissed the sides of her lips and her chin. Her own amazement at their union was plainly written upon her features and evident in her innocent words.

"Aye, sweet. With our joining it shall always be as it is now." And Star Hawk knew that never in his years of having other women freely give themselves to him, had he ever felt as he had in these past moments.

"Then whyever have we waited so long?" she breathed, thinking about the times that they could have shared this special act since knowing each other and greedy now for all those moments that had been wasted.

Star Hawk lightly kissed her upon the tip of her nose. "Augh, my beautiful Silver Star. Have you no little shame?" he laughingly asked her as he snuggled his body about her smaller frame, finding her softness already pulling at his loins.

"Nay, not when I now have known such pleasure," Jessica replied, moving a bit upon the mat to accommodate him and feeling some small measure of soreness. But thinking of the feelings that his body had evoked in her, all such thoughts of pain were cleanly swept from her mind.

"I wished not to take you before our joining, to show my love and inner feelings toward you—my respect for your body and the desire that I hold to make all right between us." He spoke softly, caressing her fragile jawline with his long finger, and sending a slight shudder over her form.

For a moment, at his words, Jessica's features turned serious. "We truly are man and wife?" She

122

thought of the ceremony, so different from the one that she had always envisioned would take place between her and the man she would one day wed.

The ebony eyes sought out her own and held them with a tender regard. "Forever," he assured her. "We are joined by the Great Spirit, who led me to find you, who knew of our destinies from the moment of our birth. I think there is little difference between the white man's God and my own. Ollie Bengiman taught me of this white God, and I am sure that He also witnessed our joining and heard the prayers of our shaman. To bless our joining."

Jessica lightly kissed him on the lips. "I have thought also this same thought. I but would wish to forever stay as we are now." She sighed as she relaxed back against the furs that were now scattered about the sleeping pallet.

Star Hawk thought back to earlier this evening when Silver Star's life had been threatened by one of his own people, and for a second a blinding fear settled over his heart, a premonition of sorts that spoke of pain and loss. But quickly, as her silver eyes glowed softly, he was lost within their shimmering depths. Taking her lips once more, he forgot all but this woman whom he so fiercely loved. With a soft sigh he whispered, "You are the beating of my heart, my reason for breath, my Silver Star."

"I love you, Star Hawk," Jessica said aloud, knowing all of this man now: that he was tender and giving, loving and kind to her at all times. And then, having also seen the savage fury that had settled over him when she had been threatened, she stated these words firmly and surely, knowing that she was binding herself more fully to him. And with this knowledge she rejoiced as she realized that she did fully love him. There was no reason to her feelings for loving an Indian, but when this man looked upon her with such a softness and his gentle ways sheltered her from all of the world outside, she knew that she had little choice. Her heart was lost to his keeping.

They made love again, a more languid, slower union than the first, their hands seeming not to be able to feel enough of other's body, their kisses caressing and exploring. Time seemed to stand still as the pair upon the soft bed of furs sought out the wild esctasy that only they could share, and again, as Jessica felt herself slipping from the hold of reality and spiraling toward the summit of fulfillment, she clung to her mighty warrior, her body swirling upon the crest of pleasure with him.

There was no time for talk, so great was their discovery of passion. Star Hawk, rising from the sleeping mat, strode naked toward the fire and stoked the glowing ambers. Then, without a thought to his own comfort, he left the cabin for a moment and returned with a pouch of water. After warming the liquid he went to his wife's side, and with a cloth from his pouch, he tenderly washed her body, his strong fingers wiping the warmed cloth over her breasts and across her belly. And then with the gentlest of touches, he bathed the flecks of blood from her inner thighs, her proof of virginity.

His tender ministrations sealed her love for him within Jessica's breast, and as he finished with the bathing and tucked the warm furs about her body, his dark ebony gaze held hers for a moment before he set the water and cloth aside and climbed back upon the pallet next to her. He held his love throughout the rest of the night, as though he feared that if he let go of her, she would flee from his side.

The following morning, as the small shafts of sunlight came through the taut hides stretched across the window openings, Star Hawk awoke. His first conscious thoughts were of the woman wrapped so snugly against his body, and turning his head to gain a better view of her, he drew a deep breath.

Many times in the days that it had taken him to bring Jessica to his village he had awakened next to her, but never had she appeared as she did this morn. She reached out to his heart with her innocent loveliness. The curls of her fiery hair wrapped about her body and curled about his arm, the sweetly scented. Her perfect features tilted toward him, left him tracing each gentle outline. The pale sweeping lashes dusting delicately against her rose-hued cheeks sent a desire over him to gather her tighter against him and to kiss her closed eyelids. But he forcefully held himself in check, enjoying his leisurely viewing of her. Her lips seemed to pout in the most provocative fashion, her small, firm chin was laid trustingly against one of the soft furs of their bedding. Her features seemed heart-shaped to him at this moment, and he knew that if his gaze were to roam under the covers, he would find only perfection there also. And for a moment he felt the full power of her beauty. He had never felt this overwhelming of his senses from any other being.

With a small, sleepy moan Jessica snuggled closer against his side, seeking out his warmth. With a tender smile Star Hawk wrapped his arms about her, and he also fell back to sleep.

It was a short time later that Jessica stretched out full length upon the sleeping pallet, her eyes still held

125

shut as she luxuriated in her well-being. She felt the happiness of one well loved, and as she felt the hard form next to her a small smile came to her lips.

"I see that you have finally awakened." Star Hawk bent over her and kissed her sweetly in a morning greeting.

Opening her silver eyes, Jessica wondered for a second if she had truly dreamed the wondrous delights that she had shared with this man the night before, but as she felt the heat of his loins touching fully upon her thigh she knew that no dream could have compared to what she had felt.

His hands gently glided across her body stoking the embers that still glowed warmly from the night before, and as his mouth covered hers he rose above her, spreading her thighs and delving into that most desired shelter of her warmth.

Jessica felt her body rhythmically responding to his with a passionate melody that gave life in some far-off corner of the world. He swept her higher and higher, soaring and then gliding as though upon the mighty wings of the hawk that he had been named for, and they both searched for rapture's pinnacle amongst the fleecy setting of the billowing clouds.

For what seemed the passing of an eternity, their bodies moved together, stroking and satisfying all cravings, waiting only for that indescribable moment's pleasure when they would cascade together upon the downy aftermath of love's brilliant embers. And as the soft cry of her release filled the small cabin, Star Hawk's shuddered, and he clutched the woman of his heart in his fierce embrace.

Floating back to reality upon the caress of the most delicate thistle down, Jessica opened her silver eyes and viewed for herself the love glowing in the

126

black eyes before her. And she also saw herself reflected within those depths—and the love that she felt for this man built with each passing moment. "Good morning to you also, my husband," she lightly breathed against his ear.

And with a chuckle he smiled full into her face. "Never has there been a finer morning, my sweet. I love you with all of my soul."

Feeling the swift sting of tears touch her eyes, Jessica whispered, "And I you, my love."

Star Hawk reached a finger out and gently wiped at the drop of liquid slowly going down her cheek. "There is no cause for tears for what we feel between us. Do you find a measure of pain in our union?" He wished to know all of her feelings and the reason why she would weep at such a special moment as this.

"Nay," Jessica shook her head slowly, seeing the concern in his regard of her. "I but have such overwhelming feelings within my heart for you, I cannot keep from weeping," she said truthfully.

Kissing away the lingering tears, Star Hawk pulled her into his embrace. "My love for you will allow only joy. I would never see you hurt or saddened."

Responding to his gentle words and tender kisses, Jessica smiled fully into his loving face, amazed at herself for having found such a man to truly claim as her own.

Snugging her warmly beneath the furs, Star Hawk left the cozy lair of their sleeping mat and began to build the fire, his ebony eyes smoldering with a warm glow as he viewed his wife watching his every move as he went about the cabin.

"You surely did a fine job of building this cabin, Star Hawk." Jessica rose upon her elbow. Now, with the daylight, she could see more of the structure.

Star Hawk smiled at her praise of his handiwork, and going to his pouches he pulled out foodstuff. "It is good to have a woman who appreciates her husband," he smugly retorted as he sorted out the food that he would prepare for their first meal together.

"I can do that." Jessica started to rise, but with his eyes upon her and the shaking of his long black hair, she stilled.

"I wish to cook this morn for you, Silver Star. I would have you rest and only waste your strength upon tending your husband." Again, the suggestive grin covered his features.

"I do know how to cook, though," she replied. "Cloud Dreamer has taught me much in these many weeks that I have lived with her."

"I am sure she has, my flower, but your husband also can prepare a meal for his family."

"It is as well, then." Jessica lay back in the warmth of the pallet. "I am pleased that I have a man who can bring me meat and then also cook it for me." She giggled lightly at her jest, and Star Hawk also grinned widely, knowing that if this were to be her desire he would do exactly as she wished.

It was not long before the small cabin was filled with the warmth of the fire and the delicious smells of Star Hawk's breakfast. Going to the sleeping mat, he pulled Jessica from the confines of their small nest. "All is ready, my sweet." He kissed her upon the cheek, his glowing eyes going down the length of her naked body and feeling his blood beginning to boil once again. "Cover yourself, love, or the meal will surely be cold before we attend it." His finger gently traced the outline of her full bosom, delighting in the way the rose-hued nipple perked at his caress.

Quickly obeying, she picked up her wedding dress, but as she would have made to pull it over her head Star Hawk took it from her hands. "Your clothes are in one of the pouches."

"You thought to bring them?" she asked as she started toward the bags resting on the floor. "I forgot completely about all but the moment of our wedding," she murmured, as she went through the pouch and found one of the deerhide dresses that Cloud Dreamer had given her.

Star Hawk chuckled as he watched her bare backside going across the room, and as he gained her side he smiled upon her. "That is exactly how I like to keep my women. Forgetful of all, except me." His perfect white teeth shone down at her from his handsome bronzed face.

For a moment Jessica stopped in her dressing, thinking of his words and then of the Indian girl who had attacked her the night before. "Are there more of your women that I should be warned against?" Her silver eyes turned to him with a touch of humor in their depths but also a small amount of seriousness. She had completely forgotten Bright Lilly and what had taken place last eve. And now, when he spoke of his women, was he truly jesting? she wondered to herself.

Holding her tightly against his chest, Star Hawk murmured, "You are the only woman of my heart, Silver Star. Bright Lilly is but a foolish young maiden. Do not think upon her or any other. I will not allow any harm to befall you."

Jessica did not in the least doubt his words. Had he not already showed her his protection? And did she not know that without her interference, Bright

Lilly would at this moment be dead? She had complete trust in this ability to care for her—what she did not know about was the other women of his tribe. She had not thought before their wedding that this virile, handsome man must have the young women of his tribe casting their eyes upon him. Already one had shown that she was willing to kill for him; what of any others?

No more was said on the matter, though, as Jessica pulled the dress over her head and she and Star Hawk sat near the fire and ate their meal.

It was early in the afternoon when Star Hawk led Jessica out of the cabin. Holding hands tightly, they went for a walk.

"It is so beautiful here," Jessica breathed as they stepped away from the clearing that had been made for their joining lodge. The mountain loomed before them in such a dense display of forest green and snow-capped peaks, that it was breathtaking.

"Each summer my tribe moves up the mountains where the game is plentiful and the air is cooler. You will love it there, Silver Star." He gently pushed a tendrill of the fire hair away from her pinkened cheek.

Jessica was sure that she would indeed love the high mountains. The valley that his people now were in was beautiful, so near the river's edge, but here, in the vastness of the mountains, she found a gentle peacefulness. It was as though there was no other world except this one that her husband belonged to.

"You are so sure that I will fit in as you wish?" Jessica lightly questioned him as he was helping her to step over a fallen tree limb.

Star Hawk looked upon her with a warm regard. "Remember when I told you that my people would

130

be your people?" She slowly nodded her head, and as they started back upon the path on which he was leading her, he continued. "You will fit in with my tribe because I have accepted you, and also because you are willing to please me."

A small smile was his answer, and it seemed to fill his heart. "I hope it will be as easy as the picture in your mind," she said.

"If you are able to see within your mind yourself as my woman and the mother of my children, living in my lodge, then it will be so." His statement left little room for doubt, and as they approached the stream that was fed briskly by the mountain water, he stopped and kissed her lightly on the mouth. "Can you swim, Silver Star?" he questioned as he let her loose from his grip. And at the nodding of her head, he grinned. "The stream is deep in several places. Let us spend the rest of the afternoon here among the shelter of the trees.

Jessica smiled her pleasure as she looked about the area. The stream was lovely, meandering along the foot of the mountains, and the greenery of the trees and the lush, sweet grass too added a picturesque setting for an afternoon of idyllic play.

With the help of her husband Jessica was soon out of her moccasins and dress, her body glistening golden as the afternoon sun sparkled through the thick coverage of the tall trees. But still not feeling totally comfortable with the feeling of freedom that came with not wearing clothes in her husband's presence, she hurriedly rushed to the stream, wading out into the cool depths until she submerged up to her neck.

Within a mater of seconds Star Hawk stood upon the bank, naked. And he stood there looking at

Jessica for a moment, she again admired the long, sinewy muscles of his body, the narrow hips and broad shoulders, the bronzed muscles of his long legs rippling with unleashed strength, and again she felt her heart racing. The man was her husband — what a difference between him and those who had come before her at Sweet Oaks and asked for her hand. Her Cousin Edmond would be furious at this moment if he could but catch a glimpse of this magnificent man she had wed. There was not a thing ill favored about Star Hawk, and at the memory of his body upon the sleeping mat with her own, she blushed.

The afternoon was given over to frolicking play as the young couple swam and teased, their bodies touching often as they enjoyed the coolness of the water gently enveloping them.

It was as the sun was beginning to lower that Star Hawk carried a breathless Jessica to the lushness of the early fall grass, and with the tenderness of one who loves, laid her beautiful body out before him, his large hands gently spreading the dampened red-gold curls about her, his dark eyes devouring in their intensity as they boldly swept over her lush form. And then, with a growl that seemed pulled from his very depths, he rose above her.

The surroundings of the hidden glen seemed to heighten the couple's awareness as their ears filled with the forest noises, the burbling stream gently rolling away, the soft cooing of a dove calling to her mate and the gentle breeze shaking the canopy of trees overhead. Even the earthy smells of grass and forest glade stoked their awareness of each other, and Star Hawk's long black hair dripped droplets of water upon Jessica's breasts. And then he lovingly licked and kissed the moisture away, and she nearly disolved against him as he filled her with his throbbing urgency.

There was a tender arousal to their love play, a slow, seductive pulsing that swept them to the outer boundaries of delight. Star Hawk's body slowly melded back and forth against his bride's, lips nipping and tantalizing as he stroked the love chords of her nether regions. His eyes watched with a burning fire as she was brought to heights of rapture and then slowly floated back down, but again and again he swept her along, not giving in to his own storming desire, but holding back until, at last, as Jessica screamed his name aloud and her body writhed and convulsed beneath him, he allowed himself to vault over the plateau of rapture as the violence of his passions overswept him and left him shuddering and gasping aloud, "Silver Star."

As the glowing embers of love's aftermath swept over the pair and they lay side by side, their hearts entwined and beating swiftly with the languid assault to their senses, Star Hawk lightly caressed Jessica's cheek, feeling the softness of her flesh once again under his large, hard hand. "What is it that you miss from your past life, sweet?" he softly questioned, surprising her and turning her face to look upon him. She saw the dark eyes watching her intently.

With a small sigh she snuggled more fully against his side, luxuriating in his hardness. "I guess, if anything, I miss Marcy the most," she quietly responded, her silver-blue eyes looking now to the trees that lay above their heads and gently waved with the late afternoon breeze coming down from the mountains.

"The black woman who came for you when you

were in the forest?" His dark gaze held many questions.

"Aye, she was much like a mother to me." Jessica remembered all of the times as a child, and then as she had grown into a young lady, when she had depended upon Marcy. And the old black woman had always been there for her. Her loving arms had always wrapped Jessica with their warmth and caring. Much as Star Hawk's did now, she mused to herself.

"And your own mother and father, what of them? To leave you to the care of a kin that would send old men to your door to seek out your virtue?"

"They died in an accident over a year ago. Always Edmond had seemed most kind and concerned about my future while my father lived, and he being my only kin here in the colonies, it was natural that my father would leave my care to him. But it was only a small space of time before Edmond showed his true interest in my welfare. He desires control of my father's wealth. That is why he has placed before me such disreputable men, hoping that I would choose one that he would be able to control. I think that he would have even found some way to eliminate me altogether, except for the fact that my father's will states that if something should happen to me before I wed or come of age, that all would go to my mother's only living brother."

Star Hawk listened attentively, his arm only tightening about her when she spoke of her fears that her cousin wished her harm. "And your mother's brother? Does he know of this evil cousin who wishes control over your property?"

"Nay, he lives somewhere in Europe. There is a large sum of money set aside in case the need should arise for my father's attorney to seek him out. Word was sent of my parents' death, but there was never a response." Jessica had wished so often in the past, after the death of her mother and father, that her mother's brother would come for her, but she had given up all hopes as the months slowly passed.

"Then it is only the old black woman that you regret leaving behind? What of your home? Do you not care that your cousin will have a free hand over all that now?"

Jessica had not truthfully thought about this matter. So much had happened to her so quickly that she had barely had time to think of anything except learning the ways of Star Hawk's people and the strange new feelings that she harbored for him.

"I do miss Marcy. But all that I had seems far off in the past now. My pretty clothes and my nice home at Sweet Oaks do not seem nearly as important as my being here now with you."

Bending over her, Star Hawk kissed her most gently. "I will think upon what you have told me about this cousin. Your properties are vast. Perhaps one day you will be able to help your people with such wealth."

And at that moment Jessica again remembered the words that he had spoken to her of his people becoming also her people. With a smile of pure bliss she hugged herself against his strong chest. Here was safety from all harm. A wise man who was loving and good. She would never regret falling in love with him.

For the next two weeks the newly wedded pair remained at the cabin at the foot of the mountains.

Their days were filled with long walks, playing in the stream as the warming sun shone forth in the afternoons, and then later lying upon the soft grasses and making love. Afterwards, in the quietness of their surroundings, they learned about each other—now and in the past. Their nights were given over to their passions and their tender budding love, drawing closer together and building a bond that would in future days remain unbendable.

Star Hawk taught Jessica how to hunt and to fish, delighting in the feel of her soft, yielding body next to his as he stood close behind her and helped her to pull back the bow string and take aim at a deer. But as her arrow would veer off to the side of the animal and she would giggle in relief at not having hit the beautiful creature, Star Hawk would take her into his arms and kiss her lips soundly, laughing along with her, for this time was for pleasure and enjoyment.

There was the afternoon that she stood at his side in the middle of the stream with a sharp spear held high as she took aim at a large fish. With the forceful thrust of her spear, she slipped, her footing taking her with a splash into the cool depths. As she came to the surface, spitting and sputtering, her dress sodden, Star Hawk laughed loudly at her antics, and then, seeing the pout of her ripe, full lips, he took her in his arms and sampled the tempting morsels. This led to other play, and within moments they were naked in the stream, their passions astir as they sought out the rapture of their touch. This afternoon was well sealed within their memories, for they had lingered in the water, then moved to the edge of the stream where he lifted her and carried her to a grassy spot, intent upon bringing her to the highest peaks of ecstasy that he was capable of. And they had lost themselves completely to the delight of their new-found love.

And so it was that now, with a tender sigh, Jessica laid her head upon her husband's sturdy shoulder, their last few moments of lovemaking leaving a sweet calm over both of them as they lay together upon the softly cushioned sleeping pallet.

"I wish we could stay here forever," she breathed, her fingers entwining the long, silky tresses of his ebony hair.

Tenderly kissing the soft fingers near his face, he agreed. "If only it could be, Silver Star. But the world still goes on about us, and my father bid me not to linger but for this short time. His braves are getting restless and there is talk among the other tribes of holding a large council to discuss our problems." He didn't tell her that their main problem was the infiltration of the numerous white men into their hunting grounds.

"Then you will have to leave when we get back to the village?" Some small fear was reflected in her eyes, and Star Hawk quickly tried his best to reassure her.

"There will be those times when I must go with the other braves of our tribe on hunting parties, and there will also be times when my father will send me on a mission such as the one that I was upon when first I saw you." Here again he kissed her fingers.

"Oh," was her soft reply.

Pulling her body up close to his, he tried to console her. "You will be safe in my father's village. You are my wife, and his daughter now, and none would dare to harm the wife of Star Hawk." He thought that perhaps the attacks of Cunning Wolf and Bright Lilly still lingered frighteningly in her thoughts.

It was not her own safety that Jessica was thinking of, but the dangers that could be lying in wait for her husband filled her mind with a terrible vision. "It is you that I am thinking about, Star Hawk. I could not bear it if some harm befell you." Her words were barely more than a whisper as they touched upon his ears.

"There is no reason for you to worry about me when I leave our lodge, my love. I have been trained from a young age to be a warrior—strong and invincible. And with the knowledge that you are waiting for me in our tepee, no harm could ever come to me. Nothing will ever separate us."

Still not so sure, though his words were very convincing and Jessica had seen for herself the strength that her husband possessed, she could not quiet the feeling of unease that had settled upon her. "Will we be as happy in our new tepee as here?" She tried to change the direction of their thoughts, hoping that she could bring a lighter mood once again around them.

"We shall always be happy together." Star Hawk grunted in satisfaction as he threw a long leg over her shapely thigh.

"We have very little in our tepee." She grinned at his charming face. "I am afraid that there will be little besides our sleeping mat."

"Your husband is a rich man, Silver Star. We will get the things that we need and you desire." He lightly rubbed the silken softness of her hair, admiring the way that the burnt tresses seemed to glow and come alive within his grasp.

"And wherever will we purchase the things that we need?" Her interest was aroused now with his words.

"I have already thought upon this matter," he easily replied, lingering over his words in the hopes of drawing her interest more fully. "I thought that perhaps we would go to the Bengiman trading post."

"I can go also?" Jessica rose up upon the pallet, her excitement visible as she thought to this excursion with her husband. She did not think so much about the trip as she did about the fact that she would be by Star Hawk's side. He would not be leaving her as quickly as she had at first thought.

"My friend Ollie will be pleased to meet you." He kissed her upon her softly pouting lips, enjoying her excitement at such a small gift. "We will leave to go to the trading post in the rising of two suns. I cannot stay from my father's wishes for too long."

Jessica nodded her head, content for the moment that she would still have her husband to herself. She would worry about his safety when he left her side whenever that time came. But for now she would think only of their returning to the village with the morning sun, and then she would make plans to travel to the trading post with Star Hawk. Perhaps there were things that Cloud Dreamer was in need of and she could bring them back for her. And at the thought of seeing the kindly Indian woman once again, she relaxed back against the pallet.

"You are happy now, my little wife?" Star Hawk leaned over and grinned down into the contented features, and as she nodded her head, he took hold of her lips, covering them with his own.

Feeling the same sweet ambrosia of passion sweep over her body, Jessica gave herself over to her husband, his strong hands upon her body, his kisses boldly roaming freely over her face and bosom, their bodies straining together hungrily. Jessica moaned softly under Star Hawk's exploring, practiced hands, his fierce, fevered kisses now showering her as she clung to him and gave herself wholly to his wondrous passion, becoming so thoroughly enmeshed in its intensity that she found herself returning it with a wild and free abandon that thrilled her husband.

She moaned aloud with pleasure as his hands moved over her body, slipping smoothly over her limbs like the merest butterfly's touch. He was now slow and deliberate in his caresses, making her forget all at the moment but the two of them, until she writhed and twisted within his hold and pleaded aloud with him to take her without further delay. But still he proceeded at a slow, measured pace, sending her emotions, enflamed and thrilling, spiraling upward. Her passion mounted until she became like a wild thing, quivering, biting, clawing at his shoulders and back. Yet he only laughed aloud, the husky sound swirling above their heads and mingling with her purring sighs, and nibbled lightly with his teeth at her smooth, slim throat, at the satiny flesh beneath her full breasts, at the smooth, flat belly, and onward to her shapely thigh. She convulsed with passion, which he evoked as her hand moved downward and closed over his throbbing manliness. He shuddered and took her fiercely, carrying her with him to frenzied, breathtaking heights that finally burst around them, shading them warmly in the aftermath of contentment.

Chapter Five

It was on a cool, brisk windswept morning that Jessica and Star Hawk set out for the Indian village, leaving behind the idyll of their lovers' retreat. With a last glance in the direction of the cabin where they had shared so many wondrous hours, Jessica sighed aloud.

"We shall return, Silver Star. Do not look so sad." Star Hawk came to her side on his large black stallion which stood much taller than her mare.

Though his words were meant for comfort, Jessica felt a chill of premonition shuddering over her body. Not speaking of these dark feelings, she smiled softly into his loving features.

"When the summer comes and the tribe goes into the mountains, we shall stay here once again," Star Hawk offered, knowing full well what she felt, for he also was reluctant to return to his village and share their lives with others. These two weeks had been the most wonderful of his life, and he was assured even further that all he would ever need to make him happy was this woman at his side.

It was well into the afternoon when the couple made their way into the Indian encampment. Many of the tribe came forth to greet them, calling out to Star Hawk, and to Jessica as well, for they fully accepted her as the wife of their chief's son.

When they came to their large tepee, which had been erected in the center of the village near Golden Eagle's own lodge, Star Hawk helped Jessica to her feet and took hold of the horses' reins. "I must tend to the horses and then speak to my father. I will not be long."

Jessica smiled at his concern. "I also wish to visit Cloud Dreamer and see if there is anything I can do for her. I will start a fire in our lodge." She started to enter the entrance flap, and as she did, she felt Star Hawk behind her. He entered with her and pulled her into his arms. She whispered against his mouth, "I thought you had things to see to?"

"Yes," he sighed, taking her lips in a lingering hold. "But you are ever first in my thoughts." His hands lightly brushed the tendrils of golden hair from her face, his touch caressing and loving.

"What a wonderful husband you are." Jessica felt her body tremble next to his, experiencing the same stirring in her breast each time he touched her.

"And what better wife could a man ask for?" He grinned down upon her. "You are most beautiful and obedient. You come first to my lodge to warm it before doing your own tasks."

Jessica heard the laughter in his tone and smiled back into his handsome face. "Aye milord, whatever you would desire will always be my first duty." She seductively drew her body closer to his hard frame. With another grin, she felt the stirring of his manhood boldly pushing against her belly.

Chuckling aloud, Star Hawk gently put some distance between them. "You make me forget everything but you, Silver Star. My mind forgets all thoughts of my horse and my father when you are in my arms." For a moment he was reminded of what his father had said about his white woman making him weak and keeping him from being a strong leader of his people.

Seeing the serious look cross his face, Jessica watched his dark eyes look at her from head to toe. "I was but teasing, Star Hawk. I would never keep you from your duty or from your father." She spoke softly, feeling for a moment tears coming to her silver eyes. This was the first time she had felt she had displeased her husband.

Seeing the unhappiness come over features that only moments past had been so beautiful with joy, Star Hawk felt his heart constrict. "Oh, my heart," he gathered her back into his arms, "I have no fear that you would keep me from what I must do. But truly you are my very first care." With a light kiss he stepped away from her. "I will build the fire for our lodge, before I see to the horses."

Again knowing happiness with the realization that this man was truly hers, Jessica watched as he built up a small fire in the shallow pit in the center of the floor. As he did, she began spreading out their sleeping mat, smoothing the lush furs invitingly on the pallet.

With his task accomplished, Star Hawk let his ebony eyes watch the movements of his young bride. "What else could a man ask for in life?" he softly questioned aloud. Drawing her gaze to him, he responded to his own question. "A warm fire, a beautiful woman, and a soft bed."

Jessica laughed aloud, "You are wicked, Star Hawk."

"Aye, sweet." He joined her laughter. "Do not linger long at Cloud Dreamer's tepee. I wish to find rest early this evening." His tone changed from that of laughter to a husky growl that left Jessica warm and flushed.

In a short time Jessica returned to their lodge. She had only visited Cloud Dreamer for a few minutes time, telling her about the time she had spent alone with her husband and about their plans to go to the trading post.

Cloud Dreamer had promised she would consider what items she was in need of, and then, after being instructed to return on the following day to help with some medicines, Jessica took her leave, already eager to be with Star Hawk after only this small separation.

Jessica arrived back at the lodge. Star Hawk was still visiting his father, so she took this time to prepare a small supper for them. Her silver eyes were frequently drawn to the hide flap, expecting it to be drawn away at any moment by her tall, handsome husband.

It was almost dark before Star Hawk managed to leave his father's lodge and go to his own. Golden Eagle had received word of a council meeting among several tribes, and his plans were for his son as well as several of his strongest warriors to accompany him to this meeting. There was much to prepare for such a meeting. Golden Eagle, now with his advanced age, was depending more upon his son. Star Hawk himself would stand before the other tribes and, with the help of his father's wise counsel and his own wisdom, he would tell of everything he had learned of the whites in his travels. Golden Eagle knew that an understanding of one's enemy was crucial and that such understanding among opponents was rare.

Raising her eyes from the soft hide of rabbit fur she was fashioning into a pair of moccasins, Jessica smiled as her husband entered their tepee. Surely he was the most handsome of men, she thought once again as her eyes took in his bronzed body and dark eyes and hair. Each time she looked at him, she felt the swift beating of her heart.

Bending over the small pot near the fire, Star Hawk fixed his meal as Jessica sat relaxed and watched each movement of his sensual body. He came near to the mat she was sitting on, his ebony eyes watching her for a moment before he spoke.

"Is all well with Cloud Dreamer? There is nothing amiss?" From the moment that Star Hawk had promised he would bring meat to Cloud Dreamer's lodge for her care of Jessica, he had taken an interest in the elderly woman, as though she were a part of his family.

"All is well, my husband," Jessica replied softly as she watched him eat the bowl of food she had prepared. "And your father and mother? What of them?"

"They are also well," He grinned down at her. "I did not think I would be so long at my father's lodge, but there were matters he wished to discuss."

"I also had things to tend to." Jessica held up the nearly finished shoe for his inspection.

It was almost as though they were shy with each other now that they were in their village and their own lodge. Feeling the slight tension, Star Hawk set

145

the bowl aside and held out his hand to his young bride. "Come to me, Silver Star." His voice was a silken caress, his dark eyes touched her with a heated longing.

With a slight blush, Jessica set aside what she had been doing and slowly rose and went to his side, her silver eyes looking up into his dark gaze. "What would you have of me, Star Hawk?" she softly questioned.

"I would have this gone between us." With a single movement of his strong hand, he pulled the tie at the shoulder of her dress, baring one breast as the material fell from her shoulder.

Jessica stood still before him, enveloped in the heat of his devouring gaze as it rested on her full, ripe breast.

With no further words, he eased the tie from the other shoulder. As she stood before him with the soft, creamy skin of her upper torso gleaming with a golden hue cast by the firelight, she heard his soft, indrawn breath.

Star Hawk gently unlaced the bindings of the braids that captured the long, softly lustrous curls of fiery gold. His large hands smoothed the mass and captured a fragrant tress to his cheek. With a large sigh, he spoke of her beauty. The overwhelming effect that she had on his senses left him trembling with the sheer intensity of her nearness.

Jessica seemed to drown beneath the soft spell of his tender words. Her body leaned toward him, a fire beginning to grow in the pit of her belly and leaving her breathless with her desire for this man.

Still Star Hawk would not be hurried. His hand slowly reached out and untied the strap of rawhide that was tied about her waist, allowing the doehide

146

dress to slip to her ankles.

For a wild, reckless moment Jessica wanted to throw herself upon him, consumed by her maddening hunger to feel her bare flesh against his, to forget the outside world and to know only the joy that she found when she allowed love to flame in her heart.

Star Hawk gently held Jessica back, he slowly allowed an adventurous hand to descend lightly across her belly. Jessica gasped aloud as his intimate caress traced a sweet, tormenting valley from her rose-tipped breast to her waist. His long, tanned fingertips seared her skin, leaving her with a throbbing, burning need. Her body belonged only to him, responding, melting for him, demanding fulfillment. As a rippling spasm of pleasure caught her, she heard herself utter his beloved name. Winding her fingers through his raven hair, she brought his lips toward her own.

"Silver Star, my love burns brightly for you," he raggedly breathed next to her lips, the dark heat of his smoldering gaze pouring over her. "You are as a fire in my blood, flaming ever higher and never quenched. I can think of little else but you in my arms, willing and warm, held tightly to my chest."

In his gaze, Jessica saw all of her past reflected, and at that moment she knew she had found her place. She would never regret or turn back. This man was all that she would ever need. It didn't matter what tomorrow would hold. She needed him as a woman needs a man, giving and sharing, creating a new beginning that would only strengthen their love.

He drew her with him to the fur-covered mat. "No matter what the future, Star Hawk, I shall always be yours. My heart beats only for the sound of your name. No matter distance or time, you shall ever be in my heart. I love you so much . . . I love. . . ."

Her lips were clasped tightly with his as her words filled his ears. Star Hawk lay his wife on the furs and his body held tightly to hers, raising his senses to an inflaming peak that denied all but that moment.

With heart-stopping tenderness, Star Hawk kissed Jessica for what seemed an eternity, languidly tasting her sweetness, losing himself in the flood of pleasure that roiled over his body.

They came together in perfect union, a blending of bodies and souls. Jessica fiercely clung to Star Hawk, her moans of delight filling his ears and circling around the tepee. The rhythm of his lovemaking brought her from the dim realms of delight to the spiraling clouds of sheerest ecstasy.

And as their senses converged, clung and sought, they were swept away. She was beyond understanding as she tasted his bronzed, manly flesh beneath her lips. His muscular body strained under her touch as she stroked his corded neck and molded back. She succumbed to his touch, arching her body to meet his thrust, each thrust driving her to a new maddening pleasure of delight. As the fiery sensations continued to build, each one more intense than the last, Jessica lost all reasoning, and she escalated toward a towering, climactic surge.

The entire world seemed to split asunder, bringing sweet, breathless, and satisfied release. Jessica clutched her bronzed warrior as the showering brilliance of full contentment pierced her being. At that moment, time and space seemed to cease as they became one, bound together in an unreality that only the two of them could share.

A ragged sigh of contentment filled Star Hawk's

chest as he pulled Jessica into the circle of his arms. "Sleep well, my heart," he murmured next to her ear as he lightly kissed that delicate spot. She also sighed softly and molded her body more fully against his. He knew a moment of consuming love that threatened to tear his chest in twain. His love for this woman was beyond mere words.

The noise and confusion of everyday life in the Blackfoot village woke Jessica. She lay silently in the security and comfort of her husband's arms and the warm furs of the sleeping couch. For a moment she studied the handsomely chiseled features of the man she loved.

With his face turned toward her, Jessica lightly smiled, knowing the pleasure of being this man's wife. He was a mixture of things to her. She had seen the savage warrior, and the gentle and concerned lover. She looked at those closed lids and thought of the dark pools of warming cinders that were now hidden. Her eyes lowered to his lips, the firm but oh, so sensual tilt that even in his sleep stirred her with thoughts of their slight pressure on her own. His skin was smooth and hairless, the golden-bronzed hue seeming to call out for the touch of her fingers. For a slight moment her hand reached out of its own accord, the desire to touch him throbbing throughout her body.

He stirred slightly and Jessica pulled back, not wanting to disrupt this moment of undisclosed survey. He seemed so innocent and young to her in his sleep, and for a moment she felt tears fill her vision. Life with this man would always be lived to the highest limits. He would fight off his enemies with bloodlust. Even facing death he would stand proud and bold, and this thought above all others filled her with a cold dread. What would she do if she lost him? In this small time that she had known his love, she had felt alive and wanted. What would she be if he were taken from her? Could she go on as before? Could she breathe the same air and walk the same earth knowing that she would be forever separated from this man?

The fierce snarling of two dogs fighting outside of the tepee pulled Jessica from this line of thought and awoke Star Hawk. His first reaction was to pull Jessica into his arms and snuggle her warm, soft body tightly against his own. "Good morning, my love," he whispered as he lightly kissed the nape of her neck.

"And a good morning to you also, my sweet," Jessica smiled, trying hard to forget the black thoughts that had swept over her moments before.

"What evil lurks in that lovely head?" Star Hawk sensed there was something bothering his bride and looked intently at her as he rose up on one elbow.

"It is nothing. I was but watching you in your sleep."

"And did I make a sour face, or do my looks not appeal to you, my Silver Star?"

"Nay, you are indeed quite handsome." Jessica blushed at this confession.

"As I think you are beautiful." Star Hawk kissed her parted lips. "But there was something troubling you. I wish you to confide in me in all things, my love. We are one now, and what plays falsely on your mind does the same with me."

His tone was so soft that it stirred Jessica's heart. "I did not mean to start off our day together with

150

bad thoughts. I was but looking upon you and the thought came to me of what I would do if I ever lost you." This time, the tears came fast and stinging, blurring her vision and leaving her body trembling.

"Oh my, Silver Star," Star Hawk soothed, his hand gently caressing the smooth skin of her neck and feeling the coolness of the amulet. "My love will never leave you. You are everything to me. Even death cannot part us. I would fight all evil to reach your side. Do not waste your time with dark thoughts of what tomorrow will bring. The Great Spirit counts the days that we are allowed and he alone rules our fates. He is the one that brought our paths together, and he will protect us."

"I am sorry," Jessica sobbed, knowing that he spoke the truth and that she worried needlessly. But deep inside there lingered intimations of separation that left her chilled.

"There is no need to be sorry." The black eyes held hers. "What is between us we can share. There are no secrets. Your fears are my own, and I shall take them to my heart. I can only hope that you will trust in my strength. I will do all in my power to keep you happy."

Jessica clutched him closely to her, knowing the truth of his words. His love was strong, and she had but to trust him. "I love you." She brushed her lips over his and soon the outside world was forgotten, all fears and hurts wiped away within the gentle love play on the soft couch. Only with their gentle caresses could the pair forget everything but themselves. And as Star Hawk took her to him she melted with the fire of his touch, their love sealed in their hearts for all time.

The rest of the day was spent in hurried activity as the couple prepared for the trip they would take the next morning to the trading post. In the afternoon Jessica went to Cloud Dreamer to help the elder woman with her tasks.

As she entered the lodge of the healing woman, she was greeted with a wide smile and a small jar with a dark mixture in it.

"What is this, Cloud Dreamer? Some of your medicines or one of your potions?" Jessica questioned as she took the jar and looked inside.

"It is a gift for you, Silver Star."

"A gift for me? But what is it?" Jessica could not fathom what it could be.

"It is for your hair and skin." the elder woman began to explain.

"But surely I cannot put this on my hair and body. It is as black as mud. Whatever does it do?" Again she looked inside the jar.

She chuckled at the girl's incredulous look. "It is to darken your skin when you go to the trading post with Star Hawk. Surely you have thought of what others would say if they saw a white woman with a brave such as your husband?"

Jessica had to admit that she had not thought about this at all. With all of the excitment of preparing to go and thoughts of being alone with Star Hawk again, she had not thought of what anyone would think of her traveling with an Indian. "But why should it matter that I am with Star Hawk?" Her chin jutted out with the defiance she felt toward anyone who would belittle her love for her husband.

"It should not matter, but I am afraid it will if the white man sees you. It could be dangerous for you and your husband. The white man can be very foolish and would perhaps think that you had been taken and were being held against your will. Will you not at least try this and change your coloring only a small bit?"

The wisdom of her words touched Jessica. Slowly nodding her head, she agreed. "I will put it on before we leave the village in the morning. Thank you, Cloud Dreamer."

The old woman smiled with pleasure at Jessica's agreement. "You are a wise daughter and a good wife. Come now, it is time we set to work." She turned her back and bent toward the bowls placed in the fire. She sat down and began to stir several containers.

Jessica grinned at the elder woman's words. It was the first time that Cloud Dreamer had called her daughter, and Jessica glowed at the small compliment. Quickly, she went to her side and began to help her. Cloud Dreamer gave her directions and explained each herb and its healing potential.

It was late in the afternoon when Jessica walked though the village. She let her eyes fill with the sights she was beginning to love. She smiled at a group of half-naked children racing about playing their games. Their straight black hair and shiny black eyes glistened with the freedom and happiness that only children know. She glimpsed a mother sitting before her lodge and nursing her papoose. Jessica softly called to her, asking after the child's health and marveling at the beauty of the tender scene before her. There was the happy chatter of squaws visiting and laughing as they tended to their outside fires. There were racks of meat drying in the sun and hides stretched between tall cottonwood poles. All seemed alive and well as she filled her mind and senses with the sights and smells of this Indian village. As her slow steps took her to her own lodge, she caught sight of Star Hawk sitting crosslegged outside their tepee. His dark head was bent in concentration as he worked his knife over a new bow he was fashioning.

Life seemed to tranquil and peaceful here in this Blackfoot village. Her past life seemed far from her at this moment. She was no longer Jessica Star Coltin. She was Silver Star, the wife of Star Hawk.

Sensing her presence, Star Hawk looked up from his handiwork, and his face broke into a large smile. He saw the peaceful smile in her face and the thoughtful look in her silver eyes. Without having to hear the words, he knew something of her thoughts, for he himself had walked through his village and known the same thoughts that were filling her mind.

"Is there something good to eat in your jar, wife?" he laughingly questioned as she advanced toward him, her full hips swinging in a manner that made him forget the hunger in his belly.

"You may have a bite, if you wish." Jessica bent and placed a kiss on his brow and held out the jar for his inspection.

He grimaced and drew back from the dark concoction. Her tinkling laughter filled the air.

"I will fix something in a minute, Star Hawk," she laughed as he looked at the jar.

"What have you there, my love? Some evil mixture to entrap a weary soul?" He looked at her with curiosity.

"Cloud Dreamer mixed this for my skin and hair. The dye of the walnut, I believe."

"You will not cover yourself with this." Star Hawk

rose to his full height as he envisioned the gold-fire hair that he loved so well and the creamy golden skin turned dark and ugly like this mixture in the jar. "Tell Cloud Dreamer that you do not need this." He was determined that he himself would seek Cloud Dreamer out and tell her she was not to be advising Jessica on ointments for her skin and hair. Perhaps the healing woman did so for other womean of the village, but Jessica was different and did not need such cosmetics.

"It is to darken my skin and hair when we go to the trading post, Star Hawk. It will wash off."

For a moment Star Hawk considered her words. Quickly understanding the value of the mixture now, he smiled again. "You had me scared, wife. You should have told me quickly what you would use the mixture for. You are sure that it will wash off?" Again his eyes went to the jar.

"It will wash right off, I am sure."

"You do not have to do this, Silver Star." For a moment Star Hawk felt his anger rise at the thought that his wife had to hide her beauty because she was white and he was an Indian.

"But it will be fun." Jessica instantly saw his pride and desired to put his mind to rest. She would do anything in her power to keep him safe, and if her being white was a threat when they were away from this village, then she would not hesitate to cover her body with this mixture.

Dinner that evening was never eaten. As the couple entered their lodge, their hands instantly reached out to each other. Long into the night their soft moans of ecstasy circled about the tepee. Nothing else mattered but each other. No problems from

155

the outside world could penetrate the cozy cocoon of love they had formed. Theirs was a love that few had known. From the very outer boundaries of their worlds they had found each other, and now they were one, their love and souls blending and joining, never to be pulled apart.

Chapter Six

The Bengiman trading post looked like a fort. Its outer gates stood open for business. The post itself was a two-story log building, the upstairs the living quarters, and the downstairs, one large room, its walls lined with shelves of foodstuffs, sacks of flour and sugar, and the everyday utensils needed for survival in the wilderness.

It was a slow two-days ride for Star Hawk and Jessica to get to the post, and they slowly walked their horses into the large outer yard. Jessica's eyes glistened with excitement as she watched all the activity.

This was the only outpost of "civilization" in the area. It was the place that whites, be they trappers or farmers, came and sought each other out for trading purposes. There were several Indians lingering about the outside walls. A small group of braves stood about drinking from a bottle of whiskey, and a middle-aged woman stood off to the side as though awaiting for her turn of the potent brew. Star Hawk's dark eyes looked upon the group for only a moment, and Jessica saw a quick flash of contempt on his face. He did not extend a glance of recognition to the other Indians, and though Jessica knew that they were not of the same tribe as her husband, she wondered about his actions.

Tying their mounts to the hitching rail in front of the store, Star Hawk helped Jessica from Red Wing's back and took the bundle of pelts and hides from the back of his own horse. Waiting for a moment for Jessica to step behind him, he went through the front door of the post.

Looking about the large dark airless room, Star Hawk slowly took in the three men sitting across the room at small table playing cards. His glance went to the opposite side of the trading post and settled upon the two bearded trappers near the wood stove. He swiftly took their measure, and reaching out, he pulled Jessica to his side.

Following the instructions that Star Hawk had given her early that morning Jessica kept her darkened head lowered, not wishing to draw any attention to herself and perhaps endanger her husband.

His head held high with the pride of his people, Star Hawk strode across the wood floor, drawing the eyes of the other men toward himself and his wife as he stepped to the counter. He pulled the bundle of furs from his shoulder, and untying them for the man behind the counter to examine, he asked softly, in perfect English, "Where is Ollie Bengiman?"

The man behind the counter was small of stature. He wore wire-framed spectacles on this thin straight nose and had thinning, dull brown hair plastered down thickly with hair oil, which lent him a sweet, pasty smell. "Old Ollie been gone now near on to a month, Injun." The little man pulled the bundle apart, his eyes gleaming at the richness of the furs beneath his hands.

"When will he be back?" Star Hawk was disappointed, for he had wished his good friend to meet Silver Star.

"Naw, he ain't a-going to be a-coming back to these here parts. He took ill, he did, and had a yearning to go back home. So he sold the post to me fur a tidy sum and is probably this minute sipping a brandy and eating some warm mutton stew."

For a moment Star Hawk felt a deep loss. Ollie had told him about his home, which he had left behind in that faraway land called England. And at the thought that he would never again see the kindly man, he felt somewhat downhearted. But only for a moment did he allow himself to feel saddened. Fate took people in different directions. He had learned much from Ollie Bengiman and was glad that he had known the older man. But his friend had another life now, and so did he.

"I am in need of supplies." He spoke again to the small man, and as the man nodded his head in agreement that he would be more than willing to exchange the furs for whatever Star Hawk wanted, Star Hawk gently spoke to Jessica in the Indian language.

Star Hawk had directed Jessica to pick out the things that she desired, blankets, clay pot, pans for cooking, and any foodstuff that she wished. With a smile directed toward her husband, Jessica set out to do as he bid her, her silver eyes going over each shelf and deciding what she would be needing for their new home and also keeping a watchful eye for a gift for Star Hawk's mother and also something special for Cloud Dreamer.

159

The group of men in the trading post had remained quietly watching the Indian brave and his squaw as they had come through the front door and then up to the counter. Now, after the tension of the first moments were passed, one of the two men sitting nearest the stove rose to his full height and approached Star Hawk. "You from the hills out yonder?" he questioned, nodding his head toward the Blackfoot hills that had been the home of Star Hawk's people for long years past.

Star Hawk looked the tall, broad man over before slowly nodding his dark head.

"Don't speak much do ya?" the man said. "Not like those Injuns outside, ha?" His eyes left Star Hawk and went to Jessica as she was reaching up to a top shelf and pulling down a bulk of colorful material that she knew Singing Moon would love. "She be yer squaw?" The trapper questioned, this time not even looking at Star Hawk but keeping his gaze fully upon the trim figure of the woman across the room. "A mite pretty to be a redskin, ain't she?" His greedy eyes went over the softly tinted dark hair and the roundness of her form.

Star Hawk did not even sound a reply or in any fashion indicate that he had heard the man as he bargained with the small man behind the counter; however, one eye held his wife in view at all times.

"How much ye take fer the squaw?" The man boldly spoke out to Star Hawk, taking a step closer toward him. "The Injun women about this old post are a might old and used up, if ye be knowing what I mean."

"My wife is not for sale." Star Hawk turned his full dark gaze upon the man who was speaking to him, the steel-cold black depths taking in the other's

160

full measure with a single glance.

"Hows about I be giving ye a couple of bottles of whisky and maybe I be throwing in a rifle." The man's eyes again went over the Indian woman. "I bet she be knowing how to warm a man just right in the cold days ahead." His laughter boomed within the large room, and the man who had been sitting near the stove with him moments ago fully agreed, his own deep voice blending with his friend's.

"I wish only to get my supplies and leave. My wife is mine and mine alone!" The words came from deep within Star Hawk's chest, and the force and volume left a cold chill hanging in the air.

Quickly, her arms laden with the things she had selected, Jessica started across the room and to Star Hawk's side and observed the hard look of the man standing before him.

As she passed by the one who sat near the stove, she felt her upper arm grasped in a tight hold, and for an instant her gaze rose to the washed-out green eyes before her. Just then she heard his intake of breath, and she quickly bowed her head. Within a second Star Hawk was at her side, his large hunting knife drawn and held to the man's hand that held her arm.

"Take your hand from my woman!" The statement was uttered in a cold, deathlike tone. As the pressure of the steel blade increased and blood began to drip down the man's hand, Jessica was quickly released.

The man nearest the counter took a step toward the Indian couple but quickly stopped in his tracks, as the blade was now held in his direction, Star Hawk's ebony eyes chilling as they looked upon his face. "Silver Star, gather what you have and go to the horses." Star Hawk did not take his eyes from the

161

man in front of him, and as she left the large room, he slowly went back to the counter and waited for the owner to tell him the worth of his furs and the total of the supplies that he had received.

The man near the fire sat holding his bleeding hand, tying a neckerchief about it and moaning softly with his pain. "Ye needn't have done that to old Sam there, Injun. He weren't but funning." The large man nearest Star Hawk spoke aloud, his eyes still watching the cruel-looking hunting knife that Star Hawk held firmly grasped in his hand.

As the proprietor wrote down some figures, making a long tally of the furs and goods, Star Hawk looked over the paper swiftly. Seeing the man was being fair, he nodded his dark head, taking the small pouch of coins that the man held out to him for the difference of his sale. But before putting the coins away his dark eyes set upon a small music box sitting upon the counter, and throwing down the required amount, he placed this also with some of the supplies that were still on the counter.

Sticking the money pouch into his breechcloth, Star Hawk then turned toward the man next to him. "It is good that your friend still has his arm intact. If he had not released my woman, I would have cut it from his body. No one touches the wife of Star Hawk. And you are lucky that I do not cut your own tongue from your mouth for the words that you have spoken of her." He felt rage and burned for revenge. Revenge against any man who would dare insult his Silver Star.

The man quickly stepped back as he viewed the full fury of the tall, bronzed warrior before him. He had fought many Indians in the past, but never had he seen such hatred and consuming rage as he now beheld in the eyes of this man who stood before him.

"Now listen here. I'll not be having any bloodshed here in me store. Ye be on yer way now, Injun, and Lonny, ye best be seeing to yer friend before he bleeds to death. I don't think he's getting the bleeding to stop." The small man behind the counter looked first to the Indian and then to the shaggy trapper, his voice commanding for one so small.

With a large sigh, the trapper turned away from the black glare of the Indian and started toward his friend. "There'll come a time, Injun, we'll meet up again," he threw over his shoulder as he walked away from Star Hawk.

"I will await that time, white man," Star Hawk spat, and then taking up the supplies on the counter, he left through the front door and made his way to his horse and to Jessica's side.

"Ye be sure crazy, Lonny," the small man shouted as Star Hawk left the store. "Did ye be hearing him say his name be Star Hawk? He be the son of Chief Golden Eagle himself. Ye be wanting the whole of the Blackfoot tribe down here upon our heads? He told ye he wouldn't be parting with his woman, what ye and Sam be thinking yer doing? Ye be the cause of me store being burnt down and me goods all stolen; I meself will be killing ye!"

"How'd I be a-knowing the Injun is Golden Eagle's son? One of them red devils looks like another to me."

"It ain't just Golden Eagle ye would have to be a-worrying about, but that there young buck Star Hawk himself they say has earned more coup than even his father. He'll be the next chief, and the stories about him are already heard among all the tribes in the area."

163

Lonny didn't say another word with this bit of information, but as he looked at Sam's wound his friend grabbed him by the shirtfront and pulled his head down toward his own, whispering something in his ear that brought a feral gleam to that one's eyes.

Star Hawk's temper quickly cooled as he and Jessica went out through the gates of the trading post. How could any man stay angered, he questioned himself as he looked upon his wife's soft concern-filled face. She was so lovely as she raised her silver eyes toward him, wondering what had happened between him and the men in the store after she had left. And as she saw his angry features relax somewhat, she smiled tenderly at him.

"Thank you so much, Star Hawk, for all of the lovely things that you bought. Our lodge will be the most beautiful of the tribe." Jessica fingered the colorful ribbons that her husband had put in her hand when he had come out of the store, and with this simple gift she knew of his warm love.

"There is no need to thank me, my sweet. What makes you happy makes me happy also."

For a time they spoke of the things they had purchased and the sights that they had seen at the trading post, both avoiding speaking of the two trappers. But as the day wore on they put the incident from their minds and enjoyed the forest and the closeness of being together.

They camped early that evening near a small stream. After settling their horses and the pack horse that Star Hawk had brought along to carry the goods, they started a small fire, and then, as though with a single mind, they started toward the stream,

Star Hawk anxious once again to see the fire-gold tresses that he loved so well, and Jessica hurriedly reaching the stream in order to wash the day's grime from her body.

Star Hawk stood at the edge of the stream and watched his young bride pull her clothes from her body and wade into the icy-cold water. With the lilac soap she had purchased at the trading post, Jessica now rubbed a creamy lather over her body and hair, delighting in the feel of the soft, luxurious substance. She allowed the scent to fill her nostrils as she inhaled deeply.

As though the sight of her beautiful body was much too tempting, Star Hawk quickly shed himself of his breechcloth and followed her into the water, the coolness settling over his large frame as he came to her side. "What have you there, my love?" He looked upon her with her hair lathered. The sweet aroma attacked his senses and drew him toward her.

Jessica laughed gayly as she wiped the bar of soap across his chest and let her hand go slowly over the straining muscles.

"What a fine brave you shall be, milord, smelling of lilac." She giggled again as she saw his dark eyes upon her.

But with a squeal Jessica was pulled into the strong arms, her full breasts held tightly to his chest and the lather of the soap slipping between their bodies.

"I think I like this soap of yours, wife."

Standing upon her tiptoes, Jessica placed her lips upon her husband's, her body slowly and seductively rubbing against his.

With a moan of savage need Star Hawk gathered her slim form up against his body in a tight hold, his

165

own mouth slanting over hers and his tongue seeking out the sweet ambrosia that lay in wait. Relinquishing all into his fiery touch, Jessica was swept up into the tempestuous storm of desire that left her body trembling with her want.

As his long fingers delved and interwined in the gold tresses, Star Hawk drank of the intoxicating sweetness of her mouth. This woman, his Silver Star, was all that he would ever need, he told himself. She was a rare jewel, a beautiful treasure, one that should be adored and cherished forever. And as the warm glow of passion flickered and kindled to full wakefulness, his hands moved slowly over her smooth flesh.

When his lips soon abandoned hers, Jessica tried to seek them back and cling to them, wanting the delicious feeling of his mouth against hers to last forever, but his warm breath skipped across her cheek and lowered to the slim column of her throat and then down further to the fullness of her breast, gently sucking at the rose tip, which strained as though with a will of its own toward him. Jessica could but moan aloud as she cradled his raven head against her body, overwhelmed by the manly scent that seemed to be invading her senses, the hardness of his muscular body, and the tantalizing feel of his mouth and hands upon her.

Star Hawk carried her to the bank of the stream and for a time they lay together, relaxed and unhurried, touching and tasting of each other.

He drew her slim form over him, his passion-filled eyes blazing as his hands roamed freely over her body and brought her to a bursting passion's edge. She rose above him, her body writhing to a primal rhythm that beat with a sensual melody in her brain.

166

She felt a craving over her entire being as her hands splayed across his broad chest, her lips seeking his and her fire hair surrounding them with a delicate curtain of spun gold. Her body moving and seeking, her breathing ragged and gasping as her body came up and down, up and down, she lost all reason to the swirling and overwhelming feelings descending upon her. The rapturous sensations stoking the fire within her skyrocketed toward the outer bounds and shattered intimately upon the fleecy clouds, leaving her breathless and perspiring atop him.

A low chuckle emitted from Star Hawk's throat, and with an easy movement he pulled his wife beneath his own body. "The pleasure that you have given is uncompared, but now it is my turn." His voice was low and husky, his dark eyes devouring as his lips caught hers in a tender hold.

As he again looked into her eyes he held her spellbound for a time, and with a gasp as he entered her she called out his name. "Star Hawk!" It was a caress, a plea.

"Do not move," Star Hawk whispered next to her ear. "Take the pleasure that I would give." As he slowly began to move his lower body, his lips and hands began to wander to the sensitive areas of her body. Chills danced along her spine as she forced herself to remain still.

When his mouth closed over one nipple, his tongue teasing the tip, his teeth gently tugging as he suckled, she cried aloud from the sheer ecstasy of it. His mouth charted a damp path from one breast to the other as his fingers roamed freely over her belly and ribs and his body moved to a timeless beat of sensual pleasure.

"Star Hawk!" The shout came from her lips. "Star Hawk, please!" She did not know at that moment whether she was begging him to stop or to continue with his divine torture. Her head was thrown back and moving from side to side, her lips parted, her entire body aflame, as at last she was consumed by the powerful vortex of passions blooming deep within.

Held in the throes of passion, spasms still quaking over her entire body, Jessica cried aloud with the total force of her pleasure, and Star Hawk also sought his release. Their rapture rose higher and higher, until Jessica felt a towering surge rippling, growing, as if upon a gigantic tidal wave washing over her, drowning her in its ecstasy as she pulled Star Hawk into its glowing center with her and they spun into its magnificent vortex together.

Adrift at last upon the fleecy clouds of sated passion, Jessica settled happily into his strong embrace, her head upon his shoulder, his arm wrapped about her waist possessively.

"How I love you." Jessica breathed aloud as she lightly traced her finger over his jawline, her breathing still ragged.

Rising on his elbow, Star Hawk traced his lips across the damp tendrils of her hair at her temple as he kissed her. "And I love you, my heart."

"Nothing will ever change this, will it?" Jessica still felt insecure with this newfound love. It had taken her so long to find the right one for her, and her feelings were growing to such tremendous heights for this man, that she was frightened each time she felt this overwhelming love touch her heart.

"Can the trees stop their growth? Can the birds stop their delicate song in the spring? Can the mighty mountain move itself from one place to another?" And at the negative shaking of her head, he added, "Nor can our love ever change. Each day I find more love within my heart for you, Silver Star. My entire life centers around your love for me, for without it, I would be nothing." For another moment his lips held hers in a tender hold.

"I feel the same, and that is why I fear so greatly of something causing a separation between us. I love you so much." Jessica spoke her heart.

Knowing from past experiences that Jessica's most inner feelings usually brought about her tears and hating to see them more than anything else, Star Hawk kissed her fully upon the lips. "I have a gift for you, Silver Star." He grinned as she looked at him with surprise.

"A gift?" she questioned. "Something that you got at the trading post?"

"Come and fix our meal and then I shall show you what I have for you." Star Hawk pulled himself to his feet and extended her a hand.

"Fix you something to eat?" Jessica looked upon him incredulously. "You tell me that you have a surprise for me and then tell me to wait?" She rose to her feet, standing before him naked and beautiful in the afternoon's fading light.

"Does your husband not deserve his sustenance?" he smiled.

"Why yes, but. . . ."

"But what, my love?"

"Why can you not give me the gift first and then I shall prepare our meal? There is little difference."

Star Hawk saw the excitement in her face. "Perhaps I could be talked into letting you have the gift first." His dark brow rose, leaving his message quite

169

clear.

With a shout of joy Jessica threw herself against his chest, her kisses raining over his face and broad chest. "Name your price, milord."

Star Hawk chuckled deeply, his arms wrapping about her waist and then lifting her up he started toward the small camp they had made earlier. "I guess that I can collect my payment later."

"Then you will give me the gift now?" Her silver eyes sparkled at the thought of the surprise waiting for her.

"How could I resist?" He put her down near the fire and handed her her clothes. "Dress while I get the gift and something for our supper from the packs."

Quickly Jessica complied, hurriedly dressing and keeping one eye upon the direction that her husband had taken. He was so wonderful, she thought as she brushed out her waist-length hair that curled about her slim body.

Within a few minutes Star Hawk was back at her side, one hand filled with the food for their meal and the other held behind his back.

Jessica looked at her husband with a glowing warmth in her silver eyes. He had still not put on his breechcloth, and his body looked primitive and virile as he came toward her and then stood so tall and proud before her.

Seeing the way her eyes looked over his body, Star Hawk smiled softly at her, his arm bringing the tiny silver music box forth for her inspection.

Jessica looked from the music box to her husband's tender visage, and with a soft cry she molded her body against his. "Oh, thank you, Star Hawk. It is lovely." Tears flooded down her cheeks.

170

"Tears, my sweet?" Star Hawk wiped them from her cheeks. "I will have none of this or there will be no more gifts for you. I can bear anything but to see you weep."

"My tears are for joy, you are so good to me." Jessica tried to stifle the sobs that were filling her chest.

With a simple movement Star Hawk lifted the lid of the box and a soft, delicate lullaby filled the air. "When I saw it I knew that I had to have it for you. I have taken you away from so much." Star Hawk knew that she had had all of the comforts that the rich white people had, and that he had made her leave everything that she had known.

"All I care about is that I am at your side. This gift is more precious to me than anything that I have ever owned." She took the music box from his hand and held it to her chest as though she would never part with it.

"Yours words fill me with great joy, Silver Star. Your happiness means everything to me." His lips touched upon hers with a tender caress.

It was only a small time later, their meal complete and their bowls washed and again packed away, that the couple lay upon their sleeping mat, and with a contented bliss they held each other tightly and listened to the night life of the forest. The sound of crickets chirping, an owl far off in the distance searching for his own meal, and the scampering of squirrels and other rodents taking cover for the night, settled the couple into a world that they gladly shared.

"When will you have to leave the village again with

171

your father?" Jessica's soft voice broke the quiet as she held her breath awaiting his answer.

With a light kiss upon the nape of her neck, Star Hawk spoke. "There is a council meeting of several tribes, and my father wishes me to speak to the chiefs. It will not be for three weeks before we leave the village." He awaited her answer, and as she remained quiet he looked into her face. "You will be safe in our lodge, Silver Star. There is no need for worry."

"And you will be safe also?" she finally questioned him.

"I will be as safe as any other. We do not go to war, we only go to the council and speak of the things that are upon our chiefs' minds."

"Then I will not worry." Jessica tried to smile, but all that she could do was to form her trembling lips into a small semblance of the smile that she would show him.

"You are a good wife then, my Silver Star." He pulled her close to his chest and kissed the fire curls at the crown of her head.

"That is all I ever wish to be for you." Jessica softly replied.

Their talk was stilled with her answer as she turned into her husband's loving arms and he swept her away with him to the farthest reaches of the planet, where the brilliance of love's sweet ecstasy spun slowly about them, wrapping them in a velvet cocoon of love's lingering embrace.

The night passed them by as they were lost to all but the touch of the other, and then, their bodies sated, they slept, their limbs interwined, their breaths lightly mingling, as even in sleep they remained as one, united in their love, inseparable in their hearts.

The next afternoon brought the couple to the Blackfoot village, and though they regretted that they were no longer alone, the sight of the faces of the women and men that greeted them were welcome. Jessica was daily beginning to become a part of this tribe of people, and with a soft and yielding heart she gave herself and gladly received that which was bestowed upon her, accepting her husband's people and learning from their guidance and gentle ways.

Singing Moon was one of the first to make her way to her son's lodge, and with a wide grin Jessica presented the bolt of cloth to her mother-in-law. And Singing Moon, with a look of awe, slowly reached out a hand and lightly felt the cloth. "It is lovely, my daughter." She spoke softly, not taking her eyes from the bolt of material, the colors holding her gaze spellbound.

"It is a gift to you, Singing Moon." This statement brought the older woman's gaze full upon Jessica, who nodded her copper tresses. Singing Moon hugged her daughter-in-law tightly and crystal tears sparkled deep in her black eyes.

"You are good to this old woman, my daughter." She finally spoke, and then pulling herself together, she looked down upon the many fine things that her son and his wife had brought back from the trading post. "Your tepee will be beautiful with all of this." She bent down and lightly touched a large pot that would be used for stews in the winter.

Star Hawk smiled proudly at his mother's words. "My wife is wise in the ways of trading." And then, going to Jessica's side, he eased his hand about her waist.

"Your wife is indeed very wise," Singing Moon agreed, her dark eyes looking at the pair and easily seeing the love between them. She could not remember a time when she had seen her tall and handsome, but often foreboding son looking so happy. The joining with this woman surely must have been the right thing for him. Perhaps he was correct when he spoke of Silver Star as being the other part of his life cycle.

When Singing Moon left the lodge, Jessica and Star Hawk set about putting away the goods they had gotten. When they finished, Jessica lightly kissed her husband. Then, taking the new, brightly decorated leather bag that she had gotten for Cloud Dreamer, she went in search of the woman who had befriended her from the first day she had arrived at her husband's village.

Jessica found Cloud Dreamer in her lodge sitting next to her fire and stirring the contents of a boiling pot. After calling from the entrance flap, she stepped into the cool interior. "Are you cooking your dinner?" Jessica greeted her.

"I am making some medicine that will halt Cross Feather's cough. It has gotten worse in these past days, and I, as well as his woman, grow tired of hearing the sound coming from his chest."

"Is there anything that I can do?" Jessica quickly questioned. Since coming to this village she had learned a lot from Cloud Dreamer, and she rather enjoyed helping the older woman with her healing.

"There is little to do, Silver Star. Come and sit with me. I have missed you these past days. Tell me of your trip. Did you cover your body and hair with the mixture that I prepared for you?"

Sitting crosslegged next to the elder woman, Jessica laughed aloud. "Yes I did use the mixture, and even Star Hawk was impressed, though he did fear that the color would not wash off."

"But it did, and all went well?" Cloud Dreamer kept a hand stirring the pot as she spoke to Jessica.

Nodding her head in answer and not wishing to speak of what had taken place at the trading post with the trappers, Jessica held out the leather bag toward her friend. "I got you a gift, Cloud Dreamer, for all that you have done for me."

"Thank you." Cloud Dreamer took the bag, and with aged and wrinkled fingers she went over the beaded design. "It is very beautiful, Silver Star. I will treasure it always, as it came from you with love."

Jessica eased over and lightly kissed the leathery cheek. And no more words were needed between the two.

"You will come to my lodge tomorrow and help me to pick wild herbs in the forest. We will leave early; it is not far that we shall go, so we shall not be gone too long."

"Of course I shall come and help you. I would not miss such a day." Jessica smiled at her excitement at being once again back at the village and getting to help Cloud Dreamer.

A short time later Jessica left Cloud Dreamer's lodge and made her way back to her own. Star Hawk was not in the tepee, and Jessica was allowed a time to herself, able to go over in her mind what had been happening to her in the past weeks. Life now held meaning for her. She loved and was loved. She had friends here in this village, she had a home here in her husband's lodge. All that she needed Star Hawk had seen to it that she had received. Never in her life had she ever been so happy. Only the thought of Star

Hawk's having to leave her side filled her with dread.

But with his entrance into the lodge at that moment there was no more time for such thoughts. All simple thoughts and reasoning deserted her when this man stood before her. He filled her mind and body but with one thought, and that was of love.

Chapter Seven

Wrapped in the warm embrace of tranquil love, they passed their days swiftly. Jessica and Star Hawk gently eased into their lives as husband and wife. They learned more of each other with each day that passed, loving all that they discovered and delighting in each other.

Star Hawk spent his days hunting and fishing, enjoying the life of one who willingly stayed near his lodge. His dark eyes constantly watched for the slim, willowy sight of the fire-haired woman of his heart. Jessica, after tending to the duties of taking care of her husband's lodge and preparing his meals, would go to Cloud Dreamer and help her ready her medicines and at times would accompany the older woman. Jessica felt her days were full. But all too quickly the hands of time were passing.

"You will not be gone long? You promise?" Jessica questioned, trying her best not to cry when she thought of Star Hawk's leaving her.

"You know I will not stay longer than needed. I too will yearn to be back here in our lodge and beside you." Star Hawk knew well of her fears of being left alone in his village and her worries over his own safety. But he had to go with the other braves and his father. Golden Eagle was a mighty chief of the Blackfoot nation and could not turn his back on this meeting with the other tribes. Many important issues would be discussed that could affect their lives. Star Hawk knew that he would have to accompany his father as he had in the past, for Golden Eagle was depending on him more now than ever.

Jessica looked up from the deer hide that she was tanning and Star Hawk glimpsed the crystal droplets of tears in her silver eyes. "I guess I will keep busy helping Cloud Dreamer, and the time will pass quickly." She willed the tears to still. She did not wish for Star Hawk's memory of his last night with her to include her weeping as a foolish woman.

Squatting down next to her, Star Hawk caressed her soft cheek. "The time will pass quickly, for the Great Spirit knows of our need for each other. It will be but two weeks. Not such a long time, my love." He dreaded the time away from her as she did, but he spoke the words that he hoped would ease her heart, and then he reached over and kissed the dampness from her eyelids.

"Any time will be too long," Jessica sniffed, but now with his arms around her she felt again the security that he always seemed to bring her. She wondered at this feeling of total contentment that came over her each time she was in his arms. If only she were as sure as he that all would be well. At least she could feel somewhat reassured that he would not be going to war against any other tribe. It was, after all, only a meeting of the tribes, and he would be with Golden Eagle and many of the braves from their village. "I imagine that this first time will be the hardest." A trembling smile touched her lips as she tried to show him that she would be brave.

178

At that moment Star Hawk glimpsed his wife's total innocence. She appeared as a small, forlorn child, looking up to him and trying to put on a face that would please him. With a low moan, he pulled her tightly against his chest. "You will be safe here, Silver Star. No harm will befall you. I have asked Spotted Pony to watch over you while I am away from our village."

"I do not fear for myself, Star Hawk," she whispered softly against his hard chest. "I only dread the time that you will not be here beside me. And you will be careful?" Again she thought of his being hurt in some fashion. "You will not risk yourself foolishly in any way?" She remembered now all of the stories she had heard since being in this village of her husband's daring feats. Cloud Dreamer herself had told Jessica the story of when her husband had faced a huge bear with only his hunting knife. There were many other stories coming to her mind. She had heard of the time when he had gone alone into a Crow village to avenge the death of a boyhood friend. He had killed the Crow Indian in front of his own lodge with the entire village looking on and then had mounted his stallion and slowly ridden out of the village, as though daring them to follow and give fight. With such thoughts as these filling her mind, her heart beat at a frantic speed, her hands clutching tightly to his back.

"Silver Star, Silver Star, do you not know that I would never foolishly let any harm befall me? You are my very breath. If I were not able to return to your soft arms, my very soul would cry aloud with my loss. I would wander the star path forever wailing with fury, and not even death would keep me from returning to your side. You are my very heart. If the very blood in my veins were to spill forth on the earth, the

179

Great Spirit himself would surely know of my pain of leaving my love and he would restore my life to me. Do not fear, my little love, for now that I have you, I will not risk myself. I shall return to your side."

A large sigh reached his ears. She felt somewhat better, but she knew that she would not feel fully at ease until Star Hawk was once again here in their lodge.

Star Hawk pulled her face to his with his finger under her chin. His ebony eyes held her silver ones with all the love and warmth his body was feeling at this moment. "I love you with every fiber of my being. You are everything to me, breath of my breath and heart of my heart. My very blood pulses through my veins with the sound of your name. From the beginning you were meant to be mine, and such a love will last throughout all time." His words were soft, and his lips gently lowered, catching hers with such a tender, consuming touch that she felt herself melting against him, forgetting everything but his touch.

Jessica denied him nothing. Her lips opened under his, sharing and giving, drinking fully of the love that had bloomed between them. With heart-stopping tenderness, Star Hawk kissed her for what seemed like an eternity, softly tasting her sweetness at first and then fanning to flame the emotions of their souls.

Jessica's own mouth accepted greedily the attentions of his. Her tongue traced his even, white teeth, and then, gently intruding, devoured the taste that was his alone, seeking and touching in primitive arousal that assured Star Hawk that as close as they were at this moment, it was not enough. Her body arched to fit itself to the unyielding contours of his. Her hands roamed over his smoothly bronzed skin and the muscles of his back, setting him aflame with

180

his need for her.

His lips slowly abandoned hers and Jessica tried to bring them back, wanting the wondrous feel of his mouth to last forever. His warm breath roamed across her cheek as he sought the smoothness of her small earlobe. He whispered, "It is time to seek our mat, wife." He stood to his full height, his arms wrapping around her, and he carried her the few feet to their sleeping couch.

Without a word, he disrobed his young bride, his breathing was erratic when she at last stood fully naked before him. She had a beauty that stirred him beyond all reason. Her smooth, golden plane, so lusciously outlined in the firelight, stoked his senses to their fullest. He reached out, and with a touch as soft and gentle as the brush of a firefly, he caressed her firm breasts, marveling at such perfection as the rose taut peaks strained toward his hand. With her small gasp, he went further, lightly letting his fingers roam over her smooth, flat belly and softly rounded hips until they touched her womanly softness, probing into her depths and leaving Jessica moaning softly.

"You stir me as no other ever has. I can never seem to get enough of you, Silver Star," Star Hawk murmured, his hands and lips searing every inch of Jessica's flesh, his mind swirling with the feel of her beneath his hand. "You are a burning fire in my blood."

Jessica's breath caught in her chest as his kisses rained on her breasts, his tongue circling and tempting each pink peak. His knowing fingers probed deeper, leaving her trembling with a deep hunger that originated from her very core. She was aflame with his touch, her body ablaze with need for him. His bold caresses were sweetly tormenting, leaving her

181

quaking beneath his loving assault.

Star Hawk's body came alive, ignited by the breath of passions' fire. With a small movement, his breechcloth fell to his feet. As Jessica's small hand boldly reached out and lightly roamed over the flat muscles of his stomach and gently splayed over his thigh, Star Hawk growled low in his chest, pulling her down on the soft fur pallet beside him. Her hand again traced his body, and he felt himself tremble with flaming desire.

Inhaling the warm, male scent of her husband, Jessica boldly let her lips kiss and titillate his broad neck and down his hard chest, her breath erratic as her hands and mouth worked their wonder over his magnificent body. Her light kisses fed the gnawing, aching hunger of his fierce passion, and her gentle caresses created new searing cravings, which mounted as she gently wrapped her hand around his throbbing, pulsing maleness.

A groan of sweet animallike torment passed from his lips, and he could hold back no longer. He swiftly rose above her, spreading her thighs, his velvet-black eyes looking deep into hers, and forged their bodies together. He quivered with the sheer erotic sensations that their joining created. The molding together of flesh to flesh pulled them toward a frantic, pulsing rhythm, searing them together as he plunged deeply into her softened depths, seeking fully the ultimate pleasure of total intimacy. Together their rapture soared heavenward, gliding on the downy wings of the flying hawk that Star Hawk had been named for, laying claim to the snowy peaks of the mountaintops, sharing the depths of unbounded ecstasy. They did not think of tomorrow, but only of the moment. They were as one, their bodies molded together, their hearts

182

swiftly racing, rounded hip touching narrow hip, soft, shapely thigh touching muscled, flexing thigh. Time stood still for this man and woman, husband and wife. No boundary of color or race intruded in this cozy lair, no thoughts of separation or what the day after would bring. Only their unique love existed, only their breath mingling with a feather touch. They were Star Hawk and Silver Star, created and living only for each other.

With the slowly dawning reality of fulfillment gently easing about them, they lay gasping, their wondrous passion spent at last, their bodies' needs appeased for a short time. Star Hawk enfolded Jessica in his arms and pulled the furs around them. He turned to her with a loving, tender smile. "This night will linger in my thoughts throughout the days ahead." He kissed her forehead tenderly and settled his large frame against her side.

With a small, wicked grin, Jessica looked at her husband. "The night is not yet finished, my love, and I will have you remember what will await you upon your return." She kissed his lips, warmly and passionately.

"Oh wife, you indeed will be hard to leave," Star Hawk chuckled, delighting in Jessica's body so softly molded against his own.

"I wish that you would never have to leave me." Jessica sighed aloud, feeling somewhat better now after their lovemaking but still dreading the two weeks that lay ahead without Star Hawk. She would miss his strong body lying next to her on this soft couch at night, and she would long for his tender smile during the days while she would be about her work either helping Cloud Dreamer with her medicines or tending to something here in their lodge. He had become a part of her days, and she did not know what she would do with herself without him.

"You would soon grow bored with me underfoot all the time if I were to stay here in the village with you day in and day out." He grinned, trying to put her in a lighter mood.

"Truly, I never would." Jessica looked at him with serious intent that bespoke the fact that she was taking him at his word.

"I was joking with you. You are truly a treasure, Silver Star. I would never allow you to grow bored with me. I would keep you here on our sleeping couch forever if I could. But our people need me, and also I fear we would starve to death if I stayed abed and did not go out hunting to seek fresh game for our pot."

Jessica lightly giggled, snuggling closer to his warm body. "I would willingly see how long I could endure such torture." The image of lying forever in this man's arms filled her thoughts with a truly wondrous picture.

"My love, I have seen your appetite, and I think you would yield swiftly." He nipped lightly at the trim column of her sleek neck.

"You have seen but my appetite for your love." She seductively pressed her young, full body against him.

Star Hawk's mind spun, but as he looked into her face he lost himself to the love he felt for her. "We have so little time, my Silver Star. Even if the Great Spirit would allow us a hundred thousand years together, that is still such a small span of time for me to love you." His mouth covered hers, slanting down upon those soft petals and losing his very soul to the splendid power of love that spun goldenly about them.

Their love raged on as the hours of the evening

184

slowly passed by. Their murmurs of love and their soft moans of fulfillment drifted about the tepee as the fire dimmed and gutted. Finally, with sated bodies and contented hearts, they fell at last into peaceful slumber, their limbs intertwined, cheek laid against cheek.

Star Hawk woke with the dawn's first light. He turned his head and his eyes filled with his wife's beautiful face lying softly against his shoulder. Her flame-gold hair softly lay about her heart-shaped face and brushed gently against his cheek and chest. Inhaling the sweet, clean fragrance of the silken strands, he held his dark eyes tightly shut, remembering the hours they had spent last night. His wife was beyond belief. She was everything any man could ever want, a seductive vixen who lay soft and willing in his arms. A proud, strong woman who would stand faithfully by his side throughout the days of their lives.

Lightly he placed a fleeting kiss on her brow, not wishing to awaken her and make their parting that much harder. He quietly eased himself from the soft sleeping couch. He would miss her fiercely in the days ahead. His little Silver Star had found a place within his heart that no other had ever touched. She was his complete world, and at this moment he wished fervently that he could stay here with her and forget about the outside world. He would be forever content to lie in her arms and think only of the budding love that he had in his heart for her.

But this was not to be. The changes taking place all around them had to be dealt with. He could remember the times when he had never seen a white man. When he had been a youth, all that he had thought of was learning the ways that would lead him one day to be a strong warrior. But now life had changed for his people and he could not turn his back on them. They needed him to be strong and worthy of their trust. He could not hide himself away with his woman.

Bending, he pulled the breechcloth around his loins, his dark eyes still gazing at Jessica. Her sleep-filled face was beautiful to his eyes. Holding this in his memory, he silently went through the flap of the tepee. At his whistle his horse came at a gallop from the back of the lodge. Within minutes he was surrounded by the large band of warriors who would be going with him and Golden Eagle to the council.

Jessica awoke a short time later. Stretching out on the sleeping mat, she reached out a hand for her husband; but instead of his hard, warm body, she but touched the soft furs of their pallet. Silent tears made a path down her creamy cheek. He was gone, and now she was all alone. "Oh please, Star Hawk, hurry back to me," she softly cried aloud and then turned her head to the furs that had nested her husband during the night. His scent still clung about her, giving her security. Tired from her lack of sleep during the night, and now with the torment of Star Hawk's leaving, she drifted into a troubled sleep, dark, ebony eyes and bronzed skin drifting in her dreams and leaving her with a feeling of emptiness and wanting.

The days slowly passed by. To Jessica, whose days were kept busy with visiting Singing Moon and Cloud Dreamer, each hour seemed to go by at a slow, almost motionless pace with the absence of her husband. Her evenings were spent alone. She would sew for hours near the small pit fire as she worked on the shirt she was fashioning for him, then she would wearily retire to her lonely sleeping couch, feeling the

186

absence of Star Hawk throughout the night.

During the dark hours of the night, she would awake with his name on her lips as she lay dreaming of his kisses or his gentle hand caressing her cheek. Upon waking, she would realize that she had been dreaming, and she would softly weep aloud in the empty lodge.

In the morning Jessica would go to the river and wash, gather wood for her lodge fire, and bring water for cooking. Since Star Hawk's departure, the Indian called Spotted Pony had made his presence known to her, assuring her that he was always near if she were in need of him. This fact helped Jessica feel more at ease, but truly she was already feeling a part of the Indian village. Everyone was kind to her, respecting her as Star Hawk's wife. The only one that made her feel in the least uncomfortable was the young Indian maiden Bright Lilly, whom, upon occasion in the mornings, Jessica would pass as she went to the riverbank. The other girl looked hostilely at her when they chanced to meet, and Jessica knew that she still harbored feelings of hurt and betrayal.

Most afternoons she spent first visiting Singing Moon for a short time, and then in Cloud Dreamer's lodge. This time of the day she enjoyed best, when Cloud Dreamer would give her a task that would keep her mind off her longing for her husband.

This afternoon was no different as she sat next to the old Indian woman and helped her fill small pouches with brown powder that they had crushed the day before from plants. The powder would lessen the pain of a wound.

"You have learned much in these past weeks, Silver Star. I think it is time that you go with me to the tent of Buffalo Runner. He is an old man and has a fever

187

of the chest. At times it is hard for him to breathe, and his wife is also old and cannot care for him properly. And also, it is time that the elders of our tribe saw your hands helping to heal their ailments. At times they are set in their ways, but there will come a day when they will have to turn to you with their complaints."

Jessica was excited about being allowed to help Cloud Dreamer with her healing, even if only to watch. She would learn more, and she would also have something to occupy her. So this afternoon as the sun slowly began to lower, she felt her spirits rising somewhat with the plans for the morrow.

She reached her lodge and sighed aloud with relief that she had not forgotten to light her fire before she had gone to Cloud Dreamer. There was a chill in the night air that had forced her to wrap her arms around herself as she had made her way to her lodge. It was warm in her husband's tepee, but as she looked about, she was once again struck by the loneliness that seemed to linger in the pointed structure.

It would be best, she thought, if she went to sleep early this evening. She would need her sleep so she could help Cloud Dreamer tomorrow. So thinking, she stood before her couch and pulled her dress from her body. Her hand touched the coolness of the silver amulet tied around her neck. This had been the first gift from Star Hawk, given to her with his love and protection. With a small smile, Jessica slipped beneath the soft, warm furs. Reaching to the floor, she lifted the small music box. Easing up the lid, she shut her eyes as the soft, tinkling music filled the lodge. The one hand lightly held the music box as the other touched the amulet around her neck, and she slowly drifted into sleep.

The next morning, Jessica hurriedly made her way to Cloud Dreamer's tepee. After helping the older woman pack her medicines, she silently walked along with her to the tent of Buffalo Runner.

As the pair stepped into the lodge, all was quiet except for the deep, slow rattling of the old man's chest. He sat near the center fire and was propped into an upright position by numerous furs and mats that allowed him to breath more easily.

"I have brought Silver Star with me today," Cloud Dreamer announced as she looked across the room at the old woman called Dashing Rabbit. "She is wise in the ways of healing. The Great Spirit has given her much wisdom to help her people."

Both sets of black, piercing eyes were directed at Jessica, but Cloud Dreamer paid no heed as she set about making the old man more comfortable and pulled from her sack the things that she would be needing. "Take this bowl and go to the riverbank, Silver Star. Fill it with the blackest mud you can find. We shall make a binding for his chest with the mud and herbs that will make heat penetrate into his body and loosen his chest."

Jessica did not linger but was quick to do Cloud Dreamer's bidding. For a moment in the lodge she had thought that the old man or woman would demand that she leave their home, but Cloud Dreamer's directness had not given them the chance to speak before the healing woman was giving out orders.

She was only gone a short time, returning quickly with the bowl of mud that Cloud Dreamer needed. After she had mixed some ground herbs and a small pouch of white powder into the bowl, she proceeded to put the dark mixture over the old man's shrunken chest. "This will pull out the evil spirits and allow the good to come back," Cloud Dreamer mumbled aloud as she set about her work.

With this completed, she bound the old man's chest with a warm fur and pulled it tight with rawhide strappings. "Your chest will ease soon, Buffalo Runner. Now lie back and try to rest. I shall mix you a drink to help you sleep."

The old man did as he was told with one eye on the white woman. He knew that the young woman was the bride of Star Hawk and that Cloud Dreamer was teaching her all of her healing secrets. But still, he was an old man, and he had ever been wary of those with pale skin.

"We will be needing water to warm over the fire." Cloud Dreamer looked across the lodge to the old woman who was still sitting in the same position as when they had first entered. She knew that the elderly woman was not capable of making the trip to the river, and for a moment Cloud Dreamer wondered about this old couple's son, Laughing Otter. Was his wife seeing to the needs of her husband's family as she should be doing? Eyeing the water bucket near the tent flap, Cloud Dreamer motioned Jessica toward it. The young girl saw that it was empty, and with a smile she hefted it in her hand.

"I shall fetch a bucket of water from the river." With that, she turned and was gone.

"Silver Star is a good daughter to an old woman." Cloud Dreamer spoke as she began to mix together some of her potions.

The older woman across the room looked at Cloud Dreamer with a strange, growing light in her dark gaze. "Do you truly think of this white woman as a daughter?"

"She is the daughter that I never had. I do not see the whiteness of her skin but the love in her heart. Our people are hers now that she is wife to Star Hawk. And as a good daughter, she sees that I have plenty to eat and drink. Her husband hunts for my lodge now, and Silver Star comes each day to see to my needs."

"She is a good daughter, then," Dashing Rabbit replied. "Our own son's wife comes only when she must. Our lives now are spent and useless. We can but tell stories to the young and lie about our lodge." Her voice was sad and listless.

Cloud Dreamer decided she would speak with Star Hawk about this elderly couple. Their tribe always honored the old. It was not fitting that this couple should have to endure such treating these last days of their lives. Star Hawk would speak to Laughing Otter about his family and perhaps the son would see the treatment of his family at his wife's hand. A good beating would be what the lazy woman deserved. A small, thin smile came across Cloud Dreamer's lips with this thought. Yes, she would speak to Star Hawk as soon as he returned.

Jessica set the water bucket down beside Cloud Dreamer, and her eyes followed each movement of the elderly woman, watching which pouch she pulled the small brown leaves from that she placed in the small bowl of water which she placed near the fire to warm. "These leaves will bring a deep sleep and allow the body to heal."

As the mixture was warmed she brought it up to the old man's lips. She raised his frail head and made him drink.

"We shall leave now and let your husband rest."

191

Cloud Dreamer began to pack her medicines. "Silver Star will return this afternoon with a pot of stew for you both to eat. As a good daughter, she cooks well and is willing to share." She smiled first at Jessica and then at Dashing Rabbit.

"I thank you, Cloud Dreamer, for your help. And you also, Silver Star. You are welcome here in my husband's lodge." The old woman raised herself from her sitting position and slowly made her way to the two women. "Our chief's son is a lucky man to have such a fine wife."

Jessica smiled with happiness, not knowing what could have caused this woman to be so warm toward her. When she had first entered this lodge, the woman had seemed cold and forbidding. "Thank you, Dashing Rabbit. I will return this afternoon."

Jessica left Cloud Dreamer to make her way back to her own lodge and cook the stew that she would share with Cloud Dreamer and Buffalo Runner's lodge. Her heart felt lighter as she made her way, remembering each word that Dashing Rabbit had said to her. With each day that passed, she was becoming more accepted into her husband's tribe, and one day she would know that she fully belonged.

A full week had passed since Star Hawk's departure. Now, with the added job of accompanying Cloud Dreamer to tend the sick each day, Jessica was finding her days passing quickly, and in the evenings she fell into an exhausted sleep. Sometimes she stayed up throughout the night with a sick child. One evening she had gone with Cloud Dreamer to the birthing lodge, and she had not found her sleeping couch until the early hours of the morning.

"Buffalo Runner is growing worse, and I cannot leave his side today." Cloud Dreamer spoke softly as she stuffed an assortment of medicines into her pouch and started from her tepee.

"Is there anything that I can do?" Jessica questioned, her heart going out to the old man and woman whom she had grown to care about in the past few days.

For a moment Cloud Dreamer thought of what she would be needing. She did need the leaves of the sleeping plant, but she wondered if she should entrust such a job to this young girl. "There are plants at the foot of the mountain that I need for a sleeping potion. These will ease Buffalo Runner's slumber. Do you think that you could ride to the mountains and bring them back?"

Jessica quickly nodded her copper head. It was but a morning's ride to the foot of the mountain where she and Star Hawk had spent such a glorious two weeks. She could quickly get the plants that were needed and be back before dark. "Tell me what is needed," she said, knowing that there would be a need for her to hurry to bring the plants back to help the old man sleep this night through.

Cloud Dreamer quickly described the type of plants that they would need and cautioned Jessica to dress warmly, for the days were growing colder, and the nearer one went to the mountains the cooler the air became. She also told her to take some food along. After this she left the girl to fetch her horse, Red Wing, her own thoughts worriedly going back to Buffalo Runner's tepee. She could already hear the old shaman singing to the Great Spirit and requesting that he stand beside Buffalo Runner and ease his great pain.

Jessica wasted little time, but went to her lodge. She

193

took a warm fur in case it got cold, and threw some dried venison into a pouch. She then went to find Red Wing.

For a moment she thought of telling Spotted Pony of her plans, but as she did not see him, she cast this thought aside. There was a need for her to hurry. She would get to the mountains and gather the plants and be back in the village before Spotted Pony even missed her.

It was a cool, brisk morning, and Jessica kicked Red Wing's sides, enjoying the feel of her mare's warm body beneath her legs and the feel of the long flanks stretching out at her command. She traveled the same trail that she and Star Hawk had the day of their joining, and once again Jessica felt the full impact of her husband's absence. She let herself remember the evening that she had ridden in Star Hawk's arms to their lover's retreat. As the mare daintily picked her way through the forest, Jessica could again imagine the feel of the gentle touch of the copper hands she loved so well. She could see the deep blackness of his warm eyes on her, and with a terrible longing, she felt a tear slip from her silver eyes. Only a week had passed, and still there was another to go before Star Hawk would return to her. How could she endure, she wondered, lost deep in her own thoughts.

With a startled gasp, Jessica felt her mare pulled to a halt. Before her, sitting atop their horses, were the same two trappers who had been at the trading post. The one who had grabbed hold of her arm now held tightly to Red Wing's reins.

"Release my horse!" she demanded, feeling the trembling of her body with quick, settling fear. But she held her own and used her haughtiest tone as her silver eyes glared at the pair before her on the path.

194

"See there, Lonny. I be telling ya that she weren't no Indian. See them eyes? She be the same little ole gal that the fancy gent been asking around about and offering such a high reward. Woowee!" He slapped his thigh with his free hand. "We'll be as rich as sin just as soon as we get her back to her cousin."

The large brute called Lonny still looked a bit skeptical, his eyes shifting around the forest as though at any moment expecting company. "I be a-seeing that she ain't no Indian squaw." He looked at the flame-gold hair pulled back into two long braids and hanging to her waist, and the creamy, smooth skin that at the trading post had been a darker shade. "Aye, perhaps yer right, Sam. But I ain't a-going to feel any easier until we get ourselves out of these here woods."

Jessica could not speak as she listened to the pair. The one called Sam had spoken of a reward and returning her to her cousin. Edmond must have posted a reward for her return. Well, she would not go. She belonged with her husband and his people, not back under Edmond's thumb. "I think you have made a mistake." She looked at the man holding her horse's rein. He seemed more in control of the situation at the moment. "There is certainly no reward posted for me. I am not who you think. My husband is Star Hawk, an Indian of the Blackfoot tribe. If you will release me now, there will be nothing said and you will be able to return to wherever it is you are from without any harm befalling you."

Sam also looked around at her words, as though he had forgotten for the moment just how close to the Indian village they were. "Yer sure right, Lonny. We had best get going quick like." Without saying a word to Jessica, he took her reins and tied them to his own saddlehorn.

"No!" Jessica gasped aloud. When she saw his intent, she jumped from Red Wing's back and started to run back down the trail the way she had come. She was not about to go easily with these two horrible-looking men.

"Catch her fast!" Sam shouted as Lonny also jumped from the back of his horse. With a few easy strides, he was upon her. "She be our fortune now, don't be forgettin'."

Jessica screamed as the large hands cruelly wrapped around her upper arms and she was jerked hard to the barrellike chest. But as quickly as the scream left her lips, Lonny covered her mouth with a thick, beefy hand.

"We'll have to tie her, Sam, or she'll be bringing the whole Indian tribe down on our heads."

"All right, just be quick about it. Her buck, that Star Hawk, might be following her."

In a few moments, Jessica was slung over the back of her horse, her hands tied and a rag around her mouth to halt any more attempts at screaming.

Jessica tried frantically to pull her hands free, wiggling them back and forth. She even tried to throw herself off of Red Wing's back, but to no avail. She was as trussed up as the turkey for a holiday meal and could not do anything but endure the horrible ride as she was bumped and jerked, her eyes only able to stare at the ground.

That first day, there was no resting for the threesome as the trappers hurriedly tried to flee from the Indian territory. It was well after dark when Lonny finally called the horses to a halt. "We got to let the horses have a rest, Sam, or we won't be going too far in the long run."

The other man nodded his head in agreement. "All

196

right, but don't be building no fire until we are further away from that Blackfoot camp. I don't take kindly to the thought of having my hair lifted over a white woman that ain't no better than a dirty Injun-loving squaw."

Sam was the one who untied Jessica and helped her from her horse. Leading her to a tree and telling her to sit, he again tied her hands.

"Please," Jessica looked at the man, hoping for some compassion from him. The weariness of her body overcame her, and as he pulled her hands behind her back, she thought that they would snap in two from the pain. With no response from the trapper, she tried again. "At least may I keep my hands untied for a while?"

"Can't take the chance that you be trying to run again," he grunted, and turning his back to her he went to help Lonny tend to the horses.

Jessica caught a sob in her chest. This was a terrible situation she was now in. What was to become of her? Fear filled her silver eyes, and she watched the two men as they stood near their horses and spoke in low tones.

She tried again to wiggle her hands free, but, as earlier, it was no use. These trappers knew well how to tie a knot that would not untie easily. Soon their voices reached her.

"Use your head, man." The angry voice of Sam came across the space to Jessica. "Ye can't be at her when we're going to be getting such a handsome price for her return. Ye be thinking that her kin will pay us if she ain't all in one piece?"

"I'll not be hurting her none. Just a little romp is all I be wanting from her. It's cold as a witch's ass this night and she be a lively piece to warm my bed roll."

"Lonny, ye best be forgetting that Injun lover. She

197

ain't fur ye. All she would have to do is tell that dude of a cousin of hers and he won't be a-giving us anything for the trouble of fetching her to him."

"Yeah, I reckon as how yer right. But it sure as hell has been a long time since I had me a woman with her good looks." Lonny threw Jessica a glance of anger and longing as he pulled his saddle from his horse.

"After that red devil has had her, I doubt she be worth the worrying over," Sam grunted, pulling the sack that held their supplies from the saddle. Taking out some dried jerky and some hard biscuits, he slowly made his way toward his captive.

"Here, girl, eat this." He threw the food in her lap and then begrudgingly untied her hands.

With a sigh of relief, Jessica rubbed her wrists where the ropes had bitten into her tender flesh. "You have surely made a terrible mistake." She tried once again to reason with this man.

"Naw, I don't be a-thinking so, missy. Yer name is Jessica Coltin. I got me a picture right here in me shirt." He pulled from beneath his dirty leather-fringed shirt a wrinkled piece of paper. Watching the silver eyes staring back at him with startled surprise, he held it out for her to see. "See, there ye be, nice and pretty. Yer cousin left it at the post some time before you and that buck come fer yer supplies, and I wouldn't have recognized ye, except when I grabbed yer arm and ye looked me in the face. I knew that instant that ye weren't no true Injun. Them silver eyes of yers gave ye away, that's fer sure. I be remembering yer cousin saying as how ye had silver eyes and golden-red hair. I got ta thinking that ye could have somehow dyed yer hair and skin and I reckon that be just about what ye did." His large mouth broke into a toothless grin as he watched her face. "Don't ye be a-worrying none, though, all me and old Lonny boy here be a-wanting is that big reward. We'll see that ye get to yer kin safe and sound. Though I bet that yer cousin, being the fine gentleman that he is, don't be a-knowing that ye been a-living with a savage, does he?"

Jessica did not answer, but now the full reality of her situation hit her. She was going to be returned to Edmond, and when he heard about her and Star Hawk, he would undoubtedly figure out some horrible torment to inflict on her. "Please, you must listen to me," Jessica implored the trapper. "I can make sure that you are paid well if you will return me at once to the Indian camp. Star Hawk will give you all that he owns."

Before she could say anymore, Sam threw back his head and guffawed. "Yer Indian buck wouldn't be a-giving me nothing, 'cepting his skinning knife if he were to meet up with me and old Lonny. 'Tain't no way that I'll be a-taking ye back that way. No siree, you're off to your kin whether ye wish it or not. As fer meself, I don't be thinking yer worth a plugged nickle, seeing as how ye been living with a savage and yer a-wanting to return to him. Ain't ye got any shame about ye?" With this he turned from her and went to where Lonny was sitting and eating his own meal.

Silent tears slipped down Jessica's face. Shame? She indeed had none. Star Hawk was her husband, and she was not ashamed of this fact. She loved him. He was a man, she never thought of him as anything else. Forgotten was the food in her lap, as she thought of the love she was being taken from. Star Hawk would not even know what had happened to her. Perhaps he would think that she had been stolen by another tribe of Indians or even that she had been killed by an animal. Her heart ached with the horrible pain of knowing that she was being taken far away from the love she had found.

Was this small space of time all that she and Star Hawk would be allowed? Had the cruel twist of the fates been so heartless as to separate her and her love now while their hearts were so tender? Wrenching sobs shook her body with these thoughts. It would be another week before Star Hawk would return to the village and find that she was missing, and in that amount of time she would be returned to Sweet Oaks and to whatever fate Edmond would mete out to her.

Even as her body demanded that she sleep after the grueling ordeal of the day, she still sobbed aloud from the depths of her heart. The two trappers only grinned at their fortune in finding such a prize, their visions of riches obscuring all but their greed.

The camp was quiet as the woman and her captors finally slept, the two rough men taking turns as they watched out for any intruders that might venture into their midst. The moon was high in the darkness of the clouds when a soft noise like the snapping of a twig caught Sam's ear. Lying on his back with his hand on the trigger of his rifle, he allowed his breathing to remain normal as though he were lost in the depths of a deep slumber.

Spotted Pony quietly crept up on the small camp, his dark eyes searching out the area and finally settling on the woman tied and sleeping next to a large tree. With the sighting of Silver Star, his anger overcame his caution, and as he took a step into the encampment, a single twig snapped under his moccasined foot. For a moment he stilled, holding his breath, his dark eyes quickly going to the two trappers and watching for any sign of movement.

He would have to kill the two men, he told himself,

for his honor demanded it of him. He had been en-trusted with the care of Star Hawk's woman and he had failed his friend. That morning after he had watched her go to Cloud Dreamer's tepee, he had gotten caught up in a game of chance with a group of braves. Never being one to turn his back on gambling, he had gone to Laughing Otter's lodge and stayed the morning through.

It had been with some surprise that he had found Silver Star gone from the village, her horse Red Wing not in the corral. He had approached Cloud Dreamer and found that Silver Star had gone to the mountains for healing plants, and he had felt secure that she would be safe. It was rare that anyone violated the Blackfoot territories. There were those among their tribe who had never seen a white man until Star Hawk had brought his beautiful captive into their midst. So he felt confident that his charge would meet with no trouble. But remembering the words that his friend Star Hawk had spoken to him about carefully guarding his Silver Star from all harm and knowing that he would not be fully at ease until he was assured that she had gathered her plants and was returning to the vil-lage, he set out down the trail through the forest on the back of his white and brown spotted pony, expecting to meet up with Silver Star at any time.

It was not far down the trail, however, that Spotted Pony came across signs of a struggle. His black eyes scanned the area, noticing the tracks of two horses that had been shod and then the prints of Silver Star's Red Wing. Seeing that the tracks led away from the trail and toward the forest, he hurriedly gave pursuit, know-ing that he could not return to his village without the woman of Star Hawk.

As all remained quiet in the camp, Spotted Pony

thought of how stupid the white man could be, allowing himself to fall asleep while he was still in Blackfoot land. Slowly, he drew his knife from his breechcloth, and on soundless feet he drew near to the two large, snoring men. He would delight in taking the lives of those who would dare steal the woman of his chief's son. With this thought he crept closer, closing the distance between himself and the men in seconds. As he was about to easily slit the throat of the man closest to him, he felt a mighty, hurtling ball hit him full in the chest, and he flew several feet backwards, his mind recoiling with the fact that he had been shot.

Sam jumped to his feet the instant he pulled the trigger at the Indian crouching over Lonny. "Got him, by damn!" he shouted, slapping his thigh with a loud noise.

"What the hell?" Lonny also jumped from his bed roll, and as his eyes caught the blood-soaked Indian, his mouth formed a perfect circle.

"That Injun was just about to slit yer throat fer ya, Lonny, old boy." Sam grinned and kicked Spotted Pony to see if he was still alive. Finding no movement, he turned his back on him and began to gather up is bed gear. "Get the horses saddled. I knew that we were still in them redskins' territory."

"Is that there the one that the gal been living with?" Lonny questioned, his hands fumbling in his haste to gather up his own bed gear and get his horse saddled.

"Naw, this here is a different one. But I reckon that he were alone or the whole lot of 'em would have come to skelp us."

Lonny nodded his head in agreement.

Jessica had been pulled from sleep by the loud booming noise and the men's voice. It had been a few hours since she had fallen asleep, so her body demanded more rest, but forcefully she pulled her eyes open, seeing the horror unfolding before her. Spotted Pony lay only a few yards away from her, a large gaping hole in the center of his chest, and the two trappers were hurriedly saddling their horses. "Oh God," she wept aloud, knowing that Spotted Pony had only been trying to save her and return her to the village of her husband. These two vicious men had killed him because of her. "No, no!" she cried over and over until she felt the hands of one of her abductors untying her and pulling her to her feet.

"Do ya have to be tied again and thrown over yer horse, gal?" Sam questioned Jessica as he heard her cries and saw her tiredness. "If ya don't be a-trying to run off or jump from yer mount, ye can ride astride."

Jessica could but nod her head, her eyes drawn without will to the lifeless body of Spotted Pony.

Again, they hurriedly fled on horseback, but now the trappers were more cautious, resting only for a short time and then again riding until they were weary and hungry. At last they were out of Indian territory, and with this knowledge the pace seemed to ease somewhat and the men's manner became more relaxed in their watchful vigil.

Jessica felt her trepidation mounting with each day that passed. Her body was numb from sheer exhaustion. She was beyond tired; she now felt a part of her horse, Red Wing. Her thoughts replayed over and over the image of her husband's dear friend lying dead on the cold earth, and the fact that she was the one responsible for his death added to her grief.

The countryside now had a more familiar look as the trappers traveled down the Mississippi and toward

New Orleans. With each mile they traveled, Jessica knew that they were drawing closer to her Cousin Edmond. But with her weariness of body and soul, she could do nothing but hold on to the saddlehorn as her captors led her closer to her fate.

Chapter Eight

The council meeting had gone well. The Blackfoot nation had gathered and reaffirmed their feelings about the influx of whites who were plaguing their lands. The several bands once again pledged their unity, and after days of listening to the elders speak and seeing the sacred ceremonies performed, the chieftains went back to their own tribes.

Star Hawk was elated on the ride homeward, his thoughts constantly upon the woman who awaited him in his teepee. Jessica's fire hair and smooth, creamy skin occupied his thoughts at almost every moment. Even at the council of the high chiefs he had been hard-pressed to keep his thoughts upon the problems of his brothers. He wanted nothing more than to turn from the gathering and return to the woman of his heart.

But now, finally, after eleven days of being away from his village, he was at last on his way home. His heart beat fiercely with each step of his mighty black stallion, but he forced himself not to leave his father and the group of warriors he traveled with, for he really wanted to set out on his own and push Night Cloud to his fastest pace.

Golden Eagle knew well of his son's impatience to be home as they rode through the forest, and with cool agate eyes he spoke to him of the things that had passed at the council. "Our nation has always been bold and strong, my son. I would not see the influx of these whites flood our lands and kill our game. We shall watch carefully over our lands from this day forth, and the whites who come on our sacred hunting grounds will know well that they are trespassing."

Star Hawk nodded his dark head in agreement, knowing that there had to be an end to the influx upon their lands of these people or his own children and grandchildren would one day have to fight to survive. They had heard at the council that other tribes, who were sometimes their own enemies, were having to fight for their lives and their food because of the whites who had swarmed over their lands. Knowing well that Golden Eagle was a wise chief who was seeing to the future and desired only to protect his people, Star Hawk had to agree with him.

Golden Eagle watched his son's reaction to his words with a wise regard. He had been proud of Star Hawk at the council, for his son had spoken well, along with the other warriors who one day would be chiefs of their tribes. He had stood tall and proud in front of his peers, his voice strong as he spoke of the things he himself had seen on his journeys. He had told his people of the whites who swarmed over the land as though they were a plague of locusts. He had seen for himself the land that once had belonged to proud people now being plowed and farmed by the white settlers. He spoke of protecting his people, but he also spoke of the need for peace. Yes, Golden Eagle was very proud of his son, and one day Star

Hawk would be a mighty leader. He no longer thought of the white woman he had joined with as making his son weak. She was an adopted daughter of his tribe, and he now thought of Silver Star as a gift from the Great Spirit. There was a mystical quality about her. Her silver eyes and her hair of fire spoke to him of a cooly burning depth. She was strong, and he had heard much of her healing powers. Singing Moon spoke to him often of her strength and love for their son. Perhaps she would bring to them the grandchildren that he and Singing Moon had been longing for. His blood was strong with a son such as Star Hawk, but he longed now for the laughter of children to fill his lodge. He held in his heart the desire to teach his grandsons how to hunt and to fight, as he had taught his own son.

"It will be good to return to our lodges." A dark brow rose in Star Hawk's direction. "In my youth I cared for nothing but hunting game and fighting our enemies, but now I but long for the comfort of my wife and my lodge." He now smiled fully upon his son.

Star Hawk also smiled, knowing that his father even at his age was stronger and more active than many of the younger warriors. He never complained. More than likely his father guessed his own impatience to be back in the village and was only expressing his own feelings for him. "I also cannot wait overlong to be back at my lodge." He grinned fully.

"Augh yes, homecomings can be wonderful, my son." Golden Eagle chuckled as he kicked the sides of his buckskin horse, pulling the stallion away from his son.

* * *

It was three days and nights of traveling before the group of warriors returned to their village. And with the late afternoon sun slowly lowering in the blue-clouded sky, Star Hawk and his group set upon the sloping rise of ground and looked down upon the peaceful Indian village. Star Hawk's thoughts went back to another time when he and his beautiful captive had stood upon this same spot. Silver Star had been frightened of what was laid out before her that day, and he could remember his own heart going out to her trembling body. With a swift kick upon Night Cloud's flanks and with a war cry upon his lips, he swiftly set out ahead of the others. But his excitement was infectious, and soon the large group was beside him, his own father in the lead.

Pulling Night Cloud to a halt outside of his tepee, Star Hawk had eyes for none in the village as he hurriedly jumped from his horse's back and pushed the flap of his lodge aside. He strode through the opening but was brought up short. Jessica was not there. There was a coldness in the tepee. No fire had been lit, and as he slowly walked toward the small pit in the middle of the floor, he saw that it had been several days since it had been used. For a frightening moment his dark eyes went about the space, but seeing all in order, he turned toward the entrance. Perhaps Silver Star was with his mother or with Cloud Dreamer. Of course she did not wish to be alone with him gone and was staying in the lodge of his mother or Cloud Dreamer. His heart was beating at such a rapid pace that he felt his very chest ready to explode. For a moment a dread filled his body that left him cold and frighteningly empty, but with a will he forced these feelings from him.

As he was bending to leave the lodge, his father

and Singing Moon stepped inside. The look upon their faces told him more than any words that something was amiss.

"Where is Silver Star, mother? Has she been staying in your lodge or that of Cloud Dreamer?" For a moment he thought to push them from in front of him and go through the village and look for himself, but his father's look of pity stilled him.

"It was but two days past." Singing Moon softly spoke aloud within the chilled tepee. "Cloud Dreamer sent Silver Star to the foot of the mountains to gather healing herbs. Buffalo Runner was very ill and Cloud Dreamer could not go herself for the needed plants."

"My wife?" Star Hawk felt a chill course through him with each word that was being spoken. "Where is Silver Star?"

"I do not know, my son." Tears were now coursing down Singing Moon's cheeks as she viewed the pain that was displayed openly upon her son's features. "She left early that morning and did not return."

"What of Spotted Pony? Did he not go with her?" Star Hawk could not believe what he was being told.

"We have not seen Spotted Pony, either. He left after noon of the same day. He had been playing games with some of the braves and finding her missing from the village he set out after her. There are braves out now scouting the forest for any signs that will lead them to their whereabouts."

Star Hawk looked from his mother to his father. The pain that was filling him was like the torture of a thousand piercing knives cutting into his flesh.

"Silver Star." The name came from the very foundation of his being when for a moment he felt the full impact of his loss.

209

As though shaking himself from the swirling clouds of doom that circled about him, Star Hawk felt the pressure of his father's strong hand upon his shoulder. "We shall go now and look for Silver Star and Spotted Pony."

Star Hawk nodded his head, his body beginning to fill with a cold rage, with the thought that any harm would dare to overtake his wife.

As they stepped from the lodge a group of braves pulled their mounts to a stop before them, one of the braves in the lead holding the reins of Spotted Pony's horse and the body of Star Hawk's friend tied to its back.

A young brave by the name of White Fox was the first to speak, his dark eyes locking with Star Hawk's and seeing the pain there. "We found the trail of your woman going toward the mountains, but it was not far before we found the prints of two other horses and could see signs of a struggle. We followed the trail that lead to the forest for some time and then came to a place where two men and your woman had camped. We found Spotted Pony's body in their camp, his horse was nearby."

"And what of Silver Star? Was there no further sign?" Star Hawk felt a deathlike chill engulfing him as he saw the body of his longtime friend and knew that he had been trying to protect his wife and that this resulted in his death.

"We saw signs that someone had been tied to a tree." White Fox could see the pain in Star Hawk's eyes turn to hard, cold flint as he was given his answers. "The camp was hurriedly broken. Your woman's horse was being led by one of the men. We followed for another day, but we knew that Spotted Pony must be properly cared for and prepared for

210

burial. We will again go with you, Star Hawk, to find your woman."

"I will find my wife." Star Hawk spoke, his voice now as cold and chilling as his dark eyes. "I thank you for your offer, but Spotted Pony must be tended, and I will be able to travel quicker alone."

White Fox and the others nodded their heads as they agreed with his reasoning. Without another word they took Spotted Pony's body to the lodge of his parents.

"You must eat and rest first," Singing Moon beseeched her son.

"I will eat, but I cannot rest until I have my wife back at my side." Star Hawk spoke softly and then turned back into his lodge.

Golden Eagle led his wife back to their own lodge where Singing Moon hurriedly began to prepare food for her son and her husband.

Star Hawk in his own lodge let his dark eyes roam about the tepee. How empty and cold it now seemed to him, as he bent and slowly sank down upon the couch of furs that had been their bed. He felt such a loss that he wished to cry aloud to the Great Spirit with his fierce pain.

He could see the beauty of Silver Star as she had sat upon this couch and sewed upon a piece of fur, he could envision her bending over a pot and preparing their meal. He could almost feel her softness within his arms as she had bent down to him and pressed her sweet, giving lips upon his own, her rounded, soft body lying full against him as she lovingly assaulted his senses. And for a moment, Star Hawk felt his total loss at the hands of the thieves who had dared steal his woman. As he pulled a beaver pelt up close to his face and smelled the sweet, clinging scent of his wife, his loud, piercing war cry filled the small circle of his lodge. He would find the men who had dared to lay hands upon his wife and he would make them pay dearly for each second that they had held her from him. He jumped to his feet, his hand still holding the soft fur, and again he let his gaze circle the home that he had shared so happily with his bride. "I am coming, my Silver Star. I will find you, no matter where you are. I cannot live without your love, for you are my life and my heart." A lone tear slid down the strong, smooth cheek before he again straightened, and throwing the fur on the couch, he turned and bent to his war paints. The silver and black lines upon one cheek and three black ones on the other. Straight lines of silver from forehead to chin, lending a deathlike quality to his appearance. His cold, black eyes looked for his war axe and a large hunting knife. Tying a silver and then a large red feather in a downward position about his forehead with a thin strip of leather, he turned from his lodge and started to his parents' tepee.

By the time Star Hawk entered the tepee of Golden Eagle, Singing Moon had a bowl of food waiting for her son. Both pairs of dark eyes looked upon Star Hawk as he hurriedly ate the food.

"You still wish to go alone to find Silver Star, my son?" Golden Eagle sat down upon his couch across from the fire. "Any of the warriors of the tribe would be honored to ride with you upon this journey."

"I know that any one of the braves from our village would gladly go with me, but I think it will be best for me to go alone. It may be some time before I find Silver Star and the men that took her away."

"You will not return then until you do find her?" Singing Moon questioned. Her deepest fear was that the men who had taken her son's wife would go far away and that Star Hawk would search to no avail.

Star Hawk's dark gaze rose to meet his mother's. "I shall not return to my village until I have Silver Star at my side. How can I return without my heart? The Great Spirit gave Silver Star unto my care as a wondrous gift. I should have seen better to her protection." And for a moment Star Hawk thought of the pain that his wife must be feeling. Had the two men hurt her in any way? Was she weak and worried with fear of the unknown at this very moment?

"Do not blame yourself, my son, for the actions of those that reach out with a heart of evil." Golden Eagle saw the pain-filled thoughts raking over his son's spirit.

For a moment Star Hawk wondered at the hand of the Great Spirit. Surely Silver Star was a priceless gift given to him. Could the gods so easily take out of his hands the one that they had given to him?

Before any further words were spoken a voice from the front of the tepee flap called out to Star Hawk. Rising to his full height, the young warrior stepped from his father's lodge, his dark gaze settling upon Bright Lilly as she stood rather nervously before him.

"I have heard that you had come back from the council, Star Hawk." She spoke softly, her dark-honey warm eyes looking up into his handsome face and knowing once again the trembling of her heart when she was in his presence.

Star Hawk looked upon the girl as though not truly seeing her. "What is it that you want, Bright Lilly? Do you perhaps know something of Silver

213

Star?" For a moment he thought that perhaps this girl knew something about the two men who had taken his wife. Again in his mind he could see her hand raised with the sharp knife in Silver Star's direction.

"I know nothing about the woman Silver Star. I wished only to speak with you for a moment. I am sure that Silver Star wished to leave our village, Star Hawk. Surely she was not used to the hard work of our women, and when you left the village to go to the council meeting she saw her chance to flee."

Star Hawk's features turned dark and unreadable as he listened to this young maiden.

"You will need a woman now, Star Hawk. One who is used to Indian ways. One who will not bring shame upon you and will help you in the years to come. Surely you see that I have much to offer you." It took some loss of pride on Bright Lilly's part to come to Star Hawk and to say these words. But she saw her chance now with Silver Star gone, and she could not afford to wait. Perhaps she could dissuade Star Hawk from giving chase to his fleeing wife. None would ever fault him if he turned now to Bright Lilly. After all, Silver Star was but a white woman.

"My wife did not leave her people willingly, Bright Lilly."

"Her people?" Bright Lilly gasped aloud. "She is not of our blood. She is white, our enemy."

"She is the daughter of Cloud Dreamer, and she is my wife. We are as one. Silver Star is not our enemy. Those that would bring a slur upon her name are my enemies. Do not seek me out to cast any doubt upon my wife. I go now to find her and to bring her back to her people and to her husband's lodge. For once

214

and for all, Bright Lilly, realize that what was between you and me, though it was very little, is now over. My heart and my arm belong to only Silver Star."

"But she is not worthy. . . ."

"Do not bring any further shame upon yourself with the words that you would bring forth. I go to find my wife, the woman of my heart."

Tears broke from the dark eyes, and with the finality of his words she knew that all of her plans and her hopes of being Star Hawk's woman had been dashed. Even if he did not find Silver Star he would never again turn to her. He was surely lost to her forever.

Before leaving the village one last time, Star Hawk went into his lodge, his dark gaze going about the enclosure as though expecting to find Jessica humming a light tune as she set about her work, but with only the coldness of the empty lodge and the memories of days gone past, he started to turn back toward the entrance flap. A faint glimmering caught his eye as he stopped to go outside, and striding toward the sleeping couch, he reached and picked up the small silver music box that he had given to Jessica, his mind filling with the love that they had shared that evening in the forest before he had given her his gift. With a slight movement of his hand he lifted the lid, his ears filling with the sounds of the sweet, gentle music that he had heard often in this lodge, when Jessica would sit at her sewing. With a soft sigh he tucked the music box in his pack and left the lodge in search of White Fox, seeking out the warrior to hear again what he had found in the forest.

Before the darkness of the night encircled him, Star Hawk had picked up the tracks of White Fox and the warriors of his tribe. He did not slacken his pace, though, even with the twilight of night closing in about the forest. White Fox had told him where they had gone, and Star Hawk hoped to make faster time by pushing his horse slowly during the nights and still traveling during the day. His thoughts were consumed with his need for speed. Silver Star was out there somewhere with two men who had already killed Spotted Pony when he had tried to protect her. He had to find her. The beating of his heart pounded aloud with his thoughts. He had to find her!

Strong, unyielding hands pulled Jessica from the back of Red Wing. "We're here now, and ye had best keep yer mouth shut until we got our gold in our hands," Lonny spat aloud as he pulled Jessica up close to his filthy body.

Able only to nod her understanding, Jessica tried to keep her knees from buckling beneath her weight as she was dragged along between the two men. They were in the back of some alley, and with a slight knock upon a door, she was pulled into a dark, musky-smelling backroom.

"We be here to talk to Mr. DeVaugn." Lonny spoke loudly to the small black man who stood inside the doorway.

"Yer too late to be catching Master Edmond, sir." The black man looked the dirty threesome over with a disdainful look of loathing for their unkempt appearance. "Ye be coming back tomorrow and he be here at his office."

"We ain't waiting till tomorrow. Ye best be telling me where I can find DeVaugn tonight." Lonny looked at the small black man, his anger mounting by the moment. He was tired and wanting a drink and the last thing he intended to do was keep this woman for another night. He needed a woman in his bed, not a pretty Injun-loving piece that he couldn't touch.

"But sir, Master Edmond he done gone home. Iffen ye got business with him, ye best come back in the morning."

"Where's he live?" Sam questioned, his hand going to the hilt of his knife at his belt. As the small black man saw his movement, he quickly told them the address of Edmond DeVaugn. It was surely not worth taking a knife in his belly to remain silent.

Once again climbing onto Red Wing's back, Jessica was led down the streets of New Orleans. Her will seemed almost broken as she quietly submitted to the two trappers' orders.

It was only a short time later that the trappers and Jessica stood inside Edmond DeVaugn's library. "I wish to thank you gentleman most sincerely for escorting my cousin home." Edmond stood behind his desk and carefully counted out the amount of gold that had been stated in the reward poster for the return of Jessica.

Lonny and Sam both greedily looked at the slim, dark-featured man who was placing the gold coins into a small leather pouch. "She were a hard one to be a-finding, that's fer sure." Lonny wiped at his mouth with the back of his hand as his mind filled with the thoughts of the whisky he would be able to buy with such an amount of money.

"And you say she was living with an Indian?" Edmond's dark gaze once again went over his silent cousin. His disgust was evident in his expression as he let his gaze go over her matted braided hair and dirty deerskin dress.

"She be claiming that the filthy red devil was her husband," Lonny supplied. "It were truly our God-fearing duty to bring her out of that degradation. Her being a white woman and all."

"Aye, you both did a fine job. I thank you again for bringing her to me, gentlemen. And here is the promised reward for my cousin's safe return." Edmond threw the pouch across the desk, his dark stare holding the two trappers with a large amount of distrust.

Lonny was quick to reach out and heft the pouch in his large fist. "Yes siree, it surely was our God-fearing duty to see the little lady out of that heathen village."

Edmond's gaze was again drawn to Jessica as she sat so quietly across the room from him. The last time he had seen her at Sweet Oaks she had been a beauty. But looking at her now, he would not even know she was the same woman. She had been living with an Indian. A stinking, dirty savage. And if these two men were correct, she claimed that the red devil was her husband. A seething rage began to fester within him as he remembered all of the gentlemen he had brought to her, any one of them would have made her a suitable husband. But she had been too high and mighty, and had rejected all who had asked for her hand, and now she claimed to have been wed to an Indian.

Clearing his throat loudly in the quiet room, Lonny spoke out. "Iffen that be all, govna, me and old Sam here have a might of celebrating to be doing this fine eve. It ain't often that we run across such a generous payment for our work."

218

"Yes, yes, of course, I am sure that you both have much to attend to." Edmond rose to his feet from the chair behind his desk. "I shall see you to the front door."

"Don't be a-bothering yerself. Me and Sam here can be remembering where we come in from." Lonny started toward the door and out through the front foyer, Sam close upon his heels.

Edmond DeVaugn stood near the library door, his dark gaze fixed upon his cousin. "You have certainly caused me great concern, Jessica. You cannot imagine what terrible thoughts were going through my mind when I first learned of your disappearance. Why, in fact, I traveled halfway across the state posting the reward posters. It is lucky that those two trappers came across you and brought you back to New Orleans."

For the first time Jessica raised her head, her chin held upward as she let her silver gaze settle upon her cousin. "I did not wish to be returned, Edmond. I wished to remain in my husband's village."

"Nonsense!" Edmond sputtered, seething at her defiance.

"Nonsense, is it? Do you say that a wife should not remain at her husband's side? Was it not your desire that I marry?" Jessica felt some of her inner strength returning to her, and though she had ever been wary of her cousin, she had never bowed down to him.

"Aye, you are right there, Jessica. I do indeed wish you to wed. But certainly not to a savage, and not to just any man, either. The man for you will have to be found with careful consideration."

"Listen to me, Edmond." Jessica slowly rose to her feet and faced her cousin. "I am already married to

219

Star Hawk, and nothing will ever change this fact."

For a moment all of the fury of the past months descended upon Edmond DeVaugn, and grabbing hold of her arm, he jerked her up tightly to his chest. "A wedding to a savage can easily be forgotten. The whole episode will be forgotten, and you will from this moment forth do exactly as you are told." The pressure upon her upper arms was increased and caused her to wince with the pain.

Trying to pull away from him, Jessica gasped, "Nay, I shall never forget Star Hawk!"

As though her flesh were contaminated, Edmond slung her back toward the chair she had been sitting on. "You will do what you're told or there will be grave consequences, Jessica." And for a moment he stood glaring down at her as he let his words settle for their effect.

"I have many friends in high places, and thus far I have been informed that the Blackfoot lands have pretty well been left alone by the military and even the white settlers. But let me assure you that the right word in the right ear could well change all of that. It would take very little for an official to take it upon himself to invade these lands and to put an end to this village that you have been living in."

Jessica could not believe her ears, and as she looked at her cousin with total disbelief, she felt her body beginning to tremble. He would have Star Hawk's village invaded, and the loving people she had grown to know and to love slaughtered, just because of her?

"I see that you take my meaning?" Edmond stood back from her and watched her facial expression clearly detailing all of her feelings. "Let no doubt linger in your mind, dear cousin. If you do not do as

I tell you, or if you try to flee from my company, I will be forced to speak with a major friend of mind who owes me a large favor and would be glad to do my bidding. And if this means having a village of savages wiped off the face of the earth, so be it."

"You couldn't," Jessica exclaimed, her hand clutching at her throat with the terrible visions that he had conjured up in her mind.

"I very well could. I will not be thwarted again. You will go to London with the morning tide, and there you shall wed Earl Henry Locksbin. While you have been away many opportunities have presented themselves, and the earl of Locksbin himself has informed me that he has need of a young and beautiful wife to act as hostess to his many guests at Locksbin manor."

"But. . . ." Jessica started to protest, but was quickly halted.

"There will be no arguing. You will do as you are told or I shall have the pleasure of making sure that the Indian village no longer exists."

Jessica could say or do nothing that could possibly threaten the lives of her husband's village. Could she live one day with the knowledge that she had caused the death of Singing Moon and Cloud Dreamer, the two women she had learned to love as though they were her own mothers?

"I see that you are going to be wise and do as you are told. Prunella will show you to a guest room and have a tub sent up." Edmond went back to his desk and sat down, his gaze rising from a stack of papers to Jessica as she still sat in the folds of the chair. "I will send a boy out to Sweet Oaks this eve to bring your clothes to the ship. There will be little time to purchase anything, for we leave on the morrow. You will have to make do with what you left behind when you ran off."

"Could we not wait a few days and I could go to Sweet Oaks myself?" Jessica questioned, desiring to see Marcy and all that she had loved while growing up one last time.

"And what then, Jessica? Will your Indian lover sneak to Sweet Oaks and try to steal you away once again?"

Jessica's features paled. "Star Hawk was gone from his village and will not return in time to steal me away."

"You are quite right there, my dear," Edmond glared across his desk at her, "for with the morning we shall set sail. Now leave me to my work, your presence is unsettling and your appearance is not welcome. Prunella will meet you in the hall."

She was dismissed and she knew she had to obey. She could not chance angering her cousin into doing something that could well affect the Blackfoot tribe. Her cousin was not one to make idle threats. He had always been vicious and cold, and she knew that he would carry out the threats upon Star Hawk's people if he was forced to.

The large, buxom housekeeper called Prunella awaited Jessica as she stepped from the library. "If you will follow me miss, I shall show you to your room. The water for your bath is already heated and will be brought up shortly." The woman kept her distance from the dirty girl, her nose held disdainfully in the air as though a certain smell offended her.

Jessica could but follow the housekeeper up the stairs and into the bedchamber, her thoughts so desperate that she felt the sting of bitter tears. She would be leaving for England the next day, without ever seeing Star Hawk again. And he would never know what had happened to her; perhaps he would even believe that she had deliberately run from him. But she was powerless to do anything but to comply with Edmond's cruel demands, and in so doing she was forever lost to the wonderful love that she had found in Star Hawk's arms.

Chapter Nine

Star Hawk's pace never slackened, for he knew that he already was at least two days behind Jessica and her abductors. He followed their tracks, which were easily read, for one of the men's horses had a broken shoe. He could easily see that they also were going at a grueling pace. He came across no camps, but now and then saw where the small group had halted for a few minutes to eat or to rest their horses. He knew that Jessica would be exhausted from such an ordeal, and his anger increased with every mile he traveled.

It was on the sixth day that Star Hawk pulled his stallion, Night Cloud, to a halt outside of New Orleans. The tracks of the three riders went into the city. Having had little sleep in the past week, Star Hawk climbed from Night Cloud's back and decided to rest for a short time before he ventured into New Orleans. He tried to reason in his mind what the two men were up to. Why would they bring his wife to this city? It was certainly close to the plantation he had stolen her from. Were her abductors bringing her back to her home? Had someone found out her identity, and was she at this moment at Sweet Oaks and perhaps waiting for him to come for her?

He was weary of mind and body, and his thoughts were going in crazy directions, he told himself as he lay down on his sleeping mat and shut his eyes. If he did not rest, he would be no good to Jessica or himself.

"I told ye, Lonny, that woman would be the sure ruination of the both of us." Sam cussed as he and his longtime friend headed out of New Orleans. Their pockets were now emptied, and his head was bursting from the hangover he had had the day through.

"It weren't my fault that the wench stole me pockets clean. How'd I be aknowing that she and her boyfriend played this game with her gentlemen friends? She sure were a pretty one, though, Sam. Ye have to be admitting that. In fact, she were almost as pretty as that Injun-loving gal we brought back to her cousin. I ain't never going to be forgetting that gal, no siree."

Sam shook his head, not believing that anyone could be quite as dumb as Lonny. Why, they hadn't been in town a full week before he had lost all of their money. Loose women and gambling had always been Lonny's downfall, and Sam should have known to keep hold of their gold himself. But Lonny had sworn, as he had other times in the past, that he would guard it with his life. That was almost what it had cost his friend. He had come into the backroom of that inn and caught the wench and her boyfriend over Lonny's prone form, the girl going through his pockets and her friend standing over Lonny with a large club. Why, iffen he hadn't scared the pair off,

225

there would have been no telling that they might have done to old Lonny.

"I reckon we'll just have to be spending another winter trapping. I sure was hankering, though, for a warm fire and a good woman to keep me warm when the snow started falling."

"We can always get on back to the trading post. Them Injun women are mighty warm on cold nights. For a little trinket and a drink for their buck they'll be doing most anything ya wants." Lonny grinned widely.

"I had me fill of Injuns. I were wanting meself a white woman." Sam was still angry at his friend. After all the work of bringing Jessica Coltin to her kin and almost getting his hair lifted by that red savage that night in the camp, Lonny had to go and lose all of their gold. And now here they were once again heading back into the wilderness.

"Let's go up a short ways and make camp. My head's killing me and I'm needing some sleep."

"Sure, Sam, whatever you say." Lonny followed behind Sam, his thoughts once again on the girl who had set him up for the plucking. She sure was a looker, that gal; she sure was.

The voices of the trappers were not loud, but with senses attuned from youth to live in the forest and to guard against enemies, Star Hawk awoke, the slight noise of the two horses making their way pulling him from his much needed sleep.

As though one with the forest, Star Hawk climbed on Night Cloud's back and headed in the direction of the sounds that had disturbed him. His reasoning was not clear, but an inner voice of caution told him to use all of his cunning.

Minutes passed and then Star Hawk, with the aid

of the bright moonlight shimmering down through the thickness of the trees, saw the outline of the tracks that he had been straining his eyes to find. With a quiet movement, he slid from Night Cloud. Bending down, he studied the prints in the earth.

There were only two sets of hoof prints, but there was no mistake that these were the same prints that Star Hawk had been following for the last week. The only ones that were missing were Red Wing's.

His heart hammering in his chest, Star Hawk remounted, his thoughts on the two men ahead of him. What had they done with his woman? Had they left Jessica in the town of New Orleans? With iron control, Star Hawk forced himself to think only of his enemies, the two men who were slowly making their way deeper into the forest.

Velvet blackness surrounded the forest. The only sound was that of a lone owl screeching with victory as he swooped down on his evening meal. The small camp that the trappers had hastily set up was quiet, the small fire burned low to only light embers, and a slight snore came for Lonny's chest as he was lost in the peaceful realms of slumber.

Star Hawk had left Night Cloud in a small ravine, and on silent feet he slipped through the forest, his dark eyes ready for danger. He waited behind the brush for what seemed an eternity watching the pair of trappers as they slept, his entire body filled with boiling rage.

He had watched earlier as the pair had sat beside the fire and ate their supper, recognizing their shaggy, rough appearance. They were the same two who had been in the trading post. The larger of the two had been the same one who had grabbed Jessica's arm and the other had questioned him about a price for his bride. Cursing himself for not taking their lives that very day, Star Hawk had to hold himself back from charging into the camp at that moment and doing so now. But this was not the way to find out what they had done with Jessica. He would have to use caution and cunning to capture the two unaware and to force them to tell him the whereabouts of his wife.

Now was the time, Star Hawk told himself, as the camp lay in darkness and quiet. On silent moccasined feet he made his way to where the two men were sleeping, his large hunting knife drawn and in the other hand his war axe held high, ready at the slightest breath to descend on the head of his unlucky opponent.

As he drew near, a moan and a large grunt from one of the men pulled his steps to a silent halt. He remained on the outer edges of the camp, his body held at the ready to make his attack. The one large trapper rolled out of his sleeping mat. Stretching and sleepily itching at his underarm, he slowly made his way toward the outer brush, nature's call pulling him from his sleep to seek his release.

Star Hawk watched for only a short moment to make sure that the other trapper had not been disturbed, and then with quick movements he stalked his prey. Slipping up behind the large man, he thrust his large, deadly hunting knife to the man's throat. His mouth was only inches from the man's ear as he softly whispered, "Do not move or make a sound, or you are dead, white man."

Lonny jerked his breeches together, his red-veined dark blue eyes enlarging with his fear as he felt the Indian's breath along his jawline and the feel of his steel blade at his windpipe. "What ya be wanting,

228

Injun? We ain't got nothing but our horses. No furs or whiskey." Lonny tried to figure out why this Indian was attacking him in the dark hours of the night. Never in his deepest thoughts did he imagine that the Indian was Star Hawk and that he had followed the trappers' tracks to regain his woman.

"I told you to be silent. I will not say this again." The pressure of the blade increased, causing a thin line of bright red blood to seep from the sliver-thin wound. Star Hawk silently eased a long leather thong that had been fashioned into a noose over the man's large head. Pulling this tightly about his throat, he took the blade away. Looping one end of the leather over the tall branch of a nearby tree, he jerked tightly, causing Lonny to gag. Both of his hands rose up in protest, trying to find some case for his breathing.

In a second, though, Star Hawk had grasped both the man's hands, and these also he tied with a leather strap in back of the large man. Pulling the leather noose a bit tighter and forcing Lonny to stand on the tips of his boots, Star Hawk whispered once again near his ear. "Do not struggle or you will die. Your friend will join you soon." With this he left the large trapper immobile, his very life balanced on his efforts to stand on the tips of his toes.

Going back to the camp, Star Hawk saw that the other man had not moved in his sleep, his loud snores filling the small area with a noisesome melody. All too quickly the snore turned to sounds of confusion as Star Hawk stood over the sleeping figure and sharply kicked his large thigh.

"What in tarnation is it now, Lonny?" Sam grunted as he jerked himself upright upon his sleeping mat, his rifle coming with him from under the furs and pointing at the figure above him. As his pale green eyes saw the figure of the Indian astride him, he tried to pull the trigger, his vision unclear from sleep but knowing at once that it was not Lonny above him.

The rifle went off with a resounding boom, but Sam found the weapon flying away as the Indian gave a savage kick to his hand. In a split second, the Indian was astraddle him, and a large, evil hunting knife was at his throat.

"Where is my wife, Silver Star?" Star Hawk's rage sounded in his voice, and with an uncontrollable urge for vengeance, he clutched the front of the trapper's shirt, his knife held tightly.

"My God, it be you," Sam gasped. Thinking quickly of pacifying this avenging savage, he lied. "Me and Lonny ain't been seeing yer woman since that day at the trading post. Maybe iffen ya take that knife away from me throat, we can be talking about this." His voice begged for his release.

"You lie, white man!" Star Hawk spat out the words, his savage fury beginning to overtake him. "You came to my people's land and you stole my woman, and before you die, you will tell me where she is!"

The bold words chilled the large trapper as he lay prone beneath the towering form of the Indian clutching the knife.

"What ya do with Lonny?" His light green eyes scanned about the camp in desperation, hoping somehow his friend would be able to help save him from the clutches of this death grip.

"Your friend's fate will be your own." With this, Star Hawk pulled the large man to his feet and shoved him along in front of him to where Lonny was standing below the tree limb, his body stretched so as not to lose his life.

As Sam took in the desperation of the moment, Star Hawk gave a loud whistle. Within seconds Night Cloud was at his side, his nostrils flaring at the scent of the white men next to his master, and his hoofs kicking up the turf.

Star Hawk murmured some words in the Indian language that seemed to calm the large beast, and as Night Cloud drew closer to the towering Indian, Star Hawk reached into the leather sack that had been tied across his back. Pulling out more of the leather strips, he stood close to Sam.

"Take your clothes off your body, white man." The order was given in a cold, steellike command.

"What?" Sam responded, not believing what he was being told to do. "I can't be taking my clothes off. The weather be too cold." This was the only thing he could think to say with the pressure of the knife on his windpipe.

"Do as you are told, or you will die now," Star Hawk seethed jerking the knife slightly. A long trickle of blood glistened in the moonlight.

Sam remembered painfully another time at the trading post when he had suffered from that cruel knife, and without a second attempt to plead with this man holding the knife, he hurriedly began to pull all of his clothes from his body.

When he stood stark naked in the enclosure of the forest, with only shafts of moonlight glistening off his milk-white body, Star Hawk ordered him to lie on the ground, his legs and arms stretched out. With hasty motions, Star Hawk tied each leg and arm with the leather straps to stakes that he had pounded into the ground with his war axe.

231

Lonny had watched silently as the Indian staked out his friend. His only thoughts at this moment were of keeping the pressure of the leather thong off his windpipe. But as Star Hawk cut the leather bindings from his hands and with a swift slash cut the leather strap from the branch of the trees, Lonny fell to his knees, his hands quickly going to his throat and pulling the strap about his neck loose.

"Do like your friend, white man," Star Hawk ordered, again his bold knife going to Lonny's throat and replacing the leather.

Lonny had instantly recognized Star Hawk when he had strode toward him with Sam under knife point. Star Hawk's size and looks set him apart from most other Indians. With the cold dread of horror in his gut, he knew that there was little to save himself and his friend. "Listen, Injun, we didn't do nothing," he began to plead.

"Take off your clothes." Again the order was given in a cold, steel voice.

Lonny quickly began to comply, and as he pulled the articles of clothing from his back, he tried his best to convince Star Hawk that he had made a mistake. "There ain't no reason for you doing me and Sam like this, Injun. Iffen yer still mad about what happened at the trading post, we're sorry we made a mistake. We didn't know how ya felt about yer woman."

Star Hawk did not respond to his pleadings nor to those of his friend as he laced the leather about Lonny's ankles and wrists and staked him out next to Sam.

The sun was rising in the eastern sky when Star Hawk stood between the pair of trappers. His face cold and unforgiving. He crouched down first next to Lonny. "You will tell me where you have taken Silver Star."

"You got it all wrong, Injun." Lonny's large blue eyes went from the Indian to his friend, "We ain't seen no Silver Star. You got the wrong fellas."

Without warning, Star Hawk slashed his knife across the trapper's broad, hairy chest. A quick flash of brilliant red welled from the shallow slice. Then, turning to Sam, Star Hawk stated, "I followed your tracks from our land. You stole my woman and took her into New Orleans. What did you do with her?"

Sam looked at Lonny with terror as the other trapper lay whimpering in his pain, his large shaggy head rolling back and forth. The only way that he could see they would have a chance to come out of this with their lives was if they could convince this Indian he had made a mistake. Sam knew that admitting that he and Lonny had taken Jessica would surely mean their deaths. "It weren't us, Injun. Them tracks must have been made by two other fellas." The pale green eyes locked with the piercing black ones as Star Hawk reached out with his long knife and sliced it across the white belly, opening the skin across the wide expanse of flesh.

Sam screamed aloud with fear and the stinging pain of the swift cut.

"One of your horses has a broken shoe. Your tracks were followed by Spotted Pony from the trail near our village, and when he tried to protect my wife, you killed him." Again the knife was drawn across first one trapper's body and then the other. As their shrieks of terror filled the small area, Star Hawk added, "It will do you no good to lie, white man. You killed my friend and stole my wife."

Lonny was the first to realize that all their plead-

233

ings would be to no avail. "She were a white woman. She didn't belong with no Injuns, but her own people," he shouted out between pain-filled breaths.

Again, the knife made its mark on his large body. "Where is Silver Star?"

"Her name is Jessica, and we took her back to where she belongs. To her kin."

Sam was shouting for Lonny to shut up. He knew surely, with their confession, that the Indian would not spare them.

This was all that Star Hawk needed to hear. Rising to his full height, he gazed down on the bleeding men. "Your time is short. You should spend the hours left you by seeking forgiveness from the Great Spirit for the evil deeds you have done." With this, Star Hawk again whistled for Night Cloud. Without a backward glance at the two men who would in a short time be food for the hungry wolves, he kicked his stallion's flanks and headed in the direction of Sweet Oaks.

The trappers had said they had returned Jessica to her kin, so he could assume that they meant they had taken her to the plantation where he had first seen her.

With some jubilation, his heart beat now with a steady tempo. His Silver Star was well and would be waiting for him to come and seek her out. He would take her back to his village, and once there, he would never again allow any harm to befall her or anything separate them ever again. She was a part of him, and he could not live without her. He could not wait to hold her soft body tightly against his own. The memory of her soft voice came to his mind as she spoke of her great love for him. With these thoughts, he pushed Night Cloud to a faster pace.

The *Ruby Heart* rode high atop the ocean waves. The sleek ship, one of the Coltins' finest, made its way straight for the docks of London. As her trim bow rode high and proud, Jessica lay locked in her cabin, her own ship now her house of prison, her days of endless solitude becoming a torture that few could have borne.

There was little to do except pace from porthole to cot. Jessica's thoughts were consumed with the life that she had left behind. Images of Star Hawk were ever present in her mind. The only respite from her isolation was mealtimes when her cousin would bring a tray and then stand back quietly as she ate her food.

He had made a habit of waiting for her to finish after the first few days aboard ship when Jessica had refused the fare, her stomach turning and heaving with the slightest smell of each meal. But as it soon became apparent that the little nourishment she was refusing was quickly affecting her beauty, her cheekbones becoming more pronounced and her slim form becoming even more trim, Edmond had taken it on himself to force the issue. He stood over her three times a day now until everything on the tray was consumed, his stern face and threatening warnings of what he would do if she were to take ill or could not go through with the bargain he had struck, slipping easily from his lips.

At first Jessica had to force herself to choke down the first few mouthfuls, but as her stomach adjusted, it was easier for her to endure. She had told herself often in the past two weeks that she would have enjoyed nothing more than to allow herself to starve

235

to death, as she knew she would never again see her love. Edmond's dire threats against Star Hawk's people kept her from such a deed, though. And as the days slowly passed, a new thought began to play in the corners of her mind. She began to realize that the upset of her belly might be due to something else. Since she had first lain with her husband she had not had her monthly time, and she began to suspect that she was to have Star Hawk's child.

With the thought that perhaps a small life was in her body and that she would at least have a part of Star Hawk, even though she had been taken away from him for the rest of her days, she found a small measure of peace. At night as she tried to sleep on the small cot, she would gently rub her flat abdomen, imagining its budding growth in the months ahead. Though all seemed lost to her, she now had something to hold on to.

There was a knock and the door was pushed wide. Jessica was pulled from her thoughts as she stood gazing out at the limitless sea. Her Cousin Edmond strode boldly into the cabin, and quickly taking in her trim form, he set the tray that he bore down on a small table near her cot. "Your dinner is a bit late this evening, Jessica."

She did not reply but stood watching as he set about arranging her plate on the table.

"I would like to talk to you for a moment while you eat." Edmond straightened and waited for her to do as he requested.

Complying with his orders, as she had since she had stepped foot on the *Ruby Heart,* Jessica sat down primly on the bed. Taking up her fork, she bent over her plate, her eyes avoiding those of her cousin.

"I am relieved that you have thus far given me little trouble, Jessica. And I must tell you that I regret you have to be locked in your cabin, but for your own sake I think it a necessary precaution. Once we reach London, you will have much more freedom." He had at first feared that she would do something foolish such as throw herself over the side of the ship, but now, as he watched her heartily eat the food on her tray, he knew that she was made of stronger stuff than to waste her life so easily. "When we reach port, we shall take rooms at a suitable inn and you will see to your wardrobe. It will take some time for the arrangements to be made with the earl of Locksbin, so you will have plenty of hours to shop and see the sights." He hoped that she would be pleased with this announcement. He did not truly wish to be unkind to her. As long as she did as told and did not interfere with his plans to wed her and hold control over all of the Coltin wealth, they would get along just fine. But if he was forced, she had already seen that he could be ruthless, and he would not hesitate to use any tactics he had to in order to gain what he desired.

With the finish of her meal, Jessica daintily wiped her lips with the edge of the linen napkin. The smug look on her cousin's face was too much at the moment for her to bear. "I am afraid that your plans will have to be put aside for a time, dear cousin."

Quickly Edmond's dark eyes clouded over with caution. What did she mean, his plans would have to wait? "You are in no position to dictate to me, Jessica. I hold the trump card and will see you do as you are told." He was satisfied that she would do anything to see that no harm came to her Indian friends.

"But you see, Edmond," Jessica rose to her feet and slowly shook out her dress, taking her time before she spoke again, "there is one card in the deck that you did not plan on being dealt. I am with my husband's child, and I shall not wed until after the birth."

"You lie!" Edmond gasped aloud, not believing she was speaking the truth.

"I am afraid not. I was not sure at first, but with each day that passes I am more assured that I am correct."

For a moment Edmond looked around the cabin as though expecting some form of answer to this new problem to jump out in front of him. "When we reach London, you will be checked by a midwife." He stated this like a threat, but at her slow smile and the nodding of her copper head, he knew that she was speaking the truth. She was too confident, he thought, realizing that she, in fact, *must* be speaking the truth. "If you are truly with child, I see no reason to wait to wed. It would be more fitting to have the ceremony as quickly as possible. Henry will still not object when he sees your rare beauty. He more than likely will also demand that the wedding be done with all haste."

"But that is not my wish, cousin," Jessica boldly stated, her silver eyes challenging the darker ones across from her. "I will not marry another man until Star Hawk's child is delivered."

"Perhaps, then, I should send a message to my major friend," he tried to threaten.

"Thus far, I have done all that you have demanded of me, Edmond, and I shall even do as you wish and wed this man whom I have not as yet seen. I care little for anything if I cannot be with the man I love.

But I will tell you this one thing. I will not be forced to wed another until my husband's child is delivered. Even your cruel threats will not sway me in this decision. And if you try to force me, I shall shout out from the highest post that I am being forced against my will to marry a man I do not want."

Edmond started to stammer out a protest, but Jessica quickly silenced him. "If you leave me for this time and allow me to have my child in peace, I shall willingly comply with your wishes. It is up to you, Edmond, but I will not relent in this one thing. I am to have Star Hawk's child alone because I have been taken from him, and I will not have a strange man calling me wife during this time."

"We shall have to make up a story of your being widowed in the colonies, then." Edmond's sharp mind began quickly to think ahead. They would say her husband had been killed in at boating accident and she, being left with child, had had only her cousin to turn to. The pair had come to London for her time of confinement, and perhaps for a short holiday. Yes, perhaps this story would work, and then after the child was born, Henry Locksbin himself could deal with the half-savage brat.

"I do not care what you say. I only want this time to have my baby and the assurances that the child will be brought up properly. After all, he will be your kin. I know your feelings about Indians, but remember, he will be innocent." Jessica watched her cousin's face as he, with a sour look, glanced at her waistline.

"Of course, the child will be taken care of. We can perhaps say that your husband was half-Spanish. That will account for its dark looks when it is born." He left out that he for one would be more than glad if she lost the child before she bore it, or that if Henry Locksbin happened to arrange for the child to be given away after he wed Jessica, he for one would quite understand. "Surely, as you say, the child, above all, is innocent," he added, hoping to assure her that he would comply with all that she desired. With this he hoped that she would be more compliant to his demands.

"Then we understand each other, cousin." Jessica said. Now that she had won this small victory, she felt herself breathing easier. She had feared this confrontation, not being sure that Edmond would give in to her demands. But now that she would have her way, she at least would have these few months to live a life of some small peace, and she would have Star Hawk's child. It would be a comfort to watch him grow and see to his needs. She would willingly give the babe, and then the child as it would grow with the years, all of her love, the love that she had given his father and the love that she could only share with the one of her heart. She would perhaps marry a man of Edmond's choosing in the end, but her heart was her own, and now it was her baby's.

Chapter Ten

The forest glade lay quiet as Star Hawk led Night Cloud along the narrow path that would follow through to the outer grounds of Sweet Oaks plantation. His ebony eyes looked about and envisioned another day when he had glimpsed a beautiful, innocent young woman picking a basket of herbs and plants. He had hidden himself behind the trees and in spellbound wonder he had watched her, not believing that any woman alive could be so lovely. But his Silver Star had been, and now with racing heart his eyes went from the path toward the large brick house.

Was she at this moment inside and wondering when he would be coming for her? Was she thinking of him as he was her? He had to force himself not to kick Night Cloud's flanks and hurry him to the front porch and then jump from his back and barge through the front portal. He would find Jessica and they would never be parted again.

It was now late afternoon, and with a deep sigh of resignation Star Hawk slid from Night Cloud's back and forced himself to settle down until dark. Then he would be able more easily to approach the house and seek Jessica. He knew that if he allowed his true desires to override his caution he could cause harm to Jessica with the hue and cry that would be sounded over the plantation. The servants would set upon him and force him to defend himself, and though he would like nothing better than to face Jessica's Cousin Edmond, he surely wished no harm to any of the people who had cared for Jessica while she lived here at Sweet Oaks. So thinking, Star Hawk rested against a tall oak, while his gaze held upon the activity at the house as he waited for darkness to descend.

Though in fact his wait was not long, to Star Hawk it seemed an eternity before he left the cover of the forest and slowly made his way toward the plantation house, his steps taking him to the same trellis that he had climbed before. His body responded as it had before, as with ease he went up to the second-story window of Jessica's bedchamber. The room was in darkness as he slowly raised the window and placed a leg over the sill.

For a moment Star Hawk stood outlined against the dim moonlight shining through the glass pane, but as he adjusted his eyes to the darkness of the room a small noise like that of a person gently whimpering came to his ears, and as he looked about he made out the form of a woman. His chest seemed to throb with his heartbeat as at first he thought that it was Jessica, but as he took a step toward her, he knew that it was not his wife. The figure sitting hunched over in the chair was of a much heavier build than Jessica, and the hair appeared dark and short, not the gold-fire tresses that he had seen so often shimmering in the moonlight.

"Why do you weep, woman?" Star Hawk silently stepped in front of the woman in the chair placed next to the bed in the center of the room.

Marcy jumped back in the chair in her surprise at being found here in Jessica's chambers. "Who you be?" She held back a deep sob, her large hands grabbing hold of the chair arms for some kind of support.

"I am here to find Silver Star. Where is she, old mother?" Star Hawk could sense her fear, and he talked softly so as not to frighten her.

"I don't be knowing no Silver Star," Marcy gasped as she sensed that this man was not like any man she had ever known before. "What you be doing here in the miss's bedchamber?" And then she realized that this man must have come through the window, for she was sitting upon the chair closest to the door.

"Silver Star is my wife, old mother."

"Well, she ain't be in here in Miss Jake's chambers. You done gone and made a big mistake." Marcy tried to see his features more clearly but could make out little in the darkness. "Ye best be leaving the same way you done come in, or else one of the other servants will be hearing us talking and run fer help." She felt her apprehension increase and hoped that her warnings would be taken as a threat and that this strange night visitor would leave quickly.

"Silver Star spoke to me of the woman called Marcy and how when she had been a young child the one called Marcy had given her the name of Jake. Where is Jessica, Marcy?" Star Hawk remem-

243

bered all that Jessica had told him of this black woman and how she had loved her.

"You be meaning that this Silver Star is the same as my honey child?" Marcy sat up closer to the edge of her chair, her dark brown eyes widening. "But you be saying that this woman Silver Star is yer wife, does that be a-meaning that . . . ?" She could not finish her question.

"Yes, old mother, Jessica is my wife. Where is she? I thought to find her here in her bed and waiting for me to come for her." Star Hawk's eyes went about the chamber as though seeking out a small spot that he had not seen, where his wife could be hiding.

Marcy felt her heart accelerating with his words. "Why, Miss Jake ain't here, master." She quickly jumped to her feet and made to light the candle upon the night table next to the bed.

"But the trappers said that they had returned her to her kin. I thought that I would find her here at the plantation." Star Hawk thought at once of returning to the trappers, and if they were still alive, forcing the truth from them.

"Whoever these trappers be they spoke the truth. Miss Jessica was done brought back to her cousin." Marcy turned about after lighting the candle and threw her hand up over her mouth as she observed the towering, fierce-looking Indian, his war paint smeared across his features and his feathers tied in his long hanging velvet-black hair. "But you be an Injun. You can't be Miss Jake's husband," she finally gasped.

"My wife's name among my people is Silver Star. I am her husband, and she is my woman!" Star Hawk allowed no doubt to linger in the black

244

woman's mind.

Marcy slowly nodded her dark head, her eyes now roaming over the man before her with a critical tilt. She had to admit that he was quite intimidating standing so tall and powerful before her, his deerskin shirt fringed with leather and his leather leggings tightly drawn over powerful-looking thighs and secured beneath his moccasins. "You truly be Miss Jessica's husband, then?" she whispered needing to hear it one more time.

"Yes, old mother. Jessica is my wife, my heart, my very reason. I must be rejoined with her."

"Oh Lordy, Miss Jake surely gone and done it now." Marcy moaned loudly and dropped her large bulk back into the chair.

"Where is she, Marcy? Is she here at the plantation?" Star Hawk held his breath as he awaited her answer.

Shaking her kinky black head, Marcy dabbed at her eyes with her handkerchief. "Master Edmond done gone and taken her away."

Her words came as though a physical blow to Star Hawk, and for a moment he had to hold himself still to hear her out. He wished nothing more than to run and find Night Cloud and somehow find this Edmond and recover his wife. "Where has he taken Silver Star?" he questioned firmly.

"It were but a week past when a boy come out and gathered all of Miss Jessica's belongings, and he said he done heard Master Edmond's housekeeper saying as how his master and Miss Jessica were going to sail on a ship the next morning for London. He be saying that Master Edmond done plan to marry his cousin off to some earl." Again

Marcy mopped at her eyes. "That why I be here in Miss Jake's chambers. I done thought fer sure that Miss Jake was lost to us forever. Her cousin had tried so many times in the past to wed her to one of them awful men and I done thought that all was lost."

"This place called London is far. It is across the mighty seas. I have a friend who has a home there."

"Then you be going there and bring my baby child back?" Marcy looked up with a new hope burning in her dark eyes.

"Yes, old mother, I will travel to this place called London and find my wife. I will send you word when we are back in my village." There was no doubt in Star Hawk's mind of what he would do. He had no choice; he had to go to this place called London and find Silver Star. He could not live his life without her. He was only half a man without her beside him to complete his life cycle.

Marcy looked upon this man with a new respect, seeing the love burning in his ebony gaze for the young woman she had raised from an infant. "You can't be going to find Miss Jessica a-looking like that." She again rose to her feet. "You couldn't even get to the docks in that town called New Orleans like you is. Why the white man would be hanging you first chance he got."

Star Hawk quickly realized the truth of her words, and slowly nodding his dark head, he said, "Old mother you will help me to gain my Silver Star?"

Marcy laughed aloud at his question. "Yes siree, this old mother will help you to get your Silver Star." Again she chuckled. "You just be sitting yourself down and I'll be back in a minute." She rushed from the room, leaving Star Hawk alone as she ran to the old master's chambers.

She was only gone a short time. She returned with her arms laden with men's breeches, shirts, and shoes, her other hand holding a pair of scissors and a hand mirror. "I used to cut the old master's hair every month fer him, though it sure weren't as pretty as your'n." She did not stop to question Star Hawk about permission to trim his long sable locks, but without a moment's hesitation she cropped his full head of hair, the black strands falling about his feet as he sat in the chair and allowed her ministrations.

"You gots to be washing that paint off your face now, master, and take off them heathen clothes and put on this pair of breeches and shirt. I reckon as how you be Miss Jake's husband and all, the old master wouldn't be minding iffen you share his clothes now that he be gone."

Star Hawk only had time to eye the buff-colored pants and the white silk shirt before Marcy was pulling him to his feet and helping him out of his leather shirt and leggings. Soon he was dressed in the white man's clothes, and after she had poured water from the pitcher on the night stand into the wash bowl he washed his face clean of the war paint. Marcy held the hand mirror out for him to view the new man she had helped to create.

Star Hawk's features did not in the least show his feelings as he looked into the glass. He walked over to Jessica's dressing table and held the hand mirror at an angle to see all sides of his hair and clothes. Slowly he nodded his head. "I will look as the other white men now."

Marcy chuckled as she stood back and looked at the handsome man standing before the mirror. Yes siree, she could surely see now what Jessica had seen in this heathen. He stood straight and tall in front of the dressing table, his dark hair trimmed about his shoulders and lying against the snow-white shirt, a few of the buttons opened to allow a glimpse of bronzed chest. The buff-colored breeches that had been loose upon the old master fit this young warrior like a second skin, molding about his thighs and buttocks in a manner that drew a sigh even from her old heart. "Ye be quite handsome, Master Star Hawk," she stated proudly. "But ye gots to be putting on these here boots and then we better be seeing iffen we can be finding any gold coins in Miss Jessica's things. She used to have some coins tucked away in her top drawer. You be needing some iffen ye think to get to that place called London."

"I have some of the white man's gold." Star Hawk went through his things and held up a leather pouch clinking with the coins inside.

Marcy grinned widely. "You sure be a strange Injun, that's fer sure. 'Taint no wonder Miss Jake grabbed ahold of you, yes siree."

Star Hawk grinned back at the large black woman and then started toward the door of the chamber. "I had better use the door—I might tear these clothes climbing out the window."

Marcy, still smiling, nodded her large head. Her joy was high, thinking that this man somehow was going to bring Jessica back from that faraway place.

"Do not worry, old mother." Star Hawk used this name for her as he knew that Jessica had thought

248

of her as almost a mother. "I will find Jessica and I will send you word." With this he quickly left the chamber and was down the stairs and out of the front door before Marcy could carry her large bulk down the hallway.

"Thank you Lord, thank you. For giving my honey child such a good man," Marcy mumbled as she climbed down the stairs and stood at the front window and tried to see into the darkness of the night and single out the figure of Star Hawk.

Star Hawk whistled for Night Cloud as he started toward the small forest glade. As the mighty beast came to his side he shied away, the scent of the white man's clothes not familiar, but as Star Hawk soothed him with Indian words, the horse settled down and allowed him to mount him without showing his temper, which Star Hawk had seen much of when the horse had been young and untrained.

Heading straight into New Orleans, Star Hawk arrived upon the docks of the city in the late hours of the night. He spoke softly into Night Cloud's ear, after removing the blanket and halter. He spoke of home to the horse and then with a stinging slap on his rump he called to him to find his way back to the village. Knowing how well his animal was trained, he felt confident that he would go home.

At this hour of the night several taverns were open along the waterfront and the noise of the carousers could be heard in the streets. Star Hawk made his way along the docks. He was not quite sure how he was to find a ship that would take him to London, but his black gaze searched out each ship in every corner of the quay, feeling a need for great haste in this new adventure of crossing the seas.

It was with some strange luck that as Star Hawk was walking across a deserted portion of the docks the whisperings of several men drew his attention.

For a moment Star Hawk stilled, his black eyes searching out the dark corners and then finally settling upon a small group of men huddled together near a stacked bunch of crates.

"Hey you, what you be doing here alone at night?" a voice softly called out in his direction.

Star Hawk did not answer. His hand slid to the hilt of his large hunting knife that he had secured to his waist.

"I be talking to you, mister," the voice called out once again.

"I am looking for a ship." Star Hawk responded this time, thinking that perhaps some luck was with him and these men would be able to help him find a ship to England.

"We are all looking fer a ship, mister. Why don't ya be coming over here a bit closer so as we can get a better look at ya?" This was the apparent leader of the group.

Still thinking that these men could help him, Star Hawk did as the man requested, his steps taking him fearlessly to within a few steps of the motley-looking group.

For a few minutes the men looked Star Hawk over, and then the one who had called out to him spoke once again. "My name be Joshua, me friends just call me Josh, and this here fellow is Scotty, and here be Robbie and Billy. Christopher is the tall one standing over there by the dock rails. He's waiting for his doxy to bring him some news.

250

And what be your name, mate?"

For a moment Star Hawk looked upon the small group of men, seeing much in their grinning faces as the one called Josh pointed each out. There was a desperateness about them that was not lost on Star Hawk. "Hawk," he finally responded.

"That be a strange name, but it seems to sit upon ya quite well with what I can be seeing of ya." Josh took in the dark features and at once was reminded of the cunning creature that was called a hawk. "So ya be looking fer a ship, are ya?"

Star Hawk nodded and the man called Scotty stated, "Perhaps he would like to be joining up with us. We be looking for a ship, too."

"What do ya be saying ta that, mate?" Josh questioned, but before Star Hawk could answer there was a small commotion as a young, full-figured blond woman came running down the docks. As she set her eyes upon the tall, thin man called Christopher, she threw herself into his arms, her lips hungrily kissing him full upon the lips. "There now, let that be a-showing ya just a little of what ya going to be a-missing iffen ya go through with this scheme," she said as she seductively rubbed her body against his.

"Here now Tess, me girl. There's little time fer the likes of this." The man called Christopher set the young woman from him, but his long arms held to her shoulders. "Tell me what ya have learned this night, Tess, and say it loudly so me boyos here can be hearing all."

"The ship called the *Fair Bella* be the one that ya be a-wanting. Her captain and most of the crew are far into their cups at the tavern, and when I be

251

filling the captain's cup of ale he told me as how there not be but a few men aboard. Her hull is full of cargo to be delivered to Port Royal and the larders are full of food. She sets sail with the morning tide, and that be the reason for the captain's having one last drink before he takes back to the seas."

"Ye done good, Tess girl." Christopher bestowed a handsome smile upon her. "I'll not be a forgetting ye."

"Ye best had not. Ye better be remembering old Tess here that's a-waiting fer ya when ye finds that fortune yer a'looking fur." She once again pressed her full body against him.

"Ye bet, Tess, that one fine day I'll be a pulling up to that tavern in a fine, big carriage and taking me love for a long ride."

Tess giggled loudly as she envisioned herself stepping into a fine carriage. "It will be swell, Chris me boy. Only ye had best now be a-watching that charming face of yourn. I'd be a-hating for anything to happen to ye."

"I'll be fine now, lass, but you best hurry back to the tavern and keep an eye on that captain and his crew." And as she instantly turned about, lifting her dark wool skirts to avoid the mud and horse dung about the docks, he shouted after her, "Take care, Tess girl, I'll be back fer ye one day soon. And then, turning to the small group of men, Christopher strode toward them. "Ye heard her lads. We had best find the *Fair Bella* before her captain has his fill of ale and makes his way back to her."

All heads nodded in agreement, and as Star Hawk watched, the group started off down the wharf. "Are ye with us, Hawk?" the one called Josh called over his shoulder as he noticed the tall man looking after them.

Star Hawk did not quite understand what these men were about. "I need to find a ship to London," he stated.

Josh halted his steps, and for the first time with the small light coming off a ship's lantern he looked upon this stranger amongst them. "Ye be looking a bit strange fer being a swell, but it makes no never mind to any of us. We all be renegades or outlaws of one kind or the other. And iffen yer a mind to throw yer lot in with the likes of us and give us yer help this night, me and the lads here will be doing the same fer ye. We'll be seeing that ye get to the fair docks of London sooner or later."

This was all Star Hawk needed—the promise that he would get on his way to where Jessica was. "I will help you, then." Star Hawk hurried his steps up beside the group, and with a slap upon his back given to him by Josh, they went down the dock.

The *Fair Bella* was a trim-looking schooner, secured closely up to the loading docks on the New Orleans quay. As the small group approached they saw only the dim lamplight of a single lantern in the captain's cabin.

"What we going to be doing first?" It was Billy who sidled up to Josh and softly questioned him.

"We be going to sneak aboard and find the men. We must be overpowering them silently and then tie them up and hide them along the quay, so as not to raise a hue and cry. Enough of ye know how to handle a ship, and once we're out to sea we're home free."

Now Star Hawk understood better what this

253

small group of men was about. They were stealing this ship called the *Fair Bella*. And Star Hawk, himself not caring about the means of his own transportation, quickly knew what had to be done, and without any hesitation he began to pull his boots off and then his white satin shirt. Drawing his knife from his breeches, he motioned for the men to stay where they were as he quietly made his way over the plank and onto the ship.

Josh and his group of men watched for a few moments with bated breath, none daring to disobey this man called Hawk and follow him, but as a chilling sound circled the area and sent goose flesh prickling over their spines, as one they rushed up the plank and onto the ship.

What met their eyes was a sight to behold. There upon the main deck stood Hawk, his fierce war cry erupting from his lips as men charged him from different directions. With practiced ease, the tall, bronzed man routed them, throwing them over his head and flying across the deck one after another.

Josh was the first to react as he shouted for the others to hurry and clear the deck of the ship of the men Star Hawk was overpowering and see quickly to the securing of the *Fair Bella*. A gleam of respect lit his light blue eyes as he looked upon the fearless man before him.

Star Hawk hurriedly drew a ragged breath from his exertion and then set to helping the others clear the ship of the crew. They had decided to tie the men and leave them upon the docks until their captain and the rest of the crew of the *Fair Bella* arrived. Star Hawk had no regrets over his actions as he helped to tie the stunned men. He had lived his life defending himself and his people, and now he was determined that he would do whatever needed to be done to once again claim his wife.

It was only a short time before the *Fair Bella* was quietly slipping out to sea, her decks dark and silent as she left the port of New Orleans. Star Hawk knew nothing of the running of a ship, so he stayed to himself out upon the deck as the group of men hurriedly rushed about, raising sails and making the *Fair Bella* seaworthy.

As the lights of New Orleans slowly became dim specks off in the distance, Josh approached him. "Ye did a fine job, me friend." He again slapped the broad back. "We would surely have had injured men if it was not fer ye. Because of this, me and the boys have been talking."

Star Hawk was silent as he watched the other man's every movement.

"We thought as how we be needing a strong cap'n who ain't be a-fearing anything, and me and the boys as a single man decided that ye be the one fer the job."

"I know nothing of running a ship." Star Hawk was surprised at this man's announcement. "I but wish to reach London and claim what is mine."

"That be fine, Hawk." Josh grinned widely. "Me and the boys have all sailed afore, so we can run the ship. You ain't got to be a-doing a thing excepting helping us out when we're in a tight spot."

Not quite understanding why this group of men would elect him to such a high position, but knowing that from birth he had been raised to be a leader of men, Star Hawk slowly nodded his head.

"Fine, then that be settled. The old cap'n's cabin is a bit of a mess, but Billy and Robbie are setting about now with the cleaning of it. There are maps

255

and ledgers that we can go over later, and I be thinking that we should be going on to Port Royal to get rid of this cargo. We got a rich load of cotton and sugar, cap'n. All we need do is anchor off of one of them small islands in the Caribbean and repaint this old tug and give her a new name."

Star Hawk nodded his dark head. It would appear that this fellow called Josh had already planned everything.

"Since ye be the cap'n, me and the boys thought as it be only fitting that ye be the one to come up with a new name for the ship," Josh stated as he started down the companionway toward the captain's cabin and Star Hawk closely followed him.

"We'll name her the *Silver Star*," Star Hawk replied, not having to think for even a moment about a name. His heart and soul as one, he thought of nothing else.

"That be having a right lively ring to it," Josh grinned as he opened the portal and stepped back for Star Hawk to enter before him.

Star Hawk's eyes went about the large cabin, and as he observed the two men trying to tidy up the appointments, he quickly noticed his shirt and boots near the bed.

"The maps and ledgers are here upon the desk. Me and Christopher will see iffen we can't be making out our way to set the course for one of them small islands." With the added light of the cabin, Josh now looked fully over this man who had appeared so strangely amongst their group. He was even taller and larger in the light, his piercing black eyes looking bout and taking everything in. If it were not for the fact that the night-black hair was trimmed neatly about his shoulders, Josh knew

256

that he would have wondered about this man's origins. But shaking his head, he reasoned that perhaps this Hawk fellow was a half-breed of some kind. But, no matter, this was of little importance. What truly mattered was the fact that Hawk was on their side. Josh had seen the vengeance of his blade, and he knew that he surely would never care to be on the opposite side of the wicked-looking weapon. "I think we should be picking up more men to add to our number, cap'n."

Star Hawk agreed with all he said, and as his dark gaze fell upon the books and open charts and maps on the top of the desk, he thought of Ollie Bengiman who had taught him how to read and write. All this information that he held stored in his mind would now be put to work.

It was a few hours later that Star Hawk, Joshua, and Christopher sat about the desk and fully agreed upon their course. They would head straight away for the closest small island to Port Royal, and once there they would anchor and set to the repairs of their ship, which they now spoke of as the *Silver Star.* Once in Port Royal they would sell their stolen cargo, and with the profits hire on more men, pick up another cargo, and set sail for the London docks.

The three men were relaxed and in a high mood at the finish of their work about the desk, and as Josh rose to his feet and stretched his body, his light blue eyes fixed upon the other two. "Hows about a drink or two, boys? We done a fine eve's work, I would be saying. It ain't often that the likes of us find ourselves owners of a ship, and her laden with expensive cargo."

Christopher fully agreed, and as Scotty entered

the cabin he called to him to join them for a drink. Star Hawk, though, declined the offer. He had learned well from his years at his father's knee, and he had seen too often in the past what strong drink had made many a red man become. "I think I will go on deck and get some air." He started to the portal. "There is much to be done with the morning, so do not drink for long." He had given his first order as captain, and all the heads in the cabin nodded in agreement.

Star Hawk stood near the rail and breathed in the salt-fresh sea air. He was at last truly on his way to find his wife, he thought to himself. Perhaps the way would be detoured now and then, but he was on a ship, and soon it would be heading for London. And once there he would somehow find his old friend Ollie Bengiman, who would surely help him to find Jessica.

Jessica. The name seemed to linger in the very air as a slight chilling breeze stirred across the sea. As Star Hawk stood barechested, his naked feet spread far apart, his dark eyes looked far out toward the darkness of the swirling seas. Nothing would stand in his way of finding Jessica. If he were forced to tear the whole city of London apart, he would. And he prayed to the Great Spirit that he would be allowed to have stand before him the man who had caused him and his wife such pain, Jessica's cousin, Edmond DeVaugn. He would have the full score settled before he could return with his wife to their village. He would not allow this same thing to happen in the future. He would put an end to the one she called kin.

The docks of Port Royal were teeming with the hurried activity of a busy port. Ships of every description and from every nation were going in and out of the harbor of the small island. As the *Silver Star* made her way into port, Star Hawk and Joshua stood upon her decks and watched as the men rushed about. Their plans were to spend only a short time upon the island, only long enough to empty the cargo from their hold and to scour the island for able men to man the *Silver Star*.

Star Hawk felt his impatience rising with each hour that passed as he waited for the ship to be tied securely to the wharf. They had spent more time than they had expected at the small island they had anchored off as they painted the *Fair Bella* and changed her name to the *Silver Star*. There had been no life upon the island to distract them, but with only the few men aboard the *Silver Star* it had taken longer to change her from the ship she had been into the fit-looking schooner she now was. With each day that they lingered, Star Hawk had chafed at the delay. His dark visage was seen about the ship at all hours of the day and night as he prowled about, his thoughts constantly on the fate of his wife.

Joshua had tried to question his new captain about his life and what it was that he was hurrying to London for, but all that he received in response was a dark, penetrating stare, and then Star Hawk turned about and stood near the railing of the ship. His life was his own, his ultimate destination was kept secret.

This manner of keeping to himself was respected by the men. He was respected for his strength and his quick ability to see into a problem. For indeed,

Star Hawk knew nothing about the running of a ship, but his mind was quick, and it was he who directed the men on the cleaning of the ship and the painting of her hull. He had even drawn a picture of twin shooting stars, and this scene Scotty had painted with silver upon the forward bow of the *Silver Star*, the twin stars shooting forward out of the ocean's depths as she swiftly skimmed over the waves. Star Hawk had also formulated their plans for landing on the island of Port Royal. His orders had been given that morning, in the hopes that they would be quickly finished with their business there and then be on their way to London.

Joshua and Star Hawk would leave the ship first and find buyers for their load of sugar and cotton. It would be left to Christopher, Billy, and Robbie to see to the unloading, with the help of any men they could hire along the docks. Scotty's job would be to scout about the island for men who were willing to sign on the *Silver Star* for their voyage to London. And in the meantime Star Hawk and Joshua would find another cargo at a good price to purchase and take to London.

All had quickly agreed as Star Hawk had given out his instructions that morning, and then the ship was docked and Star Hawk dressed once again as a gentlemen in the buff-colored trousers and white satin shirt. With Joshua at his side, in clothes that had belonged to the previous captain, he started down the quay.

It was only a short time before an elderly gentleman of medium build approached the pair. "Good day to you, gentlemen," he greeted them, pulling his top hat from his head and allowing his bald pate to shine in the startling sunlight. "I take it that you are from yonder ship?" His gray brow rose with his query. "You are new to our island." And as Joshua would have questioned him, he held up his hand. "I am the governor of Port Royal, and each day I visit the docks and see what new ships have arrived."

"Ye be the govna?" Though Joshua was well dressed this day, his manner of speech was still that of a man of little means.

Governor Darby gave Joshua a look of surprise, but before he could think upon the matter further, Star Hawk spoke up. "Yes, we are new to your island. My ship sails mostly from Europe to the colonies."

The governor looked at the tall, dark man with the dignified air as he nodded his head in thought. "Your ship? Is it full of cargo from the colonies?"

"Aye, we have our hold full of sugar and cotton. We had hopes of finding a buyer this very day, for we are anxious to once again be out to sea."

"Well then, perhaps you are in luck." Governor Darby grinned. "As it is, there was a ship expected three days ago that has not arrived in port. She also was bringing sugar and cotton. But I am sure that her buyers would be more than happy to arrange a suitable transaction with you."

"If you would be good enough then to direct us." Star Hawk started to move, but the look on the governor's face indicated that he had more on his mind.

"Why don't you gentlemen follow me to my office? We can have a goblet of my best brandy and talk over a bit of business."

Joshua started to protest, but Star Hawk's look

261

quickly held him quiet. "Your office is nearby?" Star Hawk questioned. With the shaking of his head the elderly gentleman started down the quay.

"As I said, I am often here upon the docks so I keep a small office down here to conduct my business with the ship's captains and the like."

Star Hawk was beginning to understand what the governor was after, though he kept his thoughts to himself. Joshua's expression made it plain to see that the younger man was not at all sure of what was going on.

"Take a seat gentlemen, take a seat." The governor directed the two men to comfortable chairs near his desk. "We shall have a bit of brandy and then we shall get down to our business at hand." He began to pour three goblets with the amber brew.

"I care for nothing, governor." Star Hawk relaxed back in the chair, his dark gaze holding the governor's. "And I wonder if we could not come right to the point of our business together. You see, we are rather pressed for time." All these delays were more than Star Hawk could bear.

Governor Darby handed Joshua a goblet and then he took the chair behind his desk, his green eyes taking in the large, dark man across from him. "Well, it is rather awkward, but I will come right to the point. We welcome trade here in Port Royal, but I must explain our expenses are rather high. It is costly to keep peace here in the Caribbean, what with the pirates and buccaneers these days roaming the seas. We try to keep our port as profitable and peaceful as possible, and this costs money."

"Now we are at the real point of our business

together." Star Hawk sighed aloud. "And what is your price for our entry into your port and to sell and purchase new cargo?" The man must indeed be quite rich, Star Hawk thought to himself, if each ship in the harbor paid a fee to him.

"It is a reasonable fee," the governor stated as he twined his hands together upon the top of his desk. "I will also help you to get rid of your sugar and cotton and find something to fill your ship. We try to keep our captains happy so that they will return often to our island. And as you can see by the busy activity about the docks, we do just that."

Joshua could not believe his ears. The nerve of this little baldheaded dandy bribing them. "I'll be damned. . . ."

Star Hawk sat up in his chair, and directing a dark look at his friend, he touched his arm. "If the price is reasonable, governor, then of course we shall be willing to pay a price to keep your peace. You will have to understand, though, that we cannot donate to such a cause until we have sold our cargo."

Governor Darby, at Joshua's outburst, had been set to call in the two men who waited behind a door to the back of his office, but with Star Hawk's reasonable manner he relaxed back in his chair. "Of course, captain, there is no hurry. Enjoy our island while you are here, and I shall have some buyers this very afternoon come to your ship. They will also know of cargos that you may be interested in purchasing."

Star Hawk rose to his feet and so did an indignant Joshua. But before they reached the door the governor added, "I will visit your ship myself after the completion of the selling of the cargo."

Nothing else was needed to be said until Star Hawk and Joshua stepped out into the sunlight. "Ye shoulda told the old coot to go to the devil, Hawk. He's more of a thief than them pirates he were talking about."

"He'll help us get rid of our cargo and will give us no trouble. The governor won't even be asking to see our ship's papers. All he cares about is his gold. And as long as he is not asking too much, what is the harm? After all, we did steal the ship and the cargo." Star Hawk tried to talk reason to his friend.

Joshua nodded his head slowly, but still the idea of having to pay tribute to this balding governor sat badly with him. "He had just best do what he be saying, then. Iffen he don't be sending no buyers this very day, we'll not give him a cent."

Star Hawk absently agreed as his dark eyes looked out upon the streets of Port Royal. He knew with little doubt that the governor would keep his word. This was the man's livelihood, and he knew all its ins and outs. He was well aware of who was in need of what cargo, and with the right word given, Star Hawk knew that the governor could have any number of gentlemen vying for their sugar and cotton.

"Then I think I be going and finding Scotty, Hawk." Joshua knew that he would more than likely find his mate roaming through the taverns of the island, and at this moment he wished nothing more than the cool security that could be found in a tavern with a mug of ale wrapped in his fist.

"I shall go back to the *Silver Star,* then, and help Christopher and the boys. If you are not back by the time the buyers arrive, I will get the best price."

Joshua more than gladly left this affair to the man he knew as Hawk. He did not have either the patience or the head for such affairs. And seeing how easily Hawk had handled the governor, he felt his respect for his captain grow even more. "I'll be trying to get back, but iffen we ain't back by dark, you and the lads had better come a-looking fer us. The last time me and Scotty were together in a tavern we almost didn't leave with our skins intact. That be the time that we first met Christopher. Me and Scotty, we were both well into our cups, and this fair-haired wench come and sit right down upon me lap. Well, me being all fired up and all, I began to talk real pretty like into her ear, when along comes her man. And I tell you now, Hawk, I done thought I was a goner. He had to be all of six-foot-six, and near as broad as ye be. When he pulled the girl from me lap, me and Scotty both jumped to our feet, even though we done be knowing that we were in a tight fix. And just when I thought he was going to cuff me a good one, along comes Christopher, smiling and stepping between the giant and meself.

" 'Well what we got here laddy's? he be questioning, and then, when he spots the lass standing off to the side, he grabs her arm and starts pulling her through the back door of the tavern.

"Well, I be swearing that I seen fire shoot from the woman's man, and off he runs after the pair. That was when me and Scotty both ran for the front door, and when we were out in the street, who meets up with the both of us but Christopher. And he been one of me mates ever since."

"I can well see now why you may be needing

help this eve. But try to make it back to the ship," Star Hawk grinned. The last thing he wanted to do was have to comb the waterfront taverns for Joshua and Scotty. It would suit him well to finish their business in this island and then be back to sea and on their way to find Jessica.

Early that afternoon, as Governor Darby had promised, two gentlemen arrived upon the decks of the *Silver Star*, and after only a very short time, Star Hawk held several pouches of gold, indeed a fair price for their cargo. He also struck a bargain for a load of assorted goods, no questions being asked as to where the gentlemen had obtained such articles as French lace and Spanish spices. More than likely, Star Hawk knew, the goods had been stolen from other ships, but all that he cared was that the *Silver Star* leave this port with her hull full, so that Joshua and his cohorts would make a fair profit and he could get to London.

The only drawback in the deal was that it would take at least three days for all of the goods to be loaded onto the *Silver Star.* When he balked at the delay, the gentlemen had assured him that he could not be arranging another cargo any sooner.

So, by the end of the afternoon, the two gentlemen and Star Hawk stood upon the deck of the *Silver Star,* and with a handshake, they parted with some satisfaction.

With no choice left to him, Star Hawk set about helping Christopher, Billy, and Robbie with the unloading of the cargo. Christopher had found several strong and able men willing to make a good day's wages, and the large group of them now carried the crates and bales from the hull of the *Silver Star* onto the docks where the two men Star Hawk had sold the cargo to had men awaiting to load it into wagons and then drive it to their warehouses.

The work was backbreaking, but it left Star Hawk with little time to worry over his own tormenting problems. He gave himself over to the lifting and tugging, his body straining as he exercised his all, and by the time the darkness of twilight began to settle about them, he and the rest of the crew of the *Silver Star* were more than willing to call it a night.

After eating a meal hastily prepared by Robbie in the galley, the men decided that since Joshua and Scotty had not as yet appeared, they should go out into the town and find them.

Star Hawk held back somewhat from this idea, but the other men pulled him along as they started up on deck, electing Billy to stay aboard ship and watch that no intruders snuck aboard. Billy, being armed with a flintlock, insured that the *Silver Star* would not as easily be stolen as the *Fair Bella* had been.

Star Hawk had only time to put his shirt back on his back when he was ushered off the ship by her crew.

"Cap'n, I hope ye be bringing that big knife of yours fer surely as we're on this island, our boyos are in some kind of trouble. Did ya be hearing about the time when I first met Joshua?" Christopher questioned as the small group made their way along the quay. But as Star Hawk did not answer, he proceeded to tell him the same story he had heard earlier that day from Joshua, and by the

267

finish of the tale they were standing in front of the first tavern that they had come upon.

Star Hawk had never cared for the white man's idea of entertainment, and as he stepped into the small, smoke-filled tavern, he again thought about the indulgence of the whites. They grew lazy and fat with their style of life, not holding anything back, but giving vent to all of their desires.

His dark eyes circled about the dimly lit interior as Star Hawk looked about for his crew. Christopher and Robbie went boldly up to the room-length bar.

"I'll be having me some of your good whiskey," Christopher called to the bartender, "and me friend here will be having some of the same." He then looked at Star Hawk, but at the negative shake of his head, he began to question the barkeep about Joshua and Scotty.

It would appear that the two men had, earlier in the afternoon, been in the tavern, talking to men about signing aboard the *Silver Star* and drinking whiskey as though there would be no tomorrow.

And with this information from the bartender, Christopher's laughter filled the room. "I be betting that them boyos be knowing well enough when tomorrow gets round and their heads be spinning and their guts be rolling."

As Star Hawk stood quietly waiting for the two men to finish their drinks, a young, rather thin girl sidled up to him. "Ye be a-wanting ta buy a wench a drink, mister?" Her eyes looked admiringly at the tall, well-proportioned figure of Star Hawk, and liking very well what she was seeing, she eased one hand boldly out and rubbed the material over his heart. "Unless ye be a-wanting to go on upstairs."

She looked hopefully at him.

"I do not drink nor waste my coins upon such. And I do not wish to go anywhere with you." Star Hawk spoke frankly, not caring that his words seemed to hurt the young girl.

"Mill here knows how to show a fella a real good time," she tried once again.

"Leave the cap'n be now, lassie." Christopher pulled the girl by the arm toward him, and with an easy motion he slanted his mouth across her own. "Now, this be for your trouble." He threw a few coins upon the bar, and after one last drink from his glass he motioned for Robbie, and the men left through the front of the tavern, the young girl's eyes still following the figure of Star Hawk hungrily.

"Ye not interested in her type, cap'n?" Robbie ventured as they walked out into the night air. "Perhaps there be a brothel here on this island with a cleaner type. In New Orleans some of them houses have beautiful, sweet-smelling women that most do anything for the right price."

"I have a woman," Star Hawk boldly stated, not elaborating any further but putting a quick ending to the discussion.

Robbie and Christopher both looked at their captain with some wonder, but neither had the nerve to question him further about his claim to have a woman. But they each wondered privately about the woman who could belong to such a man.

It was in the late hours of the early morn that the threesome finally entered a tavern toward the far end of the city and heard Joshua's booming voice. "I be saying you're a liar!"

"I ain't, neither. There ain't a man on this island that can be beating old Isser here in a fair round." Another voice boomed over the hubbub of the tavern.

"And I be saying that me friend right here, me mate Scotty, can whip yer man in no time flat," Joshua again shouted, but as he looked at the man he was boasting about, he saw Scotty, slowly, as though melting, slide from his seat to the floor.

"Yer friend there ain't in much condition to be doing much arm wrestling; hows about you taking old Isser on?" It was a large, blustery man who was shouting across the tavern at Joshua. Joshua, though the drink had lent him bravery, knew that the man called Isser would more than likely break his arm in two and enjoy doing it. But at that moment, when he had to make a decision either to try and back out of this argument with this large fella or to go ahead himself and at least try, Joshua's blue eyes fell upon the three men entering the tavern. "And I be still calling ye a liar," he shouted as he set his gaze upon his captain. "Me cap'n be here now, and he be the one that can cure you and your friend of yer bragging ways."

Star Hawk groaned inwardly as the words touched his ears. He had hoped to avoid any conflicts of this nature, but now as all eyes in the tavern fixed upon his tall form, he could see that there would be no way out.

"Why, Isser be taking that dark-skinned fella and showing him how to lose and how to be liking it best in the end," the large man shouted as all in the tavern parted and made way for the threesome to make their way to Joshua's side.

Christopher and Robbie both wore wide grins on

their faces as they heard Joshua's words. For after
the number of drinks they had consumed going
from tavern to tavern, they also were in the mood
for some good excitement, and what better than to
watch their fierce captain beat this man who was
supposed to be the best in the islands.

"You said that you would be back at the *Silver
Star* by dark." Star Hawk looked sternly at Joshua,
but seeing his lopsided grin, he could not remain
mad. "It is time that we return to the ship. Billy is
there as guard, and the hour grows late." Star
Hawk did not wish to be entangled in this game of
fun with these drunken men.

"What be the matter? Yer cap'n there be a bit
yellow?" the large, burly fellow snickered at
Joshua.

With a drunken movement Joshua tried to set his
fist into the large face, but he was not quite sure
upon his feet and he all but fell to the floor.
Robbie caught him by the cuff of his shirt.

"Watch what ye be saying now, lad," Christopher
warned. "Our cap'n here be the strongest man
upon the seas, and though he ain't of a mind to be
proving it here and now, you know it's the truth."

"Why, ye scuffy bunch of sea louts," the large
man shouted. "Isser be the strongest, and all of
Port Royal be knowing it."

This seemed to be too much to bear for Christopher, and turning toward Star Hawk he said, "Ye
be hearing what he called us, cap'n. Are ye going
to let him get away with it or not?"

Star Hawk saw there was little way out, and
looking at the faces of his crew, from Joshua's
mad, angry pout to Christopher and Robbie's
knowing looks, he slowly nodded his dark head,

271

his hands quickly unbuttoning his shirt and handing it to Robbie.

There was a small gasp of surprise at the bulging muscles of this small group's captain as he stood facing the man called Isser.

Without a qualm, the large man who was pitting his friend against all comers swept a table clear of mugs and plates. Sticking a large finger into his mouth, he pulled it out wet with spit and drew two small circles upon the face of the table. "Put yer elbows there, boys, and don't be moving 'em."

And as Star Hawk sat down and complied, the man called Isser followed suit. The tavern was alive with shouts of encouragement and bets were wagered over the hubbub of voices.

With calm black eyes Star Hawk took the full measure of the man across the table from him. Many times in his life at his village he had played games with the other warriors to measure one another's strengths. And he could at this moment remember a time when he had faced a brave who had been much larger than himself. He had prayed that day that the Great Spirit would give him the power to concentrate and to allow all of his strength to be centered in his body and focused upon his opponent. Now he did the same thing: silently, he offered up a prayer to the Great Spirit to lend him the power to face this foe, to muster his strength into his upper body, and allow him to endure these moments.

At a shout given by the larger man, the two adversaries' hands came together. "Now don't be a-turning your bodies, boys, only use your arm muscles," the large man directed as he turned and placed a bet upon Isser to win.

At first the two seemed to sit still, their hands locked, their eyes meeting with stares as each sought to feel out the strength of the other.

It was Isser who tried to make the first move to break his opponent's hold and bring home the victory, and with all of his strength he bore down upon Star Hawk's arm, leaning his full weight upon his upper chest and forearm.

"Foul, foul," Joshua cried aloud to the roomful of men. "Ye be saying not to use yer whole body and yer man there be doing just that." He shouted at the large man and the whole of the tavern turned to a roar.

Star Hawk was undaunted, though, by the man's efforts, and he easily withstood the worst that Isser had to offer. His gaze was still set upon the other man, as though waiting for something to clue him toward the finish.

Again and again Isser tried to pull Star Hawk's wrist to the table. One time there was a hush across the room as Star Hawk's hand seemed to lower, but just as easily he righted it, causing a sweat to break out upon Isser's forehead. "Ye be losing this time, bucko," Isser shouted as he tried once again to unleash all of his strength and bear Star Hawk to the table. But as though his efforts were wasted, Star Hawk withstood them.

With Christopher, Joshua and Robbie shouting him onward, Star Hawk at last seemed to grow weary of this game. With a simple ease he applied a small amount of pressure at a time upon his opponent, until with gradual movements Isser's hand was borne down to the table. As his knuckles brushed against the wood a shout of victory was given up by the crew of the *Silver Star* and also by those who had bet on the dark-featured captain.

Star Hawk did not say a word to Isser or his man as he rose to his full height and looked at Joshua. "Bring Scotty and let us get back to the ship." He took his shirt from Christopher and slowly drew it on as all in the tavern stood and watched this coolness.

"You cheated!" Isser boldly stood in front of the man who had bested him. "Ye leaned yer body full upon yer hand. That's how come ye won!"

For a moment there was a hush over the men in the tavern, even Isser's large friend looking in wonder at Isser. They had all seen the captain win fair and square. But it would appear that this was all that Isser had, this claim to being the best arm wrestler upon the island, and he wasn't about to lose this honor easily.

Star Hawk turned as though he would leave the tavern with his friends, but he was pulled up short as Isser reached out a large hand and grabbed hold of his shoulder. "I say 'twas unfair, man, and I'll be having you say it too."

With a shrug Star Hawk rid himself of the hand upon him. "I do not cheat. You did lose." And with this he turned about again, thinking to have finished with this man.

"Watch out cap'n!" Joshua shouted out as he saw the enraged look upon Isser's face and the beefy hand drawing back into a tight fist.

With the natural instincts of one used to defending himself by his wits alone, Star Hawk turned about upon a bended knee, his own fist swinging high and upward and landing full upon Isser's jaw. And with the blow the big man was felled like a dead tree in the forest.

"Ye needn't be a-doing that," the large friend of Isser's shouted and charged forward into the group circling Star Hawk.

But with a much faster hand Star Hawk drew out his long hunting knife, and the eyes of all the tavern fixed upon the wicked-looking gleaming blade.

Absolute quiet filled the room as Star Hawk and his crew stepped toward the door, the large friend of Isser keeping his distance from the towering, dark-featured captain holding the hunting knife.

"We'll be seeing ye now, laddies," Christopher shouted to the crowd of men circling about them, not a one daring to make the break and approach Star Hawk.

It was with a large sigh of relief that Star Hawk stepped into the cool night air. And as the crew of the *Silver Star* laughed companionably and repeated aloud what had taken place back in the tavern, Star Hawk kept his thoughts to himself. It would appear that his quest to find Jessica was leading him into another world, and though he had to admit that he did like this small group of men, he was becoming increasingly anxious about his stay on this island.

"Cap'n, me and Scotty found several men who will be at the *Silver Star* with the first morning light. We should be having enough for a fit crew when we be setting sail again." Joshua broke into Star Hawk's thoughts.

"We don't sail for at least three more days," Star Hawk replied, but as he glimpsed the lights starting to catch fire in Joshua's blue gaze, he added, "There will be little time to spend upon the island. After this eve I think that we should be all staying aboard ship unless there is business to attend."

Slowly the group of men nodded their heads in agreement. Though the allure of drink and women was great, not a one of them desired to confront their captain on the matter.

"Whatever ye be a-saying, cap'n," Joshua answered for the group.

It was almost two weeks before the *Silver Star* finally left the docks of Port Royal. There was a delay in their cargo, and then also Governor Darby held up matters with his demand upon Star Hawk's time. His hope was to delay the ship from leaving the harbor, thus ensuring their return in the future. The gold coins that Star Hawk had handed over to him were a welcome addition to his chest, and he invited the captain of the *Silver Star* to his own home and out to dine. He hoped to bring about a friendship that would, in the years ahead, bring him in a large profit. But, in fact, all that this accomplished was to further inflame Star Hawk's already frayed nerves.

On a bright, clear morning the *Silver Star* left the dock, her plans to travel straight to London with but one stop on the way, as a portion of the ship's cargo was designated for the island of Martinque, and there another cargo awaited them.

Star Hawk was powerless but to sail the tide in the direction that would best suit the crew of his ship. After all, it was Joshua and his friends who had gotten him this far and had also given him a place of honor amongst them. He could not easily set aside their needs. With the exchange of cargos at Martinique, they were sure to make a tidy sum.

He was hard-pressed, though, as he stood beside the railing and watched the lights of the phosphorous sea foam. The silver streaks flashing through the water in the cover of the night brought to his mind the memory of silver eyes looking upon him with love and adoration. Then, the fullness of his loss would settle over him, his body longing for the feel of his woman, the sound of her gentle voice touching his ears. He felt as though he was lost, without an anchor to hold him down, without Jessica at his side. The part of his heart that she had filled seemed to cry aloud with its pain for her being, for his own refilling.

Chapter Eleven

The carriage traversed the deeply rutted dirt road with a rolling, seesawing gait, throwing the occupants about on their seats and forcing them to clutch out the side windows for support. The day was cloudy and a drizzling rain poured steadily down on the countryside, adding to the discomfort of those foolish enough to travel.

Edmond DeVaugn sighed aloud in his discomfort, his dark eyes on his cousin as she tried again and again to steady herself. She was lovely as ever this morning, dressed in an ice-pink silk gown. Her burnt copper tresses had been curled up into a becoming coiffure with small gentle wisps of curls around her face and ears and longer, fuller tendrils hanging down her delicate neck. Yes indeed, Edmond admitted, his cousin was by far one of the most beautiful women in the whole of England. Even with her now noticeable condition, she was still beautiful, perhaps even a bit more so, her face having a special glow that he had not noticed before she had found herself with child.

Her pregnancy had little hindered him in his pursuit to find her a husband, *and* one with his own means, who would give him no problems about the running of the Coltin wealth back in the colonies. In fact, Jessica's added beauty seemed to make her even more alluring to the opposite sex. She now seemed almost too tranquil and was little interested in the happenings around her. Since they had arrived in London, the young men had flocked about the small townhouse that he had rented for himself and his cousin. Edmond's ace, though, had been the earl of Locksbin. All of his plans had centered on this one man's becoming so entranced with his cousin that he would make an offer of marriage. He had certainly not been disappointed. The old earl had sat in the small parlor at the rented townhouse, and when his jaundiced, blurred eyes beheld the fair Jessica, he had been spellbound, devouring each of her assets with a lingering, hungry perusal.

Jessica had remained demure and quiet throughout the visit. Her back was rigid as she sat primly on the small settee, and she would seek only to answer a question put to her by the old earl. She seemed not in the least put off by his age or his appearance, Edmond now reflected. But as he thought, he remembered the slight, noticeable shudder that had swiftly swept over her body as Henry Locksbin, starting to take his leave, had bent his sagging form, and taking her hand in a strong grip, had planted a wet kiss on it. As he had let her hand drop back to her lap, he had pulled out his lace-edged handkerchief and wiped at the dribble of spit on his chin.

There had been little discussion between the cousins of Edmond's choice of husband for Jessica. She seemed complacent enough as long as she was allowed her time to carry her child until delivery. And this Edmond could not fight, though he had been hard-pressed to convince the old earl of this. For, in fact, Henry Locksbin had been single for the past twelve years, and though he was old, he still felt his blood become inflamed when he was around a young, beautiful woman. Some even claimed that old Henry was quiet lecherous when it came to women. He had spent much gold in the past years on his mistresses, but always he had seemed to tire of them quickly. In fact, he was as much a glutton for beautiful women as he had always been for strong drink and wine. And so it was that when he had been sent word from the colonies of the beautiful Jessica Coltin, he had agreed that if she were all that Edmond's contact had claimed, he would indeed offer her marriage. There was much, he had to admit, that he needed a wife for. There were always numerous guests at Locksbin Manor, and he much preferred the countryside to the squalor and fast pace of London. With a wife at the manor, he would not have to roam so much to seek his pleasure. At the age of sixty-eight, he wearied more easily trying to live a fast-paced life.

The very next day after the visit with Henry Locksbin, Edmond had been approached by the old earl on the matter of setting a hasty date for the wedding. There was a gleam in the old earl's eyes whenever he spoke Jessica's name, and Edmond was hard-pressed to convince the earl that his cousin was in mourning for the death of her imaginary husband and that she surely could not wed until after the birth of her child.

At first Henry Locksbin had been taken back at Edmond's bold announcement of cousin's condition. He had not noticed anything except her exceptional beauty the day before. Though he had heard the stories circulating that Jessica Coltin had recently lost a husband, he had not known whether to discount them or not. But now, being told that his future bride was also carrying another's child, he was not as sure as he had been a short time ago.

Edmond assured him quickly enough, though, that once the child was delivered his cousin would be more than willing to wed him. He had even insinuated that if the fact of the small infant bothered him, there were ways to take care of such a problem. He left this subject up to the old man, knowing that his mind was sharp and that he would figure out what would be best to do with the brat when it was born.

It was finally settled, after a lengthy discussion, that one month after Jessica delivered, the wedding would take place at Locksbin Manor. Edmond had held out papers for the old earl to sign that read that he would allow full control of all the Coltin wealth to remain in Edmond's hands. Once the earl signed the papers, Edmond had sat back with a sigh.

"You will find my cousin a treasure, Earl Locksbin. She has been raised carefully and herself ran a large plantation house. She should be a valued asset to your name and home." Edmond had sipped at his glass of port as his eyes settled on the older man.

"I care not a wit for the value of anything other than her abilities in my bed." The earl did not mince his words.

"And I am sure there also you will not be disappointed, my lord." Edmond grinned at the old man, though he did wonder where the old fellow got his zest.

"Perhaps the fact that she has known a man already will be in my favor. Damn nasty business at times to have to break them in. Only a month ago one of the maids at the manor jumped from the third-floor chamber window. She was a stubborn wench, and several times I had to take the lash to her. She couldn't seem to read my moods quite clearly. Oh well, she is gone now and better forgotten."

Edmond was quickly learning what type of manor the old earl resided over. There had been much talk among the group that Edmond went about with of the things that took place out at Locksbin Manor. There were talks of orgies and all manner of lecherous affairs taking place behind the cold stone walls. There were even those who claimed it was old Henry himself who had ended his wife's life when she had gotten too old to please him.

Even with all of these rumors, Edmond was not opposed to handing over his cousin into the old earl's keeping. Jessica had proven a liability that he needed to see securely kept in place. He could not afford to take her back to the colonies and chance that she would disappear again. His threats thus far to cause her Indian friends' destruction were keeping her in her place, but there would be no telling what control he would have over her if she were again to meet up with this Indian lover of hers.

Once again, he was brought back to the present moment as his eyes settled on his cousin across the carriage from him. Yes indeed, he would have his finish of her very soon. One month after the child dropped he would be going back to the colonies and to his own way of life. The Londoners lived a frivolous lifestyle that he was little accustomed to. In fact, he had spent more money in these past few months than he could ever remember spending at one time in the past. He had always been rather thrifty. In the past he had always had to work for every cent that he had acquired, and not until he had become Jessica's guardian had he found himself with any true wealth. So it was natural to him to be tightfisted with his coins, and in London this attitude was frowned upon.

"Would you know how much further we will be traveling?" Jessica questioned Edmond as her hand clutched the window frame of the vehicle. The jouncing of the carriage caused an upset to her belly that was quiet displeasing.

"It should not be much longer," Edmond answered, rather surprised that she had spoken to him. He could count on two hands the number of conversations they had had together since their arrival in London.

"We surely should have postponed this trip to Locksbin Manor for another, more pleasant day." Jessica complained. For a second she thought she would be ill as they hit a large bump that nearly threw her to the other seat.

Edmond, seeing the paleness of her face with

this last jarring of the vehicle, was quick to react. With his gold-headed cane, he rapped on the ceiling of the carriage. Sticking his head out of the window and being instantly pelted with cold droplets of rain, he shouted for the driver to be more careful with his driving and to avoid some of the ruts and bumps.

Jessica did not indicate any appreciation for his kindness. Everything that had happened to her since the day she had left Star Hawk's village to do Cloud Dreamer's bidding had been her cousin's fault. He had posted the rewards for her and he had forced her with horrible threats to travel with him to London. Now they were traveling to Locksbin Manor, where she would again be forced to endure the vile and insulting advances of the old earl.

Edmond had told her of the plans that he and the earl had made for her wedding date, a month after the birth of her baby. Though she detested the foul-breathed, rheumy-eyed old man who would be her husband, she was powerless to do anything about it. She was forced to submit because of the dire threats that her cousin held over her true husband's people. Every time she thought to bolt or to show her temper, she imagined the small children playing in her husband's village. She would see Singing Moon smiling and sewing for her husband, Golden Eagle, or she would see Cloud Dreamer helping her people. Could she possibly be the cause of their deaths, she would questions herself, and quickly she would put a grip on her emotions.

Shortly after arriving in London she had realized that the best way for her to not be affected by what her cousin was plotting for her future was to build an icy seal around her heart and feelings. She could draw some inner strength from her coolness, acting as though she were unaffected by everything about her. Her only inner happiness was the fact that with each day, her child grew healthy and strong in her womb. Star Hawk's baby was growing fast, as her shape attested. Her gowns that she had had made in London were all in a fashion to allow for her pregnancy.

"Earl Locksbin is expecting us today. This foul weather attacks the countryside at regular intervals. You had best get used to it, dear cousin. I would think that you would be most anxious to see the home that your husband will be taking you to after the birth of the child."

Drawing her icy encasement around her as though it was a cloak, Jessica stonily looked at her kin. Her face was quiet and cool as she looked at him as though she was seeing straight through him.

Edmond felt a slight shiver course down his spine at her look. Turning his head back toward the window, he settled himself back against the seat of the vehicle. Let her act any way she desired. It would not be too much longer and he would be well rid of her.

With a shout heard over the downpour, the driver steered the team of horses up the long lane leading to Locksbin Manor. The house itself looked like an ancient castle. It sat high atop a hill and overlooked the grounds like a large, towering sentinel.

Quickly, a large bevy of servants rushed out into the downpour and toward the carriage, help-

285

ing the occupants down and then up the stone steps to the house.

Inside the large black-and-white marbled foyer, the housekeeper took Jessica and Edmond's cloaks. "If you will be good enough to await his lordship in the parlor." She spoke in a stern, no-nonsense manner and directed them to the large formal parlor where a group of people were sitting about.

A small hush filled the room as Jessica and Edmond stood in the portal. But when one of the guests rose to his feet and called out to Edmond, the room seemed to take on a more natural feel.

"Well, Edmond, old chap. Henry didn't tell us that you and your lovely cousin would be joining us for the week. It would seem that the old earl is full of surprises these days." With this, James Smelf winked at Jessica as though he and she shared a great joke of some kind.

Jessica felt her features flame as the group in the room all looked at her. Everyone knew that she was to be the bride of the old, lecherous earl.

"Since my cousin will be the lady of the manor shortly, we thought a visit would be proper." Edmond strode inside, taking Jessica's arm and steering her to a group of ladies on the sofa. His manner was relaxed and unaffected by James Smelf's remark.

The ladies in the parlor were mostly young and attractive, and as Jessica advanced on their group many jealous eyes were directed at her. All knew that the quiet and cool Jessica Coltin had come quickly into their midst and had quite suddenly captured one of the most powerful and richest men in all of England. Though most frowned on

Henry himself, all were envious of this intruder's luck at gaining the earl of Locksbin.

Jessica sat primly on the sofa next to a young woman with flame-red hair, dressed in a black evening gown speckled with glittering sequins across the bodice. Her clothing, as well as several of the other ladies', seemed a bit out of place for an early morning gathering.

"So you are Jessica Coltin? I have heard much of your name these past weeks." The woman's cat-green eyes rose to the handsome face of James Smelf, letting Jessica know instantly who had been bandying her name about.

Jessica did not attempt to answer the question put to her, but she coolly looked at the woman, and in so doing, drew all eyes in the room to her.

"And you are also to marry our dear Henry." A tinted brow rose on the powdered forehead. Then, as the eyes roamed over Jessica's pink satin gown and for a moment rested upon the bulge of her abdomen, a slow, lazy smile came over the full red lips. "It would seem that between Henry and the child you will quite have your hands full, my dear. I do hope for your sake that you will be able to keep up. We here all know well of Henry's insatiable appetite." Her grin broadened at Jessica's paling features, and she looked around for agreement from the other women, who, without hesitation, all nodded their heads.

Jessica felt her fury rise to monumental heights at the insult from this painted tart. She started to rise to her feet and give all in the parlor a good piece of her mind, when she felt a hand come down on her shoulder.

"My cousin well knows her duty toward her

husband. I doubt that he shall find fault in her abilities." Edmond stood over Jessica, and with his hand on her he could feel the quivering of her flesh as she held back her unleashed wrath. "Jessica knows how to behave, for she well knows what consequences her disobedience could cause."

Jessica knew full well what Edmond was talking about. In his sly way he was warning her to behave herself or Star Hawk's people would regret her actions. Gasping a large breath of air into her lungs, she clutched her hands tighter in her lap, forcing herself to refrain from venting her response on the redheaded woman sitting next to her.

"I do fear, though, that I should apologize for my dear cousin's quiet manner. The ride was rather wearying for her delicate condition, and she is not feeling well."

"What is this I hear?" A voice boomed from the entrance to the parlor. "Did I hear you correct, Edmond? Does my future bride feel unwell?" Henry Locksbin's rather unkempt form made its way to the back of the sofa where Edmond DeVaugn stood behind his cousin.

"It was the ride to the manor and this damnable damp weather, Earl Locksbin. After a small rest, she will be her old self."

"Nonsense," Henry mumbled as he made his way to Jessica and peered down at her with his red-veined, jaundiced eyes. "She looks fit enough to me. By damn, she looks quite lovely." His hungry eyes went from her copper curls to the tips of her tiny pink slippers, bringing a bright flush to Jessica's smooth cheeks.

"What say you, my friends? Does not my young

bride-to-be look most entrancing this morning?"

All sounded their agreement of Jessica's beauty. The women murmured low praise, but the gentlemen loudly voiced their thoughts at Jessica's appearance, to the delight of the earl and to the utter humiliation of Jessica.

"Here, here, Clair, make room!" Henry Locksbin pushed on the red-haired woman's forearm for her to scoot down the sofa and allow room for his heavy bulk next to Jessica. "We have barely had a moment together since the agreements have been made for the wedding. I had thought that we would have a small hunt before the dinner hour, but Edmond is quite right about this horrid weather. Today will not be the day to give chase to the fox. Perhaps upon the morrow the sun will be shining." As he spoke he pulled his handkerchief from his vest pocket and dabbed at his drooling underlip. His eyes fell on Jessica's full bosom, and slowly his hand inched toward her lap and her clutched hands.

Jessica felt utter revulsion at his nearness, the smell of garlic and stale wine hitting her full in the nostrils and unsettling her stomach. At the touch of his fat, soft hand on her flesh, a hot, suffocating flush settled over her. Bringing her free hand to her throat, she tried to swallow back her nausea. Feeling somewhat faint, Jessica pulled her hand from her would-be-betrothed's. Her breathing shallow, she rose to her feet, and with all eyes on her, she tried to flee the parlor. "I fear my cousin was correct. I do feel unwell. If you could please have someone show me to my chambers?" She dared say no more with the fear that she would vomit right there on the parlor floor.

With a low curse, Henry rose to his feet, but seeing for himself the terribly pale features of his bride-to-be, he quickly rang for the housekeeper.

As Jessica was led from the parlor and to her bedchambers on the second floor, the woman who had been sitting on the sofa next to her, Clair, simpered to Henry, "You must get used to such things, dear Henry. A child can bring all manner of upsets into one's life." A small giggle escaped her lips and was joined by the laughter of the other guests.

"We will be finished with the brat soon enough. As soon as she is delivered, she will find her time so taken in her husband's bed that she will barely know that a child even exists." Henry also laughed aloud at his witty remark.

Jessica heard everything as she slowly followed the slim, stern housekeeper. Stinging, wet tears quickly came to her eyes, and her hand protectively went to her middle.

"Follow me, miss." The housekeeper turned to make sure her charge was behind her and quickly she glimpsed the crystal droplets in the silver eyes slowly making a wet path down her creamy cheek. "There, there, miss. That will do little good. The plan is well set and flowing into motion. All you can do now is make the best of the affair." Mrs. Borden had been in the earl's household for the past fifteen years, and she had learned quickly that if she wished to retain her good job, she had to harden herself to the cruelties of the earl and his guests. And the only advice that she or anyone else of this household could offer this young girl was to brace herself to try and get by with what was offered her. More than that, none could offer. The old earl's wife, Martha, had been much like this one here today, young and innocent. But that had been quickly taken from her when she was placed in the earl's keeping. He had used her hard and roughly. He had even on occasion, while deep in his cups, allowed others to visit her bedchambers. The whole of the household had heard the pitiful cries of their young mistress. One day, Martha had taken all she could bear and had thrown herself from the staircase. That had been her only way out, and now she was at peace, but here was another to take her place. Turning, Mrs. Borden took Jessica's arm, "Watch your step now, child." She patted the arm with affection, though she still remained cool and impassive. It did not pay to be interfering with the gentry, especially in his lordship's affairs. There had been others at the manor who had disappeared or mysteriously found their deaths, and Mrs. Borden did not wish to be one of their like.

The bedchamber was decorated, as was the rest of the manor, in fine taste, with dark, rich furnishings. The wood floor gleamed with a high sheen and the cream-colored draperies and coverlet accented the chamber well. As Mrs. Borden stepped into the room she went to the large, imposing bed and pulled back the satin coverlet. "Let me help you out of your gown, miss." She went to Jessica's side and started unbuttoning the tiny buttons down her back.

Jessica let the woman help her, and after she had pulled off petticoats and slippers and had allowed the housekeeper to brush out her hair, she was finally allowed to lie back on the goosedown bed.

"Thank you very much for your kindness." Jessica spoke softly to the elderly woman in an unemotional voice.

For a moment Mrs. Borden's heart went out to the young woman. As she thought again of the visible bulging of the young woman's stomach, she hurried to the door. Making sure that it was tightly shut to any outside ears, she went to the side of the bed. "Miss, I would not say anything under the circumstances. His lordship's business is his own and all, but I am wondering when you seem to so ill favor the match between yourself and the earl, well, I am wondering why you are here? Will the father of the baby not wed you?"

For a moment Jessica held her silver eyes tightly shut. This was the first truly caring voice she had heard since her arrival in London, and she wished nothing more than to cry out the whole horrible story of how her cousin was forcing her to marry the earl in order to save her husband's family. But instead, with the fear that somehow her words would get back to her kin, she softly replied. "Aye, I was married to the babe's father."

She did not have to finish. Her words went straight to Mrs. Borden's heart as she envisioned this poor young thing as a widow, her husband in his grave at an early age and leaving his bride heavy with child. "Oh, my dear, I am so sorry. But is there no other way for you? You have no one else to turn to?" The thought of this young thing and her baby here in this manor sent cold chills down her spine.

Again the tears touched deep in Jessica's eyes as she was forced to shake her head. "There is only my Cousin Edmond, who has arranged the marriage between Earl Locksbin and myself. There is nothing I can do," she finished with a note of despair.

Mrs. Borden herself felt the dampness in her own eyes, but she held herself in check. Patting Jessica's arm lightly, she started toward the portal. "I shall bring you up a tray in a little while. But for now, get some rest. There will be little going on here at the manor this miserable day. Tomorrow is when all will be abuzz, what with the ball and all tomorrow eve." With this she stepped into the hall and only the faint clicking of her heels could be heard.

Jessica sighed wistfully as she huddled beneath the coverlet trying to find some small measure of warmth. It had been Edmond's idea to come here to Locksbin Manor for the ball tomorrow night. He had insisted that it would be only proper that they stay at Locksbin Manor for the rest of the week. "After all," he had stated, "you will soon be the mistress of the manor and wife to the earl. What reason would we not have for staying?"

Jessica had not been able to state her true thoughts on the matter with Edmond's dark gaze on her. She was powerless but to do as he ordered her. It had also been Edmond who had ordered her gown for the affair. Grinning at her, he had stated boldly, "Not a man at the ball will be able to take his eyes from you. The gown itself will stoke Henry's pulses to flame and he will be chafing at the bit for you to hurry with your delivery."

Jessica had gasped aloud when she had first tried the gown on. Never had she exposed so much flesh. The bosom was cut low, to expose all but the very tips of her generous breasts. The silver shimmer of the material undulated and swirled about her with each step she took, even her pregnancy hindering little the effect the daring gown had upon the eye.

Swift tears flowed down Jessica's cheeks without end. She was but a pawn of no consequence in her cousin's foul game of control. What kind of life would she have here in Locksbin Manor, and wed to a man such as the earl? His crude manner and vile ways were known to all and not lost on even her innocent nature. She would be forced to do as he commanded of her once he wore the title of husband. And what of the child? Her hand swiftly went to the small mound, and there, for the slightest moment, through all of her heartbreak, she thought she felt a small stirring. Was the baby himself knowing her hurt and deep sorrow, and was he, as his father had so often in the past, offering her comfort?

But there was little comfort to be found. Henry Locksbin would care little for a baby not of his own loins. And what protection would she be able to offer such an innocent being? She knew that nothing on this earth could hold her back from trying to give Star Hawk's baby the love he would need, but what she feared was the strength of the man she would be wedding. Henry Locksbin was not a man of gentle manners and ways. He was ruthless and corrupt, given to any means to gain his own end. How long would her own strength last against such a one?

Without even being told, she knew that she would give all that she possessed, but that that would not be enough. If only she could flee, she thought, her heart so heavily burdened and her

294

raking sobs shaking her slight form. If Edmond did not hold such a terrible threat over her, she would not think twice of taking flight for her child's safety. But with Edmond's cruel threats to Star Hawk's people, she could not chance escape at their expense. She was trapped as surely as ever a soul could be, and all that she had were her dreams for escape.

In her dreams she could be at peace, and only there in the darkness could she forget the cruel world around her and remember the smells of the forest, the feel of the river's cool water against her skin, the touch of a tanned hide dress against her flesh, and the love in the ebony gaze that seared her soul. Only there could she let thoughts of Star Hawk fill her mind. He was her strength, though he was so many miles from her. She could again feel his caress, his love words whispered into her ear, his gentle, loving hands on her body and the heated flame of his mouth on her own. Only in the deepness of her sleep did she allow such thoughts, for to dwell on them throughout each waking moment would surely be her utter destruction. How could she survive having known such a love and knowing that she would never see that darkly handsome face again?

The *Silver Star* pulled into port with the slow descent of the sun, and as the darkness of night shrouded them and the seeping fog came off the river and encircled the docks of London, her captain stood on deck, his legs braced apart to steady him, his agate eyes looking far off into the distance at the twinkling glitter of the lights of the city.

Here was this faraway place called London that was harboring his Jessica. He would find her here with her cousin and whoever else stood in his way. But he would find his wife and bring her home.

"What shall we do now, cap'n?" Joshua had quietly made his way to his captain's side.

Pulled from his thoughts, Star Hawk looked down at this white man who had befriended him. "Do, Joshua?" His fine dark brow arched. "You shall see to your cargo, and if it is your desire, you shall buy another to replace it."

"And you, cap'n, what will ye be a-doing now that we've reached the London docks?" Joshua, thus far, had not approached this dark, brooding man about his past or what would await him at the end of their journey.

Looking deeply into Joshua's face, Star Hawk sighed aloud as though the weight of the world were upon his broad shoulders. "I have a friend here that I must find, and with his help I will find my wife."

The silence on the deck seemed ominous with the soft words from Star Hawk's lips. "Your wife, cap'n?" Joshua questioned with some surprise. "She be here in London? How is it that she ain't by yer side?" He could not imagine a man such as this towering mass of strength not holding on to what belonged to him.

"She was brought here by her cousin. But this is nothing that concerns you or any other. I will find her."

"No sir, cap'n," Joshua blurted, and with the dark eyes on him, he quickly explained. "I be a-meaning, me and the boys already talked this over.

296

For we be a-knowing that something were amiss with ye, and that whenever we reached London ye would be setting the matter straight. And seeing as how ye have more than once come to our side in our time of need, we ain't about to let you go at this alone. Iffen yer wife be here in this fine town, then me and the boys shall be a-helping ye to get her back. Cousin or nay, cap'n, we'll be at yer side."

At that moment Star Hawk could not deny this friend. He did not know what it was he could be facing here in this town of London. If he were in the forest of his homeland he would have quickly cast the offer of help aside. But here in a land that he knew nothing about, he was forced to admit that perhaps he did need the help that was being offered "There is a man whom I knew in my youth. He had a trading post, but he came back to London, which is his homeland. He will be able to help me find Jessica."

"Jessica." Joshua said the name softly, like a whispered caress, evoking images of a beautiful woman languishing away without the man that she loved at her side. "What is this man's name, cap'n? The boys will scour the very streets of this fair city to find him."

Perhaps Joshua was right. It would be a lot quicker to find Ollie Bengiman with the crew of the *Silver Star* looking over the city together. Already it had been too long that Jessica had been gone from him. The weeks were quickly turning into months. "His name is Ollie Bengiman. He had spoken of coming back to London and opening his own tavern." Star Hawk remembered back through the years when his older friend had sat

297

before the wood stove and told him stories of his youth and how one day he was going back to the city of his boyhood with his pockets full of gold to open his own inn or tavern.

"Then we'll be finding him fer ye, cap'n. Me and the boys are needing a good night out on the town and what better reason than to be searching fer yer man, this Ollie Bengiman. As soon as we find out something, cap'n, we'll be sending ye the word."

Star Hawk smiled gratefully at his friend. "I will stay aboard ship this evening and await your return."

Going back to the captain's cabin, Star Hawk paced about the small area of the chamber like a prowling, caged cat. His thoughts were in a quandary. He desired nothing more than to take some form of action, to go through the town in search of what had been taken from him. But he knew there would be little use in leaving the ship until he heard word from Joshua. He had to find Ollie Bengiman, for he would know exactly how to go about locating Jessica and her cousin. She was here in this town called London; so close, and yet so very far away.

Long into the early hours of the darkened morning, Joshua hurried across the London docks and made his way to the *Silver Star*. His feet were quick as he went over the planking of the docks and to the decks of the sleek ship. Seeing the dim light of the lantern beneath the captain's cabin door, he boldly pushed his way into the small chamber. "Cap'n, sir, we think we done found yer man," he hurriedly gasped as the portal was thrown wide. Seeing Star Hawk at his desk and his head raised questioningly in his direction, Joshua knew that he had awakened him. "I be sorry fer disturbing ye, cap'n. But that man that ye be needing, that Ollie Bengiman, me and the boys we think we done found him."

Star Hawk jumped to his feet, his mind cleared now with Joshua's words. "Where, Joshua?" He questioned softly, already going to the chair and picking up his jacket that had been thrown over its back.

"We be hoping it be the right man, sir, though to be stating a fact, this here man be awful feisty. Why, he be saying he don't be knowing any sea captain by the name of Hawk, and he even threatened to toss me and Robbie from his inn. I be telling him, cap'n, that iffen he ain't the man yer looking fer, that when ye get to his inn ye be teaching him a lesson or two in manners." Joshua was now more angry at the memory of the stout, gray-haired and bearded man's actions than he was excited that he might have found the captain's man.

"And what did he say to your threats, Joshua?" Star Hawk questioned, remembering Ollie Bengiman standing up to any that stood before him with all the ferocity of a vicious bulldog.

"Why, the old loon be shouting for me not to linger me steps, but to be quick and bring me captain so he can be showing ye a lesson as well as the rest of us." Joshua truly hoped that this wasn't the man that Star Hawk was seeking, for he would delight in nothing more than to watch his tall, avenging captain mop the inn with the small brute that ran it.

Star Hawk did not speak his own opinion, but

299

followed Joshua off the ship, along the docks and then through the city, nearing the outer edges of London. "However did you find this inn?" he softly questioned as the sun slowly began to rise.

"It weren't me, cap'n, it were Billy and Robbie. They always were a pair, and this evening they sets off on their own with the directions I be giving them about this man yer after. Late into the evening Billy found me in a tavern and drags me along after him to this inn, he being sure that the fellow is the one ye be looking fur, 'cause his name be Ollie, just like ye said. Meself, though, cap'n, I ain't so sure. Mayhap there be many about this city with a like name, and this here fella needs but to be taught a lesson on treating the crew of the *Silver Star* with a bit more respect." He left out telling that he was of the opinion that Hawk here was surely the one to be giving out this well-deserved lesson.

It was still some time before they approached the small inn sitting quietly in a large yard surrounded by towering trees. Toward the back, a stable could be seen. Star Hawk took everything in, thinking to himself that if this indeed was Ollie's inn, he had done quite well for himself. The place seemed in keeping with his old friend's good taste and ease of manner.

The inn seemed quiet as the pair went to the front double doors. Joshua pushed boldly inside, his chest puffed out and his manner brash, as he now feared nothing with his captain at his side.

The bottom portion of the inn was empty, except for Billy and Robbie dozing off in chairs near the hearth. "Where be that innkeeper, now?" Joshua shouted loudly, startling both of the crew members of the *Silver Star* to their feet looking wild-eyed about them. Upon seeing their captain and Joshua, they relaxed once again. "Perhaps he be in the kitchens," Robbie said as he rubbed the sleep from his eyes. "It be so long since ye left, he might have taken his bulk to his bed.."

"Here, now, what be the noise here in my inn?" a booming voice called from the back portion of the inn, and a short, brawny man of late middle age and a rough disposition came through a doorway, his face turning red as he saw who was causing such a disturbance at this early hour in the morning. "I be telling you to keep yourself from my inn. There are decent people here asleep from their weary travels, and here you be down here shouting aloud and trying to wake the whole of the inn."

"That be the man, cap'n." Joshua spoke sourly as he watched the innkeeper start toward them.

"Who is this?" the short man questioned as he drew closer. "Is this the one that you claim I should be knowing?" His gaze went from Joshua to the tall, dark-featured, neatly dressed man at his side. "I told you already that I don't be knowing any captain with the name of Hawk." As he said this, of a sudden his eyes enlarged like twin saucers and his mouth dropped open wide. "It can't be. I must be seeing things," he finally gasped, his body now standing directly in front of Star Hawk.

Star Hawk smiled broadly. "You are not seeing things, good friend. It is truly, I, Star Hawk."

The two old friends came together in a mighty hug of love. And as the crew of the *Silver Star* watched in wonder, they also marveled at the name their captain had called himself.

"What the blazes are you doing captaining a ship?" Ollie questioned the moment he was able to breathe, after enduring the tremendous hug he had been given. "Why are you not with your father and the tribe, lad? They are all right, aren't they?" Ollie was so full of questions that he seemed to sputter out all in one breath.

"My father and our people are fine, old friend. But there is much that I must speak to you of. I need your help, Ollie Bengiman. Not unlike how, as a young boy, I needed your wisdom in many things, I now ask again that you will be a true friend."

"Of course, of course, lad. You have come to the right person. You were much as my own son when you lived with me those winters. I would not turn you away now when you have come so far." He still could not formulate any kind of idea of what could have brought this young Indian warrior all the way across the seas. "Come on out to the kitchens, lad. There is a warm fire in the hearth, and Nell is already baking bread. We can talk out there and share a cup of tea." Ollie looked at the other men, and with a large sigh he said, "I am sorry, men. I did not know that your captain was my dear friend Star Hawk. You should be telling a man what you're about," he blustered at Joshua, as he remembered how brashly this younger seaman had spoken to him earlier. Then, turning back to Star Hawk, he murmured, "Your crew are welcome to share the warmth of the kitchen also."

The crew of the *Silver Star* nodded their heads in agreement with the elder man's words, their anticipation piqued as they followed their captain and his friend into the back of the inn. Not a one of them would voice his thoughts, but each vowed that he would have paid a year's wages for this very invitation. Each man of the *Silver Star* had some curiosity about their quiet, brave captain, and with each step toward the kitchen they knew that all of their questions might be answered in the next few moments.

Star Hawk was directed by Ollie to a small table nearest the large wall-length cooking fireplace. His crew was each given a mug of warmed cider at the long wood table in the middle of the kitchen that was used for the everyday activity of the inn. The cutting of vegetables and the preparing of food was set aside to the opposite end by the large, smiling Nell, and she set about putting thick slices of fresh-baked bread on platters with jelly or jam at their side. When she looked about and saw that all in the kitchen were either eating or drinking, she turned about with a sigh and started back to her morning's work.

"Now, lad, tell me what has brought you so far from your tribe?" Ollie sat back in the chair a steaming mug of tea in his fist. His warm green-flecked eyes rested on the young man across from him with something akin to love.

Not knowing where to begin his story, Star Hawk sat quietly for a moment. Now was the moment that he had been waiting for for so long, and as the quietness of the kitchen surrounded him and the eyes of all of his friends were upon him, he felt the full burden of his loss. "I went to your trading post a few months ago but was told that you had left for this country," he started.

"Aye, I had told you often in the past that one day I would return to my homeland and buy an inn." Ollie watched his every feature, trying to read more into the few words he had thus far spoken. But he wondered fleetingly how his returning to England could have affected the young warrior.

"I went to the trading post with my wife, Silver Star." Star Hawk had not spoken of what had happened with any other person, and now, at the sound of his love's name, and telling this friend what had taken place, he felt the heaviness of his heart.

It was Scotty who opened his mouth to gasp out the name "Silver Star," but he was quickly elbowed in the ribs by Christopher, who silenced him before a word was spoken.

"Your wife, lad?" Ollie spoke softly; it was the only sound in the kitchen. Even Nell was held still with her sharp knife in hand as she was starting to cut strips of bacon.

"There were two trappers that day in the trading post who offered to buy Silver Star. Of course, I refused them, and there were some angry words."

Ollie could well imagine the fury of this young man at an insult such as this from two white trappers. Star Hawk was a man of honor, as his father Golden Eagle was, and if he had taken a wife to his sleeping mat then he held her as a part of himself. He did not say anything, though, as Star Hawk took a sip of the hot tea. Then, with his ebony eyes upon Ollie once again, Star Hawk spoke.

"I was called away shortly after this to a council meeting with a number of great chiefs, and I left my Silver Star with my tribe. She was watched over by my friend Spotted Pony."

"Aye, Spotted Pony, I remember that rascal quite well." Ollie smiled as he remembered Star Hawk's young friend. The pair had ridden into the trading post many times together when they had been younger.

"He is sleeping now with the fathers. His path has walked the star path, and he is in the hunting paradise with the Great Spirit," Star Hawk softly mumbled. Then, without waiting for this to sink in, he added, "The trappers came near my village and stole my wife. They killed Spotted Pony when he tried to protect her."

"Sweet Christ!" Ollie exclaimed aloud, the horror of what had taken place swirling around him.

"I found the trappers. Their souls shall forever follow the path of the evil one, crying in anguish for their foul deeds." The words were spoken so coldly that all in the kitchen caught their breaths, a stony chill now settling about them.

"And your wife, son?" Ollie softly questioned, pulling himself from the coldness gripping Star Hawk and seeing more into the young man's soul, feeling some of the pain that was searing his very heart in two.

"That is why I am here, Ollie Bengiman, my friend. My wife is here in your country. I have come to find her and bring her back to our lodge."

Ollie was now somewhat confused. What would an Indian woman be doing here in England? How had she made her way from the colonies to this land? "Are you sure, lad, that she is here? How could she have. . . ?"

Star Hawk supplied him with the answers to his

questions before he could get them out. "Her cousin is an evil man and hired the trappers to find her and bring her to him. He paid them much gold for her return and when he had her, he forced her to go with him on a ship which came to the London docks."

"But lad, I still don't understand." Ollie was still bemused, as were the men of the *Silver Star* who by now knew that their fierce captain was in truth an Indian warrior. All now looked upon him in wonder at why an Indian would steal his cousin and then come to England with her.

"My wife is a white woman." Star Hawk made his gaze hard and piercing as it traveled about the room and then settled on his friend. "Her name is Jessica Coltin. Her cousin's name is Edmond De-Vaugn."

Ollie Bengiman sat back in his chair as though all the wind had been knocked out of him. Then, slowly, he shook his round head as everything seemed to settle upon him and he digested all that the young man had told him. "It would seem then, lad, that there is indeed a bit of a problem. Are you sure that the lass wishes to be returned to your people? You know, lad, that it is a hard life for a white woman with people not of her own kind."

Star Hawk looked deeply at his old friend, trying to take in the effect that his words had on him. Seeing in those eyes only love and the desire to help, he slowly nodded his head. "Silver Star is the only woman of my soul. She was taken, and she fought her captors. She told them of her love for her husband and that she did not wish to return to her evil kin. My people are her people, as she and I are as one."

The group of men in the kitchen could only imagine how Star Hawk had been given the information about his wife's abduction. It could only have come from the men who had stolen her, and shivers coursed down their spines at the thought of the ordeal that they had surely undergone before finally confessing their crime.

"What can I be doing then, lad?" Ollie did not hesitate in his offer to help. This was his friend and he had been given a foul hand. Anything he could do, he would. With a single voice, the crew of the *Silver Star* all shouted in agreement that they also could be counted on,

Star Hawk did not hesitate. He had been raised with the understanding that if a friend was in need, you reached out your hands in any way you could. And these men in this warm kitchen, he knew, were all his friends. It did not matter that he was an Indian warrior who would one day lead his people against their own kind, and that he was joined to a woman of their own race and was trying to find her to bring her back to his people. All that mattered was that they were bound as friends. "I thought you could find out where this Edmond DeVaugn lives. If I can find out where he has taken Silver Star, I can myself reclaim her."

"I wonder why this cousin has brought the lass all the way to London?" Ollie absently ran his fingers through his graying strands of hair as he thought of the best direction to take to find this Edmond DeVaugn.

"He has brought her here to join her with another," Star Hawk stated, bringing Ollie's eyes back to him.

"Does he not know of you, then?"

"He knows, for the trappers and Silver Star herself told him. He cares only for the wealth that her name brings, and as he is placed as her guardian, he wishes to marry her to a man who will allow him to keep what is hers."

Slowly nodding his head, Ollie lightly drummed his knuckles on the small wooden table. "I can see how he would not wish her to wed you, now. He must be careful with the choice of her husband if the outcome is a great deal of wealth."

"I care not for the gold of the white man. I care only to regain my wife."

"Aye, but this Edmond DeVaugn does not know this," Ollie stated wisely. "First, I will visit my solicitor. He is well known to the hobnobs of London, and if this Edmond DeVaugh and his cousin are of an elite standing, he will surely know of their whereabouts. He stays on top of all this class hubbub. I believe he himself was a third or fourth son to a lord or a duke or something of this nature." Without a second thought, Ollie rose to his feet.

"I will go with you," Star Hawk stated, also rising to his towering height.

"Your men can stay here and relax and eat a hot meal. We may indeed be needing their help. There is no telling the circumstances that are surrounding your wife. We may be needing all the help we can find."

Star Hawk did not respond. If he could find out where Jessica was, he would bring her back to his side alone if he had to. Nothing would keep him from regaining her once he knew where she was.

Willis Swineheart sat back on the top of his desk and grinned down at his client. "I see that you have heard of the fair Jessica Coltin also, Ollie. She is the very talk of London these days."

"What do you mean, Willis? I was but wondering if you knew of her or her cousin, this Edmond DeVaugn." Star Hawk and Ollie Bengiman had wasted no time in finding his solicitor, Willis Swineheart, and after a few pleasantries about Ollie's inn and the general weather, Ollie had questioned Willis lightly about Edmond DeVeugn, claiming that he was having some business dealings with the gentleman and was wondering about his character and also that of his cousin, a Jessica Coltin. But he had been taken by some surprise by the extent of Willis Swineheart's answer.

"Why, upon the tongue of the most simple peasant woman, is the fact that Jessica Coltin has suddenly appeared from nowhere and is to wed Earl Locksbin."

Ollie gasped aloud, "The earl of Locksbin is to marry the lass?" He, along with all of London, knew of the earl of Locksbin. His cruel ways and lecherous exploits had been rumored about his inn from its first opening.

"Aye, and they say the girl is quite heavy with child, too. But you know how rumors circulate, Ollie. You can't be believing all that you hear. It is a bit strange, though, that the wedding is not for another couple of months. They say Henry is quite smitten with the innocent young thing. I myself feel only pity for her at his hands, but there is no accounting for the taste of others."

For a second Star Hawk felt his muscles tense as this man spoke about his wife and claimed that she was heavy with child. He felt his heart hammering in his chest and his hands circled the arms of the chair he was sitting in as he forced his features to remain normal. Ollie had warned him that under no circumstances was he to act out of the ordinary. There was no telling about a man like Willis Swineheart. He was one of the upper class, and though he was Ollie's solicitor, he could still only be trusted so far. So with a great effort of will, Star Hawk took a deep breath as he kept his thoughts to himself. His midnight-black eyes held on the man as he lightly answered Ollie's questions.

"There is much gossip about London these days, Ollie. I do know, though, that if you have had dealings with Edmond DeVaugn, you had best beware. They say that right after his cousin weds the earl, he will again set sail for the colonies. Many say that his time here in our town has been a bit flippant. He comes and he goes with those of the upper crust, and he often invites people to his townhouse. Rumor there says that he was offering his pretty cousin up as a tidy tidbit, and the best nibble was the earl's." Willis Swineheart coughed aloud with laughter at this jest, not in the least knowing of the mortal danger he was in by talking in such a manner about Star Hawk's wife.

But Ollie Bengiman knew full well, and seeing the heat surface in Star Hawk's features, he quickly questioned, "You know where this townhouse is where he and his cousin reside? I think perhaps I should pay a small visit and better understand the man."

310

"Aye, the townhouse is not far into the city, but you would be wasting your time to go there this week."

At Ollie's questioning look, he responded. "The rich are not like you and I, Ollie, my friend. We have to stay in the city and scratch out our living, while those of the upper class can adjourn to the countryside and relax among the gilt and glitter of their peers."

Ollie took his meaning clearly and also heard a touch of envy and loathing in his tone. It was plain to see that Willis Swineheart had been deeply hurt by his peers in the past. "Do you know where they have gone for the week, then?" He held his breath, awaiting the answer.

"Not a place that the likes of you or I would be invited to easily." He had no grin now as he answered. "The earl of Locksbin is having a ball tomorrow evening. All of the city will be arriving at his door this afternoon and tomorrow. His country castle will be awash with the best that London has to offer, and there, I am sure, is where you will find Edmond DeVaugn and his charming cousin. Not that you or I would be there. It would be hard indeed for us to be getting through the front doors."

"Well, I was just wondering about the chap, you understand. Perhaps when he is back in the city, I will meet up with him." Ollie quickly made himself appear only slightly interested in the man in question.

"Well, Ollie, if there is a legal question or anything that I can be handling, don't be hesitating to ask me. I am right here in my office whenever you need me."

311

Ollie smiled and stepped to his feet, his large hand extended toward his solicitor. "I appreciate the time you have taken already for me, Willis. Come by the inn and share a mug of ale with me soon."

"I'll be doing just that, Ollie. My missus sometimes could try the very saints with her nagging. My only escape at those times is with a mug of ale and a good friend to share it with."

The two men laughed and made their way out of the office, Star Hawk following with his thoughts in a whirl. Jessica and her cousin were indeed here in London, but now he was still not quite sure where she was.

Once away from the solicitor's office, Ollie looked at Star Hawk with a troubled face. "You understand all that he said, lad?"

Slowly Star Hawk nodded his dark head. "We still do not know where my wife is." He spoke softly, as though nothing else mattered except that he find Jessica.

With a sigh, Ollie patted him upon the shoulder. "That is no problem, lad. The whole of England knows of the earl of Locksbin. His manor lies outside the city, along the coastline. The problem will be getting Jessica out of the manor house. You heard Willis call it a castle, and by all accounts, it is staffed and armored like one. There are guards stationed about the grounds, they say, to keep out unwelcome visitors, and there are many within the manor itself. Perhaps it would be best if we let this week pass and then rescue your wife when she and her cousin return to the city."

A fire of coal-black passion stirred in the ebony eyes as they looked down on his friend. "My wife is at this place called Locksbin Manor, and I shall find her. You have done enough, my friend, with finding out this information. I thank you."

Ollie grabbed hold of Star Hawk's arm. "Wait a minute, Star Hawk. I am not about to let you go into a situation like this all by yourself. You will be needing all the help you can muster, lad. I will be right by your side." Ollie had voiced his safest opinion of the situation when he had said perhaps they should sit easy and await the return of Jessica and her cousin, but with Star Hawk's answer he knew that safety was one of the lesser thoughts in this man's bold life. He lived every day by his wits, and when treated unfairly he retaliated in kind. There would be no delay from this young warrior. He would set his plans and go after his wife.

Star Hawk smiled slowly at first and then more fully. "It is hard to find one that is a true friend." He spoke softly.

"That is the truth, lad, but I am thinking that you have yourself quite a few now, counting those waiting at the inn for you. And we will be needing each and every one of them. We had best hurry and make our plans, for the best weapon we shall have on our side will be surprise!"

Chapter Twelve

Jessica Coltin stood before the tall gilt-framed dressing table mirror and could not help but marvel at the reflection of the woman looking back at her. She was dressed from head to foot in shimmering silver, her gown fitted tightly across the sheer bodice and revealing the deep cleavage between her breasts. The satin material was gathered to produce a high waist that made her pregnancy less noticeable, and swirling about in yards of the gleaming silver cloth. She wore silver bracelets that had been given to her by the old earl himself. That very afternoon a servant girl had brought the jewelry to her chamber with a note attached, requesting her to wear the gifts at the ball that evening. Her fire tresses had been fashioned and twirled into perfect ringlets, forming a crown upon her head, and within each curl was placed a sparkling silver hairpin, whose twinkling caught the eye whenever she moved her graceful head. Even her slippers were of a silver material complementing the gown, with high heels of sequin-sparkling studs. As Jessica looked at her reflection, she did not know the woman who gazed back at her. How could anyone look so lovely when she had a broken heart? Not caring about the happenings about her, she silently wept for the love that had been stolen from her.

Those with her in the chamber had no clue as to the lovely woman's inner feelings. With a sure hand another servant lightly rouged the creamy cheeks, her voice mumbling about the paleness of one so lovely. But Jessica barely heard her words, her mind now consumed with thoughts of the evening ahead.

Jessica had stayed in her rooms since the day before, still claiming illness and begging to be released from the activities of the day that had been planned for the rest of the many guests who had arrived at Locksbin Manor. Only one time had Jessica ventured from the chamber, and that had been to find Mrs. Borden, to request that a cup of tea to be brought to her room.

It was while she had slowly made her way down the hallway that she came face to face with Henry Locksbin. And at the moment that his red-veined eyes had fixed upon her, Jessica had felt her flesh begin to crawl. His eyes leisurely went over every inch of her bosom before focusing upon her face, and then he pulled out a lace handkerchief and began to dab at the dribble upon his lower lip. With his other hand he reached out and took one of Jessica's ice cold ones.

"Edmond told me this morning before the fox hunt that you are unwell again today?" His voice had a coldly inquiring edge to it that had unnerved her altogether and had set her limbs atremble. "My last wife was never caught with child, so I have little understanding of the ways of a woman in this condition." He had spoken the words almost to himself as Jessica stood there in the hallway before him, her face ashen now at his nearness and his intimidating bodily threat.

"However, I have heard several enlightening stories in the past weeks of women with their time so heavy upon them. It would appear that everyone has some thought upon the subject of our union." And with this his beady eyes settled upon the mound of her belly that was visible through her day dress. "Some even have told me that the tightness in such a condition is much likened to that of a sweet young virgin."

Jessica gasped aloud at his vulgarity and tried to pull her hand free from his firm grip.

A loud laugh filled the hallway as Henry Locksbin saw the terror in her silver eyes. He enjoyed nothing more than witnessing such fear in a woman's gaze; it excited him, driving his passions ever higher. "I am sure that there will be a time to experience all before the vows are spoken, my pretty," he whispered next to her ear as he kept his pudgy hand clasped about her wrist. "I would hate to waste such an experience. Who knows, you may not again be in a like condition. And it would be a shame to let a chance slip of such rare delight and pleasure as I have been hearing about."

Cold chilling terror descended about Jessica as she tried once again to break his hold upon her. He was a vile, filthy, old, flesh-sagging man with

316

a lecherous look in his eyes, and his handling of her was worse than anything she had ever endured in her past. "Please," she almost whimpered, as she tried to reclaim her hand from his keeping.

"Aye, I shall do that my lovely." He grinned down upon her fear-filled silver eyes. "I shall indeed please you well. Be sure that you are well enough for the ball this eve." He released her hand and stepped back from her side. "Unless that is, you would rather I join you in your chambers and we could hide away from my houseful of guests?"

Jessica swallowed convulsively. "No, no, I shall be well enough to attend," she finally got out between her trembling lips.

"I would hope so." Henry Locksbin stood near the head of the stairway and started to step downward. But with a raised brow he turned back to the beautiful woman in the hall. "Perhaps we shall find some time this night after the ball. So much goes on during such affairs that I am sure none will wonder at our disappearance."

Jessica could only stare after him with horror as he turned and made his way to the bottom of the stairway and to his guests lolling about the first floor of the manor, his loud laughter filling her with swift revulsion as she turned about and slowly made her way back to her chambers, all thoughts of tea fleeing from her mind.

"You're just as lovely as I have ever seen any grand dame be looking ma'am," the servant marveled as she stepped back and gazed upon the incredible beauty of the woman in the silver gown, her loveliness transcending anything that she could voice with her limited vocabulary. "A right picture of a fairy princess ye be now, ma'am. Why, the earl will be keeping his eyes upon ye all of this here eve," she went on, trying to praise Jessica's beauty.

Jessica paled even more at her remark as her eyes also looked in the mirror at her reflection. Whatever could she do to save herself from the lecherous earl? She could not throw herself from her chamber window and seek the freedom of her soul—she now had Star Hawk's baby beneath her breasts, depending upon her for its life and she could never deprive it of that life. She could not flee, for to do so would surely bring destruction upon the heads of Star Hawk's people. What was there left to her but to submit to the abuse that was being foisted upon her?

As she looked upon the beauty of the gown and the elaborate coiffure of her hair and realized the extent of the special treatment her appearance was receiving, she knew all that it would mean to be the wife of a wealthy earl. She knew that she would give it all up for the one man whom she loved with all of her heart. She would gladly have worn the simple dress of the Indian women, worn her fingers to the bone cooking and cleaning hides, slept upon the cold ground and endured all that nature could hurl at her, if she could only have been at Star Hawk's side. There was nothing left for her in this white man's world, except betrayal and anguish.

The thousands of lighted candles glittered like

brilliant shimmering diamonds as they sparkled high above the ballroom floor, bedecking with splendor the swirling couples across the dance floor, in a marvelous kaleidoscope of color and contrast.

"You are, as usual, the most beautiful woman in the room, dear cousin." Edmond DeVaugn raised his glass of sparkling champagne toward Jessica, and with a slanted smile he sipped at the light, bubbly liquid in his glass as his dark eyes strayed to the valley of her swelling bosom.

"I certainly do not feel very beautiful," Jessica responded softly as they stood to the side of the ballroom, nearest the french double doors, her nerves in such a tangle that she did not even notice the lustful glance of her cousin.

"That is because of your condition. You will learn to adjust and to relax soon after the child is born. Could you truly ask for a better life than you see before you?" The hand that held the glass of champagne motioned to the huge gathering in the ballroom, and as Jessica let her silver gaze go about the room and observed the women, bejeweled and gowned in the richest of cloth, and the men, escorting them across the ballroom floor in elegantly tailored suits of the most stunning colors, she wanted to weep. This was not her life. Hers was a simple nature, needing no pomp and no ceremony.

But none of this could she speak aloud to her cousin, lest he think that she was referring to her husband's people, for although she was submitting to all of his plans, he could easily get into his mind that it would be best to eliminate Star Hawk

319

and his tribe anyway. With a soft sigh she realized that she would forever think of her husband as Star Hawk. No matter who her cousin forced her to marry, she had only one man, and he had been taken from her. The beauty of the night when she had stood beside Star Hawk and the old shaman of his tribe had joined them as one came to her mind swiftly, and the memory burned within her breast as though a piercing knife had struck.

"Cheer up, sweet cuz. One would think that you are not happy." Edmond's tone held a brittle note that contained implications only Jessica could understand.

"I am sorry, Edmond," she tried to respond in a light tone. "I have not felt well, but I shall try to exhibit some form of delight with my surroundings."

"Do that then, Jessica, for the earl has been glowering at you the evening through. You would not wish for him to change his mind about the marriage now, would you?"

If those simple words would come true it would be the happiest occasion in Jessica's life. But again she had to hold back her thoughts as she lightly shook her head at her cousin.

"Come then, sweet Jessica." Edmond took her cold hand within his own. "Dance this set with me and show everyone that you are not as dull and ill tempered as you have thus far appeared." He gave her no leave but to follow him onto the dance floor as he took her hand and swirled her across the floor, allowing her to lose herself in the rhythm of the softly flowing music in the company of the many guests of the manor house.

And indeed, with the music Jessica did lose herself, if only for a few seconds, her thoughts going far away and taking her to the cabin at the foot of the mountains. There, under the velvety darkness of the sky, the stars enhanced the earth with shimmering light. She remembered the soft, tranquil songs of the night crickets. Most of all she remembered how Star Hawk had taken her to his strong chest, his lips holding her own in a gentle pull upon her senses; the way his hands brushed across her naked flesh like the touch of a satiny brush of a butterfly's wing; the way their bodies joined and floated upon the fleecy clouds of no tomorrow. Alone and in love they had melted all barriers and scaled the outer walls of obstruction, their love climbing high upon the ladder that led heavenward and exploding with a fiery brilliance with the stars about the galaxy.

It was back to cold reality when the music came to a halt, and Edmond took his hand away, leaving Jessica standing in the middle of the ballroom floor. She was now cold and alone. It had only been a dream, she told herself as another came before her to take Edmond's place and again she was led about the dance floor. She would have naught but her dreams forever to content herself with, she told herself as a young man politely spoke to her as he now led her about the ballroom floor.

Was she not Miss Jessica Coltin? The woman who was soon to wed the earl? The young man had questioned, and with a sigh and her affirmative answer he had complimented her upon her beauty, his bold eyes telling more of his thoughts than his complimentary words. Everyone knew that in time the old Earl Henry's women became fair game to whomever that the earl would permit to participate in the hunt. And it was certain that this young man would be one of the first in the long line that would be waiting. For this woman would truly be worth any wait, the young man thought to himself.

One dance lead to another, and Jessica found herself swirling about the ballroom upon the arms of many young men. Until finally she had to beg for a moment to catch her breath and for a drink of something cool.

Her partner was the young son of nobility, and desiring nothing more than to please the young woman in his arms, he quickly nodded his head and offered, "Perhaps some champagne would be a welcome, then?" He smiled, entranced with her radiant beauty.

"Nay, lemonade would better suit me," she smiled, grateful for the young man's kindness toward her.

"I will be but a moment," he stated, and after helping her to a soft chair against the wall, he hurried to do her bidding.

Jessica sighed with some relief as she was allowed this small time to rest, and for a moment she forgot the sorry plight that had brought her to Locksbin Manor. She watched the many couples on the dance floor, enjoying the music as her dainty slipper tapped along with the melody. As her silver gaze fell upon the elderly matrons sitting in a small group near the opposite wall from her, she smiled at them, watching their fans lightly moving over their mouths as they whispered gossipy bits of information one to the other behind their small squares of embroidered lace and edging.

"I see that you are indeed feeling much better," Henry Locksbin said as he broke into her small reprieve from the harsh reality of her life. "Your cousin assured me that you were, and as I was watching you from the alcove, I saw for myself the pinkness of your glowing cheeks and the movement of your steps upon the dance floor."

He must have been spying upon her from the curtained alcove, Jessica thought as her frightened eyes went to that spot nearby and then back to the man at her side. "Yes, thank you, I do feel somewhat better," she finally stammered, "though I am sure that my coloring is from the turns about the dance floor."

"And I must say that you dance divinely," Henry complimented her as his eyes went to the expanse of bosom that was showing.

Jessica felt her body begin to shudder at his compliment upon her dancing abilities. Always there seemed to be undercurrents to his tone that left her chilled and frightened.

"Your body, even though swollen with child, seems so sensuous and free to the rhythm of the musicians, it makes me wonder about your other abilities, as well." His voice was low and suggestive, and again the lace-edged handkerchief was pulled from his pocket and he wiped away the small dribble coming from his lower lip.

Jessica drew herself back in her chair as she witnessed the fired glare he directed at her. "My lord, I must beg you to understand." She tried to remind him of their bargain to wait until after the birth of her baby before he would claim her as his wife.

But before she could finish the young man came back. "Here is your drink, my lady." He proffered the glass of cool lemonade and stood before Jessica, his eyes going from her now pale features to the earl standing so near to her chair, and he observed the small, set eyes looking upon Jessica with a lustful glaze.

"Away with you, young pup!" The earl waved his dampened handkerchief in the young man's direction as though shooing him away, but the latter's eyes were riveted upon the woman in the chair.

"But sir," the young man started, "the lady is sitting this dance out with me instead of taking a turn upon the dance floor."

"Begone now!" The earl of Locksbin shouted, and drew the attention of most of those in the room, causing a small miss in the music as one of the musicians looked across the floor.

The young man knew well enough when to leave the scene, and with a stiff bow first in the earl's direction and then in Jessica's, he was gone.

"My lord there surely was no call. . . ."

"Do not rebuke me, my lady." He cocked a brow upon her, and with a bold move placed his hand upon her naked forearm above the silver bracelet that he had given her that afternoon. Taking the chair next to her own, he sat as he rubbed the tender flesh with his pudgy thumb. "I see that you are wearing my gift," he said as his eyes went over the smoothness of the skin beneath the silver circlet.

"It is quite lovely. I thank you for it and the necklace." Jessica gulped back her fear and revulsion of him.

"They are indeed dim compared to your beauty," he breathed near her cheek. "When I purchased them I thought of your petal-soft beauty. I even imagined what they would look like upon your creamy, smooth body, with them your only covering."

Jessica, feeling many sets of eyes upon the earl and herself, thought to make light of his manner. "I am afraid that you surely make jest of this encumbered form of mine, my lord." She looked first upon his face but then quickly away as she saw the steaming lust boldly displayed upon his features.

"Nay, I make no jest, Jessica." The fingers again boldly caressed her smooth skin and drew a quiver of revulsion from her. "I spoke to you this day of my thoughts upon your condition." Again the dark eyes shifted from her face and lowered to her midriff. The protruding of her belly was barely discernible under the abundance of the silver material of her gown. "You far outshine many a fair maiden with a much slimmer figure."

Not knowing what to say, Jessica again tried to put the manner of his pursuit to her in a lighter mode. "You do indeed jest now, my lord. There are many here who would easily stir the eye of such a man as yourself."

"Only you, fair Jessica, at this moment stir my eyes and every other portion of me." Taking a firmer grip upon her upper arm, the earl pulled her up tightly against his chest. "Come with me now to my chambers!"

"Nay, I cannot!" Jessica balked at his horrible invitation and tried to pull her arm out of his grip.

For a man of his age, the earl was strong where the pursuit of women was concerned, and without a blink of his dark, small eyes he held on to her arm, not caring if any were watching his actions, for he was too gone in his lust and need of this woman. "Aye, you will come with me, my lady." He stood and pulled her from her chair, and in so doing knocked the chair backwards upon the dance floor.

Jessica desperately looked about for some kind of help, but those who were watching looked upon the old earl and his young betrothed with some kind of queer enjoyment for the moment. When Jessica's eyes found theirs they turned their heads, afraid to venture into this line of play with the earl of Locksbin. He was a most powerful man, and all those here in his home this eve were aware of what could well happen to them if they stepped between him and the woman he was to soon wed.

"But the ball is still being held," Jessica finally gasped, thinking of this as her only out for the moment. If only he would release her for a time, she would think of some way in which to free herself from his vile hold upon her.

"The ball is at a finish for the two of us this eve. This whole silly affair was but for this present turn of the hand."

Jessica looked upon him as slow dawning came to her. "You mean that you held this entire affair just to. . . ."

"Indeed, you are quite correct, my dear, just to. . . . But we shall see what there is to just to . . . in a short time now. Come with me!" He pulled at her as he started from the dance floor.

Trying to think of anything to sway him, Jessica shouted aloud, "But Edmond!"

"Edmond was quite delighted with my plan, so do not worry about your cousin."

Jessica gasped as she pulled back, "No I will not go with you!" For the first time she thought of herself as more than her cousin's chattel to be bargained for and passed about without any feelings of her own. The price that her cousin had set upon her was too high. Even for the man she loved and his people she could not submit to this vile old man's lust. "There has been a terrible mistake made. I will not go with you, and I shall not wed you. Your very touch fills me with loathing and revulsion."

Now all attention was fully drawn to the couple as the earl of Locksbin with a glare jerked Jessica up tightly next to him, his hand upon her back, punishing in its forcefulness. "You will do as you are told. You are not the one to change your mind. You shall be my bride, and if you do not come willingly with me this eve there will be many a night that you will regret your hasty actions."

Jessica looked about with panic at the faces around her as she tried to see the features of her cousin, but he was nowhere about, and she reasoned that he had probably disappeared knowing that the results of this evening would be what they now were. Again she tried to pull free from the earl, but as he placed his other wrinkled hand upon her other arm and began forcefully to drag her behind him, she felt her entire body beginning to grow weak, her mind beginning to cloud with her fear and the horrible thoughts that were swirling about in her brain. This vile, ugly man was going to take her to his chambers and there do to her what no other man but her husband had done, who had only touched her with love. The earl of Locksbin had no love for her—only a fierce, horrible lust that consumed him.

It was with a cry of utter despair and fright that Jessica slowly began to slip to the marble floor. But as her senses blurred and a fuzzy haze of unreality settled about her, she imagined the arms of her abuser being pulled from her and a towering, vengeful force standing boldly over her.

The words seemed to float to her ears out of her haze and touch her heart like a burning cinder. "Take your hands from my wife, you filth." And as the earl was forcefully shoved across the ballroom floor, everyone stepped back and gasped aloud as one, the music stopped, the laughter died away, the tinkling of glasses stilled, and a hush settled on everything as all eyes were directed to the magnificent man standing tall and bronzed over the fallen silver angel.

Now a long, wicked blade was drawn as the avenger stepped toward his victim and the earl of Locksbin lay panting with his own terror at the sight standing above him. "Stop him!" he whimpered aloud to any who would do his bidding, and as a few brave souls made as though to move in his direction to defend him, a shout was heard from the french double doors, halting all steps.

"I would not be so much as daring to breathe a light breath, if I were you, my laddies." It was Ollie Bengiman standing there boldly, with Joshua at his side, their fists wrapped about twin barrels of pistols aimed at the chest of anyone who would care to take their dare.

"They are but two," the earl shouted now as he took in the situation with his frightened eyes.

"Not quite," came a call from an open window, and then another and still another, until all the crew of the *Silver Star* were stepping into the ball-room or perched outside a window, with either flintlock or pistol held in their hands.

For a blinding second Star Hawk began to reach down to the fat old man with hate and vengeance stamped across his features. He had watched through the alcove where he had slipped in from the window and had observed the treatment of his wife at this vile man's hands. His heart at this moment desired nothing more than this man's blood upon his knife, his life taken from his fat, wrinkled body. But as he would have reached out toward him, a small moan came to his ears, and thinking of nothing else at that moment but his woman, his splendid body went to Jessica, and with an ease he bent down and gathered his Silver Star to his chest.

For a second Jessica truly thought that she had passed miraculously from this life into another. She felt the firm, naked arms of her lover, his breath softly caressing her cheek, his warmth

329

seeming to shield her from all hurt, and as she opened her eyes slowly and focused them upon the cherished face above her own with a cry of joy, she clutched her arms about his strong neck. For it was the same beloved face that had come out of the large group of Indians, that night of her marriage, it was the same boldly painted face of the man she loved with all of her being. "Star Hawk," she wept aloud against the smooth, broad chest that she loved so well, "Take me from this place, please take me home."

No more words needed to be said. Star Hawk needed to hear no more than these loving words. The whimpering fat earl lying upon the ballroom floor was forgotten for the moment as the tall, proud Indian warrior's ebony eyes blazed into the silver jewels of the woman in his arms. "You are safe now from all harm, Silver Star. None will ever again take you from my side." And with these words, some inner prick of memory stirred. "Where is your cousin, Silver Star?" he lightly questioned, holding her against his chest as his dark eyes went about the crowded ballroom.

Jessica did not have to look about to know that Edmond was not here at the manor. She had not seen him for hours, and according to the earl he had been privy to the obnoxious man's foul plans. Obviously he could not face his cousin knowing that the look in her eyes would hold him guilty. "He has fled to the city, Star Hawk."

Without another word Star Hawk turned to the tiny alcove and swiftly disappeared with Jessica through the velvet curtains, a twitter of excited voices now erupting throughout the ballroom as, just as swiftly, the men with the guns held upon the earl's guests also disappeared from sight.

The earl, seeing that he was safe now that Jessica's husband had gone from the ballroom, rose to his feet. "Sound the alarm!" he shouted to the group in general as they all stared at him. "My guards on the grounds will find them and make them pay for this insult." He brushed harshly at the dirt upon his puce-colored jacket and matching pants, his sputtering now turning into screams as he called aloud for his guards.

The housekeeper, Mrs. Borden, was the only one to respond to his calling, though, and with some dignity she offered, "I am afraid, sir, that the guards have been overpowered and are all now tied up in the front parlor." Seeing her employer in such a state, a small gleam of something akin to glee sparkled in her eyes; indeed she was the one who had opened the portals and allowed Miss Jessica's husband and his men free run of the house.

More gasps of surprises were now sounded as the guests heard what the housekeeper was saying, and small groups now formed and speculated upon what they had just witnessed. Many of the elder matrons' fans fluttered as they whispered, "Did you see what that man was wearing, Sybil? The large one that took Earl Henry's bride to be?"

And the reply, "It must have been some form of underclothing, my dear. And did you see that body? I swear, if my James had ever looked like that I would never allow him out of the house."

"My dear, if your James looked like that dark

331

Adonis you would have to be fighting the women from coming to visit." Then there was tittering behind those matronly fans, and more smirks and giggles, all in agreement that the bold, impressive stranger with the paint of silver and black streaks upon his cheek was by far worth all of the excitement that he had caused and well worth the spoiling of a good ball. For surely this eve would be the talk of every woman in London for months to come.

Once outside the manor grounds, Star Hawk and the crew of the *Silver Star* hurried toward the coast. Their ship was lying off to sea at anchor, and Billy was waiting for their return.

Star Hawk cradled his wife tenderly in his arms as though fearing that she would again be taken from him. His long strides kept apace with the others, and with Ollie and the crew all watching for any unexpected visitors, they were quickly at the coast and climbing into the small boats that were waiting for them.

Jessica had little time even to think as they hurried along, everything seemed to have happened by so quickly. All that she could realize at the moment was that she was, in fact, safe, she was once again being held by the man she loved and the only one she could ever love. She held to his neck, not wishing ever to release him. "Star Hawk," she whispered next to his ear, "I don't understand how everything happened." But as he seated her next to him in the small boat and wrapped his strong arms about her, she felt again the safe security that always enveloped her when she was in his arms.

"There will be plenty of time for you to learn about everything, my love." Star Hawk kept one arm about her shoulders and the other hand he tenderly placed over her swelling belly. From the first moment he had seen her next to the earl he had noticed a change. Star Hawk had devoured her with his ebony eyes the moment he had caught a glimpse of her, and the slight protruding of her waistline was not missed by his hungry gaze.

"You will be a father soon," she whispered next to his cheek, still not able really to believe that this was truly happening to her. It seemed a miracle that she was once again with her husband.

The day before when Star Hawk had heard Ollie's solicitor say that rumor had it that Jessica Coltin was with child, he had discounted the information, not thinking it possible, but now, with the excitement of the moment, with having her back and safely in his arms, he let his entire being glow with the words that she had just spoken: "You will be a father soon, you will be a father soon," his heart sang with the sound of her sweet words, his chest swelling with his pride and his love for this woman of his heart.

In minutes Jessica was once again in Star Hawk's arms as he carried her up the rope ladder and they boarded the *Silver Star*, her eyes going to the prow of the ship and reading the name Silver Star. "The ship is named after me?" As the entire crew stood about her, she shook her fire-gold head. "I don't understand any of this."

333

"Her name was the *Fair Bella*. We be thinking a more fitting one would be the *Silver Star*." It was Joshua who spoke up with a large grin. "And we be her crew ma'am, and ready to do your service, or that of our cap'n."

"Her captain?" Jessica turned and looked at Star Hawk who stood next to her and slowly nodded his head. "You are the captain of this ship?"

"I am afraid I am," he stated softly, and then after a moment, as it all settled in upon her, Jessica had a grin of her own, and soon a round of giggles escaped her as she fell against her husband's sturdy chest. "Edmond will be furious when he finds out that the *Fair Belle* has a new master."

Everyone now looked at the captain's wife as though her experiences had been too much for her. She explained, "This is one of the Coltin ships. I am truly her owner, and you, my love, are certainly her master."

Whoops and hollers were shouted as all the men broke down with laughter. Ollie Bengiman's voice was the loudest as he exclaimed with much well-deserved relief over this brush of good luck. "At least now you will not all hang for piracy," he shouted over the din.

"Indeed not," Jessica said haughtily, her hand protectively going to her husband's chest at the thought of someone's trying to harm him now that she had him once again at her side. "All that I own is my husband's, as my father's will states."

Again the hoorahs and laughter filled the deck of the *Silver Star,* and with a look of longing and long-denied passion, Star Hawk swept Jessica up in his arms. "Set our sails for the docks of London, men. Ollie must get back to his inn, and I still have a score to settle with my wife's kin. But for this night Silver Star has had much too much excitement. Her condition is most delicate, for you see, men," he paused, taking his dark gaze from his bride's and then slowly settling it upon each of the men who were now truly his closest friends, "I am to be a father soon."

The shouts now were deafening as the crew of the *Silver Star* and Ollie Bengiman pounded each other upon the back, and someone brought forth a keg of ale and passed mugs to each man, toasts being called and happiness assailing all as the *Silver Star* set her course back for the docks of London.

With crystal tears in her silver eyes, Jessica clutched Star Hawk's neck as he eased the cabin portal shut and softly secured them from the outside world. "I thought that I would never see you again." Now she finally wept aloud, her sobs shaking her body as her thoughts filled with the horror of the past months. "Edmond threatened that he would have your entire village wiped out by the army as a favor to him owed by an officer. I thought I had no choice but to go along with all that he planned. But at the last minute I could not bear the thought of that terrible earl touching me." Her wracking sobs filled the cabin as she gulped out her words, showing Star Hawk some of the terror that she had endured.

Star Hawk sat down upon the bed with her still in his arms and gently rocked and soothed her. "You are my life circle, Silver Star. No amount of time or distance can ever keep me from your side. My heart only beats when you are within my sight. Without you, my heartbeat is shallow, as is my substance and soul. You are the very link of my life, the breath of my body. Your cousin's words are like the whistling wind. They will not come about. My people are strong, and you are one of their own. A threat to you is a threat to all, and they would all stand at my side to protect you. Your cousin will be dealt with, and his threats will no longer linger but shall die upon the night breeze."

Slowly, as she absorbed his words, the terror that she had been living with began to diminish, and she responded to him. "I have missed you so much. Each moment that I was awake I thought of only you, and even while I slept my dreams were of your touch, your lips against my own."

"We are the same then, for I held your vision in my every thought. The Great Spirit has brought us together, and nothing will ever separate us again." His lips gently touched upon hers, as though he feared that he was in a dream and that at any moment he would awaken and find his arms empty. But with her soft moan of delight his lips slanted upon her own, and he pulled her against him.

"I would have you lie with me," he softly whispered next to her lips as he gently eased the glittering pins from her hair and ran his fingers through the fire gold that he had dreamed of so many long nights.

Jessica did not speak but willingly helped with his undressing of her, his large, but oh so gentle hands slipping the gown from her shoulders and leaving it lying about her ankles.

Star Hawk's breath caught in his throat as he view her lovely perfection once again. He had looked for this moment for so long that it now seemed almost a torture as he feasted his ebony gaze upon her creamy-soft skin.

A blush quickly came over Jessica's features as she felt the dark eyes upon her body. He had not seen her undressed since she had discovered she was carrying his child, and in these months her body had changed considerably. She was no longer the trim, willowy girl he had known and married. Her stomach was quite large, and even her breasts were twice their natural size.

"You are so beautiful," he breathed aloud, his glance enveloping her in a world of sheer love and desire. Lifting her, he laid her upon the bed, his large hands lingering upon her flesh as though not able to feel enough.

Jessica knew in that instant that his words were those of a man completely in love with his woman. His child growing within her body only added to the depth of his feelings. "Oh, my love, my love," she breathed, "It has been too long since I have known your love." She reached out to him and brought him down upon the bed beside her, but Star Hawk lightly resisted, kissing each one of her fingers and drawing his mouth lightly down her arms to the smooth indentation between her arm and breast.

337

His mouth seemed to set her aflame as he stood over her and licked and nibbled, and as he slowly made his way to her full, throbbing breasts, Jessica gasped and writhed beneath his ministrations, her need for him mounting to such proportions that she moaned aloud with her desire.

"You hold all of my desires within your body, you are the beauty which fills my eyes, all of my tomorrows, and my longings of today. My soul cries out for the joining of our flesh." Slowly his hand caressed the mounding of her belly, and then his lips made a path of delicious, sensuous kisses to where his child lay secured, his mouth tasting again the sweetness that was his woman's alone. "I would wish not to cause you any hurt." He looked into the passion-filled silver eyes below him, his heart beating at a rapid tempo.

"You could never bring me harm, my husband. You who love me so well could only bring me joy." Jessica welcomed him gladly to her, not wishing for another moment to pass that would keep them separate.

And as he held his body above hers and quenched the fires of her arousal with the gentle easing of his maleness, she was at last complete. She melted from within as the burning ecstasy consumed and raged. And Star Hawk, holding back in his concern for her delicate condition, was more than content to move with an ease and rhythm that delighted and thrilled, quickly losing himself in her body's softness and enflaming touch. As he brought her to the outer peaks of loves searing realms, he also tottered upon the very edges of his senses, his large body consumed

338

with raging embers of light and dark, and with a mighty groan of fulfillment and release, he was spiraled over the precipice and was left for a fathomless time hanging upon the very streaks of flashing light. And then slowly, ever so slowly, he was swept downward, drifting upon fleecy clouds of softness, until again he could draw a breath and his voice could capture the name of his love.

Jessica also knew once again the joy of total fulfillment, and as she lay gasping and clutching the strong back of the man she loved, she felt tears of joy fill her eyes and gently lie upon her cheeks. "I love you so much, Star Hawk," she wept, all the feelings of her heart expressed in few words.

Not in that moment able to express the feelings within his own breast, Star Hawk drew her closer to him, his lips tasting of the joy of her tears and their finding of each other.

For a time they were held thus, their bodies drawn tightly together, their lips kissing and tasting, but as the babe between them gently stirred within its mother's womb, Star Hawk eased back somewhat, a large grin upon his face as he placed a hand upon her abdomen. "He will be a mighty warrior and a brave leader for his people, my love." His ebony gaze held hers.

"Or she will be a beautiful Indian princess, my husband." Jessica lightly laughed and eagerly kissed him upon his strong chin.

"The first should be a son, but if he is an Indian princess, I shall be just as satisfied for the second to be a son. To have you as the mother of my children is all that I shall ever ask."

Jessica smiled into his love-filled eyes. "Truly, this is the way that it will ever be." She sighed aloud and snuggled her body next to his, for she now believed that it had been destined for the two of them to be together. How else could he have found her at Sweet Oaks, and now again here, so far away in England?

"You are truly my gift from the Great Spirit, and our children will be made by our love and ruled by his hand. Their paths will be straight and strong, they will lead our people as the Great Spirit would direct them."

Jessica felt content and at peace in this strong man's arms. Her ears were filling with his words about their future, and her heart expanded with the love that she felt for him. Surely all that he said would come to pass, she thought as she contentedly slipped into a gentle sleep.

Star Hawk smiled in his own moments of peace as he heard her gentle breathing and saw that she was asleep. His hand lay upon the mound of their creation, his senses filled with the feeling of her soft body, and his thoughts dwelt with the fact that here beneath his hand was a tiny, perfect life that they had created, lying in its mother's warmth and awaiting for the right time to greet the world and its sire.

A large sigh escaped Star Hawk as he thought about what could have been. If he had somehow not found Jessica, she and his child would have been lost to him. His hands tightened about her, and a small moan escaped her lips, but he was not yet ready to release her as these black thoughts filled him. He could not allow something

340

like this ever to happen again. There was more now at stake than his love for Jessica, there was also his child.

A fierce protectiveness welled within his chest. He would find Edmond DeVaugn when they reached London, and he would put an end to such worries. Her kin was evil and unworthy to have guardianship over such a priceless object as Jessica. Again he envisioned the earl of Locksbin's fat, ugly hands upon her, and he felt a raging black fury come over him. But as Jessica stirred in her sleep he felt the peace of her love settle quickly back about him. He could keep her from the hands of such men as the earl, but her cousin was another matter that would have to be settled. He could not chance that Edmond DeVaugn would post a reward for her capture and return to his vile hands. Tomorrow would see an end to these fears that were now filling him with a cold dread.

The morning tide found the *Silver Star* tied securely against the docks of London. Jessica stirred, and in her dreams reached out and felt the body lying so close to her own, and a tender smile graced her petal-soft lips.

Star Hawk had awakened the moment the ship had made port, and for a time he lay enjoying the vision of his wife in his arms. Her soft brow titillated him with her beauty, and as she reached out to him, he smiled. How he loved this woman. She was all that he would ever need or desire.

As though feeling the dark eyes upon her, Jessica slowly opened her silver eyes, a smile of pure happiness radiating from them. "Before I opened my eyes I prayed that I was not dreaming this whole thing, and that I would not, somehow awake and find myself back at the earl's manor." She smiled and lightly kissed him upon the cheek, now able to make light of the terror that she had been living with, as she knew for sure that she was once again safe and secure next to her husband.

"Never again will you have to fear. Each morning shall be thus for us. I shall not leave your side again, Silver Star."

Jessica laughed lightly and snuggled herself up tightly to his large frame, her belly large and imposing but gently held next to his own. "And what will the other warriors think of such a brave?" She raised a fine brow toward him. "Will they not wonder if you don't hunt or travel with them to scout for the needs of your tribe? Will I not be the one they will blame for the mighty Star Hawk's strangeness of manner when we return to our village, my husband?"

For a moment Star Hawk rested his gaze upon her, reading the wisdom in her words and trying to understand her full meaning. "You would have me leave you alone in our lodge?" His arms reached out and encircled her as he remembered the empty nights of longing with her taken from him.

"I would have the beauty of what we feel for each other grow with each new day. I would not wish to see it wither because you feel less than the man that you are. We cannot live in fear of the unknown, my husband. We must search with our eyes open for that which lurks about and threatens to devour us, and when we find that evil we must not harbor our fear of it, but set it from us so that we can go on living." She remembered her own fear at the hands of her cousin and how it had almost destroyed her, for when she had realized that the fate being offered to her was far worse than her own inner fears, it had almost been too late. If Star Hawk had not rescued her when he had, she would have been destroyed by the earl and Edmond because she had been too afraid to stand up to them.

"You are wise for your young years, my love." Star Hawk softly kissed the tip of her nose. "But your words are true, and you know me well. I would soon be but an empty shell of the man that I am if I could not face that which threatens me and live my life to the fullest. I have you back at my side now, and that is all that truly matters."

"Yes, that is all that matters," Jessica softly whispered as her lips touched lightly upon his, and they were lost for a time to the taste and senses of each other.

Each kiss, each caress was given with tender consideration, lingering and loving as Star Hawk bent above his wife, his mouth taking hers in a possessive, tender hold, his exploring heightening their steaming desires. He lightly nibbled at her ears and down over her creamy shoulders, his heated tongue enflaming and teasing, his large, loving hands growing bolder as their passions mounted. His heated breath caused her to quiver as he whispered soft Indian love words in her

343

ears, and as his mouth again lowered and roamed down her throat to her breasts, Jessica clung to him with her need.

A golden sphere of pleasant, hazy intoxication seemed to hold the pair upon the bed, Jessica's body leaning toward her husband's, not wanting him to ever release her. Wishing only for more and more food for her craving body, she wrapped her sleek arms about his muscle-corded neck and pressed her full bare breasts against the broad expanse of smooth, bronzed chest.

The incredible feel of Jessica's hard-tipped breasts and her velvety-smooth satin skin drove Star Hawk into a near frenzy of complete desire.

Jessica lost herself in the cool sweetness of his lips and moaned aloud with her desire. She was enflamed by a world of bittersweet passions, easily losing herself with a maelstorm of throbbing, sensual pleasures sweeping over her, encasing her being, surrounding her senses with the taste of his bronzed skin beneath her lips, his hard body under her fingertips, his male heat filling her and carrying her upon the sensuous journey of shared love.

With an animal growl from deep within Star Hawk's throat, his heart pulsating upon her heart, his mouth plundering her mouth, his thighs covering her silky-smooth thighs, they were joined by the act of love.

Star Hawk's lips went to Jessica's ear, into which he lovingly whispered husky, incoherent words of love and endearment. Anticipating their desired effect, his body worshipped hers with a tenderness and gentleness that left her trembling.

344

Jessica's husband's lovemaking reached deep into her soul, her body pulsating with the feel of his hard, strong body over hers and touching off explosive sparks within the very foundations of her being and bringing them up as though an erupting volcano were melting all obstacles and barriers. All that would ever matter was that they were at last together; all the world could pass them by but as long as they were one, they could endure.

And as deep within she scaled the very tips of all tomorrows and her body rose up to meet his, his name burst from her lips. "Star Hawk, Star Hawk!" Her cries circled about the ship's cabin, her hands clutching his broad tan back. And when she was saturated with love, he brought her to the very pinnacle of her womanhood.

At that same moment that she found this all-consuming climax, Star Hawk's ebony eyes gazed down into his wife's passion-filled face, and something in her look touched off a quickening feeling deep within his being. He loved this woman with his entire being. She was his life, his blood, his very breath, and as he watched her need for him being fulfilled, his large hands tenderly stroked the creamy smoothness of her cheeks, his lips once more seeking out the honey taste of hers and his body now slowly exploding into a thousand erupting cinders deep within. And with a shout of pure rapture he spilled forth the substance of his being, his body atremble as he gasped aloud from the fiery sensations.

They held each other as the magic of the moment was dispelled and settled about them. It was Star Hawk who finally spoke. "Never in my dreams could I envision such a moment." His lips caught hold of Jessica's, and for a long time they drank of their love.

"It would seem this moment that never have I been away from your side. Your presence brings me to such heights that I can but think of this time, here now, within your arms," Jessica whispered next to his lips before once again he pulled her tightly against him.

It was only a short time later that a light knock sounded on the door and Ollie Bengiman's booming voice broke upon the pleasant interlude. "Are you fully decent within?" he shouted, giving the couple a minute before barging through the doorway.

Star Hawk had only time to pull his breechcloth about his loins and Jessica to snatch up a blanket about her breasts before the door was pushed wide and Ollie strode into the ship's cabin with a large grin upon his face.

"I must say, for a sea captain you sure keep late hours of the morn," Ollie joked as he came to stand before his friend. "But I can see now that you are well rested, so I can be assuming that this is your reason." Again a small hearty chuckle escaped him.

"We are at the docks?" Star Hawk tried to keep the elder man's mind from where it was obviously going.

"Aye, for a short time now, and Josh and some of the boys have set out already to find this Edmond DeVaugn."

Star Hawk stood bold and proud before his friend, a slight smile upon his features as he remembered only the other morning when Joshua and this same raspy old innkeeper had all but come to blows. And now here was Ollie Bengiman calling his first mate Josh, as though they were longtime friends. "I will dress and go into the city myself to confront Silver Star's cousin. I cannot allow him to go unpunished for what he has done to my family."

Neither Jessica nor Ollie could deny him. Both knew that it would do little good to plead with him to turn the *Silver Star* about and go back home. The fear in Star Hawk that had to be faced and put to rest was Edmond DeVaugn. For he knew that as long as he lived there was still the chance that he would steal into his life and try to lay claim to that which belonged only to him.

"Then I will step out and allow you to dress. I brought some clothing for Jessica. They will perhaps be a mite big, but they will do until she can be getting better." He held out a pair of Billy's trousers and a shirt that also belonged to the younger man. Billy, being the smallest of the crew, had eagerly agreed to share his wardrobe with their captain's wife.

"Thank you, Ollie," Jessica responded from the bed, and then with a small smile added, "it is truly a pleasure to at last talk with you Ollie. I am afraid that last evening was quite hectic, and I did not get the chance to properly meet you, although I am still afraid that I am not quite in the proper position to make your acquaintance." She

347

looked down to the coverlet held tightly in her fist and against her chest.

Ollie beamed his pleasure down upon the young beauty in the captain's bed. Indeed, he thought his young friend had done well for himself. This was the most beautiful woman he had ever set his eyes on who also had a kind heart. This combination alone was quite rare. "You have yourself a fine lad here in Star Hawk, lassy. I wish you both well from the bottom of my heart, and if ever again I can be of any assistance, do not hesitate to call upon me."

"Are you going back to the city soon?" Jessica questioned with some disappointment. She had hoped to get to know Ollie better aboard ship.

"Aye, lassie, I have an inn to run and have already been gone far too long. Old Nell has too kind a heart and will be handing out free ale and mutton to whoever speaks a sad tale."

"I am pleased, then, that I was at least able to meet you. For my husband has spoken quite often of you in the past." Jessica looked to Star Hawk as did her husband's close friend.

"And I also thank you, good friend." Star Hawk, feeling the eyes upon him, spoke softly.

Ollie Bengiman wrapped his arms about Star Hawk and said to the tall Indian warrior, "You brought back a touch of my youth, lad. I wouldn't have missed it for the world. Now you be taking care of this young lass and the wee one that she will soon have. I taught you well how to read and write, so you had best write me and let me know what the babe be, a son or a daughter. I shall be waiting to hear the news." And with that he hugged Star Hawk tightly to him one last time and turned to leave.

A tear formed in Star Hawk's eyes with the reality of again another departing of this dear old friend. "May the Great Spirit guide your steps, good friend," he called to Ollie's retreating back.

With the elder man gone from the cabin, for a few moments the couple looked in silence at each other, but quickly Jessica jumped to her feet, and wishing to see the smile back upon her husband's handsome features, she went to his side with the clothes that Ollie had brought to her. "Do you think that they will fit, Star Hawk? Do I dare wear a man's clothes? What will people think of me," she said with a giggle. He smiled at her sally, and then with a shout of happiness that she was again in his embrace, he swung her about the cabin, her silky body filling his hands as she clutched Billy's shirt and trousers tightly to her naked form.

"You will look beautiful in anything that rests upon your lovely body." He grinned as he at last set her to her feet. "And here upon this ship I am the captain and the law, and only what I care matters, so do not worry about other's thoughts."

"I do think that it will be pleasant to be wearing breeches. It gets so tiresome wearing dresses at all times. The stays and petticoats are such a bother, I have longed so often for my doeskin dresses and moccasins," she sighed.

"You are truly a native at heart, my love." Star Hawk took up the pair of small breeches and held them out for her to step into, and with loving hands he buttoned up the front and pulled the rope belt securely about her bulging middle. Even in these men's clothes with her hair streaming about her shoulders in tangled disarray, she was breathtaking. The glow upon her cheeks added to her incredible beauty. "You are indeed quite lovely," he breathed, and as his eyes set to her belly once again, he noticed that she was well into her pregnancy. If the child were to be born in his village with all that was familiar, their journey back home would have to be taken without further delay.

"What is it, Star Hawk?" Jessica questioned as she saw the playful gleam leave his eyes to be replaced with a light of concern. "Is there something amiss?" She worried at the look in his dark eyes. Had he soon found some disfavor with her ungainly shape?

"It is nothing, my love. I was but wondering as to the time of the child's birthing. I would have him born in our village where my mother and Cloud Dreamer will be able to be with you."

Jessica smiled softly. "Do not worry. There is plenty of time. There should be at least two more months before he will wish to be freed from his warm haven."

"My child does not know how lucky he is to lie within your warm, nurturing body. I would rather be there than any other place that I can think of." He pulled her into his arms and gently kissed her lips, leaving her melting against him.

As he let his fingers run through the fire gold of her curls he said lightly, "Come and sit. I have a comb here upon the bureau." He led her to a chair, and then picking up the comb, he stood over her and stroked the tangled waves. It had been so long since he had been allowed such a simple pleasure.

The moment was destroyed as a loud knock sounded upon the outside portal and Joshua burst into the cabin, his eyes wide as he took in his fierce captain standing over his beautiful wife and lovingly brushing out her waist-length hair. "I be truly sorry, cap'n sir," he stumbled but quickly was held in his tracks.

Jessica turned to the young man with a smile, and for a second Star Hawk's dark look seared the man who had disturbed them in this moment of peace, but as quickly he noticed the excited look upon Joshua's face, and bending down, he lightly placed a tender kiss upon his wife's cheek. "I shall only be a moment, love." He walked toward the cabin door, not wishing to speak of anything disturbing in front of Jessica. "I will have the cook bring you something to eat," he added before pulling the door shut behind himself and Joshua.

Jessica sighed out her happiness as she was left alone in the ship's cabin. The ordeal she had been living in now seemed far behind her as she remembered the wonderful night of love she had experienced in Star Hawk's arms last eve and then this morn. Nothing else mattered but this man, and if she had not fully realized it before, she now knew that he was her life. She would follow wherever he would lead and be happy with the lot that he would choose for them. She needed only his loving strength to see her through.

Outside the cabin door Joshua now spoke softly

to his captain. "The bloody blackguard has done flown, cap'n. We went to his town house, and his manservant there said as how he come late last night and gathered his clothes. DeVaugn's ship, the *Ruby Heart* left the docks before midnight last."

"Did his man say where he was bound?" Star Hawk could not believe that Jessica's cousin would leave London so quickly. He had assumed that he would have planned to stay until after he had wedded his cousin off to the earl of Locksbin.

"The servant said that he left for the colonies. He told the man that his cousin would be staying at Locksbin Manor until the wedding, so there was no need for him to be waiting around. He had plenty of business to be keeping him busy back in the colonies."

"Are all the men aboard ship, then?" Star Hawk looked down the companionway as though already anxious to be giving chase to the man who had so darkly come into his life.

"Aye, cap'n, it still be early and they are all still upon the *Silver Star* and ready to find your man." Joshua also was anxious to find this Edmond De-Vaugn. He had always had a sense of fair play as far as women were concerned, and after himself witnessing the foul hands of the earl of Locksbin upon the captain's wife and seeing the innocent, sweet beauty of Jessica, he was more than ready to vent his pent-up fury. And every member of the crew of the *Silver Star* had already voiced these same thoughts.

"Then set our course for the colonies, the New

Orleans docks. Run us full sails, and perhaps we shall outdistance the *Ruby Heart* in only a few days." The rage was deep within the ebony eyes as for a moment Star Hawk thought of the man who had once again slipped through his hands. It would not be for long, though, he swore to himself.

"Aye, aye, sir. We be out to sea then right away." Joshua stood in the narrow companionway as though he still was plagued with something upon his mind.

"Is there something else, Joshua?" Star Hawk asked.

"Aye, cap'n," he said softly, and at Star Hawk's questioning look he nervously went on. "It be you, sir. Me and the boys were sharing a mug last eve and decided that Injun or not we ain't never had no better ship's cap'n. You be at our side through the thick of things and the thin of 'em, and we be a-wanting ye to be knowing that we be all of the same mind. Yer wife is safe as long as there be a one of us drawing breath, she be a real lady, we can all be telling that right off. And we wouldn't be a-standing by and watching any harm coming to her or the wee babe within her." There—he had said what the crew had told him to, and what he himself felt deep in his heart.

Star Hawk looked upon this friend for a full moment without quite knowing what to say in answer. It was not often that a white man stood at an Indian's side against other white men. But he had found out that all men were not alike. Some did not judge a man by the color of skin or race, some took a man at his worth and spirit. A slow, lazy smile replaced the serious look upon Star Hawk's dark features. "I am glad to know that my wife will be safe then, Joshua. This is all that I could ever wish. Tell the others that I thank them also."

"I sure be a-doing that now, cap'n." Joshua grinned and then stepped around the larger man and started down the companionway to see about his duties. "I be telling cook to bring that tray, cap'n. There be no need fer ye to be too long away from yer lady's side." And with that he was gone, Star Hawk for a moment longer watching his retreating back.

He marveled for a second upon his good fortune in friends, but then quickly his thoughts went back to Edmond DeVaugn. The *Silver Star* was a fleet ship, fast and sleek as the wind blew in her sails. They would overcome the *Ruby Heart,* he was sure, and then he would settle with his wife's kin. But with this thought some small stroke of fear stilled his heart. What danger could there still be here upon the seas for his young wife if they did meet up with their foe? Could he keep Jessica from harm's way? He could well trust his men to fight brave and strong, each one would give his all to protect his wife. But would this be enough?

Chapter Thirteen

Life aboard the *Silver Star* became peaceful and routine as she swept across the seas, sails filling with wind as she put the motherland behind her, her destination the port of New Orleans. To Jessica, after her horrible ordeal at her cousin's hands, life aboard ship was a wonderful dream come true. With each day that passed, her separation from her husband seemed to recede more into a remoter time. She now knew only love, the strength and tenderness of strong arms holding her tightly throughout the long nights, and the look of love and passion mixed as the ebony eyes gazed at her.

No more did she live under the dire threat of some terrible fate befalling the ones she loved in retribution for her own transgressions. She was free here aboard the *Silver Star.* She could love and be loved. She did not have to endure the threat of an unloved husband or experience the verbal and physical abuse that her own kin would have seen her suffer. No, here next to Star Hawk, and surrounded by the good men of the *Silver Star,* she was happy.

The only small blight on these joyous feelings came over her when she stood on deck and her silver eyes looked out at the sea. For somewhere out there on that large, blue vastness was the ship called the *Ruby Heart,* with her cousin on it making his way back to New Orleans, not knowing that the *Silver Star,* with each hour that passed was gaining on him.

Jessica had overheard Star Hawk and Joshua talking outside the cabin door last evening. They had spoken of their calculations and voiced the opinion that the *Silver Star* should overtake the *Ruby Heart* sometime within the next two days. This thought alone sent shivers coursing down Jessica's spine with the images it brought to her mind.

Surely, she reasoned, there would be a terrible fight at sea if they were to overtake the other ship. She had seen the dark fury in her husband's eyes and knew without being told that he would not lay the matter to rest until Edmond DeVaugn was no longer a threat. And what of Edmond himself? What would his reaction be when he found that Jessica had been rescued by her husband, the Indian, whom he loathed? Of course he would be furious, she thought, knowing him as well as she did. She knew that he himself would order an attack on Star Hawk and his crew if he were able.

And then what? she wondered quietly as she gazed at the horizon. Would they truly be free from his evil once and for all, or would her kin somehow once again be the victor? Would he again hold control over her and her child? With this thought a small gasp escaped her lips. Nay, she told herself sternly. She would fight also if it came to it. She would stand with sword in hand against Edmond DeVaugn before she would subject herself to his vileness once again. And if this did not see her through to her lover's arms for eternity, then she would give up her existence to the pulsing, rushing arms of the sea. She swore at that moment that Edmond would never own her or lay claim to herself or her child again. She would follow Star Hawk's path no matter where it led.

"You look quite serious, love. Is all well with you?" The dark eyes moved from her face to her enlarged belly with concern as Star Hawk stood by his wife's side at the deck railing.

Jessica turned from the sea to the man who stirred her soul. Her silver eyes were misted softly with her dour thoughts, but now the mingling of her feelings was easily seen as her love shone in her face. "I am well, my husband. I was but thinking of my happiness as your wife and soon the mother of your child."

"That is well, then," Star Hawk wrapped his large hand around her smaller one on the railing. "I would have you think of nothing else."

"What else could ever matter?" she whispered as her body was held next to Star Hawk's larger, sturdier form.

With her softly spoken words Star Hawk thought of what the morrow might hold in store for them, but as quickly, with her bright silver

eyes so lovingly on him, thoughts of Edmond De-
Vaugn and the fight that would ensue when they
met fled his mind. "When you look at me thus,
wife, I but have one thought in my mind." As a
slow, sensual smile came over her lovely features,
he added, "I am beset day and night with images
of you in our cabin lying softly and loving in my
arms."

Jessica felt the slow melting of her body as she
looked into the ebony eyes. Star Hawk's virile
magnetism was a strong pull of her senses. "Let
us go to our cabin, then, husband, for my own
thoughts are much like your own."

With a small squeeze of her hand, Star Hawk
pulled her tightly to his side and they slowly
started to the captain's cabin. Their glances beheld
only each other and they missed the small smiles
directed at them from members of the crew who
glimpsed the shining love that radiated from their
faces. Young Robbie hurriedly stepped out of
their way as he all but collided with them coming
from the companionway, but as the captain had
only eyes for his lovely bride, a small grin settled
on the younger man's features.

All were in agreement that their captain was a
different man since he had rescued his lovely wife
from the evil intent of her kin. Where before Star
Hawk had seemed darkly pensive and aloof, now
he laughed and joked in a companionable mood
with all of the crew. Though they all noticed that
when Jessica was above deck their captain was
possessive of her and dared any to approach her,
at least now he seemed more human to them. No
longer was he the dark, vengeful warrior that they

had known at the start of their journey.

As the pair entered the cabin, their arms encircled each other, their bodies molding as they clasped tightly with feelings of undying love. Star Hawk's head lowered and his mouth tenderly slanted over Jessica's, seeming to draw out her breath with the single kiss.

Their tongues circled and sought as they played a mating dance of love that stoked their senses and seared them together. With intoxicating slowness Star Hawk unbuttoned the loose-flowing shirt on his wife's body, and the valley of her bosom was left open to his eyes and lips. With a heady intake of her sweet scent, his lips worked a magic path along her fragile jawline, down the slim column of her throat, and to the full twin mounds of her straining breasts. His heated tongue circled and sucked as they gently latched onto a taut rosebud, and as he ministered to one, his hands gently massaged the other, until that one was also under attack by his greedy lips and heated tongue.

Jessica, as ever, was caught in the web of Star Hawk's sensual lovemaking. She was lost to all but the sensations that he was arousing in her body. She felt herself scale the heated mountains of love's towering surge as his mouth captured her breast. A small moan of pure bliss filled the air as her hands reached out and sought the satin darkness of his hair, clutching him tightly to her as he lavished his attentions on her body.

Ensnared by the heady, feverish intoxication of desire, Star Hawk's mouth left Jessica's sweet breasts and slowly roamed over her budding abdomen. He delighted in the feel of her flesh beneath his lips as his hands slowly untied the rope belt that fastened her breeches. When she stood naked before his heated gaze, his ebony eyes devoured every inch of her wondrous body. Even with child she was beautiful, still all that any man could desire. With her clothing gone, he bent to his knees before her, his lips again roaming across her belly and then down to kiss lightly the pulse of her being. Slowly he left this junction for later, his hands stroking her body as his lips kissed and nibbled her inner thighs and down her long, sleek legs.

With the feelings of exquisite sensations he was arousing, Jessica again felt the rapturous assault on her womanhood. His mouth engulfed her senses in a kaleidoscope of awakenings. She felt her body trembling and quivering, and as her moaning grew louder, he increased his feasting until she began to shudder with delight, and with a total loss of control, her passion flowed with fiery release, her hands clutching and wrapping in his hair as she held on to him to keep her quaking body from slipping to the floor.

But before her body could completely succumb to its fulfillment, Star Hawk captured her in his arms and carried her to their bed. His heated gaze witnessed the height of her passion, the searing love that she had for him, and the binding of their union. These towering realities filled him with a surging love and tenderness for this woman. Beating in his chest was the need to share everything with her, to fill her with all that he was, all that he would ever be.

He rose above her and took her, as it had ever been since their reunion, a sweet, tender assault. He was careful with her condition, holding himself in check lest he hurt her in some way, but showering his love on her with love play that left her gasping and writhing beneath his flaming skill.

Jessica pressed her body against his, caring for little except her flaming need for him. Her hands seductively fondled his back and shoulders as she pulled him more tightly to her. Her body kept a pulsing rhythm with his own, and as the merging of a building crest began to form within her and a sparkling of brilliant embers slowly began to shower inside, she knew once again the fullness of her love as she rode the stormy waves of flaming fulfillment.

Joyously, Star Hawk matched her pace as he rode out the small distance to passion's peak, his senses spiraling to heights unknown as he lost all control and reasoning for a short span of time. As they slowly descended to victory's ending, they happily clung together, their bodies and mouths interwined.

"Sweet, sweet darling love, you are truly the keeper of my heart." Star Hawk whispered next to the fire gold of Jessica's curls as he held her tightly to his chest.

There was no fear here in her husband's arms, and in his bed were only joy and contentment. With a large sigh, she let out her happiness against her husband's chest, his words of love filling her thoughts and making her complete. The only blight of her joy now were images of Edmond DeVaugn's dark shape before her eyes. "I wish that we would never meet with the *Ruby Heart* and that we could forget all about Edmond DeVaugn." Her words softly touched Star Hawk's ears.

Ever present in their thoughts was the threat of Jessica's kin, but not wishing for his wife to think of this dark evil, Star Hawk gently placed his finger across her lips. "Let us not speak of such matters. Let us only share our love for each other." He placed his hand on her abdomen and with shining eyes he kissed her brow. "My mother and father will be pleased with the news that they will soon be grandparents." He skipped the subject that often plagued their minds and held to a lighter train of thought.

"Do you truly think that your father will be happy with the news, Star Hawk?" Her silver eyes looked at the darker ones before her, trying to discern the truth. "What of his desire for no whites to be among his people?"

"He no longer thinks of you as white. He thinks of you as Silver Star, his daughter, and the adopted daughter of Cloud Dreamer. There was pain in his eyes when we returned to the village and found that you had been stolen. He would have ridden at my side in search of you if I had allowed him."

A small tear slipped from Jessica's eyes. This was all that she had ever desired—to be accepted into her husband's family and to be allowed to love and be loved.

Star Hawk tenderly reached out a long, tanned finger and wiped the crystal droplet away. "My father has longed for the sound of his grandchildren's laughter to fill his lodge. He is a wise teacher and will show our children many things."

Jessica's happiness was unbounded with the images playing in her mind of the days ahead that she would share with this man. "Our children will be most fortunate, my love." She kissed his strong chin as she snuggled her body closer in his arms.

"Most fortunate indeed to have such a beautiful and wise mother." He smiled at her.

"I am not so sure about being wise. You, my husband, are truly the wise one."

"Do not doubt your wisdom, Silver Star. Did you not wisely agree to become my mate, and do you not wisely agree on my abilities as a warrior and a lover?" he slowly boasted, his chest swelling as he spoke, his laughter held lightly beneath the surface.

"Perhaps I do agree that you are a great warrior, but. . . ." Jessica's silver eyes sparkled with her playfulness as she teased her husband.

"But . . ." he began to tickle her ribs, "but what, woman?" His hands bought her to rounds of loud laughter.

"Nothing, nothing," she gasped. He was relentless, and she tried to scoot away from him to find release. "You are truly the best husband, warrior, and lover," she finally gasped out before he was satisfied, and as she tried to catch her breath, he held her to the bed and ravishingly took hold of her lips.

"I knew that you were a wise woman," he whispered next to her lips before again taking hold of the soft, pinkened petals.

* * *

As was her wont Jessica spent most of her afternoon on the upper decks of the *Silver Star*. When Star Hawk took the wheel and steered the ship toward their destination, as he now knew how to do, she relaxed in a comfortable chair, enjoying the warmth of the sun's rays and watching the activity of the ship's life.

The crew of the *Silver Star* were most respectful in their actions during these afternoons when the captain's lady was about. Each man watched the words that easily slipped from their lips and their rowdy actions as seafaring men. If one of them were to slip and in some fashion make a mistake in his behavior, another would boldly hit him in the ribs with an elbow, while nodding toward the captain's wife and warning his comrade to beware of his manners.

Star Hawk watched everything from the wheel of the ship, his dark eyes not missing a thing going on in the small radius around his wife. He kept a possessive eye on her every movement and was filled with pride as he witnessed her glowing beauty. She seemed even more lovely to him as she grew each day with his child in her womb. Her beauty ensnared his senses and left him waiting for the moments when he could again be alone with her in their cabin.

After only a small forced separation, Star Hawk could bear no more. With a call to Joshua, he handed over the wheel and made his way to his wife's side where she stood against the rail, her fire-gold curls swirling about in the breeze and her face uplifted to the sun's warmth. "What is it that holds your thoughts, my love?" he quietly asked as he reached her side.

"You, my sweet." She rose upon tiptoe and kissed his cheek. "Always my thoughts are of you." With this they were lost for a span of time as they looked into each other's eyes. Everything around them seemed lost and of no concern, as though only the two of them existed. But it was only a small interlude this day that they had, as they were suddenly pulled apart by the shout carrying full on the breeze.

"Sail, ho!"

Star Hawk first looked at the young man high atop the yard arm and then toward the direction that he was pointing. Jessica also stared out to sea, but she made out no shape or form, only the blue-green vastness meeting her gaze for as far as she could see.

"You had best go to our cabin." Star Hawk saw her straining to see the ship and quickly thought of her safety, if, in fact, this was Edmond De-Vaugn's ship, the *Ruby Heart,* that was approaching. He now prayed heartily that it was.

For a moment Jessica looked at him and thought of refusing. She did not wish to leave his side. She would rather brave the danger with him and share whatever fate befell this man whom she so loved. But in that moment, other thoughts flashed into her mind. She would only be a hindrance if she were on deck, and what if something should happen to her and her child? Would her husband be able to stand and defend himself knowing that she was harmed? Nay, the wisest choice was to do as he told her, so with a small nod of her head and with her eyes full of love, she turned around and started back toward the companionway.

A flurry of activity settled around the ship as the call of "Sail, ho" was heard and the men saw their captain's lady start back toward her cabin. Each man ran toward the spot that held his weapons, cutlasses were drawn and made ready, knives tucked into breeches, pistols primed and set at ready, clubs brandished overhead. But as the call from their captain was heard above the din of their confusion, the crew scurried to stand before him on the deck.

Star Hawk looked at each anxious face for a few seconds, his chest swelling with pride for each one. He started to give out his orders. He wanted their attack on the *Ruby Heart* to be a surprise. Edmond DeVaugn did not know as yet that his cousin had been rescued from the cruel arms of the earl of Locksbin. He would not expect an attack here on the sea from another colony ship. They would approach with caution, and then when they drew close he would go aboard the *Ruby Heart*. Once aboard, he would give his war cry, and then the crew, with grappling hooks at the ready, would cross over and give their help. "Perhaps the deed will be at an end with the only blood spilled from myself or Edmond DeVaugn," he softly stated, which brought many murmurs of doubt from the group of men standing around him.

There were nearly thirty men now making up the crew of the *Silver Star,* and all stood listening to their young captain. Each held respectful admiration for the man who was giving out instructions. Only Joshua stood aside and waited for Star Hawk to finish. He did not like the fact that their captain wished to venture aboard the other ship alone. He would at least demand that he be allowed to accompany him aboard the *Ruby Heart*.

"Nay, Joshua, you are the one who will have to stay here on the *Silver Star,*" Star Hawk told him as the rest of the men set about carrying out his orders.

Joshua was taken aback with these words, "But cap'n, ye be a-needing me aboard the *Ruby Heart*. Why would I be staying here when the others will be following ye?"

"You are the only one that I can trust with the care of my wife, Joshua. I could not go aboard the *Ruby Heart* and leave her if not for the fact that I will be trusting you to watch out for her. No one is to pass through that cabin door, Joshua, no one!" he stated, knowing that the young man would indeed guard Jessica with his very life.

"I be doing as ye say then, cap'n. Yer lady is safe with me. I be gutting the gullet of any that dare try and take her," Joshua swore, knowing that this was the most crucial part of the attack to his captain, to see that no harm befell his woman.

Star Hawk nodded his head and then went about the ship making sure that the men had their weapons and the grappling hooks out of sight. He again went to the railing and looked out to sea.

He was now able to make out the dark shape of a ship off in the distance. Knowing that they were quickly gaining on her, he began to feel his pulses race. It would not be much longer and he would stand before the man who had dared to steal his wife and force her into the arms of the vicious earl of Locksbin. His rage increased as he stood on deck and thought of everything Edmond DeVaugn had caused to happen to Jessica. He would make him pay now for each moment of misery she had been forced to endure.

With a will, Star Hawk pulled his eyes from the ship ahead. He would need to appear a gentleman and a respectable captain of the *Silver Star,* so he needed to go to his cabin and retrieve his jacket. He would also need his knife, he thought, as he envisioned his meeting with his foe.

When he entered the cabin, Jessica flew into his arms. Her fear was obvious in her face—she had been alone in the cabin and worrying over what was taking place out on deck. "Can you tell yet if it is Edmond's ship?" she asked as she clutched him to her."

"Nay, love, we are not close enough to be sure." He tried to talk in an easy manner to settle her fears, for deep inside he was now positive that the ship was indeed the *Ruby Heart* and that shortly he would stand face to face with her kin. "Do not worry so, love." He wrapped his arm around her and brought his mouth down over her own. "No one shall ever harm you again," he whispered next to her lips. Then he drew his mouth from hers and looked deeply into her silver eyes.

"I do not worry for myself." She partially told

the truth. A part of her thoughts did center on herself and her unborn child. She would not again be forced to submit to Edmond's dealings. But mostly now her fears were for this man holding her tightly against his chest. She could not endure it if something were to happen to him. All of these thoughts were plainly written on her face for her husband to easily see.

"Have you not yet learned that nothing will ever separate us, my gentle flower?" Star Hawk gently rubbed his knuckles across her fragile jawline, his eyes delving deeply into the priceless silver-blue jewels before him. "Trust in my love. I shall be your strength," he whispered before once again taking hold of the petal-soft lips before him.

Jessica, in that moment, did. She drank of his inner strength like a drowning woman seeking to pull out his substance in this small moment of intimacy. This could well be the last time that she would have him next to her, she thought with a terrible dread, but casting this thought aside, she forced herself to obey him completely, to trust only in their love, knowing that they had to endure. His strength, as he had softly told her, would carry them through all their trials.

It was all too soon, though, when Star Hawk gathered his jacket and his weapon and left her to the utter silence of the cabin, warning her sternly before pulling the door shut behind him to stay to the cabin and to keep the door locked from within. She gave him a trembling smile and slowly nodded her copper head. Her eyes told him boldly of her love for him and of her deep-rooted fears for his life.

The *Silver Star* was a lighter, quicker ship then the *Ruby Heart,* and in no time she was closing the distance between them.

"Ahoy, ship." The shout was called across the short distance of the seas to the *Silver Star* from the *Ruby Heart.* She had little to fear from a native ship sailing the English flag. "Is there something amiss?" The call was again shouted to the quickly approaching ship.

"Our cap'n wishes to come aboard and have a word with your'n." The answering call was shouted to the *Ruby Heart.*

There were some long moments of drawn-out tension before the agreement was shouted across the small distance, and Christopher, who had been calling across to the *Ruby Heart,* smiled with the other man's words of, "Have your captain come ahead."

"All be at the ready, cap'n." Christopher grinned widely, wondering as he did at the stupidity of the other ship for allowing another to draw so close and then to agree to allow its captain to come aboard. It was no wonder so many English ships were preyed on far out at sea. "Just be letting us get a bit closer now, sir," he added, measuring the distance between the two ships and how close they would need to be to cast the grappling hooks to the decks.

Star Hawk stood on the deck with his feet braced in a proud stance and his hands folded behind his back. He also was waiting for them to draw closer, and as the *Silver Star* drew so close that there was fear that the two ships might bump together, Star Hawk leaped with a bound and landed on the deck of the *Ruby Heart*, drawing gasps from both ship's crews as all aboard watched the lithe grace of the tall, dark captain.

A tall, angular, white-haired man stepped forward and saluted Star Hawk sharply. His intelligent gaze took in the other man in a single glance and then questioned, "You wished to speak with me, sir, on some urgent matter?"

Star Hawk did not respond, but his dark eyes gazed at those standing on the deck. The man before him added, "I am Captain Sinclair. I am in charge of this vessel."

As though he hadn't heard the words, Star Hawk still looked about, and then finally he noticed the elder man's impatience. He spoke loudly and firmly so all aboard could hear. "I seek one out who is called Edmond DeVaugn. I bring him word of his cousin, Jessica Coltin."

The captain looked at the man before him whom he recognized as a ship's captain. "Mr. DeVaugn is in his cabin. I will have my first mate bring him." Captain Sinclair imagined that there was either very dire news about Jessica Coltin or that some great occurrence had taken place for her to request this sea captain to seek out her cousin here on the seas. But he himself was not one to interfere with the business of the owner of the ship he was commanding. As far as he knew, this ship called the *Silver Star* could very well be one of the Coltins' newest investments. In fact, as he looked at her sleek lines, she did look somewhat familiar; much like the *Fair Bella* herself.

Only a few minutes passed before Edmond DeVaugn stood at the captain's side. "Your man said that I was needed on deck. What is all the commotion?" Then his dark gaze met the tall figure of the gentleman standing across from Captain Sinclair. Seeing the closeness of the other ship, he looked again at the stranger.

"Aye, Mr. DeVaugn, the captain of the *Silver Star* here says that he has some words to speak to you of your cousin, Miss Coltin."

"The lady is no longer a miss, but is a married woman." Star Hawk spoke coolly, his ebony eyes holding the two men. For the one, a slow-burning hatred began to spark in his depths; the other he held in only a touch of contempt for his allowing a complete stranger to board his ship.

Edmond DeVaugn smiled at the newsbearer before him. The earl of Locksbin must have told this ship's captain to give him the news of his cousin's marriage if he were to meet up with the *Ruby Heart* on the seas. "So, the earl of Locksbin did indeed talk Jessica into wedding him before the birth of her brat." He was only mildly surprised that after the ball, the evening on which he had quietly left London, Henry had forced Jessica to wed him early.

Star Hawk had cold, steel rage in his gaze as he stood towering over the two men before him. As all of the crew of the *Ruby Heart* stood about, he chillingly replied, "And did your kin, this innocent woman put in your charge, wish to be joined with such a man as the old, vile earl of Locksbin?" A dark brow rose with his question.

Edmond was shockingly taken aback. No one ever dared to question him in such a manner, especially not a ship's captain. His features began

372

to take on a reddish tint from the anger that was surfacing, and he sputtered, "What difference to you or any other what I arrange for my family? You are right in only one thing, though, and that is that Jessica was under my care. I hold every right to see her safely married to a man of means who will well be able to care for her." He stuck out his chest in a haughty manner and looked down his thin nose at the darkly-featured man before him. "You have done your duty by bringing us word from the earl of Locksbin. Now, if you do not mind, you are holding the *Ruby Heart* up." Edmond was about to turn his back on the man and take himself back to his cabin, when the other's words held him stiff.

"Rightly I have done my duty to my own family. I have saved my wife and unborn baby from the clutches of a scheming relative and from the hands of a vile, lecherous old man. Though he perhaps had the means to take care of her, he only had in mind to abuse her and enjoy the suffering he could cause her."

The words gave Edmond full understanding. "You!" he shouted, his small, dark eyes now not seeing a handsome, gentlemanly ship's captain, but instead a tall, dark-skinned Indian. The same one who had taken Jessica from Sweet Oaks, and now, if his words were true, he had again grasped her out of the hands of the fate that Edmond himself had arranged for her.

"Aye, I am your cousin's husband." Star Hawk advanced toward his prey, his piercing black eyes holding the other with a chilling look of cold death. "You dared to take that which belongs only to me. And then you thought to leave my wife with the evil earl." As he read the true fear in the other's face he said softly, "No man touches the wife of Star Hawk and lives!"

Captain Sinclair began to stutter as he heard the words being spoken by the two men. "Gentleman, I am sure that we will be able to straighten this all out," he started, but with a leap, Edmond pushed him to the deck of the ship. Grabbing at Captain Sinclair's side, he clutched the sword that the captain had strapped on when he had first seen the *Silver Star* approaching them.

"By God, you shall not live to interfere in my cousin's life after this day," Edmond shouted as he flexed his arm wide. The sword was a brilliant flash in the afternoon sunlight as it was brandished in Star Hawk's direction.

Swift of feet and ready on the second for any kind of attack, Star Hawk sidestepped the attack easily. In a moment he was out of his jacket and standing with feet braced apart, his large hunting knife clutched in his fist. "Come and meet your death, Edmond DeVaugn. A man that preys on innocent babes and women does not deserve to live."

Still Captain Sinclair thought to put a halt to the fight. Looking at the stunned faces of his crew, he began to shout for them to overpower the *Silver Star's* captain.

All stood looking at the fierce avenger with the wicked-looking hunting knife clasped in his hand, and none were brave enough to make the first step.

Star Hawk had his eyes centered on his victim,

and he glimpsed a touch of fear and some small wonder written in the eyes of Edmond DeVaugn. He opened his mouth and let out his chilling, animallike war cry, and in seconds, the crew of the *Silver Star* were grappling the side of the ship, and men from every direction were pulling themselves over the side railings, their hands filled with their weapons.

Those upon the *Ruby Heart* looked around them like caged animals as they were surrounded by the rough-looking crew of the *Silver Star,* brandishing clubs, pistols, cutlasses, and knives. As one their eyes looked at their captain, wondering if he would still insist on their putting a stop to the fighting between the two men facing each other on the main deck.

Captain Sinclair turned beet-red in the face and then finally sputtered, "This is piracy! You will all hang for your treason!"

"Not so." Star Hawk spoke almost softly now to the other captain, his dark eyes still held on his opponent. "My wife is the owner of this ship, and as her husband, the *Ruby Heart* also belongs to me. And as such, I command that your men do not interfere with myself and DeVaugn. This is a matter that has long been in need of being settled."

Captain Sinclair measured his words carefully in his mind, agreeing, though rather slowly, that the young captain was right. Jessica Coltin did indeed own this ship, and if he was her husband all of her property now belonged to him, as well. Slowly he nodded his head, though he wondered at this man's own good sense in standing before Edmond

DeVaugn with but a knife in his hand.

Edmond saw the look of acceptance on Captain Sinclair's face, and with a scowl at the man's stupidity he boldly lunged at Star Hawk, forcing all the men to take a backward step.

Star Hawk ducked and stepped aside. With but the knife in his fist, he was powerless at the moment, except to stay away from the sharp-edged sword that was swinging in his direction.

Quickly, though, Scotty called aloud to Star Hawk and threw him his own large, dangerous-looking cutlass. "Perhaps this be making the game a bit more even," he grinned, not worried in the least when Edmond threw him a black look.

Star Hawk now held his knife in one fist and the cutlass tightly in the other. Edmond DeVaugn still advanced, for he was well educated in the art of fencing and still thought to overtake his opponent. He reasoned to himself, this man was but an Indian savage, his skills could not equal his own in the slightest.

It was Edmond, though, who a few moments later, and at the other end of the ship, was gasping aloud, while Star Hawk seemed as fresh and sprightly as though they had only just begun to fight. At that moment a small rumbling fear began to prick his heart. He would have to press his advantage and skill, he told himself, and with a shout he attacked, hacking and thrusting the sword toward the man whom he now hated above all others. He was the reason for all of Edmond's troubles. If not for this Indian, he would have had Jessica wed long ago back in New Orleans. Again he forced himself at the dark-skinned man, trying desperately to get to his body and draw his very life from his limbs.

Star Hawk read the savage fury laced with fear on the other's face, and as he held the cutlass out to deflect the blows, he drew Edmond closer toward him. So close now were they that Star Hawk could hear the other's gasping breath as though they were only sounds upon the ship. Edmond, with a gleam in his eyes, stepped in front of Star Hawk and swiped at his chest, tearing the white linen shirt and tracing a thin line of red across that wide expanse. Star Hawk now heard the shrill laughter of Edmond DeVaugn over being the first to draw blood. Edmond now began to thrust harder for the kill. With a coldly calculated easing of the hand holding the knife, Star Hawk held his other weapon high in the air, and at that moment he thrust his knife upward.

A gasp escaped Edmond, one of disbelief and horrible pain as he froze in his stance. His eyes were wide as they looked into the face of death written before him on the visage of the Indian.

"You will not harm that which belongs to me again." Star Hawk pulled the knife from the body of his enemy. As Edmond DeVaugn slipped to the deck in a pool of his own blood and slowly sank into the inner depths of death, Star Hawk did not look back, but quickly left the ship called the *Ruby Heart*. He boldly traversed the distance between the two ships and stood upon the deck of the *Silver Star*. All that he desired at this moment was to feel the softness of his wife's body next to his own and to allow her gentle tenderness to wipe from his memory the killing and fighting.

As the crew of the *Silver Star* made their way back to their own ship and set her once again to sail, Star Hawk slightly nodded at Joshua standing guard before his cabin door. No words passed between the two, but Joshua easily saw the glint of victory in his captain's dark eyes, and there also he saw something else. Was it perhaps a desire to be at peace, to see an end to bloodshed for a time?

Jessica flew into Star Hawk's arms as the portal was opened. Her silver eyes took in his haggard appearance and the blood on his shirt. "You are hurt?" she questioned as quick tears filled her eyes and a trembling settled on her body.

"Nay, I am well, and we are at last free." Star Hawk ignored the slight stinging of his chest and pulled her against him, his nostrils inhaling deeply the fresh sweetness of her hair. Her arms encircled him like a haven of pure love and softness. Here he could forget the viciousness of the outside world, for all Star Hawk had ever desired was this woman, their love, and a quiet peace.

For a time they stood clasped tightly together, allowing their pain and fears to be swept aside as they filled their senses with each other.

But this was only a short respite, as Jessica soon remembered the wound on her husband's chest and beckoned him to sit so that she could wash and tend him.

Star Hawk delighted in her treatment of him, enjoying her fussing and the way her silver eyes slid over his broad chest as she looked at the thin slice on the massive, muscled bronzed chest. "It is not serious, Star Hawk," she said as she drew the

378

sponge across him, wiping away the blood.

Star Hawk did not respond, but allowed his eyes to travel over her as she cared for him. At that moment he envisioned her tending and loving their child, and a warm contentment settled over him. He could not wait to get back to their village and resume the life that they had long been parted from. Their warm lodge beckoned in his dreams and left him with a deep wanting.

The *Silver Star* reached the port of New Orleans on a warm summer morning, and after bidding her crew farewell, Jessica and Star Hawk went to see the solicitor who handled all of the Coltin affairs. Spending some time with the elderly gentleman, they arranged for him to send a written report of all the business transactions once a month to Sweet Oaks. Star Hawk would have one of the braves from his village gather them from Sweet Oaks and bring them to Jessica. In this fashion he would set up her correspondence, making sure that all of her holdings ran smoothly with the help of Mr. Armstrong, the solicitor, who had also been a close friend of her father's. After meeting Star Hawk he softly confessed that he had had serious doubts about Edmond DeVaugn, but he explained that he had been unable to do anything to interfere with her father's will. There in his office, Jessica told the kindly man about her husband's heritage. Swearing himself to silence, he agreed to start a rumor wherein Jessica Coltin had wed a close relative somewhere in Europe and had decided to remain abroad instead of returning to the colonies and to Sweet Oaks.

One other portion of business they also attended to this day, and that was having the papers drawn up to transfer ownership of the ship known as the *Fair Bella,* now called the *Silver Star,* to Joshua, Christopher, Scotty, Robbie, and Billy. The men could do with her as they desired, Star Hawk had told Jessica. More than likely they would make runs from the Carribbean to the colonies, gaining riches and adventure for themselves.

With all of their business attended to in Mr. Armstrong's office, and with full confidence in the other man's promise of secrecy, Star Hawk went to the stables and rented horses. The same afternoon they had arrived in port, the couple slowly made the short trip out to Sweet Oaks. Jessica insisted that they would stay only a day before they would set out for the Indian village, for she longed to see Marcy before she resumed her life.

The two-hour trip passed quickly for Jessica as she excitedly looked at the familiar countryside, her joy complete as she continually let her eyes stray to the handsome man sitting so proud and tall on horseback. He had planned their future on the *Silver Star* and had quickly put his plans into motion with the help of Mr. Armstrong. Now Jessica was free to indulge in her joyful anticipation of the life ahead of her, and she felt true happiness.

The reunion at Sweet Oaks was one of tremendous joy as the young, roundbellied white girl and the old black woman stood on the front veranda and clutched each other closely, their tears and laughter mingling.

Star Hawk stood back with a wide grin upon his face as he watched the pair. Happiness welled in his chest for his wife to see her for this short time at the home where she had been raised. Then the wide brown eyes of the black woman looked at him, and Marcy straightened out her dress from the mussing it had taken as she had held Jessica tightly to her.

Star Hawk spoke softly to her. "Old mother, I have brought your daughter back home to you for a visit."

"You done surely that, master," Marcy grinned widely, her gleaming teeth starkly standing out from her dark face. "It be looking like ye got her here just in time." Her eyes were now directed at the large, swelling belly.

Jessica laughed aloud with happiness as she was surrounded by the two people she loved most in this world. "We are only here for a day, Marcy. My husband is anxious to get back to his people, and so am I." She hoped that this black woman who had raised her would understand, for she did not wish to hurt Marcy; but Sweet Oaks was no longer her home. Her home was with Star Hawk and his village. That was where she would have her children and raise them, with the understanding of the forest and of the ways of those who wished only to be left to themselves.

"But Lordy, child, ye can't be a-traipsing about in yer condition. Ye be having that youngun on the trail somewhere. Ye ain't been a-raised for the like, Miss Jessica." Marcy braced her hands on her hips and looked first at the copper-haired beauty standing before her in men's breeches and shirt and then at the man at her side, still dressed in the white man's garb and surely the most handsome male she had ever set eyes on. But as she glimpsed the look of stubbornness in Jessica's silver gaze she knew already that she had lost the battle. Swift tears came to her eyes. "I thought surely that ye be staying home where ye belong. And now I ain't ever a-going to be a-seeing ye again, nor that youngun." Tears came and rolled down the black cheeks as she remembered Jessica as a baby and how much she had loved her. She had always thought of a future helping to raise her children, too.

It was Star Hawk who placed his arm around her shoulder. "Old mother, you will know our children," he promised.

Marcy looked at this young man standing next to her and as she did the tears dried, for she trusted and believed him. If he told her that she would know Jessica's children, she thought, she surely would.

With a grin she now turned to Jessica. "Ye be bringing yerself and yer man on in the house now and don't be a-lingering out here in the heat. I be having ye both something fixed up right quick to eat and a hot tub of water sent up to yer room. Wiles ye here, honey lamb, I be making sure that ye get yer rest and eat enough fer yerself and that youngun."

Star Hawk grinned widely as he followed closely in the wake of Marcy as she ushered Jessica up the stairs. Amid her fussing and cooing, she had her settled in a comfortable chair in her old bedchamber and hurriedly rushed about to see to their dinner and have steaming water brought up the stairs with a large tub set up for bathing.

Jessica groaned aloud at all the attention she was receiving, but no matter what she said, Star Hawk would not help sway Marcy into believing that she could tend herself and that she was not some small, fragile doll.

They stayed at Sweet Oaks for two more days, for Marcy could not bear for them to leave after only the first day. But after two more days, Star Hawk took the kindly dark woman aside and calmly explained that he wished to get Jessica back to his village where his mother and their healing woman could help attend her birthing.

With this, Marcy slowly nodded her head in agreement, though there were shining tears in her warm brown eyes. She stood upon the front veranda amidst the other servants of Sweet Oaks and waved the couple good-bye.

The couple on horseback slowly kept pace as they moved away from the large brick house and entered the path in the forest glade. They passed the spot where Star Hawk had first seen Jessica gathering wild plants, and their eyes met and locked.

"This was the beginning," Jessica softly murmured.

"Aye," Star Hawk pulled their horses to a halt and for a moment breathed the sweet smell of the earth and forest. "We shall tell our child of our meeting in this special place and he will delight that the Great Spirit was so good to us." He bent and lightly placed a soft, lingering kiss on her pink lips.

"I only hope that he or she will be as lucky as we have been, my love." Jessica breathed. All of the love that she felt in her heart was now in her silver eyes as she looked at her handsome husband.

This trip to the valley where Star Hawk had months ago taken his beautiful captive was much longer than the first one when Star Hawk had held Jessica tightly in his arms as they had ridden on the back of his horse, Night Cloud. Now there was a need to travel slowly, for Jessica's condition was ever present in Star Hawk's mind. They camped early in the evenings and tried not to rush her in the mornings, and the days slowly passed.

The past two days had been even slower as Star Hawk had worried over his wife. His dark eyes were constantly going to her. Several times he had caught a look of pain on her face when she had thought his gaze was not on her, and he had also witnessed her hands clutching the back of her horse for support.

This morning they pulled their mounts to a halt on top of a grassy knoll overlooking the peaceful valley where hundreds of tepees had stood when they had been here last. Now all was silent, the lush summer grasses standing green in the distance as the rushing river flowed gently through the valley floor.

Star Hawk had worried for the past days that they would find the encampment moved to the mountains, but he had prayed that his father, for whatever reason, might have put off the move for a time yet. But he knew that with the heat of the summer the tribe would survive much better in the mountains, and always in Golden Eagle's mind were thoughts of the good of his people. Now as he looked into the valley and nothing stirred below, his dark eyes went back to his wife as she sat on her mount. There were beads of sweat on her forehead, and her shirtfront was now dampened. He had hoped that they would reach Cloud Dreamer here in the valley and that the old healing woman would be able to help Jessica in her labor. Now with the realization that this was not to be, a real fear began to settle on his shoulders.

He knew that the long trek into the mountains was a hard one, and for a woman in Jessica's condition there would be much hardship. But he knew of nothing else to do except to try and slowly make their way there. "Are you able to go on, Silver Star?" he softly questioned, his dark eyes taking in her strained features.

Biting down hard on her lower lip as a sharp pain laced through her lower back, Jessica slowly nodded her copper head. With the slight easing of her pain, her lips formed a tender smile as she looked at the concerned face of her husband. She had seen the concern on her husband's brow in the past few days, and she hated to think that she was the reason for his worry. She also had been praying that they would reach the valley in time to join the village in their move. Her time, she knew, was near, for the pains of the past two days had increased. Now, as she looked at the man she loved, she doubted that she would be able to make it to the mountains and to the village. This morning when she had awoken the pains had seemed to sear her lower back, and now they were coming more sharply and much more frequently. But she was determined that she would endure as long as she could before telling Star Hawk that they must find shelter for her to deliver.

As the long day progressed Star Hawk knew of each lancing pain that assaulted his wife. Several times he brought the horses to a halt and helped her from her mount, easing her down on the soft grass with the hopes that this would help her endure yet a while longer.

It was nearing dusk when Star Hawk looked at Jessica and for the first time she revealed the raw pain of her labor. It crossed her lovely features, her lips now swollen from her biting them together, her face pale as though all the blood had left her body. "It is only a small way to our joining lodge," he told her, but as he saw her eyes held tightly shut as a contraction lanced through her body, he pulled her from her horse and into his own lap. Gently kicking the sides of his horse, he took her to the lodge that he had built for their joining ceremony.

The front entrance to the lodge was tightly shut, and Star Hawk hoped that no animals had made the small vacant cabin their home. He carried Jessica in his arms into the dimly lit structure.

Setting her down, he quickly set about building a small fire in the shallow pit. The light from the fire sparked and sent its golden hue to every corner of the small building.

Jessica had slipped to the dirt floor when he

had set her down. Her hands were on her bulging belly as she was attacked again with a searing pain.

Running to his horse outside, Star Hawk gathered the sleeping mat and furs and quickly made up a soft bed for his wife. His dark eyes were worried as he laid her on the furs and began to help her undress. A fear had begun to grow in his heart throughout the afternoon as he had glimpsed her horrible pain, and now that fear increased. She was no longer able to endure the pain but clutched at the furs with her hands. Her lips parted, and moans like the sounds of a small animal in torment now filled the cabin.

Looking around him, Star Hawk knew that they would be needing water and a few things from their pack horse, so with loving hands he soothed the gold-fire curls from his beloved's forehead and told her that he would be back shortly. Then on quick feet he hurried to do what was needed, the whole time filled with his fear for his wife.

How was he going to help her, he wondered as he ran to the stream in the back of the cabin. He was a warrior trained in the ways of fighting and protecting his people. How was he going to help his love with the delivery of their child? He had never even known another brave in his village who had helped his woman deliver a child. Always there had been other women about for such business. Would he be able to help her now in her true time of need? What was there that he would need to do? He and Jessica had never discussed this, for they had both put from their thoughts such a thing's happening.

Hurrying back to the cabin with water and the things he had gotten from the pack horse, Star Hawk was struck with an inner quaking as he parted the entrance flap and stepped inside. Jessica lay panting, her legs apart as she strained and moaned aloud with her pain and burden. Seeing her thus, a new deep-rooted fear settled over his heart. He had often heard stories of women who had died while trying to deliver a baby. Was this horrible pain that Jessica was enduring normal? Or was something wrong and was she going to suffer before she was taken from him? A lone tear trailed down his strong, bronzed cheek with these thoughts, but as her silver eyes fixed upon him, he forced such thoughts from his mind. The Great Spirit would not take his Silver Star. Too much had already happened to them for them now to be separated. He would help her have their child. His own hands would lead his son from his nest.

Quickly he stirred himself and went to her side. Bending down, he began to bathe her face with a cool cloth. "Ah my love, my love," he softly said to her as he smiled down at her. "My son is most anxious to behold his mother's lovely face." His hand went to her bared stomach, feeling for himself the tumult going on there and taking a portion of the pain upon himself.

Jessica eased somewhat with his soothing words, and as her silver eyes held his ebony ones, she felt some strength return to her. A small smile filtered across her lips. "He is even now as his father. A mighty warrior," she lightly joked before another spasm of pain came over her, doubling her over on the pallet and leaving Star Hawk anxious.

"Think of the beautiful valley we saw this morning, my love." Star Hawk gently talked, his one hand massaging her belly as the other caressed her cheek. "Remember the forest glade where we met? Let the coolness of the glade touch you, Silver Star. Feel the breeze in your fire hair and smell the flowers around you."

Again Jessica relaxed, her eyes shut as his strong voice took her away from the torturous pain that was attacking her so viciously. She was again running free with the wind, her skirts flying about her as she ran down the path and into the cool world of the forest glade. There was peace here, there was love in the soothing voice above her, and she bound her mind with the dreamworld that Star Hawk was spreading around her. Her pain was still there, but it seemed to be some distance away. All she could hear was his voice speaking of cool, refreshing waters, the earth, and the forest. Here was the shelter, in her husband's voice and touch; here she could endure.

But as her body drew up and off of the pallet and everything inside her seemed to push downward, Star Hawk knew that it was time. Keeping his tone light, he told her of all the beauty that he had ever seen, the seas on a velvety, cool night, the stars of heaven dancing with wondrous brilliance over Mother Earth. His hands still touched and soothed, and he bent down between her legs, his eyes now seeing the tiny dark head of his child making its way through its mother's body. With a fiercely beating heart he watched as a shoulder and then another and then a small, perfect being pushed from its warm haven into the world.

With a shout that seemed to encompass all of the small cabin, Star Hawk gently picked up the tiny slip of life. As he touched his son, the baby squirmed and began to cry out his wrath at the ordeal he had just been put through. With a grin of disbelief and purest pleasure, Star Hawk's eyes rose from the baby in his hands to the woman of his heart. But as he looked at her face he still saw the pain of before. He tenderly set his child upon the end of the sleeping mat. "What is it, love?" he softly questioned as he touched again her contorted belly. He had thought that with the birthing the pain would be stilled. What was amiss, he wondered, and for a moment he forgot about his son as his black eyes looked at Jessica.

Rolling her head back and forth on the pallet, Jessica started to speak. "I don't . . ." But before she could finish, another searing maelstrom of pain rushed over her and a scream pierced the still cabin.

A cold dread of fear doused Star Hawk at the scream. As he looked at where only seconds ago his son had emerged from his wife's body, he glimpsed another small, black-haired head. "Push down, Silver Star," he gently called to Jessica, not knowing that her pain was brought about because there was not one but two children in her body. Again he began to talk to her, to soothe her as well as he could as his large hands bent over her and helped this child as it slid from its mother's body.

At last Jessica lay panting and gasping, the pain of childbearing at last over. As Star Hawk looked from the infant in his large hands to the one at the foot of the pallet, the moment was written on their memories forever. "This one is a girl." He spoke in wonder, not even truly believing his own words.

"And the other?" Jessica breathed, her silver gaze on the man she loved with all of her heart and seeing the unsurmountable joy in his face.

Star Hawk had forgotten that he had not told her the firstborn had been a son. He looked at her with a grin. "A son, Silver Star. The Great Spirit has given us a son and a daughter. Two." He said this still with wonder in his tone.

At his words a soft smile appeared on Jessica's face, and slowly her silver eyes shut. A son first and then a daughter, she thought happily before she drifted into a well-deserved sleep.

Star Hawk, still with a look of wonder on his face, set the babe in his hands down next to the other. Then, with loving hands, he tended to his sleeping wife. Later he sat back on his haunches and pulled the furs up under her chin. He marveled at his fortunes. This woman of his heart had not given him one child, but two. She had silently broken down all the barriers that he had ever known. She had unexpectedly swept into his heart and rendered him all but senseless with his desire for her and her alone, and now she had gifted him with a miracle. Twins. His heart raced as he beheld the sleeping woman. Rarely had his people known of such births. Always in the past there had been a great plan by the Great Spirit for such an occurrence. Again his dark eyes went to the babies at the foot of the pallet, now resting peacefully after he had washed them and wrapped them in warm hides.

A boy and a girl. He dared to believe his eyes. As he looked at them, the tiny, perfect little girl opened her eyes. This small movement caused Star Hawk's heart to all but still in his chest. The coloring was light, as though with tiny sparks of silver. "Sky Eyes." The name came to him as he beheld her. Looking at his other child, he studied the tiny being for a time before a smile flited across his lips. He would call his son Two Shadows, for his path would always be shadowed by the Great Spirit and he would never be alone. And there would always be Sky Eyes, his sister, as a part of him, and they would be joined to form a whole. Yes, Two Shadows would be a proud name for his son, and one day this son would be a leader of his people.

It was late in the evening when Jessica awoke from her deep sleep. Looking about, she saw her husband near the small fire stirring a pot of aromatic stew.

Like a current between them, Star Hawk felt her eyes on him. Turning, he showed a tender smile on his handsome features. "I have fixed you something nourishing to eat." He rose to his full height with a bowl of the venison stew in his hands.

Jessica watched as he came to her side. As he lowered to her, she let out a small sigh.

"Are you still hurting?" His concerned-filled black eyes looked at her face as he tried to read in her movements whether something was still amiss.

"Nay, I am but stiff and sore." Jessica smiled as he helped to prop her against the furs. As she sat up, she quickly looked at the babies at the foot of the sleeping mat. "Are they well?" she softly questioned. With his smile and the nodding of his dark head, she let out the breath she had been holding.

After helping her eat the warmed stew, Star Hawk set the bowl aside and brought the two babies to their mother. His joy was apparent in his gaze as he sat back and watched his children in his wife's arms.

"Which one is the girl?" Jessica softly questioned as she pulled back the hide that covered them.

Star Hawk reached out a gentle hand and placed it on one of the heads. "This is Sky Eyes," he said, and then looking in Jessica's eyes, he added, "Her eyes look like yours, small glittering gems of silver."

A large grin came over Jessica's face with his words, "And my son?" she questioned, already knowing that her husband had named him also.

"I thought to call him Two Shadows." At her questioning look, he responded, "Our son is a special gift from the Great Spirit, and his paths shall be always in his shadow. The other portion of his name is for his sister, so that Sky Eyes and he shall always remain a part of each other."

Jessica nodded her copper head in full agreement as small sparklings of glittering tears filled her silver eyes. How like her husband to name their children with such sensitive names. "They are beautiful names," she softly said. "But there is

393

something else I would add."

Star Hawk looked at her, not knowing what it was that he could have forgotten. "Whatever you wish, my love, I will be pleased."

"You were raised with much understanding, Star Hawk, and you are a very special man. Your father used much wisdom in allowing you to learn the ways of the white man, for they have aided you throughout your life. I would have the same for my children. I would wish for them to know also about the first part of my life. Not all of the white world is bad. My own parents raised me with much love and understanding."

Star Hawk listened to her words and measured their worth. What man could not gain from knowledge, he wondered. As he looked at the infants lying in Jessica's arms he knew that he would not be able to deprive them of the heritage of their mother. They would learn and weigh the differences between the white race and that of the Indian. They would make their own decisions one day, and he and Silver Star could only offer their own strength and wisdom. Slowly he nodded his dark head in agreement. "Our children will know both worlds, Silver Star. Perhaps they will help their people more with their knowledge."

Jessica had known that he would see the benefit of allowing their children their white heritage. "Then I would call my daughter Mary Jean in the white world, and my son, Heath." She looked again at the babies in her arms, and as they both slowly began to squirm, her eyes rose to her husband. "Thank you so much, Star Hawk, for my children. Thank you so much for showing me love."

Though all that he could ever want was right here before him, Star Hawk bent toward his wife and children. His lips slowly descended on the velvety-soft petals of Jessica's. "I am the one to give thanks, my wife. For until you came into my life, I knew nothing of the feelings that are now filling my heart. You have shown me what it means to love. I adore you so, Silver Star."

"My heart will forever be in your keeping, my love. Forever," Jessica breathed as again the lips found hers and lightly caressed them.

"Aye, forever," his whisper breathed against her parted lips.

FIERY ROMANCE
From Zebra Books

AUTUMN'S FURY   (1763, $3.95)
by Emma Merritt

Lone Wolf had known many women, but none had captured his heart the way Catherine had . . . with her he felt a hunger he hadn't experienced with any of the maidens of his own tribe. He would make Catherine his captive, his slave of love — until she would willingly surrender to the magic of AUTUMN'S FURY.

PASSION'S PARADISE   (1618, $3.75)
by Sonya T. Pelton

When she is kidnapped by the cruel, captivating Captain Ty, fair-haired Angel Sherwood fears not for her life, but for her honor! Yet she can't help but be warmed by his manly touch, and secretly longs for PASSION'S PARADISE.

LOVE'S ELUSIVE FLAME   (1836, $3.75)
by Phoebe Conn

Golden-haired Flame was determined to find the man of her dreams even if it took forever, but she didn't have long to wait once she met the handsome rogue Joaquin. He made her respond to his ardent kisses and caresses . . . but if he wanted her completely, she would have to be his only woman — she wouldn't settle for anything less. Joaquin had always taken women as he wanted . . . but none of them was Flame. Only one night of wanton ecstasy just wasn't enough — once he was touched by LOVE'S ELUSIVE FLAME.

SAVAGE SPLENDOR   (1855, $3.95)
by Constance O'Banyon

By day Mara questioned her decision to remain in her husband's world. But by night, when Tajarez crushed her in his strong, muscular arms, taking her to the peaks of rapture, she knew she could never live without him.

SATIN SURRENDER   (1861, $3.95)
by Carol Finch

Dante Folwer found innocent Erica Bennett in his bed in the most fashionable whorehouse in New Orleans. Expecting a woman of experience, Dante instead stole the innocence of the most magnificent creature he'd ever seen. He would forever make her succumb to . . . SATIN SURRENDER.

Available wherever paperbacks are sold, or order direct from the Publisher. Send cover price plus 50¢ per copy for mailing and handling to Zebra Books, Dept. 2527, 475 Park Avenue South, New York, N.Y. 10016. Residents of New York, New Jersey and Pennsylvania must include sales tax. DO NOT SEND CASH.

ZEBRA HAS THE SUPERSTARS
OF PASSIONATE ROMANCE!

CRIMSON OBSESSION (2272, $3.95)
by Deana James

Cassandra MacDaermond was determined to make the handsome gambling hall owner Edward Sandron pay for the fortune he had stolen from her father. But she never counted on being struck speechless by his seductive gaze. And soon Cassandra was sneaking into Sandron's room, more intent on sharing his rapture than causing his ruin!

TEXAS CAPTIVE (2251, $3.95)
by Wanda Owen

Ever since two outlaws had killed her ma, Talleha had been suspicious of all men. But one glimpse of virile Victor Maurier standing by the lake in the Texas Blacklands and the half-Indian princess was helpless before the sensual tide that swept her in its wake!

TEXAS STAR (2088, $3.95)
by Deana James

Star Garner was a wanted woman—and Chris Gillard was determined to collect the generous bounty being offered for her capture. But when the beautiful outlaw made love to him as if her life depended on it, Gillard's firm resolve melted away, replaced with a raging obsession for his fiery TEXAS STAR.

MOONLIT SPLENDOR (2008, $3.95)
by Wanda Owen

When the handsome stranger emerged from the shadows and pulled Charmaine Lamoureux into his strong embrace, she sighed with pleasure at his seductive caresses. Tomorrow she would be wed against her will—so tonight she would take whatever exhilarating happiness she could!

EXPERIENCE THE SENSUOUS MAGIC
OF JANELLE TAYLOR!

FORTUNE'S FLAMES (2250, $3.95)
Lovely Maren James' angry impatience turned to raging desire when the notorious Captain Hawk boarded her ship and strode confidently into her cabin. And before she could consider the consequences, the ebon-haired beauty was succumbing to the bold pirate's masterful touch!

SWEET SAVAGE HEART (1900, $3.95)
Kidnapped when just a child, seventeen-year-old Rana Williams adored her carefree existence among the Sioux. But then the frighteningly handsome white man Travis Kincade appeared in her camp . . . and Rana's peace was shattered forever!

DESTINY'S TEMPTRESS (1761, $3.95)
Crossing enemy lines to help save her beloved South, Shannon Greenleaf found herself in the bedroom of Blane Stevens, the most handsome man she'd ever seen. Though burning for his touch, the defiant belle vowed never to reveal her mission—nor let the virile Yankee capture her heart!

SAVAGE CONQUEST (1533, $3.75)
Heeding the call of her passionate nature, Miranda stole away from her Virginia plantation to the rugged plains of South Dakota. But captured by a handsome Indian warrior, the headstrong beauty felt her defiance melting away with the hot-blooded savage's sensual caress!

STOLEN ECSTASY (1621, $3.95)
With his bronze stature and ebony black hair, the banished Sioux brave Bright Arrow was all Rebecca Kenny ever wanted. She would defy her family and face society's scorn to savor the forbidden rapture she found in her handsome warrior's embrace!

Available wherever paperbacks are sold, or order direct from the Publisher. Send cover price plus 50¢ per copy for mailing and handling to Zebra Books, Dept. 2527, 475 Park Avenue South, New York, N.Y. 10016. Residents of New York, New Jersey and Pennsylvania must include sales tax. DO NOT SEND CASH.